THE GRAND GAME
BOOK 1

THE GRAND GAME

Book 1

Tom Elliot

COPYRIGHT

THE GRAND GAME

One man.
Assassin. Caster.
A new world.
And a Game that is as brutal as it is complex.

Michael finds himself in the realm of the Forever Kingdom, with no memory of how he got there and who he is. Even so, he must participate in the Grand Game and forge a new destiny for himself.

Dropped into a dungeon of monsters, and strange magics, would you survive in a Game where to lose means death?
Alone and with little more than his wits to aid him, Michael must advance as a player, slay his foes, and gain experience. All while navigating the intrigues around him and discovering his purpose.

A world of Powers, Forces, and mysterious factions. A Game with endless opportunities for advancement and power.
Join Michael on his epic adventure as he deals with the Game's challenges, the machinations of the Powers, and the ambitions of his fellow players.

The start of an exciting new portal fantasy epic!

AUTHOR'S NOTE

Dear Readers,

Thank you for reading the Grand Game. This is a self-published book. Even though care has been given to the review and editing of this novel, some mistakes may have slipped through. If you spot any grammatical errors or typos, please contact me via email.

This book also contains game-like elements. They are generally unintrusive and are integrated into the story, but beware, they do exist. Otherwise, I hope you enjoy Michael's story.

Happy reading!
Tom
Support me on PATREON[1]

---

[1] https://www.patreon.com/grandgame

CONTENTS

CHAPTER 1: A NEW BEGINNING

I fell, tumbling over and over through a seemingly endless void of darkness. My eyes stared out, but I saw nothing. My mouth was open, and my throat was raw and scraped. It felt as if I had been screaming for hours. Yet I heard nothing.

Even worse, I remembered nothing.

No, that wasn't quite true. I knew my name. *I'm Michael,* I thought. I knew nothing else. Not where I lived. Not how old I was. Not where I was from or even how I came to be falling through a void of nothingness.

But I knew who I was.

I'm Michael, I repeated. It seemed a nearly negligible tidbit of knowledge, yet it gave me a measure of comfort, and I clung to it as I plummeted downwards.

Hours passed, if not days or weeks.

I kept falling.

And kept screaming.

Eventually, it proved too much for my overwrought mind, and oblivion beckoned. Gratefully, I surrendered myself to unconsciousness and waited for it all to end.

~ ~ ~

Hands shook at me. "Wake up, boy. Don't keep the Master waiting."

I groaned. My body was riddled with pain. Not an inch of me felt free of aches and bruises, and I wanted nothing more than to return to the sweet nothingness of sleep. Shrugging away from the interloper's reaching touch, I rolled over. Escaping his attention was not so easy, however.

He tugged at me again. Stubbornly, I ignored him. That proved to be a poor decision. A brutal kick to my midriff followed, and my world went white with agony. Involuntarily, I curled up in a ball. *Vicious bastard,* I swore.

"Easy Stayne," someone else said. "I may have need of him yet." The words were mildly spoken, yet the timbre of command in the speaker's voice was unmistakable.

"Sorry, Master," Stayne said. "I'll be more careful, promise."

The pain in my center eased slightly, and I forced my eyes open. I was on the ground, on bare earth, covered with only loose bits of rock and shale. My gaze drifted upwards. A dome of white light about twelve feet across surrounded me, but beyond that was only pitch black. The darkness was unrelieved by the slightest detail and gave no hint of what lay within it.

I shivered as the memory of falling came rushing back.

My eyes darted back to the hard ground. It seemed that my plunge through the void had finally come to an end. *No wonder my body feels like one big mass of bruises.* But then again, if I had fallen anywhere near as far as I suspected, it was a miracle I was even alive.

Where am I?

I still didn't remember how I came to be wherever I was or any more of myself other than my name. *Time enough to deal with the mystery later, Michael,* I told myself. *Right now, you have other matters to attend to.*

I rolled onto my back again and found the two who had disturbed my sleep watching me intently. At the sight of the pair, a ripple of fear shuddered through my body. Both figures were disturbingly *unnatural.*

The Master... floated. My gaze flicked from his robed form to his booted heels hovering nearly a foot above the ground. My eyes widened at the sight. Still, it was not the only startling aspect of the man. What was equally disturbing was the Master's size.

He was at least nine feet tall.

I gulped and turned my gaze to the second figure, Stayne. My appetite for amazement had been sated, so I barely blinked as I took in his bleached-white bones. *He is a bloody skeleton.* A walking, talking skeleton. *What the hell is going on here?* I paused, struck by a ludicrous thought.

Is this... hell? I certainly seemed to have fallen enough. I chuckled grimly. *Maybe it is, and maybe I deserve to be here.*

"What are you cackling at, human?" Stayne asked suspiciously. His empty orbs pulsed an ominous red. "You find all this funny?" He took a threatening step forward.

I scrambled backward and out of his reach. *Now, now, Michael,* I chided myself. *Wherever you are, you are in enough trouble already. Let's try not to ruffle the natives' feathers anymore, shall we?*

"Enough, Stayne," the Master snapped. "Help the boy up."

The skeleton hung his head sheepishly and lowered the weapon in his bony hands. It was a double-bladed axe, and I hadn't even noticed him draw the bloody thing. My eyes narrowed as I stared at the weapon. The axe head was formed from an obsidian metallic substance that I didn't recognize.

Stayne stepped forward again. This time I didn't back away and only watched warily as he stuck out his arm. Cautiously, I took the offered hand, and the skeleton heaved me to my feet.

I tottered slightly, wincing as new aches made themselves known, before regaining my balance. Standing beside the skeleton, I immediately noticed our disparity in height. Stayne loomed over me. I judged his height to be around six feet, which would put my own height at just under five and a half feet.

So, I'm short, I thought. I stared down at my arms. They lacked any muscle definition. *And thin.*

"That's better," the Master said. I still couldn't see his face. His voluminous black robe covered him from head to toe. Only his steel-clad boots and leather gloves were visible.

"Welcome, Michael," the Master said.

My head jerked involuntarily at that. "You know who I am?" I asked hopefully.

The Master shook his head. "No, Michael. I do not. Your memories were wiped when you were brought here. Only your name remains. You are a blank slate and free to write your story anew in whatever fashion you wish."

"Brought here?" I asked sharply, dissatisfied by his response. "Who brought me here? You?"

"Watch your tone, boy," Stayne growled.

The Master waved his servant to silence. "No, it was not me. I do not have the power to perform such a feat. Yet." He paused. "It was the Forces of the cosmos."

At my blank look, the Master continued, "Still your thoughts and focus your attention inwards. Make of your mind a still and waiting pool, and perhaps things will become clearer."

I stared at the so-called Master in consternation, wondering if I should do as he bade. Focus my attention inwards? How was that going to help? My gaze darted from the Master to Stayne. Both were watching me expectantly.

Just how crazy were these two? And me as well for contemplating doing what the Master asked. Still, it didn't look like I was going to get answers any other way. And besides, what could it hurt to try?

With a sigh, I closed my eyes and did my best to quiet my mind. A second passed. Then another. Nothing happened. "This is ridiculous," I said, feeling foolish. "Nothing is—"

I broke off as a strange and wholly unnatural sensation rippled through me. Something—*a foreign entity? an unfathomable consciousness?*—entered my mind, and words spilled across it.

Welcome to the Forever Kingdom, Michael.

You have been brought to this realm by the Forces of Light, Dark, and Shadow to participate in the Grand Game. Through your own deeds and actions in your past life, you have merited a place as a player in the Game.

Rest assured, you made the choice to enter the Forever Kingdom willingly. To preserve your sanity and to allow you to forge your destiny afresh and unburdened by your past, your memories have been wiped clean.

Good luck, and may fortune favor your Game!

My jaw dropped open, and for long moments my mouth worked soundlessly. "What was that?" I finally managed to ask.

The Master laughed, and even Stayne seemed to share in the amusement, snickering loudly.

"*That*, Michael," the Master said, "was the Adjudicator. And you, my dear boy, are the Game's newest participant."

CHAPTER 2: THE GRAND GAME

Confounded, I stared at the Master. "What is the Grand Game?"

"All in good time, my boy," the Master assured me. "But come now, you were the last. The others are waiting."

"Others? What others?" I asked.

The Master ignored me. Turning around, he floated away. The small circle of light that had illuminated my surroundings moved with him. In fact, the light seemed to be centered on his figure, but I still could not make out its source.

With the Master's departure, the encroaching darkness swallowed me, leaving me with only Stayne's glowing red eyes for company. "Damnit," I growled.

If I didn't want to be stuck alone in the dark again, I had no other choice but to follow the Master—as he likely very well knew. Cursing whatever fate brought me here, I hurried after his departing figure and the comforting globe of light that surrounded him.

~ ~ ~

With Stayne by my side, and the Master floating before us, we traversed the darkness. I tried questioning the Master—and even Stayne again—but both steadfastly ignored me. Left to myself, I turned my attention inwards and cautiously probed my mind, feeling again for the sense of the entity that had written in it before. But as hard as I tried, I caught no whiff of the mysterious being.

Presently we came to a cast iron door set in a wall of grey stone blocks. The walls extended to my left and right beyond the circle of light the Master cast, and I could not tell how far it stretched. Stayne stepped forward and unbarred the door, and as silently as ever, the master floated inside.

I followed after.

The room within was bare of furnishing but was thankfully well-lit, with torches set all along its four walls. The floor of the chamber was paved with the same grey stones as the wall, and the roof curved high overhead with its peaked center barely visible. Seated within the room were hundreds of people.

Some were human. Many were not.

I felt barely a flicker of surprise as my eyes roved over features that my mind identified as dwarven, elven, goblin, troll, orc, and many more. I knew with bone-deep certainty that besides my fellow humans, I had never encountered the likes of any of the other species in the room.

The thought was unexpectedly comforting.

It seemed that even though my memories had been wiped, I retained some connection to who I was—or had been. *I am still me in some sense.* It was reassuring to know that I was not wholly a blank slate, that some facet of who I was remained.

At our entrance, the quiet hum of conversation that had filled the room died down, and every gaze in the chamber turned our way. Immediately, I noticed an oddity.

Everyone in the room was dressed in the same manner: in white cotton shorts and shirts. I glanced down at myself.

I was dressed in the same clothes too. "Who are these people?" I whispered.

"They are your fellow candidates," the Master replied vaguely. "Like you, they will be competing for the honor of joining my cause in the Game."

I glanced at him. "Your cause?"

Once more, he ignored me. Gliding through the air, the Master floated upwards as he made his way to the center of the room, where he stopped, hovering high above us all. "Gather around candidates," the Master said, his voice as soft-spoken as ever but somehow still reaching me from a few dozen yards away. "The last of you have arrived, and it is time to begin."

Moving quietly, I slipped further into the room and sank to the ground in a cross-legged stance next to a human woman. With her attention fixed on the Master, she did not so much as glance at me.

The Master had fallen silent while he gathered his thoughts. "As the Adjudicator himself has already told you," he began after a moment, "you've been brought to the Forever Kingdom to become players in the Grand Game." He paused. "But you are not *yet* players. You are only candidates. Before you can fully participate in the Game, you must *earn* that right."

The Master spun a slow circle, surveying the hundreds of faces staring up at him. "And that is why you are all here: to compete against each other for the honor of becoming players in my faction: the Awakened Dead, the preeminent faction in the Axis of Evil."

There was some muttering at that. *Axis of Evil?* I thought, feeling my own measure of concern. It didn't sound like anything good. Nor did the Master's faction: the Awakened Dead. I wasn't sure I wanted to have anything to do with either.

"Silence," Stayne thundered from where he lurked by the door.

The Master chuckled, a grim, humorless sound. "I sense your unease, and I can taste your fear, candidates. Worried, are you, that the Axis of Evil is not for you?"

Some brave souls in the crowded room nodded. Instinctively, I held myself still and let no hint of my own thoughts slip. From behind, I felt Stayne's eyes sweep the room, and I had a feeling that those few who had let their own unease show would soon have cause to rue doing so.

"Make no mistake," the Master continued, "it is no accident that you have been reborn within the Grand Game in the very heart of the unholy alliance. Your memories may have been wiped, but it is your actions in your past life that brought you *here*." He laughed again. "Only the blackest of deeds would have brought you to *me*. Imagine the foulest thing you could do, and I assure you, you have done it *already*."

The Master paused and swept his gaze across the room again. "Like it or not, candidates, you are well-suited to the Dark. It lives and breathes in your souls."

The Master's gaze crossed my own. "Understand this: you *are* evil."

CHAPTER 3: THE EPITOME OF EVIL

I bit at the inside of my lip, fighting hard not to despair at the Master's assertions. Was it true?

Am I evil?

What had I been in my previous life? A serial killer? A mass murderer? A rapist? *Heavens forbid, I hope not.* I searched deep within myself yet could detect nothing within me that resonated with the Master's words. But the Master was still speaking, so I set aside my gnawing worry and listened to him again. I would have to think more about my origins later.

"Regardless of how you may feel—or think you feel—on the matter," the Master continued, "if you candidates want to live, you have no choice now but to complete the task I have set before you."

The Master pointed to another barred door at the room's far end. "When we are done here, you will proceed through that door. There you will choose your first Class."

Confused mutterings followed. The Master waved away the candidates' confusion. "I see some of you have no idea about what I speak of. No matter. Your questions will be answered in due course. Those of you who have tried interacting with the Game will have found it unavailable. This is because I have blocked your access to the Adjudicator, but in the room beyond, you will find the Game interfaces available again. It will tell you all you need to know about Classes."

I scratched at my chin, noting in passing that I had no beard. I knew what Classes were—or thought I did. *It is a gaming term.* Now how did I know that? Had I played in the Grand Game before?

"Once you have chosen your first Class," the Master said, "you will move beyond the next room and into the dungeon."

My ears perked up at that. We were going into a dungeon? That didn't bode well. I glanced at my flimsy clothes. *How will we survive without any gear?*

Seeming to read my thoughts, the Master addressed my concern. "Do not fear. Each of you will be provided with two pieces of equipment before you venture into the dungeon. Two pieces, mind, no more." The Master chuckled. "After all, where would the fun be in that? Additionally, I have a gift for each of you."

The floating black-robed figure raised his hands and muttered words under his breath that I failed to catch. My brows drew down. What was he doing?

I got my answer a moment later, as from somewhere unseen, the drumming of wings filled the air, seemingly as if in answer to the Master's call.

I glanced upwards at the shadowed ceiling. Sure enough, hundreds of tiny white flying forms were looping about in a furious circle. Where had the birds come from? Had the Master summoned the creatures? And how? I was certain they hadn't been in the room when we had entered.

The Master dropped his hands, and the birds dove downwards. Passing the black-robed figure, the flock split as individual creatures honed in on a different candidate.

One hurtled directly towards me, seemingly on a collision course with my nose. Hurriedly, I shielded my face with my arm while I waited for the inevitable crash.

It did not come.

Lowering my arm, I peeked at the white form hovering in front of me.

It was not a bird.

It was a bat. A fleshless bat.

~ ~ ~

I stared in amazement at the skeletal creature in front of me. No larger than my hand, the bat held itself stationary in the air with the flapping of its delicate wings. Its bones appeared too fragile to survive against any concerted attack—or keep it airborne, for that matter—yet the creature still exuded a cold menace.

As intently as I considered the bat, it studied me in return with the two glowing orbs of arctic light that I took for its eyes.

"Well? Aren't you going to say anything, human?"

I blinked. The bat had spoken. Its words echoed eerily through the gaping cavity that was its mouth and were barely understandable. Still, the creature *had* spoken.

And why not? What's one more wonder to heap upon all the other strangeness I've witnessed?

"Uhm, hi," I said. "I'm Michael."

The bat snorted. "I know *that*. Now, do you accept the Pact?"

I blinked again. "Pact?" I asked stupidly. "What Pact?"

Before the small skeleton could answer, the Master resumed speaking. "Before you candidates, you will find the familiar I have magnanimously provided each of you with. The creatures will guide and assist you in your journey through the dungeon. And in return for this: I ask nothing. I've unblocked your access to the Adjudicator. Turn your focus inwards and query the Game. You will find the Pact just as I've described. Read the terms and accept my generous offer."

I did as the Master asked, and more words unfolded in my mind.

Gnat, a level 20 skeletal bat, offers you a Pact. If you accept the Pact, for the duration of your time together, Gnat will serve as your familiar and boost your death magic skill by +1 rank. Your familiar cannot participate in combat or defend you in any way. This Pact may be terminated at any time by either party.

Do you accept Gnat's offer?

Ignoring the strangeness of the Game speaking in my mind again, I chewed over the information it had provided. One particular aspect fascinated me beyond all else.

Magic.

The Game's message implied that in this world, I could cast spells. Despite my concern about entering a dungeon or my worry that I was the blackest of souls indelibly tainted by evil, the thought that I had magic sparked a joy in me that I found hard to stem. Somehow, I *knew* that I had never wielded magic before, and the thought of doing it in this world excited me no end.

"Magic," I breathed to Gnat. "Your Pact will let me cast spells?"

The skeletal bobbed in the air. "No, human. I cannot give you what you already have. I sense a deep well of mana at your spirit's center. You possess magic already. You only have to unlock it, and the Game will allow you to do that without my aid. What I offer through the Pact is the means to advance your necromancy skill beyond levels you could normally. Now, do you accept my offer?"

Struggling to contain my excitement, I considered the terms of the Pact again as carefully as I could. The wording seemed simple enough, and I could spot nothing suspicious or anything that hinted at a hidden meaning. Finding no reason to do otherwise, I voiced my assent. "I accept your bargain."

You have sealed a Pact with a level 20 skeletal bat. Gnat is now your familiar.

You have gained the trait: undead familiar. This trait increases your necromancy skill cap by +1 rank.

CHAPTER 4: GNAT

On the tail end of my words, Gnat glided forward and alighted on my shoulder.

Turning to study him, I asked. "What now?"

The bat shrugged its tiny wings. "We wait for the others. Once they are done, the Master will give us further instruction."

Scanning the chamber, I saw that many of my fellow candidates were still conversing with the creatures that hovered before them. A few had already sealed their Pacts and, like me, were gazing about the room.

I turned back to my familiar. "What can you tell me about the Grand Game?"

Gnat laughed. "What can I *not* tell you? All that I know of the Game could fit a dozen books twice over. You will learn more soon enough. Be patient."

I narrowed my eyes. "At least tell me about the dungeon we are about to enter."

"I know little of how the dungeon has been configured," Gnat said. "No one does. Except for the Master, of course."

I sighed.

"There is one bit of advice I can give you, though," Gnat continued.

"What?" I asked eagerly.

"Don't die. You will not enjoy the experience," he said with a snicker of amusement.

I blew out a frustrated breath and turned away to consider the strange world I found myself in. If the Adjudicator was to be believed, I had chosen to enter the Forever Kingdom.

Why did I do so? I wondered. And could I carve out a life for myself in this world? If so, what sort of life would it be? Bowing my head, I lost myself in contemplation of the future.

It was a good few minutes before the murmur of conversation in the room died down again. When it did, I saw that, but for a handful of the candidates, everyone else had accepted the Pacts offered to them by their skeletal companions.

"Excellent," the Master said, sounding pleased. "Now, as to the details of the task before you. It is simply this: find your way out to the world above. While you venture through the dungeon, you will come across further Class stones beyond the initial one you will obtain in the next room. Each of these will grant you a Class. To reveal the dungeon's exit portal, you will need to fill all *three* of your Class slots. If you are confused as to my meaning, ask your familiar after you've chosen your primary Class."

I frowned. If I understood the Master, as a player, I would have three separate Classes. How to choose them, though? And were there any synergies between the Classes that I could exploit? These thoughts ran through my mind of their own accord, leading me to believe that whoever I had been in my previous life, I was no novice player.

Perhaps, I am more suited to this world and its Grand Game than I think.

"Our time together has come to an end," the Master said. "We will not see each other again, not unless you successfully navigate through the dungeon and graduate as players. One final word before I release you: there are no rules in the dungeon. I care not if you work together—or against each other."

The Master chuckled. "You may find that killing your fellow candidates will net you more experience than slaying the dungeon's inhabitants. So, murder whomever you please. It will be all the more amusing to watch. But wait until you enter the dungeon before you embark on your sprees of mayhem." The Master's voice turned harsh. "I will not tolerate any killings within my domain."

I shivered, not quite able to believe what the Master was encouraging us to do. Warily, I gazed to my left and right and found my fellows likewise eyeing me suspiciously.

Which amongst them will try to murder me? I wondered. And could I stomach attempting to kill them in turn?

"Now, if you will," the Master said, "make your way to the next room and choose your primary Class. Good luck, candidates, and may fortune favor your Game." With his piece said, the Master rose in the air and vanished into the shadows concealing the chamber's roof.

Setting aside my disquiet, I rose to my feet and studied the room again. The Master's parting words had created a renewed stir amongst the candidates, and all around me, I saw people banding together as they sought safety in numbers.

How long have the others been here? I wondered. Judging by some of the conversations floating around me, many of the candidates appeared quite at ease with each other. Enough so that they were willing to trust their companions to guard their backs against the others.

It was only I—the newcomer—that was a stranger to all. I grimaced. *Alone or in a group, I will survive,* I vowed.

Stepping around the still-forming parties, I joined the line leading to the room's exit at the far end. As I did so, from the corner of my eye, I noticed Stayne leaving his place by the entrance and moving into the chamber.

Tilting my head slightly, I observed the skeleton. Moving unhurriedly, Stayne pulled a candidate out of the line. She was one of those who had rejected the Pact, I noted.

Stayne herded the woman to a vacant spot near the chamber's entrance and left her standing there in confusion while he moved again to the line and gazed searchingly along its length. I studied the skeleton intently, watching to see what he would do, but I passed through the exit before I could see if he had pulled anyone else from the line.

Still, I couldn't help but wonder what Stayne was about.

CHAPTER 5: THE MASTER'S GIFTS

The room beyond was as large as the first chamber, but unlike the one before, it was not empty of furnishings. Stalls lined nearly the entirety of the room. All overflowed with items, and each was manned by a single unclothed skeleton.

Before I could move further into the room to explore its depths, I was stopped at the door by another skeleton.

"Stop," the figure commanded. Whereas the other undead in the room wore little in the way of clothes, the one who had intercepted me was fully dressed in shoes, pants, a shirt, and cloak. *Everything* he wore was some shade of red. Even the staff he twirled in his hands was crimson.

As I turned his way, he beckoned me. "Come here, human."

Curiously, I stepped up to him.

"Hold out your hand," he demanded.

I stared at him, making no move to comply.

"Do it," Gnat hissed. "The gatekeeper only means to issue you with the Master's tokens. You will need them to buy your Class stone and other items from the vendors."

I glanced from the bat on my shoulder to the stalls, having an inkling now as to what purpose they served. I held out my hand. Immediately the gatekeeper dropped three chips of black glass into my outstretched palm.

Curiously, I peered at the small polished bits that I held. They looked to be made from obsidian, and stamped in the center of each was what appeared to be a crow. I drew one up for closer inspection. The details included in the rendering of the bird were exquisite. Somehow the artist had managed—

"Enough gawking!" the red-clothed figure snapped. "Off with you now. You're holding up the line."

I clenched my fist around the tokens and glared at the gatekeeper before moving away to drift amongst the stalls.

The first stall I stopped at was laden with plate armor: legs, arms, gloves, helms, and breastplates. Each piece seemed to be formed from steel and was poorly made— to my eye, at least. I raised my gaze to the stall's vendor. His gleaming red eyes seemed to be bright with excitement.

"Ah, a customer," the merchant said. "What can I help you with, sir?"

I waved my hands across the untidy heap of equipment. "How does all this work?"

"It's simplicity itself," the merchant said, rubbing his hands together. "In exchange for one of the Master's tokens, you may take any piece of armor."

In the act of picking up a helm for closer inspection, I paused. "One piece only?" I asked disbelievingly. "Not an entire set?"

The skeleton chuckled. "No, no, no. Of course not. For that, you would need *far* more tokens."

I pulled back my hands and folded them behind my back. Considering that I only had three tokens, I was not going to waste any of them on a single armor piece. I glanced at the nearby stalls. Some were filled with weapons, others with shields, some with scrolls, and yet others with trinkets and jewelry.

Walking away from the armor vendor, I headed towards a weapon merchant's stall but stopped as Gnat spoke up. "Human, I would not purchase any items until you've chosen your Class."

"Why is that?" I asked, coming to a halt.

"Items have skill prerequisites. While you may still equip an item without the required skill, you will not gain any of the item's benefits. And it is your Class that determines what skills you will have access to."

I nodded. I didn't have to ask Gnat what he meant by skills. Somehow, I understood what they were already. *I really must have been a player in my previous life*, I thought.

"How many skills do I get from my Class?" I asked.

"Classes come in three tiers: basic, advanced, and master," Gnat said. "Basic Classes give you access to three starting skills."

My brows rose in surprise. That number appeared low. "Only three?" I murmured. "You said *starting* skills, though. Can I get more eventually?"

"You can," Gnat answered. "Through skillbooks, you can add three additional skills to your Class."

"I see," I said. And I thought I did. The Class stones only started a player down a specific development path. It did not completely define him. Something else occurred to me. "Do the other Class tiers grant more starting skills?"

"They do," Gnat confirmed. "But for your primary Class you may only choose a basic Class."

"Hmm," I mused, rubbing at my chin. Recalling the Master's words from earlier, I sought my familiar's confirmation, "I can have three Classes, right?"

"That is correct, human," Gnat said. "Every player can have a primary, secondary, and tertiary Class."

"Call me Michael," I said absently.

"As you wish," the skeletal bat replied.

I closed my eyes, thinking. Seeing as how I would only enter the dungeon with a single Class, there was no need to deliberate on my choice of secondary and tertiary Classes right now, and I dismissed them from my thoughts. I would consider them later once I understood this world far better than I did now.

What mattered now was that I would only have three skills available when I entered the dungeon. That, more than anything else, would determine the strategy I pursued. *Gnat is right*, I thought. Before purchasing any items, I needed to select my Class.

I opened my eyes. "Where is the Class vendor?"

Chapter 6: Gamers' Speak

There was already a queue at the Class vendor when I got there. I slipped into line and waited patiently as it moved slowly forward.

While I waited for my chance with the merchant, I turned to my familiar. It was time to find out more about what it meant to be a player in the Grand Game.

"So, Gnat," I began, "besides Classes and skills, what other characteristics do players have?"

"Attributes," Gnat grunted. "And before you ask me what they are, you can find out for yourself. Just ask your Adjudicator."

I tilted my head to the side while I considered the bat's response. *Why not?* I wondered. Turning my attention inwards, I blanked my mind and focused on a single thought: *attributes*.

To my surprise, my efforts yielded a response, and a window unfurled in my mind.

<u>Player Profile: Michael</u>
Level: 1. Rank: 0. Current Health: 100%.
Stamina: 100%. Mana: 100%. Psi: 100%.
Species: Human. Lives Remaining: 3.
Classes: 0 of 3. Traits: undead familiar.
Skills: none. Abilities: 0 of 0.
<u>Attributes</u>
Strength: 0. Constitution: 0. Dexterity: 0.
Perception: 0. Mind: 0. Magic: 0. Faith: 0.

Every skill and ability is governed by one of the seven attributes. They, in turn, act as a cap on both your skills and the number of abilities you can learn. For every rank you invest in an attribute, you can advance your skill level by ten and acquire one ability slot.

Strength is an attribute that primarily influences a player's ability with heavy and medium weapons. Each rank you invest in Strength also increases your carrying capacity by +10kg.

First and foremost, Dexterity determines a player's ability with light weapons and evasive combat maneuvers. Each rank in Dexterity also improves your speed by +1.

Perception influences a player's accuracy with ranged weapons, as well as his ability to anticipate his opponents' moves and sense oddities in the surroundings.

Constitution enables players to increase their health and fortitude, while Mind determines a player's ability with psionic skills and abilities.

Similarly, Magic influences the power of a player's elemental spells and Faith, the strength of a player's light, dark, shadow, necromancy, and life spells.

I exhaled a troubled breath as I tried to absorb the small avalanche of information the Game had thrown my way. More surprisingly, despite all the jargon, I was able to make sense of the Adjudicator's message.

It's gamer speak, something told me.

After I worked through the information, I turned to my familiar again. "Gnat," I said slowly, "if I understand correctly, attributes limit skill growth. Correct?"

"That's right," the bat said.

I frowned, puzzled. "Then, even if my Class unlocks new skills, how do I increase them without any starting attributes? They're all zero!"

Gnat chuckled. "All basic Classes come with a trait that boosts one or more attributes."

I rubbed my chin, initial worry subsiding. For a moment, I had feared I was an irrevocably broken character. "Do all players start with zero attributes?" I asked after a moment.

"They do," my familiar confirmed.

That at least seemed fair. "Besides Class traits, how else can I earn attribute ranks?" I asked.

"At every new player level, you will gain one attribute point to spend as you desire," Gnat said.

I winced. "Only one?"

The skeletal bat nodded.

That sounds harsh, I thought. It meant I would have to deliberate long and hard on how I invested my attribute points. I could not afford to waste any. "Is there any other way to earn more attributes?" I asked.

"Attribute gems can be found in dungeons and other places in the Forever Kingdom," Gnat said. "But don't count on finding any," he warned. "They are exceedingly rare."

Hmm. "And what's this bit about 'remaining lives?' What does it mean?"

Gnat stared at me. "Exactly what it says, human. You have only three chances to prove yourself."

I didn't like the sound of that 'only.' It implied that the dungeon would be exceedingly dangerous. "So if I die, I will be reborn? Is that it?"

Gnat nodded. "You will. But as I said before, you will not enjoy the experience. It is said to be exceedingly painful."

"And what happens after I die three times?" I asked.

"Then you'll be dead—permanently," Gnat said. "And your spirit will belong to the Master to do with as he pleases. Our lord may choose to raise up your spirit anew as an undead." The skeletal bat's eyes glinted. "Or gift it to one whom he favors."

I shuddered. Seeing the eager gleam in Gnat's eyes, I didn't ask what the one so-favored would do with my spirit. I suspected it would be nothing good.

I glanced at the candidates in front and behind me in the line. Some looked excited, others nervous, and a few downright terrified. "How many of us can expect to emerge alive from the dungeon?" I asked Gnat soberly. I didn't think it would be a lot.

"No more than a handful," Gnat said. "And that is under the best of circumstances. Whatever happens in the coming days, the Master's servants will feed well."

I gulped. My chances of surviving in this new world seemed slim at best, and I wondered anew what had possessed me to enter it. But there was no more time for further talk. I had reached the front of the line.

I sucked in a deep breath. It was time to begin playing the Game and forging myself into a player. Whatever happened, I would not go quietly to my death.

I will win free of this dungeon, I promised myself.

CHAPTER 7: CLASS SELECTION

The Class merchant did not bother to look at me when I stood in front of his table. Like the gatekeeper, he was fully clothed too, but less garishly. His clothes were shaded in muted tones of grey and brown. A hood concealed his face, and gloves hid his hands. I assumed that, like all the Master's other servants, he was an undead, but I couldn't be sure.

With his head still bowed, the cowled figure reached into the bag hanging off his chair back and picked out three small objects. He placed them on the table and said, "On the table before you, you will find three Class stones. Pick one. But before you do that, drop the Master's token into the chest on the right."

I glanced at the table. Arrayed on it were three gleaming marbles of solid bronze. They had to be the Class stones. Each marble was indistinguishable from the others and provided no indication of the Class it contained.

I frowned. "How am I to choose?" I asked. "I don't know what Class each offers."

"Query the Adjudicator," the merchant said disinterestedly. "Now hurry up. I have more customers waiting."

After a moment of frosty silence, I did as the merchant bade and willed the Game to reveal more about the three objects before me. This time, I was unsurprised when it responded.

This stone contains the path of: a warrior. The warrior is a basic Class that confers a player with three skills: a heavy weapon skill of the player's choice, an armor skill of the player's choice, and a shield skill of the player's choice. This Class also permanently boosts your Strength attribute by +1 and your Constitution attribute by +1.

This stone contains the path of a scout. The scout is a basic Class that confers a player with three skills: dodging, sneaking, and a light weapon skill of the player's choice. This Class also permanently boosts your Dexterity attribute by +2.

This stone contains the path of a caster. The caster is a basic Class that confers a player with three skills: wands, necromancy, and fire magic. This Class also permanently boosts your Mind attribute by +1 and your Faith attribute by +1.

"Well," I breathed. All three Classes were strangely familiar. I had seen them before or something very similar to them. The knowledge struck a chord within me, and a nugget of information from my past revealed itself.

"I was a gamer," I murmured.

"What's that?" Gnat asked, pinning me with his gaze.

"Nothing," I muttered. Suddenly, I was certain that I had never been part of the Grand Game before, but from whichever world I had come from, I had spent countless hours playing games of a similar nature.

Perhaps that is why I chose to enter this world. A world itself that was a game? The very idea would have been intoxicating.

While I was uncertain how much my former gaming knowledge would aid me, I knew to a large extent it *already* had, helping me understand the Adjudicator's, Gnat's, and even the Master's explanations about the Forever Kingdom.

I realized something else too. Even though I did not remember exactly where my knowledge of the Grand Game sprung from, I could—and should—trust my instincts to guide me.

I glanced back at the three Class stones. *So what are your instincts telling you now, Michael?*

Naturally, my first inclination was to pick the path of a caster. Undeniably, magic appealed to me. Still, I could not be hasty. I could only have three Classes, and for better or worse, my choice now would likely determine my fate in the near future.

Closing my eyes, I quietened my mind and let whatever knowledge that lurked deep in my subconscious rise to the fore.

Casters are usually weak early game.

The thought dropped into my consciousness with startling quickness, and I frowned as I considered it. It rang true. I took in the room again. I was still the only candidate not obviously part of a group. If I was going to venture into the dungeon alone—which at this point seemed likely—I could not afford to do so with a Class that hampered me further. I bit my lip. As much as I wanted magic, I knew with certainty that now was not the right time.

Casters also depend heavily on their spells.

And spells were something else I would lack early on. If I understood how abilities and attributes were related in this Game, if I chose the caster Class, until I gained more levels, I would only have two spells at my disposal: one faith-based and the other magic-based.

With a sigh, I quenched the urge to take up the caster Class stone and turned my attention to the other two marbles: the ones containing the path of the warrior and the scout. Neither particularly appealed to me. I glanced at the open bag hanging by the merchant's side and caught a glimpse of more bronze marbles within it.

"Why these Classes?" I asked abruptly. "Are they the only basic Classes you have to offer?"

"What?" the merchant asked, finally looking up.

The skin on the merchant's face was pale, pockmarked, and... rippled. He was not a skeleton, but he was undeniably undead. Looking closer, I saw that the open wounds on the undead's face were filled with wriggling maggots.

Urgh. I bit back my revulsion and fought my instinctive desire to step back. *Is he a ghoul?* I wondered.

"What?" the merchant repeated, scowling at my poorly concealed disgust.

Breaking off from my rapt study of the undead's rippling face, I pointed to his bag. "Do those other stones contain different Classes?"

"They do," the merchant replied. "What of it?"

"Then I'd like to see some other options," I said politely.

The merchant spat, sending a glob of spit and wriggling maggots my way.

I barely dodged the disgusting projectile in time. "What was that for?" I asked with a scowl of my own.

"*That* was for you thinking I would entertain your foolish wishes. You will choose from the choices before you, or not at all!"

My jaw dropped open. "That's ridiculous!" I said. "It's not as if I am asking you to—"

"Shut up, mortal!" the merchant broke in. "The Master only contracted me to provide you fleshlings with three choices. Having to deal with your kind is disgusting enough. I will not lower myself further to bargaining with *you*." With every word he uttered, the merchant's voice rose an octave, and by now, every gaze in the room was fixed on me and the irate undead.

"Now make your choice or begone!" the merchant hissed.

Shaken by the unexpected confrontation, I looked unsteadily from the merchant to my fellow companions. Many were glaring at me in anger, and I heard not a few choice curses flung my way. Turning slowly on my heels, I walked away from the stall.

"Don't think if you come back, you will be offered a different choice!" the undead yelled after me.

Ignoring him, I kept walking, wondering as I did what I was going to do now.

CHAPTER 8: A SHREWD STRATEGY

I toured the rest of the room, drifting past the other stalls while I regained my mental equilibrium. The confrontation with the merchant had shocked me badly and hinted at some deep-seated resentment on the undead's part.

Was it only towards me that the merchant's anger was directed? Or all 'fleshlings' as he had referred to us? Whatever the case, I knew I could not afford to anger the Class vendor again. My walk through the room had confirmed he was the only one offering Class stones.

There was no way I could enter the dungeon without skills of some kind. If I did that, I was sure I would die quickly and repeatedly. I sighed. One way or the other, I would have to return to the ghoulish merchant. But before I did that, I decided I would take the time to study my fellow candidates and observe *their* choices first.

The others moved together in groups as small as three to ones as large as twenty. Some were confident and strutted arrogantly, while others appeared nervous and indecisive. But as I perused the goods the many merchants had on offer, I noticed none of my fellows dared to question the Class vendor or refuse to make a Class choice.

After selecting their Classes, the crowd of candidates moved to the equipment vendors and began equipping themselves with swords, shields, axes, and wands. Much to my surprise, some of the groups pooled their tokens together and fully kitted only a single member—usually in plate armor and with the clear intention of making the chosen one the party's tank.

I shook my head. It was a bold strategy, but I couldn't see myself placing that much trust in another, *especially* after all the Master's talk of player kills yielding more experience. Still, it was their folly to commit. Idly, I followed one such party as they made their way to the room's far end.

It had been my initial plan to enter the dungeon as quickly as I could, to run ahead of the pack, so to speak. But with me not having chosen a Class yet, that was no longer an option. And truth be told, as a solo player, I wasn't sure how wise that option would have been in the first place.

Racing ahead of the other candidates might have given me the first stab at the best loot in the dungeon, but it also meant I would have been forced to face the dungeon's many perils first while also constantly being on the lookout for attacks from the rear from my 'fellows.'

As I thought further on it, I decided that the much better strategy would be to stay at the back of the pack, especially considering how dangerous Gnat had hinted the dungeon was. From the rear, I wouldn't have to worry about being hunted from behind, and while those ahead might out-level me, I would at least be able to explore the dungeon at a slower and more cautious pace.

Slow and steady is the wiser approach, I concluded.

With my course decided, I watched the party of eight—a clanking tank and, by the look of the wands the others carried, seven casters—enter the dungeon through one of six open doors set in the far wall of the chamber. A shimmering curtain of white crackling energy hung within all the doorways.

"What is that inside those doors, Gnat?" I asked.

"Those are the portals to the dungeon section allocated for the Master's trial," the skeletal bat replied.

"Portals?" I asked.

The familiar nodded. "The dungeon does not truly lie adjacent to the Master's domain. When you step through one of the doorways, you will be teleported to one of the Axis of Evil's sectors in the Endless Dungeon."

"What is the Endless Dungeon?" I asked in confusion.

"The Forever Kingdom is formed of two realms," Gnat answered. "The aboveground world loosely referred to as the Kingdoms and the subterranean world which we are in now, called the Nethersphere. The Nethersphere stretches nearly the breadth of the Forever Kingdom and is almost wholly made up of the Endless Dungeon, so named because, as yet, no one has been able to plumb its depths."

"I see," I said. "And do all six doorways lead into the same area of the Endless Dungeon?"

"They will all lead to the same sector," Gnat replied. "But at different starting locations."

I nodded thoughtfully, and leaning against an adjacent wall where I had clear line of sight of the six doorways, I set myself to observe my fellows making their way into the dungeon, and in particular, through which door each party ventured.

~ ~ ~

A good few hours later, I was still observing the stream of candidates making their way into the dungeon. Many threw me suspicious looks as they entered the dungeon, but I ignored their glares and kept as careful a tally as I could of which parties entered which doorway.

As time passed, my familiar got increasingly upset with my inactivity. "When will you enter the dungeon, human?" he inquired querulously. He had stopped calling me by name as his frustration grew. "I assure you the Master will be most displeased if you fail to attempt the trial he has set you."

"Relax, Gnat," I said. "I told you I would enter. Just not right yet."

"When?" he demanded.

"After the last party of candidates goes through," I repeated. *And when I can be sure none of the others are waiting behind to ambush me.*

"There are no more candidates in the room," Gnat hissed. "Soon, the merchants will begin closing their stalls. You best hurry if you intend on entering the dungeon."

Turning around, I saw to my surprise that the skeletal bat was right. I had been so focused on watching the dungeon entrances I had lost track of the state of the room behind me.

I kicked off the wall. "Alright, Gnat, let's get shopping. Then we begin our dungeon crawl."

CHAPTER 9: GETTING READY

"You again," the ghoul muttered.

"Me again," I agreed, standing in front of the Class vendor.

The undead merchant looked at me suspiciously. "So, are you going to buy something this time or just stand around and complain?"

Rather than attempt to debate his unjust statement, I only nodded agreeably. "I am ready to choose my Class."

The ghoul reached into his bag again. This time instead of placing the first bronze marbles he withdrew onto the table, he sniffed each carefully until he found the three particular stones he searched for. Once the merchant was satisfied, he arranged them in front of me. "Choose then."

I inspected the three Class stones. Unsurprisingly, I saw they contained the same Classes I had rejected earlier, but I had already made my peace with that and was ready to choose.

Given that I had already ruled out the caster Class as an option, my next inclination was to go with the path of a warrior. Fighters, I knew, were powerful early on, even if they were usually less so end-game when casters came into their own.

But after giving the matter much thought, I had decided that becoming a warrior would be as much a mistake as picking the caster Class. Primarily, this was because a fighter usually depended heavily on his gear, and seeing as how I would only be able to buy two pieces of equipment, I realized I would be exceptionally underdressed for my venture into the dungeon.

On the other hand, a scout was far less dependent on equipment. As a scout, I would have the dodging and sneaking skills at my disposal. With those skills, I would have a good chance of surviving most encounters—when I wasn't able to avoid them altogether.

Or so I hoped.

The path of the scout was not ideal, and ordinarily, I suspected I wouldn't have chosen it, but given the options in front of me, I thought it gave me the best chance of surviving until I could pick up a second Class. I would make sure, I assured myself, that my choice of secondary Class was one less constrained by necessity.

"Well?" the ghoul barked, interrupting my musing.

I shook my head to clear it. Dropping one of the Master's obsidian glass chips into the merchant's coin chest, I picked up the bronze marble containing the path of the scout. "I'll take this one."

The merchant only grunted in response and began packing up his stall.

I held the marble in my hand, wondering what came next. I was about to turn to Gnat for advice when I felt the bronze stone turn warm.

Glancing down, I saw the stone turn misshapen before melting entirely to vanish beneath my skin. "What in the world—" I began.

I broke off as the Adjudicator spoke in my mind again.

You have acquired the scout Class. You have gained the base trait: nimble. This trait increases your Dexterity by +2 ranks. Your level cap for dexterity-based skills has increased to 20.

You have gained two basic skills: dodging and sneaking. Choose your light weapon skill from the list of those available.

Following the Adjudicator's words, a long line of text scrolled through my mind: light weapon skills. All of them were familiar and matched one or another of the weapons I had seen in the vendors' stalls.

Curiously though, some of the skills were labeled as 'advanced.' "Gnat, are their different grades of skills?"

The skeletal bat nodded. "Yes. As with Classes, skills can belong to any one of three tiers: basic, advanced, and master."

"Hmm," I murmured. Just on principle, I was tempted to choose one of the advanced light weapon skills—like the one labeled kukri—but while the idea of having an advanced skill was nice, some instinct warned me that such skills were matched with weapons that were usually rare or hard to come by.

I will be more likely to find a common dagger or short sword than a kukri in the dungeon, I thought.

Considering that whatever choice I made would be my only weapon skill until I picked up another Class, I decided to go with my original choice of short swords.

You have gained the basic skill: shortswords. Initial scout Class configuration complete. Remaining Class skill slots: 3. To gain further Class traits, advance your Class rank.

Hmm, advance my Class... That sounded interesting, but I left off further deliberation of the matter for later. Now that I had my Class, I was eager to begin my journey in the dungeon.

Whistling contentedly, I strolled to the weapons vendor I had picked out earlier.

~ ~ ~

Even as I took my first steps as a scout, I sensed something different about myself. My stride was surer, my feet bounced lightly off the ground, and my body felt far more coordinated.

Extraordinary, I thought. The effect, I knew, had to be a result of the two additional ranks in Dexterity that the Class had given me. On a whim, I tensed my haunches and launched myself upwards into the air.

And executed a perfect backflip.

"Wow," I breathed in awe as I landed back on my feet. I was amazed that I had managed to pull off the maneuver. Adrenaline surged through me, and my heart beat rapidly. It had been exhilarating.

As dangerous as this Grand Game appears to be, perhaps, there will be aspects of it that I will come to enjoy.

I turned my mind to the other 'gifts' the Class had given me. Merely thinking about the three new skills was enough to trigger an avalanche of data into my mind. The information felt at once both foreign and familiar.

Instinctively, I dropped into a crouch and padded forward stealthily.

You have failed to conceal yourself from the nearby entities. You have failed to advance your sneaking: skills cannot be gained in this area.

Despite my failure, I laughed. "Incredible," I chuckled.

"If you are done playing," Gnat said acerbically. "We'd best get moving before all the vendors leave."

I smiled at the skeletal bat. Not even my familiar's sour words could destroy my happy mood.

"Alright, let's go," I said.

~ ~ ~

You have acquired a basic steel shortsword. This item increases the damage you deal by 10%.

You have acquired a common thief's cloak. This item increases your sneaking skill by +3 when in dark environments.

I used my last two tokens from the Master to buy a basic weapon and the item of clothing that I felt would best suit my skill set. I secured the sword around my hip with the belt and scabbard that came with it and draped the cloak over my shoulders. So equipped, I padded towards the dungeon's entrance.

I was finally ready to enter its depths.

CHAPTER 10: THE DUNGEON

I chose the portal that I had seen the lowest number of large groups go through and stepped in front of its door.

I studied the shimmering curtain of white in the doorway, suddenly nervous. "Ready, Gnat?" I asked.

The skeletal bat snorted. "Of course." The familiar eyed me sideways. "You, on the other hand, don't appear to be so sure anymore."

I shifted from foot to foot. Gnat was right. Now that the moment had arrived, I felt fear stir within me at the thought of deliberately putting myself in a life-and-death situation.

No doubt about it: I was scared. *The fear is natural,* I told myself. I would be a fool *not* to be scared. But even knowing all that to be true, I still couldn't force my feet forward.

I squeezed my eyes shut. Thus far, I hadn't questioned too closely anything the Master had said or the circumstances I found myself in. Mostly because I was afraid I wouldn't like the answers.

I had just kept moving forward because so much of what I had been asked to do seemed so familiar and because it was easier to do as I was told rather than fight against the tide. *But,* I thought, *if I survive what comes next, that has to change.*

I wasn't sure I trusted the Master.

I had many unanswered questions about who he was and what he asked of us. Yet, here, in what appeared to be the heart of his domain, I didn't think I would find the answers I desired. But in the dungeon... There, I would be out from under the Master's thumb, and perhaps I could forge my own path.

Either way, whether to follow the Master's path or create my own, I have to enter the dungeon.

I opened my eyes. *Right. Enough delaying.* Exhaling a heavy breath, I stepped forward through the portal.

~ ~ ~

You have entered sector 14,913 of the Endless Dungeon. This area has been previously explored and is presently under the control of the Axis of Evil. This sector is a closed region, cordoned off from the rest of the dungeon. It was last populated 8 hours ago by denizens of the Dark.

Recommended player levels: 1 to 20.

Recommended party size: 4 to 6.

You have been allocated a new task: <u>Escape the Dungeon</u>. Your objective is to fill all 3 of your Class slots. Once you have done so, the way out will be revealed.

Coming out of the portal, I dropped down into a crouch. A swift glance revealed I was in a small chamber. Moving quickly, I padded away from the entrance and into the room's darkest corner.

You and your familiar are hidden.

Safely concealed, I took stock of my surroundings once more. Large cobwebs draped the room's ceiling and walls. Other than the still-glowing portal, there was no other light source in the chamber. The floor was paved with granite flagstones, and the walls were formed from rough-cut bricks. There was an open door at the room's far end, and beyond it, I spied a long corridor extending away.

Most gratifying of all, the room was empty.

The tension in my shoulders eased as I realized this. Rising to my feet, I unwrapped my fingers from the hilt of my shortsword.

I was safe. For now.

I glanced at my familiar. All this time, he had not moved from his roost on my shoulder. He had kept his presence so still and small I had almost forgotten about him. Only belatedly did it occur to me to wonder if my sneaking skill would apply to Gnat, but it had worked to cloak his presence too—which was a relief.

My relief was short-lived, though, as another worrying thought occurred to me. "Gnat, I used my sneaking skill to hide, didn't I?"

"You did," the bat confirmed.

I frowned. "Then why didn't my skill improve? Surely at my low level, even a single successful use should've been enough to advance it?"

"Most skills only advance in level when employed in combat or when used in the presence of hostiles," Gnat replied.

"Oh," I said, my lips turning down. It had been in the back of my mind to try training my skills *before* engaging in combat, but that didn't seem possible.

Seeing my disappointment, Gnat laughed. "You didn't think leveling would be that easy, did you?"

Ignoring my familiar's amusement, I returned my attention to the surroundings. I walked to the center of the room and spun in a slow circle. Nothing further of interest revealed itself. *Alright then*, I thought. *Time to move beyond.*

Hunching down, I tiptoed to the room's only exit and peered cautiously around the doorway. The corridor extended for a hundred yards before ending at another wooden door, which appeared ajar, but from this distance, I couldn't be certain.

The corridor itself appeared empty of threat. Firelight blazed golden from the torches affixed to the walls along both sides of the passage. I grimaced. As brightly lit as the corridor was, I doubted I would be able to conceal my presence once I stepped down its length.

Even though the corridor appeared safe, at equidistant intervals between the torches, doorways gaped open. Anything could be in the rooms they led into. But the only way I was going to find out what lay inside them was by venturing down the passage.

I shifted restlessly. *Entering the corridor will be dangerous.* I almost snorted in amusement at the thought. *This is a dungeon, Michael. You didn't think it would be safe, did you?*

Alright, alright, I thought and shifted forward. Then paused as a thought occurred to me. I glanced at my familiar. "Gnat, how silent can you be?" I whispered.

The skeletal bat eyed me suspiciously. "Why?"

I gestured to the first door on the right side of the corridor. It was less than ten yards ahead. "Go scout that room."

My familiar stared at me for a long moment, seeming to search for a reason why he shouldn't or couldn't do as I asked.

I waited.

Eventually, Gnat rose wordlessly off my shoulder. Flapping hard, he winged his way to the ceiling before gliding silently along its length and into the room I had picked out.

Clenching my sword hilt tightly, I counted off the doorways in the corridor while I waited for Gnat's report. There were thirteen in total.

It did not take the bat long to emerge from the first room. Flying swiftly, Gnat shot out of the chamber, but instead of returning to my shoulder, he flew into the next doorway. A few seconds later, my familiar reappeared before disappearing again into another room.

Understanding what Gnat was about, I waited patiently for him to be done. Shortly thereafter, the skeletal bat flew out the last of the passage's doorways and dropped onto my shoulder. "They're all empty," he reported laconically.

I waited for him to go on, but when he didn't, I prompted, "And?"

"And it looks like a few candidate parties have already been through the rooms," Gnat answered.

My eyes narrowed. "How can you tell?"

Gnat shrugged. "Go see for yourself."

Frowning at my familiar's non-answer, I rose to my feet, intent on doing just that.

CHAPTER 11: MOVING ON

On entering the first room, I immediately realized what Gnat meant. The stink of death hung heavily in the room. Four corpses were strewn across the floor. All appeared humanoid. One, in particular, caught my attention.

It was a candidate.

Fighting back the sudden heaving of my stomach, I stepped closer and crouched on my haunches next to the slim body. It was a dead elf.

The candidate's flimsy cotton clothes had been ripped to shreds, and three gaping holes marred his torso, exposing his innards and spilling blood everywhere. It was a ghastly sight.

I closed my eyes and breathed in and out rapidly through my mouth. When I had my nausea under control, I asked, "Gnat, why is this body here?"

I felt my familiar study me. My eyes were still closed. "What do you mean?" he asked.

"Didn't you say we had three lives? Surely this candidate couldn't have died his final death in this room: the very first in the dungeon?"

Gnat chuckled. "You *do* have three lives, but you still die as you would normally each time, leaving behind a corpse and all your belongings. Players are only reborn after their spirits manage to escape their prison of rotting flesh. This can take anywhere between a few hours to a day." He paused. "I told you: dying will not be pleasant."

I swallowed. To be dead for a few hours—or even days—sounded horrible. "Where would this elf be reborn? Back in the Master's domain?"

"No," Gnat answered. "There will be a safe zone with a rebirth well somewhere in this sector of the dungeon. The candidate would be reborn there."

I opened my eyes and glanced at my familiar. "So the elf would be separated from his party?"

Gnat shrugged. "Most likely. Unless they all die too, of course."

Harsh, I thought. It seemed that even in a party, surviving the dungeon would not be easy. *I bet all those players who gifted their tokens to their party leaders are regretting it now.* I rose to my feet and moved to inspect the other corpses close by.

The three other dead appeared to be of another species. They were uniformly green-skinned and small, with the largest being no more than three feet tall. The creatures had sharpened teeth, filed to gleaming points, and hardened black talons on their fingertips.

They were all also naked.

It seemed the surviving candidates had stripped their kills of their belongings, leaving the dead with only their small clothes. "What are these creatures?" I asked Gnat.

"Goblins," he replied.

I stared at him, considering his response. "Are they real?" I asked finally.

Gnat tilted his head to the side and studied me curiously. "Of course, they are real. Why would you ask that human?"

I shook my head, not sure myself what had made me ask the question. "How did the goblins get here? Or do they live in the dungeon?"

Gnat snorted. "No one wants to live in a dungeon, not even goblins. Although there are rumors of strange tribes in some of the more remote and unexplored regions of the Endless Dungeon," he admitted. "But as to your question, this sector of the dungeon was cleared and claimed by the unholy alliance long ago. For this trial, the Master would have populated it as he saw fit. The goblins and any other creatures you encounter will all have been teleported in by the Master's servants."

I nodded thoughtfully. *So this sector of the dungeon is part of the Master's domain too.* From Gnat's explanation, it sounded as if the Master controlled it fully. I would do well not to forget that. I swept my gaze across the room again.

Like the dungeon's entry chamber, the room was mostly unfurnished. Against one wall of the room, I spotted a wooden chest. Eagerly, I peered inside. It was empty. Disappointed, I turned my gaze upon the rest of the room. There didn't appear to be anything for me to loot. "Do you see something of use here, Gnat?"

"No," he barked. "Your fellows have done a good job stripping the room bare."

I sighed. "Alright, let's get moving," I said and slipped out of the room.

~ ~ ~

I explored each of the other rooms as meticulously as I had the first. After entering the sixth room, I became inured to the smell of death, and my stomach stopped heaving at the sight of butchered corpses and bloody entrails.

The first twelve rooms that I investigated—six on either end of the corridor—contained nothing remotely valuable. I imagined a whole host of players had searched them before me and stripped them of every useable item.

The rooms had all been configured in a similar fashion. Each contained only one piece of furnishing: an empty wooden chest. The scenes of violence depicted in the chambers did not vary much either. In each room, there were between one to three dead goblins and, in rare instances, a single dead candidate as well.

I drew some comfort from that.

For the level one and nearly naked candidates to defeat the goblin squads with so few losses meant the creatures were not exceedingly dangerous opponents. It boded well for my own chances.

The thirteenth chamber, though—the one at the end of the corridor—was wholly different from the other rooms. For one, it was three times as large, and for another, it contained plenty more corpses.

Stopping in the room's open doorway, I studied its interior intently. An open archway situated on the right wall led to another corridor and what I took to be the next section of the dungeon.

Heaped in the middle of the chamber were eight hacked-up corpses. All goblins. From blood spatters on the wall and the copious amount of blood on the floor, it seemed like a violent battle had raged in the room. Nor were the goblins the only ones that had died in the room. Near the dead goblins was a smaller pile of four white-clothed candidates—equally savaged.

Another two dead candidates were in the far left corner of the room. The pair were human and of similar size. More interestingly, unlike the other dead in the room, the two humans' bodies were *not* riddled with wounds.

How did they die, then?

I studied the layout of the room again. The two dead humans were separated from the slain goblins and candidates in the chamber's center by a good few yards.

They didn't die fighting the goblins then, I thought.

Stepping carefully into the room and giving the heaped corpses in its center a wide berth, I knelt beside the human corpses. There was a tiny glint of metal in the neck of each.

Darts, I realized. Each gleaming length of metal—no wider than my finger—was lodged deep in its victim, but the darts themselves looked too tiny to have killed the candidates. Frowning, I reached down to pull out one of the projectiles for closer inspection.

Only then did I notice the wooden chest lying beyond the corpses. It was closed. Some buried instinct cried out in warning at the anomaly. Why was this chest closed? All the others I had encountered thus far had been opened and looted.

Halfway to touching the darts, I pulled back my reaching fingers. Sitting back on my haunches, I inspected the tableau again. Given the candidates' proximity to the closed chest, they had likely been attempting to open it when they had died.

Of course, I thought, suddenly understanding what had happened to the pair. They had triggered a trap. The darts were probably coated with poison—a particularly virulent one, too, to have killed the two so quickly. *Good thing I didn't touch the darts.*

Is the chest still trapped? I wondered. I eyed the chest askance. Considering it was still closed, it likely was. But why had the other candidates not tried opening the chest after the first failed attempt? Unless...

I rubbed at my chin. I was assuming that both humans had died at the same time. But what if they hadn't? Did the two corpses represent not one but two *separate* attempts to open the chest?

I was sure one failed attempt would not have been enough to deter the other candidates from trying to loot the chest. Two failed attempts, though... that likely had frightened even the most foolhardy amongst them.

I frowned as another thought occurred. "Gnat, why is this chest trapped?"

"I don't understand your question, Michael," he replied.

"All evidence suggests the chests in the other rooms weren't trapped, so why was this one?"

"Ah," the bat replied. "By all appearances, this room contained the final encounter of the first leg of this dungeon sector. Such encounters are usually designed to provide a tougher challenge." Gnat paused. "Also, the Master will have configured the dungeon to become progressively more difficult."

I winced. "Does that mean further areas of the dungeon will contain more powerful foes?"

"Undoubtedly," Gnat replied.

I sighed. I was hoping he wouldn't say that. It meant I couldn't walk away from the chest. Even considering the risk of triggering its trap, I could not ignore the potential loot the chest contained. I would need every advantage I could grab to survive further on in the dungeon.

So how do I go about opening the chest? I wondered. *And preferably without killing myself.*

CHAPTER 12: TRAPPED GAMES

"I don't suppose you could open the chest, Gnat?" I asked.

"No," the skeletal bat replied curtly.

"Why not?" I persisted. "I mean, it's not like poison should affect an undead, right?"

Even though he had no face, Gnat managed to convey the impression that he was scowling. "Our Pact does not allow me to aid you in that manner," he said grumpily.

I scratched my head. I didn't recall seeing anything in the Pact that forbid the bat from aiding me in out-of-combat situations. Still, I had no means of forcing Gnat to help me.

Letting the matter lie, I turned my attention back to the chest. Like the ones in the other rooms, the chest was a simple top-lidded box with no locking mechanism. My gaze drifted to the two corpses. The poison darts had been driven upwards into the humans' necks, which suggested the darts had been fired from below.

The trap must have been triggered when they lifted the chest's lid. I bit the inside of my lip. Assuming that was how the trap mechanism worked, it should be simple enough to defeat it.

But if I am wrong...

I quelled my doubts and got to work. First, I grabbed the humans by their legs and gingerly dragged them away from the chest. Then I set about removing the poison darts from their necks.

I did not do anything so foolish as to use my bare fingers, of course. Stripping off both candidates' white shirts, I cut them into long strips with my sword.

With my hands wrapped in my makeshift cotton gloves, I removed the two darts and wrapped them securely in cotton strips of their own. Given how potent the darts' poison must have been to fell their victims so quickly, I was betting that some of the poison still remained on the darts. Which, if it was true, would make them very useful indeed.

I heaved a sigh of relief when I completed my work and had both darts secured in rolls of cotton cloth.

You have acquired two used darts coated with an unknown toxin.

I smiled at the Game's confirmation of my suspicion. "Good," I breathed. With the first half of my labor completed, I set about the second half of my plan.

Removing my thief's cloak, I lay flat on the floor with my back pressed against the ground. I wrapped the cloak around my right arm, shielding my bare flesh as much as possible in its thick layers of fabric.

Then I drew my shortsword and inched closer to the trapped chest. Placing myself to the chest's left—and hopefully out the dart's line of fire—I slowly extended the sword in my right hand and wedged it under the lid. The sword tip slid into place without resistance.

I held my breath, waiting.

Long seconds passed, and nothing happened. Tentatively, I pushed my sword in deeper and forced the lid to open an inch further.

I stopped again, waiting.

Still the trap did not trigger.

Growing bolder, I angled the sword in my hand downwards and gradually levered the lid open further.

A second passed. Then another. And just as I began to think the trap was no longer active, a metallic ping echoed resoundingly loud in the silence.

I froze. Moving slowly, I turned to study the room's far end. That was where the sound had come from. After a moment, I spotted the gleam of a dart on the floor. The sound I had heard was the dart impacting against the chamber's stone walls.

I grinned. I had done it. Pushing down on my sword again, I flipped open the chest's lid all the way. Two more pings echoed through the room as a pair of darts flew across the chamber. I gave it another minute before rising to my haunches and peering warily into the chest.

Congratulations, Michael! You have successfully opened a booby-trapped chest without falling victim to its lethal toxins and have gained experience.
You have reached level 2!
You have 1 attribute point available.

My grin split into a broad smile. "Well, well, isn't that nice," I murmured. I hadn't expected to gain any experience in the process of opening the chest, but I would take it. Turning my attention downwards, I studied the chest's contents.

It held only a few items. Reaching inside, I removed them one at a time.

You have acquired 2 minor healing potions. Each item restores your health by 10%.
You have acquired a backpack. This item can hold up to 10kg.
You have acquired a pack of six field rations. This item can be consumed to replenish stamina slowly over time.
You have acquired one flask filled with water. This item can be consumed to replenish stamina slowly over time.

The loot was slightly disappointing but useful nonetheless. Holding up one of the healing potions, I studied it. The potion was in a stoppered stone vial that looked like it could survive hard use. The water flask looked similarly durable.

Next, I inspected one of the field rations. Opening the foil-like wrapping covering it, I sniffed at the ration's contents delicately. It was odorless.

I only hope it is not tasteless as well. While I felt no pangs of hunger at the moment, I hadn't eaten since arriving in this world, and I knew sooner or later I would be grateful for having the rations.

Lastly, I inspected the backpack. It was a plain brown leather bag of sturdy construction that I could carry easily across my shoulders. *Handy*, I thought.

~ ~ ~

It took me only a few minutes to store all the loot in my new backpack. When I was done, I moved to the right side of the room and studied the corridor leading away from it.

Like the first passage, the new corridor continued unerringly straight and was interspersed with rooms on either side. But the second corridor did not terminate in a room. Instead, at its far end, I made out what appeared to be a four-way intersection.

I didn't step into the second corridor immediately. I placed myself in the right corner of the room and sat down cross-legged. Rubbing my chin, I pondered what I had seen of the dungeon so far.

Goblins and traps.

I still had no idea how I would fare in combat against the goblins—and I wasn't exactly eager to find out—but what worried me more than the goblins was the thought of encountering further traps. With the goblins, at least, I would have enough forewarning, but with a trap? Would I fall prey to one and die just as suddenly as the two victims claimed by this room's trap?

"Gnat," I asked after a moment's thought. "How do I spot traps?"

"There are skills and abilities that let you do so," the skeletal bat replied.

"But I don't have any of them," I protested.

Gnat chuckled. "Then you are out of luck, I'm afraid."

I sighed.

"You can try to look at things *really* hard," the bat suggested unhelpfully.

I ignored his poor attempt at wit. "What about Perception?" I asked.

"What about it?" Gnat responded.

"Will it allow me to detect a trap before I trigger it?"

"Not normally, no," Gnat said. "Perception will help you spot oddities in your surroundings, but on its own, the attribute will not give you the knowledge necessary to determine the source of the strangeness. Although," the bat admitted, "all skills required for trap detection *are* perception-based."

I frowned. Noticing an oddity but not being able to divine its source did not sound all that helpful. Still, doing so would at least provide me with some forewarning of danger. *And some warning is better than none.*

My new level had given me an attribute point to spend, and at the moment, investing it in Perception seemed the wisest course. "How do I use my available attribute point?" I asked.

"Simply will your request to the Adjudicator," Gnat said succinctly.

I grunted. *Of course,* I thought. *How else?* But before I finalized my decision, I needed to inspect my profile in more detail. Closing my eyes, I willed the Game to display my player data.

Player Profile: Michael

Level: 2. Rank: 0. Current Health: 100%.
Stamina: 100%. Mana: 100%. Psi: 100%.
Species: Human. Lives Remaining: 3.

Attributes

Available: 1 point.
Strength: 0. Constitution: 0. Dexterity: 2. Perception: 0. Mind: 0. Magic: 0. and Faith: 0.

Classes

Primary Class: Scout (basic).
Secondary Class: None.
Tertiary Class: None.

Traits

Undead familiar: +1 to necromancy rank.
Nimble: +2 Dexterity.

Skills

Available skill slots: 3.
Dodging (current: 1. max: 20. Dexterity, basic).
Sneaking (current: 1. max: 20. Dexterity, basic).
Shortswords (current: 1. max: 20. Dexterity, basic).

Abilities

None.

Equipped

1 common thief's cloak (+3 sneaking).
1 basic steel shortsword (+10% damage).

Backpack Contents

6 x field rations.
1 x flask of water.
2 x used poison darts.
3 x unused poison darts.
2 x minor healing potions.

I took a moment to study the information the Adjudicator provided. Everything appeared fairly self-explanatory, and I saw nothing inconsistent with the various explanations I'd been given thus far.

Without delaying further, I willed my Perception to increase.

Your Perception has increased to rank 1. Your level cap for perception-based skills has increased to 10.

I opened my eyes and looked around. The world appeared different. The change was nearly imperceptible, but somehow the room's shadows seemed less deep and the details on the bricks on the far wall less blurred. *My eyesight has grown sharper,* I thought.

I wrinkled my nose. Was it my imagination, or had the stink of the corpses worsened? *No, my smell has improved, too.* One by one, I inspected my other senses and noticed a change in them too. I smiled in satisfaction and rose to my feet.

Feeling better equipped to face the dungeon's challenges, I stepped into the second corridor.

CHAPTER 13: SIDE TRIP

The second leg of the dungeon had twenty rooms. Disappointingly, despite searching each chamber diligently, I failed to find any usable items in them.

Gnat's prediction proved correct too. As evidenced by the corpses in the many rooms, the dungeon's encounters had grown more difficult. In this section, the candidate parties had faced off against goblin squads sized between three and six.

It caused me to worry afresh. Would the size of the goblin parties keep growing? And if that happened, would I be vastly under-leveled when I fought my first skirmish? I was growing increasingly certain that that would be the case, and in hindsight, I regretted my decision not to join the first rush of candidates into the dungeon.

Still, there was little I could do about my decision to lag behind the others. All I could do now was try not to fall too much further back.

But despite the new urgency that gripped me, I did not let myself grow incautious and rush my investigations. Using my sneaking skill, I concealed myself each and every time before entering an unexplored room. I did not want to fall victim to a trap due to carelessness, nor did I want to miss any potential loot.

Still, I was none the richer when I reached the crossroads I had spied earlier. Standing at the intersection of the four passages, I studied the three unmapped corridors.

The first passage continued straight ahead and was seemingly unchanged from the corridor I had just explored. The passages to my right and left were both smaller and darker. No torches lit their depths, and where the corridor ahead was nearly four yards across, the ones to the right and left were barely two yards wide.

Briefly, I debated whether I should explore the darkened passages, but in the end, I didn't see how I had any choice. If I wanted to be better prepared to face the threats that undoubtedly still lurked in the dungeon, I had to gain more levels, even if it meant taking dangerous risks.

Dropping into a crouch, I ventured into the right corridor.

You and your familiar are hidden.

~ ~ ~

To my surprise, it was not pitch black in the side passage. Ten yards in, as I waited for my sight to adjust to the darkness, I noticed the ceiling was glowing.

At first, I had thought my eyes were mistaken, but after long minutes when the ceiling retained its shining cast, I realized that I was not imagining things and that there really was a light source on the roof.

Luminous crystals, I thought, finally identifying what I was seeing. They provided enough light to see but not enough to beat back the darkness. Turning my gaze forward, I studied the side passage again. The shadows concealing its depths had assumed enough definition for me to make out that the darkened holes to my left and right were open doorways.

So, despite its lack of light, the passage's configuration is much the same as the main corridor. Cautiously, I advanced further. I paused on the threshold of the first room and listened, but nothing jumped out at me, nor did I hear anything. I slipped inside.

Even in the darkness, I could make out that the chamber was empty. *Really* empty. The room didn't contain so much as a looted chest. There weren't even any dead bodies on the floor. I frowned. As empty as the chamber was, I couldn't figure out its purpose.

I spent a few fruitless minutes searching the room but didn't uncover any clue as to what it had contained. The next room was just as empty. As was the next and the next.

It was baffling.

What possible purpose can the empty rooms serve? I wondered. I was no closer to figuring out the mystery when I reached the end of the side passage—an abrupt cul-de-sac. Scratching my head in confusion, I studied the blank-faced wall in front of me. "Right, this was a complete waste of time," I muttered.

My back and knees were killing me from the sustained half-crouch I had maintained while exploring the side passage. I hadn't dared leave hiding the entire time, but now having confirmed the emptiness of the passage, I began to rise to my full height.

Your sneaking has increased to level 2.

Mid-motion, I froze.
What the—? My thoughts raced as I studied the Game message in my mind.

Your sneaking has increased to level 3.

There was only one explanation, I realized. Something was in the passage with me. Something hostile. I dropped fully back into my crouch. The agony in my overstrained limbs was forgotten, banished by a sudden surge of adrenaline. Maintaining my still posture, I strained my ears and listened intently.

Nothing.

A hostile entity has failed to detect you! Your sneaking has increased to level 4.

Cautiously, I set my hand to the hilt of my sword and ever-so-slowly began to draw it. *What is out there?* I wondered. The creature—whatever it was—was nearby, although it had obviously not been this close all along.

My gaze slid to the last room I had just exited. Had the creature been hiding in there? But no, that couldn't be; otherwise, my skill gains would have triggered when I had entered the room, not after I left it.

A hostile entity has failed to detect you! Your sneaking has increased to level 5.

The creature was clearly hunting me now. I imagined it drawing closer and pictured it striking unseen, concealed by the darkness. *Like an assassin.* A bead of sweat dripped down my forehead, and my grip tightened around the hilt of my blade. What had I done to attract the creature's attention?

My voice, I realized. *The careless words I had spoken.* I was suddenly sure that they were what had drawn the creature to me. *It must hunt by sound.*

I was assailed by sudden fear and had to bite back the urge to run and flee for the safety of the main corridor. *No! That's what it's waiting for.* Cautiously, I backpedaled and placed my back against the wall.

However, even that slight movement nearly proved my undoing.

A hostile entity has detected you! You are no longer hidden.

I don't know if it was the whisper of my cloak's fabric or something else that the creature sensed, but somehow my motion gave it a fix on my location.

I held my sword before me and, with wild eyes, scanned the darkness. A clot of blackness, darker than the rest, drew my gaze. *My foe.* It was ten yards away, and between me and the crossroads. In an odd sort of swaying gait, the creature crept along the floor towards me.

If I had to hazard a guess, I would have said the approaching menace was oval-shaped and no more than knee-high in height. But despite how much I strained my eyes, I couldn't make much more of the creature.

As I watched with mounting fear, the creature continued its unhurried approach. Did it not know I had spotted it? I was gripped by sudden indecision. Should I try to cut past the monster? Or duck into one of the side rooms? Or wait for it to close the distance?

Before I could resolve how to act, the decision was taken out of my hands. A smaller blotch of darkness separated from my foe and hurtled towards me.

More by instinct than conscious thought, I ducked. The mass of darkness sailed overhead and, with an audible splat, collided with the wall. With rising dread, I eyed the still-hissing trails of darkness slide down the wall behind me. *Bloody hell!* What was that thing?

I had no choice but to close the distance myself, I realized. I couldn't give the creature a chance to launch another projectile at me. But my limbs were locked in place, frozen motionless by the debilitating fear coursing through me.

I was going to die here.

I knew it with bone-deep certainty.

Whatever horror threatened me, I just knew it was a damned sight worse than any goblin. *I'm not ready,* I stuttered. *I can't face—*

"God damnit, Michael!" I screamed, breaking free of my downward-spiraling thoughts. "Stop thinking and move!"

Surprisingly the yelling worked. The sudden sound—shockingly loud in the silence—unlocked my frozen limbs. Screwing up my courage, I howled. Then charged.

I weaved an erratic path, with the vague notion of making it harder for my foe to hit me with a second projectile as I closed the distance to it.

One step. Two. Three. Then I was in range. My sword whipped downwards.

The blob rose off the floor and surged upwards.

Sword and darkness met, and blade sliced through with barely a hitch. The creature's body offered little resistance. It was like cutting through jelly.

But jelly doesn't strike back.

Despite being nearly sliced in two, the twin halves of the creature flowed around my blade and wrapped themselves around me.

A level 5 young black slime has critically injured you!

I screamed, and not for courage this time. Everywhere the slime's body made contact with my naked skin, cold suffused me. Cold so deep, it burned. My legs trembled, then gave way under me, and I collapsed to my knees.

A young black slime has injured you!

I howled again and felt the grip on my sword slacken. *No!* I protested. *I will not die like this.* With an effort of will, I tightened my hold on my blade and raised it to slash down. This time, I hacked off whole bits from the slime. It didn't stop the rest of the creature from continuing its attacks, though.

Gritting my teeth, I ignored the burning cold spreading throughout my body and kept hacking. It was: kill or be killed. And I was grimly determined that I would prevail.

My sword rose and fell, even as black globs of the creature continued to spread over me in a seeming attempt to encase me within itself. But I did not give up. Yanking off bits of slime with hands grown numb, I slashed onward and sliced my foe into smaller and smaller pieces.

Eventually, nearly at the end of my tether, the message I had been hoping for—and that I had begun to believe would never come—arrived.

You have killed a young black slime.

I collapsed to the floor in an exhausted heap. It was over. I had won.

Warning! Your health is dangerously low at 5%. Death is imminent.

Too tired to care, I let unconsciousness claim me.

CHAPTER 14: STILL ALIVE

I awoke in darkness.

For a moment, I didn't know where I was or how I came to be lying on my back on cold, hard stone. Then the pain riddling my body made itself known, and it all came rushing back: the slime was dead, and I had survived—if barely. Seemingly in response to my thoughts, a message from the Game dropped into my mind.

Warning! Your health is dangerously low at 5%. Death is imminent.

I lifted my head to take stock of my surroundings and gasped as even that slight movement caused new jolts of agony to rip through my body. *Bloody hell, it hurts.* But I had to move.

Stretched out on the floor, with my health hovering at nearly zero, I was a sitting duck. *What if another slime comes to investigate?* That dire thought was enough to spur me on. Panting with the effort, I rolled onto my side. "Gnat," I croaked. "Where are you?"

I heard the flap of bone wings from above and felt the bat alight on my arm. "I'm here, Michael."

"What happened?" I asked.

"You won," he replied. He chuckled. "Although you don't look so good anymore."

I was in too much pain to muster a retort. "Why aren't I healing?" I asked, focusing instead on the matter that concerned me the most.

Gnat tilted his head to the side and studied me. "Why would you?"

I glared at him. "Isn't this a game? Aren't players supposed to recover after every encounter?" Something told me they should.

The skeletal bat snickered. "I don't know what games you've been playing, Michael, but that is not how things work in the Grand Game." He paused. "In the Forever Kingdom, your injuries won't mend of their own accord. You will have to find a means to heal yourself."

What sort of wretched game is this? I wondered, staring at my familiar aghast. But complaining would do me no good. Wriggling my arms, I managed to unhook my backpack, though not without suffering multiple bouts of agony.

I dragged myself to a nearby wall and, pulling the backpack into my lap, searched feverishly for the healing potions. With trembling hands, I unstoppered the lid of the first and downed its contents.

The effect was instantaneous.

Ripples of soothing energy flowed out of my stomach and into my much-battered body. Damaged tissue was mended, torn skin grew back, and cuts and abrasions healed before my eyes. "Wow," I exclaimed, overcome by momentary euphoria.

You have restored 10% of your lost health with a minor healing potion. Your health is now at 15%.

A second later, the comforting waves of energy faded and the pain returned with a vengeance. "Well, it was nice while it lasted," I mumbled through gritted teeth. Without hesitation, I pulled out my second—and last—healing potion and drank it too.

You have restored 10% of your lost health with a minor healing potion. Your health is now at 25%.

I eyed the Game message unhappily. Twenty-five percent health wasn't much, but it was still a darn sight better than five percent. "I've got to find more of these potions," I muttered. I rose gingerly to my feet and packed away the empty vials. I had a vague idea of how to make use of them in the future.

My head pulsed suddenly, forcing me to lean on the passage wall for support. *What the—?* The moment I concentrated on the sensation, I felt more messages from the Adjudicator unfurl in my mind.

Congratulations, Michael! You have successfully defeated your first opponent and have gained experience. You have reached level 4!
You have 2 attribute points available.
Your dodging has increased to level 2.
Your shortswords has increased to level 7.

A smile broke through my grimace of pain. At least, the encounter had yielded some meaningful benefits. I tottered over to my slain foe.

The Game had called it a black slime, and in death, that was truly what it looked like. Very little remained of the creature. Its soft, gel-like body seemed to have decomposed further, leaving behind nothing but puddles of sticky, black ichor.

Glancing down at myself, I saw that much of my white tunic and shorts had been ripped and torn away. The bits that remained were streaked with black, more of the slime's remains. *Ick*, I thought, my face twisting in disgust. My thief's cloak, at least, seemed to have survived the encounter relatively intact, for which I was grateful.

"You were lucky," Gnat said, interrupting my musing.

I turned to him. "Hmm?"

"If it had hit you the first time around, you would not have survived," the bat replied.

I glanced at the wall at the end of the passage where the slime's opening salvo had landed. "What *did* it shoot at me?"

"A paralytic," Gnat replied. "Slimes use them to stun their prey before they consume them."

I shuddered. Was that why the slime had wrapped itself around me? To eat me? "Well, it's dead now," I said.

Gnat nodded.

"Pity there is nothing salvageable in this mess," I said, glancing at the creature's ruined remains.

"There will be a lair," Gnat said confidently. "And a chest."

My brows rose in surprise. "Really?"

The skeletal bat bobbed his head. "The Master designed this sector as a trial, remember. There will be a reward. You only need to find it."

I nodded thoughtfully. It made sense. Every room I had been to—besides those in this side passage—had contained loot chests, after all. I swept my gaze over the darkened passage. I had already been over every inch of the area. If the slime's lair was here, I was sure I would have found it already.

I sighed. There was nothing for it but to search again. Wincing in pain from my injuries, I hobbled deeper into the passage.

CHAPTER 15: WHAT LIES BENEATH

To my surprise, it did not take me long to find the entrance to the slime's hideout. In the first room of the side passage, out in plain sight, was a wooden trapdoor.

I eyed the hatch suspiciously. It had definitely not been there before.

Seeing my look, Gnat said, "It must have been hidden. By an illusion, most likely. The slime's death would've caused it to be revealed."

I hobbled a careful circuit around the closed trapdoor. There was a simple metal handle to lift it, but I made no move to touch it. "Is it trapped?"

Gnat shrugged. "I don't know."

The answer was not unexpected, but still less than helpful. Narrowing my eyes, I studied the hatch intently and tried to spot anything out of the ordinary.

After a minute of fruitless staring, I was forced to admit I sensed no danger emanating from it. But, of course, that could have just been because my Perception was too low. With my health as low as it was, I was not going to take any unnecessary chances. Stepping back from the hatch, I closed my eyes and willed my intent to the Adjudicator.

Your Perception has increased to rank 3. Your level cap for perception-based skills has increased to 30.

My senses grew sharper, and my awareness expanded, revealing previously unseen details in my surroundings. I inspected the hatch again. The grains on its wooden slates snapped into focus, and the streaks of rust on its metal handle were clear to see. But once again, I detected no hint of strangeness.

Alright, maybe it really isn't trapped, I thought. Standing as far away as possible, I raised the closed hatch with the outstretched tip of my sword.

The trapdoor creaked open.

To my relief, no trap was triggered. After a drawn-out moment, I peered inside the open hatch. It was darker inside the slime's lair than in the passage, but with my recently enhanced sight, I had no trouble picking out the shapes hidden in its shadows.

A wooden ramp had been placed against the edge of the hatch and extended to the floor. That had to be how the slime got in and out. The lair itself was small, less than a few yards in diameter. Alongside one wall, I made out a heap that my eyes failed to identify.

My nose, though, had no problem divining what they contained, *the remains of the slime's victims. Dead bodies.* I clamped a hand over my nose and mouth. The smell was sickening and made me reluctant to enter the lair, but something else drew my attention, a closed chest sitting at the bottom of the ramp. *Now that I cannot ignore,* I thought.

Gingerly getting onto the slide, I entered the lair.

~ ~ ~

As I had suspected, the pile in the lair contained the liquified remains of the slime's victims. Nothing remained of their bodies except bleached bones sucked dry and bits of torn cloth. From the pieces of fabric, it appeared that the slime had preyed solely on candidates.

I had wondered why none of my fellow candidates had ventured into the side passages, but it seemed that at least some must have. Yet none had managed to kill the slime. It should not have been difficult for a group of candidates to defeat the slime—once they had been alerted to its presence.

I frowned. Or had none of the candidates been able to find the creature? The slime appeared to have been a skilled hunter and one suited to stalking its victims in the dark. If the creature had only preyed on stragglers, it would not have been hard for the slime to conceal its presence while it devoured its chosen quarry.

I shuddered. I had narrowly escaped such a fate myself. When my half-hearted poking through the pile revealed no salvageable gear, I turned my attention to the true source of my interest: the loot chest.

I spent a good five minutes inspecting the chest before daring to open it. I had been sure it would've been boobytrapped, but to my surprise found it free of any traps. Inside, I found two items.

You have acquired an advanced ability tome: a summon lesser wight spellbook. You cannot learn this ability. You do not have the necessary skill: necromancy rank 3, or slots available in the required attribute: Faith. The ability tome is a single-use item.

You have acquired 1 full healing potion. This item will fully restore your health.

"An ability tome?" I murmured, studying the thick tome bound in black leather in my hands.

"They are the means by which you acquire abilities," Gnat said from my shoulder. The skeletal bat peered curiously at the book in my hands. "The spell this one holds is quite useful, but it's worthless to you, of course. Too bad you didn't choose the path of the caster."

I nodded absently. "Too bad," I said, echoing his sentiment, although as a caster, I doubted I would have managed to survive against the slime. I stored the spellbook in my backpack. While the tome was of no immediate use to me, it could still prove valuable in the future.

I turned my attention to the healing potion. It alone made my descent into the lair worth it. Without hesitation, I downed the elixir.

You have restored yourself with a full healing potion. Your health is now at 100%.

"Ah, much better," I said, smiling in pleasure as all my injuries miraculously healed and left me blessedly free of pain. Feeling far more encouraged about my chances in the dungeon now, I climbed up the ramp.

It was time to explore the left-side passage.

~ ~ ~

I snuck into the second side corridor with all my senses extended and looking for the slightest sign of danger. The left corridor was also shrouded in darkness. After only a cursory examination, I concluded its configuration was identical to the passage I had just been in.

Given that similarity, I padded quietly back into the corridor's first room and scrutinized the floor. Sure enough, after a few seconds, I spotted an oddity in the right corner of the chamber. I studied the suspect patch of ground.

Something about the flagstones covering the area in question appeared not quite right. *They're too smooth*, I realized. *Too perfect and without any of the scratches marring the other flagstones.* The difference was subtle but noticeable now that I had identified it.

No doubt about it, I thought. *That's a hatch covered by an illusion.* My emotions were mixed upon discovering the trapdoor. On the one hand, it was likely another opportunity to gain experience and earn more loot. On the other, it likely meant facing off against another slime, which I was not at all looking forward to.

But this time, I have a plan, I reassured myself.

I had thought long and hard before venturing into the left side passage and had come up with a way of defeating any slime it contained with minimal risk, but it all hinged on my assumptions being correct. I had no way of testing them before the battle. Either I was right or not. *Besides, if the worst happens, I can always hack the slime to death again. I only need to avoid its paralytic projectiles.*

Moving in a half-crouch, I placed myself in the corner of the room furthest away from the trapdoor. I looked down at the elven finger bone I held in my hand, testing its weight. I had taken it from the dead slime's lair.

Right here goes, I thought and tossed the small bone towards the fake flagstones. My aim proved true, and the bone clanked noisily over the unseen wood of the hatch. Holding myself still, I readied my weapons.

I didn't have long to wait. After only a few seconds, the hatch began to yawn open.

CHAPTER 16: A SECOND STAB

A puddle of liquid-black took form around the open trapdoor. This time around, I was able to easily pick out the slime from the surrounding darkness.

A hostile entity has failed to detect you! Your sneaking has increased to level 6.

I felt some of my rigid tension fade at the Game message. I hadn't been sure before this if I would be able to escape detection by the slime. I watched the creature pool upwards, almost as if it was tasting the air. *Listening for me?* I wondered.

Recalling how the creature had found me last time, I didn't dare move. As the seconds ticked by and the creature failed to find me, another Game message entered my mind.

Your sneaking has increased to level 7.

I smiled grimly. Increasing my sneaking in this manner was part of my plan, too. Hiding from the slime was the only means I had found for training my sneaking, and even though I knew I played a dangerous game, it was a risk I had to take.

The seconds turned into minutes and advanced my skill further, but still, the creature did not move from the open hatch.

Your sneaking has increased to level 8.
Your sneaking has increased to level 9.

Schooling myself to patience, I waited. Eventually, the creature broke its stillness and crawled out of the room—to search the rest of the passage for me, I assumed. I gave it a minute, then took a single step forward. I waited another full minute to see if my motion had been detected.

When I was certain I remained concealed, I followed the slime out of the room.

Your sneaking has increased to level 10. Congratulations, Michael! Your skill in sneaking has reached rank 1.
Your skill learning rate in sneaking has decreased. Learning rates are inversely proportional to your rank and will decrease with each new rank you attain.

I paused on the chamber's threshold as the latest Game alert dropped into my mind. This one was slightly different, but I didn't have time to give it much consideration.

Dismissing the message from my awareness, I padded after the slime. It was slowly making its way deeper into the passage, stopping at every room to search inside. I kept a good few yards between myself and the slime but made sure to always keep it in my sight. All the while, my sneaking skill gradually ticked upwards.

Your sneaking has increased to level 11.
Your sneaking has increased to level 12.
...

I continued my dangerous game, tracking the slime up and down the passage until, eventually, my sneaking maxed out.

Your sneaking has increased to level 20. Congratulations, Michael! Your skill in sneaking has reached rank 2, your current level cap. To improve your sneaking skill further, increase your Dexterity rank.

That was easier than expected, I thought, pleased that the skill had trained so quickly. But given the game's latest message, it was clear that it would become progressively more difficult to advance my skills.

With the first part of my plan completed, I moved on to the next stage: killing the slime. I took a second to confirm the slime's location. It was in the passage, moving farther away from me and towards the next room. *Perfect.*

Palming a second finger bone into my hand, I flung it as hard as I could at the far end of the passage. The sound of the bone clattering against the hard flagstone floor echoed resoundingly loud in the silence.

Not unexpectedly, the slime reacted instantaneously. Firing one of its paralytic projectiles in the direction of the noise, the creature pulled itself down the passage at a fast crawl.

Pleased with the success of my ploy, I withdrew one of the used healing vials— empty no more— and gripped it in my right hand. Hurrying forward, I narrowed the distance between myself and the slower-moving slime. When I judged I was close enough, my hand whipped forward in an arc and sent the contents of the unstoppered vial unerringly towards the still oblivious slime.

You have struck a level 5 slime with a poison dart. A hostile entity has detected you! You are no longer hidden.

The slime began turning around, and I dropped the empty vial. Making no move to draw my sword yet, I backpedaled quickly and pulled a second vial from my belt.

I held the vial at the ready as I watched the slime warily. Predictably, the creature fired another projectile at me. I was expecting the attack and danced aside easily.

You have evaded a slime's attack. Your dodging has increased to level 3.

The slime was still showing no ill effects from the dart. I had no idea if the dart's toxins would actually affect the creature. Still, I had considered using the dart worth the gamble. My biggest concern with the whole venture had been making sure I struck the creature. But in the end, the slime's soft skin and the guided trajectory provided by the vial's narrow length had made scoring a successful hit on my target a trivial exercise.

Now to see if my gamble pays off. Wondering how long I should wait before throwing the next vial, I kept retreating.

I was nearly out of the side passage and at the crossroads when the slime suddenly collapsed, and its gelatinous mass shriveled into near-nothingness.

You have killed a young black slime and have gained experience. You have reached level 5!

I stumbled to a halt in surprise. "Well, Gnat," I said, unable to conceal my grin, "that was almost too easy."

~ ~ ~

I paused at the slime's corpse. Like the first one I had killed, nothing useable remained of it, but glinting faintly amongst its remains, I spotted my dart. Bending down, I fished it out from the slime.

You have acquired a used dart.

Then I made my way to the creature's lair. I took the same precautions as before and ensured the slime's loot chest was not boobytrapped before opening it. What I found inside gave me renewed cause to smile.

You have acquired an advanced skillbook: two weapon fighting. This skill is compatible with your slotted Class and may be learned. The skillbook is a single-use item.

You have acquired 1 full healing potion. This item will fully restore your health.

Gnat peered at the items in my hands. "Well, Michael, it appears you've finally gotten lucky."

I nodded. "I have indeed."

CHAPTER 17: CROSSROADS

I made my way back to the crossroads and, finding a clean spot, sat down to think. I was intrigued by the skillbook I had found, but before I decided whether or not to learn its skill, I needed to ponder my course first.

"So, Gnat," I asked, "how do skillbooks work?"

The skeletal bat shifted on my shoulder. "In much the same manner that Class Stones do. You will acquire its knowledge directly."

I pursed my lips. "Permanently?"

"Permanently," Gnat confirmed. "Once learned, a skill cannot be unlearned."

I ran my hand over the skillbook in my lap. It was bound in brown leather and engraved with silver text on its cover. A tiny flap on the right kept the tome sealed, but it would be a simple matter to unlock it. Making no move to open the book yet, I read its Game description again.

Two weapon fighting: this skill is compatible with your slotted Classes and may be learned.

The message implied that the skills I could learn were predetermined by my Class, but I wasn't certain yet *which* skills I would have access to as a scout. Still, I could guess. "Can scouts learn magic skills, Gnat?"

"No," the familiar replied, confirming what I suspected.

"So, what skills can a scout learn?" I asked.

The bat shrugged. "The list is too large for even me to remember. The scout Class is dexterity-based and, as such, can learn most skills governed by the attribute. Many perception-based skills are also available to scouts."

I nodded thoughtfully. I would have liked to see the full list of skill options available to me before learning any new skills, but I didn't have that luxury, and truly, I couldn't pass up the chance of learning the only other skill I had found—and an advanced one at that. Besides, the skill would complement my existing light weapon skill nicely, and even after learning it, I would have two skill slots available.

Decided, I opened the skillbook.

The pages of the tome were filled with long lines of sliver script, which to my surprise, I could understand. Almost involuntarily, I began reading.

~ ~ ~

I blinked, awareness returning slowly. I had been so enthralled by the tome, I had lost track of both time and my surroundings.

I glanced down. The skillbook was gone. Before I could panic, a pulse in my mind alerted me to a waiting Game message.

Looking inwards, I perused its contents.

You have acquired the advanced skill: two weapon fighting. You may now dual-wield weapons in combat. As you increase this skill, the penalties you incur by wielding two weapons simultaneously will be reduced. Note that not all weapons are suitable for use in your second hand.

You have 2 of 6 scout Class skill slots remaining.

My eyebrows rose in surprise. Seemingly while lost in my trance, I had finished reading the skillbook and acquired its knowledge. "Gnat, how much time has passed?"

"Less than a minute, Michael," he replied.

I shook my head, amazed at how quick the process had been.

"Shall we get moving?" Gnat asked.

"One moment," I replied. "I have another matter to attend to." Closing my eyes, I communicated with the Game's Adjudicator again.

Your Dexterity has increased to rank 3.

This time, I chose to use my new attribute point to increase my Dexterity. It would allow me to keep improving my sneaking. To verify the changes to myself, I called up my player data.

Player Profile: Michael

Level: 5. Rank: 0. Current Health: 100%.
Stamina: 70%. Mana: 100%. Psi: 100%.
Species: Human. Lives Remaining: 3.

Attributes

Available: 0 points.
Strength: 0. Constitution: 0. Dexterity: 3. Perception: 3. Mind: 0. Magic: 0. and Faith: 0.

Classes

Primary Class: Scout (basic).
Secondary Class: None.
Tertiary Class: None.

Traits

Undead familiar: +1 to necromancy rank.
Nimble: +2 Dexterity.

Skills

Available skill slots: 2.
Dodging (current: 3. max: 30. Dexterity, basic).
Sneaking (current: 20. max: 30. Dexterity, basic).
Shortswords (current: 7. max: 30. Dexterity, basic).
Two weapon fighting (current: 1. max: 30. Dexterity, advanced).

Abilities

None.

Equipped

1 common thief's cloak (+3 sneaking).
1 basic steel shortsword (+10% damage).

Backpack Contents

6 x field rations.
1 x flask of water.
3 x used poison darts.
2 x unused poison darts.
3 x empty potion flasks.
1 x summon lesser wight spellbook.
1 x full healing potion.

I nodded approvingly at my player profile. Undoubtedly, I was getting stronger. I rose to my feet. It was time to move on.

~ ~ ~

I tiptoed into the main passage with my sword out and my gaze flitting from side to side. I had tried hiding, but even with my sneaking skill at rank two, the corridor was too brightly lit for me to conceal myself.

The first part of the corridor was identical to the other main passages I'd ventured into: filled with dead goblins and looted chests, and I moved rapidly beyond them. Presently, the corridor opened out into a large circular chamber.

I paused on the threshold and warily scanned the interior. By all appearance, the room had contained the final encounter of the dungeon's second leg. I could spot no movement but saw plenty of corpses.

Slipping into the room, I sidestepped through the grizzly remains while I counted the dead. Two dozen deceased goblins littered the room and nearly as many candidate corpses. In the chamber's center, where the carnage was the worst, the goblin dead were distinctly different from the rest of their fellows.

I frowned. "Gnat, what's wrong with these goblins?"

The skeletal bat looked at the six corpses I was studying. "They seem normal to me," my familiar replied.

"They're not," I argued. "They're bigger." At just over five feet tall, the corpses in question were about the height of a short human.

"Ah," the bat said. "I understand your confusion now. *Those* goblins," Gnat said, gesturing to the six with his chin, "are warriors. Low-level fighters, most likely." The familiar swung his head around. "*Those* goblins are workers." He spat. "Worthless civilians."

I chewed over my companion's words. "I'm guessing then that from now on, I can expect to see more goblin warriors in the dungeon?"

Gnat snorted. "Of course."

I sighed. "Right." I returned my attention to six dead goblins. Scattered around them were twice as many candidate corpses as in the rest of the room. From this, I gathered that the warriors represented a measurably greater threat than the workers.

The warriors were also notably more muscular than the other goblins I had encountered. I assumed that they had been better armed and armored too, but since the corpses had been stripped bare, I couldn't tell if that really was the case.

The hacked and battered remains of a wooden chest lay in the center of the corpses. I sighed again. It seemed that the other candidates had found their own way around the chests' traps. I would likely not be finding any un-looted chests anymore.

I raised my gaze to scan the perimeter of the room. There was only one other opening leading away from the chamber: a large archway on the northern end. It had to be the entrance to the dungeon sector's third leg.

Sheathing my sword, I slipped through the archway and continued onwards on my journey.

CHAPTER 18: CHOICES

The dungeon's third leg was nearly identical to the first, except this time, the rooms were all populated with warriors and not workers. But to my relief, the number of goblins in each room had reduced again to three, a more manageable group for me to square off against on my own.

I made my way through the third leg in silence. Once more, I spotted no one else. It made me wonder how far ahead the other candidates were and how quickly they had cleared this section of the dungeon. I wondered, too, about the dungeon's design. Would it remain this repetitive throughout the sector?

It was only as I entered the final chamber of the third leg that I noted a change in the dungeon's configuration: there were three exits leading away from the room. The corridors beyond were all similarly sized and dimly lit.

My brows drew down. So which one led to the fourth leg, and which two were mere side passages? Thus far, I hadn't encountered any true branches in the dungeon. There had only been one path to follow. Was that about to change?

I walked to the mouth of one of the tunnels and peered within. Right away, I noticed another difference. Unlike the other passages I had ventured through so far, the one stretching away from the chamber's exit had an unpaved gravel floor and rough-cut rock walls. More correctly speaking, it was a tunnel. I inspected the other two exits and found the tunnels leading from them to be identical.

"Gnat," I asked, turning to my familiar, "any explanation for the sudden change in the dungeon's demeanor?"

The bat chuckled. "It must mean the training phase is over."

I stared at him blankly. "What?"

"It seems that the Master chose to keep the first phase of his trial relatively... tame and uniform," Gnat said. "You'd be wise to assume that is no longer the case." The familiar gestured to the dark tunnel. "Expect things to be more difficult and varied through there."

That's just great, I thought, my lips turning down. If I understood Gnat correctly, the encounters beyond this point would be more random in nature, which could be either good or bad. Still, weak as I was, I *much* preferred predictable challenges. Those, at least, I could prepare for.

Well, there is no help for it. Picking the left tunnel at random, I ducked through it.

~ ~ ~

The tunnel meandered left and right, narrowing in places and widening at other times. I tiptoed through it, treading as stealthily as I could on the hardpacked gravel surface. The tunnel's lack of lighting served me well in that respect. Not once did I lose my concealment.

The tunnel, though, was not truly pitch black. In places, luminous crystals relieved the darkness, and in patches, glowing mushrooms grew. They provided me with enough light to see while still leaving me enough shadows to slip through unseen.

I had tried picking a few of the mushrooms, thinking they would make a good portable source of light, but after only a few minutes of being unearthed, the mushrooms lost their glow and shriveled up into dry husks. Abandoning the idea, I continued my journey.

After ten minutes, I came across the first sign that others had also been this way. A dwarven corpse lay in the middle of the tunnel. His white cotton clothes were cut to ribbons, and deep gouges had been carved through his skin.

Studying the body from the shadows, I scanned the surroundings. There was no sign of what had slain the candidate. When nothing jumped out at me after a few moments, I slipped past the body and continued my journey.

But only a few dozen yards later, I came across another dead candidate. This one was a gnome who had likewise been ripped to shreds. Feeling my trepidation grow, I kept going down the tunnel.

A little later, I stopped once more. The tunnel had widened into a small cave full of large rocks. Strewn amongst the boulders were three more bodies. Again, they were all candidates.

This time I ground to a halt. My instincts were screaming at me to turn back. Narrowing my eyes, I scanned every inch of the cavern. There was still no sign of whatever foe—or foes—had killed the candidates. "Any idea what did this?" I asked Gnat.

"No," my familiar replied, sounding unwontedly serious. "But I'd advise turning back."

I closed my eyes for a second and pondered my options. Turning back *did* seem the wiser course, but I had already gained greatly by venturing where other candidates had feared to tread.

Why not go on? I wondered. *As long as I remain concealed, I should have little to worry about.*

I wavered for a moment, weighing the potential rewards against the risks. But the thought of exploring virgin territory was too tempting to ignore. *I press on,* I decided. Slowing my advance to a near crawl, I crossed the cavern and continued into the tunnel beyond.

I had ventured only a little way farther when an unnatural noise caught my attention. I stilled instantly. Straining my ears, I waited to catch the sound again.

Grrrr... nnnch... aarrgh.

My breath caught. This time there was no mistaking the noise. It was coming from farther down the tunnel. Somewhere ahead, a creature waited. And it sounded close by.

I studied the darkness in front of me again but found no answers there. Only a few feet away, the tunnel curved sharply to the right, hiding the source of the sounds.

Unconsciously, my hand dropped to the hilt of my sword. *To go on or not? But I've already come this far. What's a few more paces?*

Mustering my courage, I padded forward and braced my back against the tunnel wall. I inched around the bend, double and triple-checking my footing before each step.

I don't know how long it took me to navigate those few yards, but eventually, I turned the corner and caught sight of what lay beyond.

I stifled my sharp intake of breath. The tunnel had widened into another cavern. This one was covered in a field of glowing mushrooms that bathed the cave's interior in a gentle blue light. Sitting in the center of the mushrooms were two nine-foot-tall figures.

The creatures looked scrawny and half-starved, with their bones showing sharply beneath their olive-green skin. The pair's teeth had been filed to points, and their filthy black hair fell to their shoulders. Both creatures wore nothing more than a small loincloth.

Yet it was not the sight of the green-skinned pair alone that caused my eyes to widen in horror. No, it was what they were doing. In the clawed hands of each monster was a... limb. A pale, soft-flesh limb that had clearly been torn off the human at the pair's feet.

I swallowed convulsively. The creatures were eating the candidate. The noise I had heard was the sound of the monster's teeth grinding down on human bones. As I watched one of the creatures spit out a small bone and blood drip unheeded down the chin of the other, my stomach heaved, and I took an involuntary step back.

A pebble shifted under my foot.

The monsters paused in their incessant chewing, and as one, their gazes swung to the tunnel mouth concealing me.

I froze.

A hostile entity has failed to detect you! A hostile entity has failed to detect you! Your sneaking has increased to level 21.

Idiot! I cursed myself. I kept my eyes glued to the two creatures. They were still watching the tunnel entrance intently, and I dared not move an iota. A bead of sweat trickled down my face.

A hostile entity has failed to detect you! A hostile entity has failed to detect you!

A heartbeat passed, then another. I was petrified but poised to flee too. If either of the creatures made any move to rise, I would break cover and run. In my scan of the cavern, I hadn't failed to notice the other dead amongst the cavern. At least a score of candidates had died here.

If that many of my fellows had failed to kill the two monsters, there was no way I was going to risk entangling with the creatures unprepared. But to my intense relief, as the seconds ticked by and no enemy revealed itself, the creatures' suspicions abated, and first, one, then the other, returned to its feeding.

A hostile entity has failed to detect you! A hostile entity has failed to detect you! Your sneaking has increased to level 22.

Not letting my shoulders sag or allowing myself another betraying slip, I edged away with carefully controlled movements.

CHAPTER 19: DEAD ENDS

I didn't stop retreating until I was back in the third leg's final chamber. I flung myself to the ground and exhaled a pent-up breath as my rapid pulse finally began to subside.

"What the hell were those things?" I asked.

"Trolls," Gnat replied succinctly.

"Trolls?" I repeated. "And they *eat* people?"

Gnat shifted uncomfortably. "Trolls eat anything. Even undead."

My face twisted in disgust. "Really? Whatever for?" Gnat opened his mouth to reply, but I waved him off. "Never mind, I don't want to know." I rubbed my face. "What I do want to know," I murmured rhetorically while I considered the matter, "is how I can go about killing them."

"You can't," my familiar said.

I snorted. "Anything can be killed, Gnat. Granted, it won't be easy. Given how many candidates those monsters killed, taking them down must be tough. But I only have to—"

Gnat shook his head. "No. I mean, *you* can't."

I paused. "What do you mean by that?"

"Trolls can only be killed by magic," Gnat said.

I blinked. *Alright, this could be a problem.* "So, I can't even hurt them?"

Gnat shrugged. "You could. You could even incapacitate them—assuming you are able to inflict damage fast enough—but trolls possess superior regenerative properties with which they can heal themselves from almost every type of damage. The only wounds that a troll cannot recover from are those inflicted by magical flames."

I bit my lip as I considered that. "How strong do you think those trolls are?"

"Trolls are rank two creatures," Gnat replied. Seeing my blank look, he explained further. "That means that even the lowliest and weakest troll is level twenty."

I whistled soundlessly. "Well, damn," I muttered. I had spied an exit at the far end of the mushroom cavern and had been hoping that once I dealt with the trolls, I would be free to explore an as-yet-untouched region of the dungeon. That possibility had been ruled out now, though.

As brightly lit as the cavern had been, there was no way I could sneak past the trolls, and considering the creatures' levels, I doubted even my poison darts would do much more than irritate them.

I let my gaze drift to the other two tunnels leading away from the chamber. I sighed and clambered to my feet. "I guess it's time to explore another tunnel," I said and slipped down the middle one.

~ ~ ~

The second tunnel snaked up and down, far more so than the first had. Maintaining a careful pace, I followed the passage's tortuous twists and turns. After only a few hundred yards, though, a niggling worry began to worm its way through my thoughts as I noticed that the darkness around me was growing.

The farther I ventured into the tunnel, the more barren it became. Even the rare patches of luminous crystals and glowing mushrooms had grown less frequent, making it harder for me to see. I frowned in concern. If the light kept deteriorating, I would soon be forced to retreat and find a light source before continuing. My worry about the worsening light so preoccupied me that I almost failed to see the trap until too late.

But whether through luck or as a result of my three ranks in Perception, when my gaze passed over a distinctly darker patch of ground, I *knew* there was something odd about it, and I crashed to a halt.

Staring at the ground at my feet, I realized I was standing at the lip of a ditch. A *very* deep ditch. Carefully, I dropped to my knees and felt out the empty void of space where the ground should be. My reaching fingers found nothing but air.

I gulped. If I had fallen, I would have been seriously injured. If not worse. *How deep is the hole?* I wondered.

Lying flat on the ground, I stretched my hands into the void as far as I could reach and, staring down, still couldn't find the ground beneath. Sidling along the lip of the ditch, I tested its depths at regular intervals, but at no point could I find solid ground.

Frowning, I rose back to my feet and stared down the tunnel and tried to measure the length of the ditch, but my eyes failed to penetrate the darkness.

"Gnat, fly along the floor," I said, "and tell me how far this ditch extends."

The skeletal bat scowled at me. "I cannot fly if I can't see."

I blinked. "Aren't you a bat? Don't bats fly in the dark?"

"I'm an *undead* bat," he groused.

What difference did that make? I sighed. He really was no help.

Why did the Master give me such a worthless familiar? I wondered despondently. *But no, that's unfair.* As little use as Gnat had been in exploring, he had been a font of information on the Game itself, for which I was more than grateful.

"Alright," I said, another idea occurring to me. "Let's head back."

~ ~ ~

I made my way back to the nearest patch of glowing mushrooms and wrenched them all out. With my precious cargo in hand, I hurried back to the ditch. Panting slightly from my exertions, I drew to a stop at its edge.

Knowing that I had less than a minute before the light from the mushrooms died, I threw a handful into the ditch, then waited in anxious anticipation. The mushrooms fell a long way before coming to a rest. And when they did, the scene they revealed caused the blood to drain from my face.

The bottom of the ditch was a long way away.

More properly speaking, the hole in front of me was a trench—a twelve-foot deep one riddled with wooden stakes that had been sharpened to lethal points and angled upwards to catch any falling body.

A tumble into the trench would have been fatal.

Indeed, from the bodies already in the trench, I saw that it had already claimed more than its fair share of victims.

"Good thing you spotted that trap before you fell in," Gnat said.

I nodded wordlessly. *Good thing.*

Gnat's words recalled me to the other mushrooms in my hands. I knew how deep and deadly the trench was now, but I still didn't know how far it extended. Winding my arm back, I began flinging more mushrooms into the hole, sending each one farther away, until one of my flung projectiles did not tumble downwards but rolled to a stop on ground at the same level I stood on.

Squinting, I measured the distance in the already fading light of the mushrooms. *Six yards.* The trench was too wide to try jumping across.

Another dead-end, I thought as the tunnel was once more plunged into darkness.

~ ~ ~

I spent a good five minutes sitting at the edge of the deadly trench, pondering a way to cross it. And though I managed to come up with a few half-decent plans, they were all fraught with peril.

While the wooden stakes riddling the bottom of the trench were plentiful, they were not so abundant that I could not pick a careful path between them. Assuming, of course, I could secure enough light to see by *and* reach the bottom of the trench safely.

My half-caught glimpse of the trench's far wall also led me to believe I would be able to climb out once I got there. There had appeared to be enough handholds for a nimble person, but again, I had caught only a single glimpse and couldn't be sure there was a viable way out.

It's too risky, I decided. With a sigh, I rose to my feet. I knew what I had to do, explore the third tunnel. If it, too, proved a dead-end, I would return and try crossing the trapped trench.

Who knows, maybe I will find something as handy as a rope. I didn't hold out much hope of that, though.

CHAPTER 20: A SURPRISING DISCOVERY

The third branch was different from the others.

Where the first two tunnels had twisted through the earth, the third one rarely varied in direction, and while it was not as well-lit as the stone-paved corridors of the dungeon, the tunnel contained noticeably more patches of glowing mushrooms than the others.

After a few minutes of slow but careful exploration, I began to cautiously hope that the third branch would at least be different. But that hope was quickly dashed.

The tunnel ahead had widened into a large cavern as its two sidewalls extended further and further apart from each other. The cavern was the largest expanse of space I had yet seen in the dungeon. Its roof arched high overhead and was dotted with luminous crystals that bathed the cave in blue light.

But that was not what made me pause. It was the murmur of voices that did. There were people up ahead. I had finally caught up to some of my fellow candidates.

Immediately, I dropped deeper into my crouch, making sure I remained concealed. I was not such a fool as to assume those ahead would look on me kindly.

Better to learn more of them before I reveal myself, I thought.

Tiptoeing forward, I inspected the area ahead more carefully. Despite its size, the cavern appeared full. There had to be a few dozen candidates within it, at least. My brows drew down. What were so many of them doing together? None of the parties that I had observed entering the dungeon had been this large.

Even more puzzling, the candidates did not seem to be on the move. Amongst the crowd of people, I spied bedrolls and tents. Even ignoring the mystery of where the candidates had gotten all their gear, I didn't understand why they would be resting. It hadn't been that long since we'd entered the dungeon, after all.

It also didn't escape my notice that all the candidates were better equipped now. I saw dwarves in full—if battered—plate armor, elves in brown leather hides and carrying longbows, humans in chainmail, and mages of all kinds sporting robes and bearing staffs.

There was a distinct undead presence in the candidates' camp, too. Bone bats winged aloft, mindless zombies shambled behind black-robed mages, and squads of skeletons roamed the camp.

As I drew closer, I began to pick out individual voices from the background noise.

"Hey! Gimme that. That's mine!"

"Haha. Not anymore."

"...long are we going to wait?"

"Until Saben gives the word..."

"...how much for that skillbook?"

"More than *you* can afford."

"...think they'll give in to Saben's demands?"

"Nah. Morin and her crew are too stubborn by far. They'll..."

"...do with the prisoners when we leave?"

"Torture them, I guess."

The snippets of overheard conversations were intriguing and left me with the impression that candidates had formed into factions—factions that didn't seem well-disposed to each other.

The mention of 'prisoners' disturbed me too, and inching even closer to the mass of candidates, I focused more intently on the pair that had spoken of them. They were on the perimeter of the camp themselves and seemed to have deliberately drawn away from the others.

"We can't let him hurt them!" the first said, sounding distressed. The one who had spoken was a dwarf clad in heavy plate armor. Tufts of his black beard poked through his helm, and his voice rumbled when he spoke.

"Keep your voice down!" the second hissed. She was a wiry human woman dressed in leather armor. "If any of Saben's goons hear you speak that way, they'll take it for mutiny, and we'll both end up with the others."

"But they are our friends, Soya," the dwarf protested.

The woman—Soya—sighed. "I know, Jah," she said, lowering her voice. "But what can we do? Saben is too strong to oppose. Even if all of us 'pledged' band together, we can't overcome his thugs. No, the best chance the prisoners have at life is to pledge themselves to our glorious leader as well."

Jah fell silent and swung his head to stare at something on his left. Following his gaze, I saw a bedraggled group of candidates in the camp's center that I had failed to notice before. Unlike the others in the camp, this group of about ten wore no armor and bore no weapons, and more tellingly, their hands and feet were bound in thick ropes.

They're prisoners, I thought. Even as I watched, six well-armed fighters walked up to the group and, without any exchange of words or gestures that I could see, began beating them.

Bare fists met soft flesh, and hard-capped boots crunched into defenseless bodies. One after another, the prisoners were left writhing on the floor, but still, the beatings did not stop. Only when all the prisoners were senseless with pain did the brutes walk away, but not before spitting contemptuously at their victims.

My gaze flicked back to Jah and Soya. All color had drained from the pair's faces, and the dwarf clenched his axe in a white-knuckled grip. Yet neither rushed to the prisoners' aid.

"You know Morin will never bow to Saben's will," the dwarf said, breath heaving with emotion as he resumed his conversation with Soya.

"I know," the woman said softly.

Meanwhile, the thugs had formed a line a little way away from their victims. Their leader—an imposing half-giant—raised his head. "This is what happens to those who follow Morin!" he shouted. "Those of you thinking to rebel: don't." He sneered. "Or do, and let me crush your worthless hides." Turning on his heel, he disappeared into the camp's interior.

The dwarf watched the retreating half-giant for a moment before turning back to his companion. "Maybe Morin will save us."

Soya snorted. "Don't count on it. She's tried once already and failed. She's just lucky her people managed to get themselves killed in the effort. Otherwise, they would be in the same boat we are in right now."

"But what if—" the dwarf began.

A hostile entity has failed to detect you!

My head snapped around at the Game message. A few yards to my right, a shambling zombie was peering with befuddlement in my direction.

Damn, I cursed. I had moved too close to the camp and had attracted the attention of one of the undead. The shadows in which I had concealed myself were still dense enough to hide my presence, but staying here any longer was too risky.

Keeping a wary eye on the zombie, I slipped away. It was time to decide my next move.

CHAPTER 21: REALIZATIONS

"What did you make of all that, Gnat?" I asked once we were safely back in the third leg's final chamber.

"It's nothing out of the ordinary," the skeletal bat said with a yawn. "The candidates usually band together for survival by rallying around the strongest."

I frowned. "What do you mean 'usually?'"

The familiar cocked his head at an unnatural angle. "What? You didn't think yours was the first group of candidates the Master has sent through his trials, did you?"

I narrowed my eyes and took a second to digest the bat's revelation. "So the Master does this regularly?"

Gnat nodded. "This is not the first trial, nor will it be the last. Although," Gnat grumbled, "the Master insists on changing the dungeon configuration each time, which only makes my job harder."

The familiar's words left me wondering exactly what his job was, but choosing to remain focused on the matter at hand, I didn't pursue his offhand remark. "Why does the Master do all this, though?" I asked. "What is the purpose of his trials?"

"The Master has already told you that," Gnat said, sounding exasperated. "The trials are a means of finding those worthy of joining his cause."

"And what *is* the Master's cause?" I asked.

"That I cannot tell you," the bat said. "To find that out, you must complete the trials first."

I rubbed at my temples in frustration. "But surely the Master can devise better methods of recruitment?" I waved my hands around at the dungeon. "All of this is so... inefficient."

"Whatever you're imagining, Michael, it's been tried before," Gnat said, with amusement tracing his voice. "The only way to find those capable of surviving the Game is by having them play the game."

I sighed. "And is the Master fine with what's going on in his dungeon? With his candidates enslaving other candidates?" That is what I concluded this Saben character was doing. The 'pledges' the dwarf and human had spoken of sounded like little more than a euphemism for slavery to me.

Gnat laughed. "The Game is ruthless, human. And to play it, you must be ruthless too." He paused. "Or you will perish."

I bowed my head, perturbed by the bat's answer. The dungeon's challenge I could accept, if perhaps not agree with. Survival of the fittest and all that. But what Saben and his cronies were doing, what the Master was *allowing* them to do, that was more than ruthlessness. That was casual cruelty of the sort that did not sit well with me.

I thought back to the Master's parting words to us. *Am I evil?* I wondered. I hoped not. Despite the Master's insistence that I was, something in me was repulsed by what Saben and his ilk did. No, it was even more than that.

I closed my eyes and concentrated on what my subconscious was telling me. My hands were trembling, I realized. And it was not from fear. *Disgust,* I thought, *is too mild a term to express what I feel.*

Rage was a better word. *I am trembling in fury.*

Whoever and whatever I had been was appalled by what Saben was doing to the candidates in his clutches. But what could I do to help them? *Nothing.* I swallowed bitterness. The candidate camp was too large, and I, by my lonesome—and significantly unequipped by comparison—was not going to be able to free the prisoners.

I opened my eyes and saw Gnat was watching me carefully.

"What are you thinking?" the skeletal bat asked almost nonchalantly.

I shrugged, instinct guiding me to keep my thoughts hidden. "Just wondering if I trust Saben's people enough to join them," I replied blandly.

Gnat snorted. "You would be a fool to do that," he said before turning away and seeming to lose further interest in the conversation.

I took a moment to ponder my options. *Trolls. Trapped trench. Or Saben's gang. Which should I tackle?*

~ ~ ~

In the end, there was only one viable choice really, and with a heavy heart, I made it. I could not sneak past the trolls, nor could I defeat Saben's gang, but there was still a chance that I could cross the trapped trench.

So, despite my reluctance to abandon the prisoners to their fate, I did just that and set about planning to cross the trench.

It took me nearly an hour to drag about a few dozen corpses from the dungeon's third leg to the edge of the trench. Finding the bodies was not a problem. There were plenty of corpses in fresh supply in the dungeon, but it was back-breaking work that left me feeling unclean for desecrating the dead.

The first half of my plan was to use the corpses to create a ramp down into the trench. One by one, I threw the bodies into the hole and piled them high at the closest end of the trench until they were nearly at ground level.

I checked the mound height with a few glowing mushrooms and verified that the slope they formed was navigable to the bottom of the trench. On the lower half of the mound, the sharpened tips of the stakes poked through, conveniently anchoring the pile of corpses.

The trench was too large for me to attempt to fill its entire length with bodies, and besides, I doubted I could have thrown the corpses far enough to reach the far end, to say nothing of how arduous and repulsive a task it would be to drag a few hundred corpses to the trench.

With my landing in the trench secured, I returned to the third leg of the dungeon and set about removing one of the many torches affixed to the wall. It was harder than I expected, and by the time I was done, I was drenched in sweat from all the tugging and pulling I had to do to free the precious light source from where it had been bolted onto the wall.

You have acquired a torch. This item has sufficient fuel to last three hours.

Finally ready to begin my crossing, I returned to the trench once more.

Chapter 22: Crossing

Standing at the edge of the trench, I stared down at the pile of bodies that would serve as my stairway. In the flickering light of the torch, the eyes of the dead gleamed as if alive and seemed to stare at me accusingly for violating their remains.

I shivered involuntarily. *That's just meat,* I told myself. *The spirits that housed them have long since fled.* Unsurprisingly, my words did little to alleviate my trepidation. Somehow walking on the dead seemed a greater desecration than carrying them.

Gnat peered around me to study the fruits of my labor. "You're full of surprises, aren't you? Think this plan of yours will work?"

"It better," I replied grimly, trying not to imagine what failure would mean. Holding the torch high above my head with my right hand, I placed one foot tentatively onto the mound of dead and tested my footing. The pile did not so much as shift under my feet.

Feeling more confident, I stepped fully onto the mound. The corpses deflated as my weight squeezed their insides out, spurting blood and offal. I swayed and felt my feet begin to slip beneath me.

Fighting the urge to panic, I windmilled my arms frantically to regain my balance. The corpse beneath me settled, and I found firm purchase again. I heaved a sigh of relief. "Phew," I muttered, "that was too close."

I glanced down at the pile of dead, realizing that while the mound looked stable, it would shift and move under my weight. I would have to be wary of my footing. The smell, of course, was awful too, but after hauling around corpse after corpse, I had grown accustomed to the stench of the dead, and it didn't bother me as much as it should have.

Bending my knees, I lowered my center of mass to better balance on the precarious mound. I took a careful step down the slope. Then waited. The corpse underfoot shifted slightly before settling.

I took another step, making sure to spread my feet and place my second foot on another corpse to keep my weight distributed. I waited. The mound did not move. My footing was secure. Continuing my crab walk, I made my way down the slope.

Not so hard, after—

Landing on something wet and slippery, my right foot shot out from under me. Before I could even think of regaining my balance, I fell.

My head and rear shot back, thumping against the mound of corpses before sliding down the slope at an ever-accelerating pace. I flung my left arm outwards and tried to slow my fall, not caring what I grabbed onto. My right hand still held the torch aloft. Keeping it burning was my first concern, and I dared not abandon it.

Realizing there was no stopping my plunge now, I swung my head forward and found myself staring at the sharpened end of a stake.

Bloody hell!

I wrenched myself right and avoided being impaled, but I wasn't able to completely throw my body out of the way. Pain—a throbbing white-hot sensation— tore through my mind as the stake punctured through my left hand. I jerked to a halt, my skewered hand acting as an unwitting anchor.

A wooden stake has critically injured you!

The torch went flying and disappeared from my sight. I had no attention to spare it, though. Anguish consumed my world. I bit off a scream. Even in the throes of agony, I retained enough presence of mind to know I didn't dare scream. Anything could be lying in wait beyond the trench.

Momentum dragged me around in a half-circle, and my feet brushed up against other wooden stakes. Thankfully, it was against their rough-cut sides and not their pointed tips.

I slowed to a halt, still dangling from the stake that had skewered me. "Gnat," I gasped, my breath heaving as I struggled to think around the pain.

"Here, Michael," my familiar said from somewhere above.

"Can you see the torch?" I asked.

"Yes," he replied. "It's still burning."

Good, I thought. *I can still survive this disaster.* "Where am I, Gnat?"

"You're almost at the bottom," he said. "Your feet are inches from the ground."

Better yet. Straining against the pain, I finally looked at the stake pinning me down. The sharpened end had gone straight through the center of my palm, ripping apart skin and tendons and exposing bent and broken bones. Just looking at my damaged hand caused me to go weak in the knees.

Get it together, Michael. You have to free yourself, and quickly. Likely upended, the torch wouldn't keep burning forever. I gritted my teeth and slapped my right hand around the stake for leverage.

Then, I pulled my left hand outwards.

My mind went blank with pain, and I nearly passed out. Clinging desperately to consciousness, I slowly drew my skewered hand off the stake. "God, that hurts," I moaned softly but didn't stop yanking on my hand. At least a foot length of stake had buried itself through me. After a torturous and seemingly never-ending few seconds, my left hand came free.

Your left hand is crippled. Your left hand is bleeding. Ongoing damage sustained. Your health is at 70% and dropping.

I released the stake from the white-knuckled grip of my right hand and dropped the short distance to the floor of the trench. "Gnat," I growled, cradling my damaged hand, "where is my bag?"

"Still on your back."

With my one good hand, I somehow managed to open the pack. Finding my last healing potion, I unstoppered it with my teeth and gulped down its contents.

Closing my eyes, I sighed as my left hand first went numb, then tingled with soothing waves as rended flesh and bone were magically mended.

You have restored yourself with a full healing potion. You are no longer crippled. Your health is now at 100%.

I opened my eyes, still high on euphoria from the healing. All I wanted to do was sag in relief, but I knew I didn't have that luxury. My gaze darted left and right, searching for the dropped torch.

It was two yards to my right and still burning. Measuring the ground between, I carefully stepped around the stakes and picked it up.

You have acquired a torch. This item has sufficient fuel to last six minutes.

The greater part of the torch's oil reserve was spilled and lost. But a smidgen still remained. Enough for six minutes more of light. *Ample time to navigate the trench and climb out,* I thought.

Then you can rest, I promised myself. Gathering myself, I set about it.

CHAPTER 23: WHAT LIES BEYOND

I was about a third of the way across the trench, moving carefully but quickly, when a glint of metal caught my attention.

Turning my head to the side, I studied the nearby gnome corpse that was the source. It was not one of the bodies I had thrown in but one of the trench's own victims. It was not the first corpse I had run across either, but it was the only one to make me pause. Rather, it was the shortsword by the body's side that did.

The gnome's body did not lay far of my course, and detouring to grab the sword would likely not cause me to lose much time. And besides, I needed a second sword. It was worth the risk.

Changing path abruptly, I swiftly made my way to the body and retrieved the sword and its sheath.

You have acquired a basic steel shortsword. This item increases the damage you deal by 10%.

The sword was identical to the one I had bought from the weapons merchant. The gnome had probably bought the blade from him, too. The dead candidate carried nothing else of value that I could see, and his armor would have taken too much time to remove. Abandoning the body, I continued onwards through the trench.

I reached the far end of the trench with only a minute to spare on my torch's light. Hurriedly, I scanned the wall before me. I had been right, I saw. There were small outcroppings of rock and clumps of dirt that could serve as handholds.

I set down the torch. I would need both hands for the climb, and there was no way I could carry it up with me. Nor did I have a means of relighting it once it died. Better to leave it here and use its last light to manage the climb.

I rubbed my hands together. *Right, here goes.* Then I set to climbing.

~ ~ ~

The climb was easier than I expected, and I scurried up the trench wall in less than thirty seconds. Pulling myself over the edge, I rolled onto my back and took a moment to enjoy my accomplishment.

I had made it. Crossing the trapped trench had been something of a feat in itself, and as a new Game alert opened in my mind, I realized the Adjudicator seemed to think so too.

Congratulations, Michael! You have successfully overcome another of the dungeon's traps and have gained experience.
You have reached level 6!
You have 1 attribute point available.

I smiled at the message. At least the Game had offered me some compensation for my maimed hand and lost potion.

Sitting up in a cross-legged stance, I took in my surroundings. The torch's light had died, and the area had been plunged into darkness once more. I could make out very little of my surroundings other than I was still in a tunnel.

Before moving on, I considered my new attribute point and briefly debated how to spend it. I was certain that I would face combat somewhere ahead, and for that, Dexterity would serve me best, but I was also concerned about the lack of lighting in the tunnel. If the darkness continued unabated, then Perception would be better.

If I can't see, I cannot fight, I thought, reaching a decision. Even though none of my skills were governed by Perception, it was still the better choice given where I was at present, and I willed the Game to advance it.

Your Perception has increased to rank 4.

Once more, my senses grew sharper. The darkness was pushed back, and I could make out more of my surroundings. I was in a tunnel, I realized, and one that was curving sharply to the right. Rising to my feet, I dropped into a crouch and padded down the tunnel to whatever awaited me.

You and your familiar are hidden.

~ ~ ~

Rounding the tunnel bend, the first thing I saw was light—light from the red-orange flames of a campfire.

I almost fell back in surprise.

My first thought was that I had been mistaken and that some other party had found a way around the trapped trench as well, but as I observed the two figures sitting beside the blazing fire, I realized they were not candidates.

They were goblins.

That realization, too, nearly caused me to flee. Surely the pair had spotted my torch when I had crossed the trench? But then I recalled that I hadn't seen their campfire from the trench either.

The tunnel bend must have hidden us from each other.

I was doubly grateful now that I hadn't screamed in the trench. The pair would have heard me for sure. Secure in the knowledge I was hidden, I studied the goblins afresh.

The two creatures were camped at least fifty yards down the tunnel, and judging by their size, they were of the warrior caste. Both were dressed in armor of sorts, but from this distance, I couldn't make out the details.

I wondered at the campfire. Nothing was cooking on it, so why did the goblins need it? Did goblins have as much trouble seeing in the dark as humans? I could only assume so. I debated moving forward to observe the two more closely but then decided the wiser course would be to retreat and consult with Gnat first.

Slipping back to the trench's edge, I listened intently for a heartbeat before turning to my familiar. "Gnat, those were goblin warriors, right?"

"Correct, Michael."

"Can you tell their levels?" I asked.

Gnat shook his head. "No, to determine a foe's level, you will need the analyze ability." He paused. "But goblin warriors are rank one creatures."

I pursed my lips. "That means those two are each level ten?"

"At least," Gnat confirmed.

Hmm, I thought, rubbing my chin. The pair were too high-leveled for me to tackle head-on. "How well do goblins see in the dark?" I asked.

"Their night vision is poor," Gnat said.

"That's what I thought," I murmured, an idea forming. I turned back to my familiar. "Thanks for the information, Gnat."

He bobbed his head. "That's what I'm here for."

"You have my gratitude anyway," I said with a smile. Slipping back into the shadows, I tiptoed back to the two goblins.

I advanced as close to the goblins as I dared, right up to the edge of the light from their campfire. Neither creature gave any indication that they knew I was nearby.

From this close, I could make out every detail of the pair. The goblins were dressed in hide armor, roughly hewn and primitively stitched together. A bow rested at each creature's side, and a pair of bare daggers were shoved in their belts.

They're archers then, I guessed.

Both goblins stared fixedly into the fire. Not once did either glance away. While I couldn't claim to be able to read goblin expressions, both archers appeared morose. One of the goblins, who I took to be the younger from his lack of wrinkles, bore an intricate tattoo of a raven on his face. *Some sort of tribal symbol?* I wondered.

Peering beyond the goblins, I saw that the tunnel continued onwards. Given the goblins' seeming disinterest in their surroundings, I didn't doubt I could sneak past them, but doing that would leave two powerful foes at my back, and I wasn't ready to do that yet.

Moving carefully, I retreated a few yards and positioned myself against one of the tunnel walls. From here, I could more comfortably observe my targets. Settling down, I readied myself to watch and wait.

The time was not yet ready to act, but it would be soon.

CHAPTER 24: EPIPHANY

I jerked awake from the light doze I had fallen into. I hadn't meant to sleep, but the long minutes of stillness had lulled me into slumber. I wasn't sure how much time had passed since I had dozed off, but I knew something had disturbed me.

I dropped my hands to my sheathed swords, poised to act. My eyes flew to the campfire, and my tension eased as I saw that the two goblins hadn't moved from their previous positions.

Then I frowned. The two goblins were still there, but *something* had changed.

A hoarse laugh floated through the air, and I realized the pair were conversing. Rising to my haunches, I crept closer.

"... why be us!"

I froze as the words reached my ears. The accent was guttural, and the words were clipped and barked. Still, they were decipherable.

I was more than a little surprised that the goblins could actually speak and even more amazed that I understood them. For some reason, I had assumed them to be primitive savages.

Shaking my head in bemusement, I crept up to the edge of the campfire and listened attentively.

"You smart, you shut up. Or Knorl smash you," the older goblin said.

"Bah! Me no fear Knorl," the tattooed goblin replied.

"Then you be stupid," his companion spat. "Knorl speaks for Master. He be chief one day," the goblin predicted.

My curiosity was piqued at the reference to the Master. They couldn't be referring to the same Master, could they?

"But why us be here?!" the young goblin whined. "Me no mewling woman!" He thumped his chest. "Me warrior!"

The older goblin snorted. "We *soldiers*. Not warriors. We listen chief. If chief say watch tunnel, we watch." He paused. "Chief says if all players die, Master gives tribe reward." His eyes gleamed. "Beeg reward. Do as chief says. Chief smart. Let dungeon kill lotta players. *Then* we kill rest."

"But me wants to kill players now!" the other goblin protested. He bared his teeth in a ghastly smile. "Especially elves."

His companion chuckled. "We serve Master. Master *always* fighting." The older goblin's humor faded, and he stared into the fire. "There be always more elves to kill," he finished, almost wearily.

"But me want—" the younger archer began.

"Shuddup!" the older goblin barked, seeming to lose patience. "Enough talking, or players hear us!"

The younger goblin muttered something under his breath, but he didn't gainsay his older companion. Presently, both goblins fell silent, and I crept away.

The pair had given me much to think about.

~ ~ ~

I pressed my back against the tunnel and leaned my head against the cold wall while I pondered what I had learned. From the overheard conversation, it was clear that the Master had not only put the goblins in the dungeon—which I had known already—he had also offered them incentives to kill the candidates.

I don't know why, but that just rubbed me wrong. The Master had been clear from the get-go about the purpose the trials served, and I couldn't fault him on that front, but what I disliked was how much of a game he was turning this into.

I suspected the Master had set the goblins to hunting us for no other reason than to provide him with entertainment. The more I learned about our mysterious 'benefactor,' the less I liked.

Do I even want to pass this trial? I wondered. I wasn't so sure anymore. Yet what would be the consequences of failure? My eyes shifted to the still and unmoving undead bat on my shoulder. Would the Master kill me? *I wouldn't put it past him.* But the Master's motives aside, had anything changed? My eyes drifted to the goblins.

No.

I still have to get stronger.

I still have to escape the dungeon.

I still have to kill the goblins.

Closing my eyes, I schooled myself to patience. Soon, the goblins would sleep. Then I would act.

~ ~ ~

For the next few hours, I kept a lonely vigil while I watched the goblins. I was determined not to lose focus again or succumb to sleep. I had no idea what day-night cycle the goblins were following, but I knew sooner or later, the pair had to sleep.

Four hours later, my patience was rewarded, and I heard the first snores coming from the campfire. *At last.*

Creeping towards the sleeping goblins, I paused at the edge of the circle of light and verified that my targets were indeed passed out before inching forward again.

Both goblins lay on their sides. A dirty sack, serving as a makeshift pillow, was tucked under the head of each. I drew my swords and edged closer to the older goblin. He was the more dangerous of the pair and had to be eliminated first. Slowly, I went down on one knee beside the goblin, my movements slow and controlled.

The goblin did not stir.

I raised my swords and held them poised above my target while I decided where to strike. Hide armor protected the goblin's torso, legs, and arms, leaving only a small part of his neck and head exposed.

The neck, I decided. *That's where I must strike.*

I narrowed my eyes and tensed my arms, readying myself to bring my blades crashing down. A long second passed. Then another. But still, my swords did not whip down. I was hesitating.

Why was I hesitating?

I've never murdered anyone before.

The thought rippled through my mind with sudden and shocking clarity. *It was true.* I knew with certainty that I had never killed anyone, much less committed murder. Despite whatever the Master said, right then, I knew I was not evil.

I am no murderer.

I glanced down at my intended victim. If I went through my plan, I would become a killer. Could I become one? Did I *want* to be one? I had not been afflicted by such doubts when fighting the slimes. But then again, the creatures had clearly not been sentient.

The goblin, for all that he was a primitive savage, was still a person. A living, breathing person with thoughts and desires of his own. But the archer was more than that. He was my foe too. The goblin's own words bore testimony to his intent: he and the rest of his tribe had pledged themselves to kill me and every other candidate in the trials.

Asleep, the goblin didn't appear threatening, but I was not fooled. Given half a chance, I didn't doubt he would slay me without remorse. My hands tightened around the hilts of my swords.

It is him or me.

I may not have been a killer in my other life, but I had no illusions: if I wanted to survive in this world, I would have to kill—and repeatedly.

But, I swore, *I will do it by my own code.*

I will not prey on the weak or the innocent.

I will kill only those that deserve it or seek to harm me. The Master and his cause be damned.

At ease with my actions, I brought my swords flashing down.

CHAPTER 25: AMBUSH

You have missed a level 14 goblin archer. You have critically injured a goblin archer. Your two weapon fighting has increased to level 2. You are no longer hidden.

I bit off a curse as the blade in my left hand missed my target completely. Thankfully though, the sword in my right hand found its mark.

Yet it was not a clean kill. The archer still lived. As my blade sliced open his throat, the goblin's eyes snapped open, and he tried to roll away. Leaping forward, I straddled his body and pinned him in place. I raised my swords aloft once more.

The archer's eyes grew wide. "Help—!" he managed to croak before my blades flew down again. This time, I struck true.

You have killed a goblin archer and have gained experience. You have reached level 7! Your shortswords has increased to level 8.

At the sound of movement from behind me, I rolled off the corpse and narrowly escaped the unseen attack of the second goblin.

You have evaded a level 10 goblin archer's attack. Your dodging has increased to level 4.

I growled in frustration. My mishap had cost me. The older goblin's cry of alarm had warned his younger companion, who was now alert to the danger and eagerly rushing to engage me again.

I bounced back to my feet in time to meet the tattooed goblin's onrushing dagger. Parrying aside my foe's weapon with the blade in my left hand, I simultaneously struck out with the one in my right.

The maneuver caught the goblin by surprise, and he was not able to bring back his dagger in time to fend off my sword. The point of my blade pierced the archer's hide armor and sank three inches deep into the lower half of his torso.

You have injured a goblin archer!

I grimaced. I had only superficially wounded the goblin. While the archer had failed to evade my blow altogether, he had twisted his torso far enough away for me not to have hit anything vital.

Favoring his injured side, the goblin stepped back and glared at me. With predatory intent, I circled him, both blades held at the ready. The archer shifted with me, keeping me front and center.

I paced a full circle around my opponent, and when the goblin still failed to attack, I darted forward myself. My blades flashed, the right one descending down from up high and the left one stabbing forward.

Even injured, the goblin proved my match. He ducked beneath my descending sword while his knife turned aside my thrust blade. I didn't let up. Dancing to the side, I slashed at the archer from the left and right simultaneously.

Once again, my foe proved equal to the task. Dodging adroitly between my blows, he stepped inside my blades and sent his dagger snaking forward.

I leaped backward and narrowly avoided being skewered. *Bloody hell! How did he do that?* I had been pressing the goblin hard, and he should not have had the time to launch his own attack. Yet somehow, he had.

From two yards away, I eyed the goblin warily. He was proving to be a much tougher opponent than I'd anticipated. In fact, if not for my two blades to his one, I feared I would have been outmatched already. As it was, I wondered if I would be able to kill the archer.

Seeming to sense my sudden concern, the goblin smiled toothily. "Stupid human. Me kill you now." He took a threatening step forward.

Before I could stop myself, I took an involuntary step backward. *Idiot! That was the worst thing you could've done.* Never show a predator fear.

The goblin's grin broadened. "You die now," he chortled and hurtled forward.

The archer's dagger was a half-seen blur as it flashed toward my face. Instinctively, I flung my left sword upwards and parried away the attack, only to be threatened anew as the goblin brought his dagger slashing back before I could recover.

I blocked the second blow with the sword in my right hand and backpedaled desperately in a bid to regain my equilibrium. The goblin followed quickly after, not giving me a chance to recover. In his battle frenzy, the archer seemed to be entirely unhampered by the wound to his side.

My foe thrust his blade forward again. Once more, I fended it away and continued my retreat. The goblin, his eyes crazed, pursued me relentlessly and launched one onslaught after another.

I wove a frantic defense with my twin blades and somehow kept the archer at bay. My plan was in tatters, and I had no thought to spare beyond the moment. Still, it was in the back of my mind that the longer this went on, the better my chances.

Eventually, the goblin had to tire. Eventually, the biting pain and blood loss from the wound to his side had to tell on the archer.

Eventually. I only had to survive until then.

The next few seconds passed in a blur as the goblin continued to hound me with his dagger, and I tread a slow circle in reverse around the campfire. Not trusting myself to spot the goblin's quicksilver blows in the darkness, I didn't dare leave the circle of light cast by the campfire.

After a minute's harried exchange, and with the goblin showing no sign of tiring, I began to wonder if it was time to flee. I was barely holding the goblin at bay, and sooner or later, his dagger would pierce my guard. *It's time to acknowledge the truth*, I told myself. *I can't win this fight.*

Settled in my course, I prepared to disengage. But as I was about to do so, I was struck by the change in my swordplay. My strokes were surer, and my grip around my blades firmer. My two blades worked less at odds with each other and more in tandem.

Where at the beginning of the skirmish, it had been a scramble to coordinate my attacks between my left and right sword, I was doing so more easily now. *My skill has grown*, I thought. *Appreciably so.*

And from the sideways flicker of my opponent's gaze, I suspected he had come to the same realization. There had been a constant stream of Game messages in my mind since the battle began, but with my focus consumed by the goblin, I had mostly ignored them.

I pulled up the three most recent now.

Your dodging has increased to level 14.
Your shortswords has increased to level 19.
Your two weapon fighting has increased to level 11.

I smiled. *So, this is truly what it means to be a player.* The advancements to my skills had happened so subtly, and intuitively, I had barely noticed their individual increases. But their cumulative effect could not be denied.

I turned my attention upon the goblin. He was still faster than me, I noted, but now I was his equal in skill, at least when it came to blades, and soon no doubt, I would surpass him.

This fight is not lost yet, I realized. I let a broad grin split my face.

The goblin sensed my renewed confidence and his strokes grew more frantic. My own, by comparison, grew more graceful as the fear clouding my mind receded, and I let instinct guide my hands.

Biding my time, I fended off the archer's attacks by rote and waited for him to slip. He would too. And soon. I was sure of it. The goblin had lost his confidence, and panic was setting in. Any moment now...

There!

In a bid to batter through my defenses, my foe had lunged forward and extended himself an inch too far.

I pounced.

Stepping into the archer's attack, I parried his dagger away with one blade and thrust toward his torso with the other. Overextended, the goblin was helpless to stop me, and the point of my sword buried itself in his heart.

You have killed a goblin archer with a fatal blow.

You have gained experience and reached level 8! You have 2 attribute points available.

Your two weapon fighting has increased to level 13. Your shortswords has increased to level 20. Congratulations, Michael! Your skill with shortswords has reached rank 2.

Letting the flurry of game messages scroll through my mind, I dropped my swords and sank to the ground.

I had triumphed again and, once more, lived to fight another day.

CHAPTER 26: KILLER

For long moments, I sat, with my head bowed, while I came to terms with what I had done and with what I now was: a killer.

It had been both easier and harder than I expected to slay the two goblins. A single thrust of a blade, and that easily a life was snuffed out.

Yet the goblins had fought hard for their lives, and the skirmish had been as much a test of wills as skill. In the end, my desire to live proved the stronger. I did not regret slaying the pair. Their deaths were necessary for my own continued survival. But I felt the weight of their spirits.

Killing is easy, I thought, *but bearing the cost, perhaps less so.*

I studied my hands. They were covered in blood, both literally and figuratively. And I stank. Dragging dead corpses back and forth, rolling down their remains in the trench, and now spilling fresh blood had all left me reeking of death—and worse.

I must be a sight, I thought.

"I'm impressed," Gnat pronounced.

I picked up my head to find the skeletal bat sitting on the corpse of the older goblin. I had lost track of Gnat in the skirmish. I narrowed my eyes and studied him. "Really?" I asked. "And why's that?" Given my recent reflections on the Master and his motives, I was not feeling too well-inclined toward his servant.

Gnat chuckled. "A candidate killing *two* warrior-caste goblins all on his lonesome? I don't think anyone has done that before. I really thought you were a goner there for sure." The bat's gaze drifted to the dead bodies. "Who would have believed you had it in you," he murmured.

Deciding to ignore Gnat's musings, I glanced around the camp. The first thing I noticed was the large wooden chest sitting next to the still-burning campfire. It had *not* been there before the fight.

"Where did that come from?" I asked, gesturing to the chest with my chin.

Gnat shrugged. "The Game must have spawned it once you killed those two."

I looked at the familiar sharply. "The Game?" I asked. "I thought you said the Master designed this sector?"

Gnat shifted uncomfortably and didn't answer immediately. "The dungeon's encounters, layout, and occupants are all the Master's doing," the bat said eventually.

My eyes narrowed. "But not the loot chests?"

"But not the loot chests," Gnat agreed. "They are spawned by the Game itself. The Adjudicator decides when a party deserves to be rewarded."

I frowned. "So where do the items from inside the chests come from?"

"Loot chests are randomly populated with items held by the Game according to an arcane set of rules known only to the adjudicator," Gnat said.

I nodded slowly and rose to my feet to study the chest containing my 'reward.' I detected nothing unusual about it, but once again, I had to wonder if that was due to my Perception being too low.

I pursed my lips. I really needed to find a trap detection skill or ability. I couldn't keep increasing my Perception indefinitely. *I'll do it once more only,* I decided. Thereafter I would start dumping future attributes into Dexterity.

Closing my eyes, I willed my choice to the Game.

Your Perception has increased to rank 6.

I studied the loot chest anew but failed to detect anything amiss. That didn't prove anything, of course. The chest could still be trapped. Admittedly, the likelihood was lower, but the possibility was still real.

I sighed. *Right, time for more rigorous testing.* Picking up one of the goblins' abandoned bows, I began the laborious process of methodically testing the chests for traps.

~ ~ ~

Ten minutes later, after warily poking and prodding the chest and carefully lifting the lid by degrees, I was sure as I could be that the chest was not boobytrapped. With only a flutter of anxiety, I swung back the lid and peered inside the wooden box.

You have acquired 3 minor healing potions. Each item restores your health by 10%.

You have acquired a basic Class stone. This stone contains the path of: an archer. The archer is a basic Class that confers a player with three skills: light armor, daggers, and a ranged weapon skill of the player's choice. This Class also permanently boosts your Perception attribute by +1 and your Constitution attribute by +1.

I stared at the marble in my hand. Finding a Class stone was the last thing I had expected. A Game message opened in my mind.

You have two available Class slots. Do you wish to acquire the archer Class?

I started in surprise. Become an archer? It was not a path I had considered, but given the equipment left behind by the goblins and my already-high Perception, there was an undeniable appeal to the choice.

"I wouldn't advise it," Gnat said abruptly.

I blinked. I didn't have to ask what he meant. "Why not?"

"It will only limit your player potential. The archer Class is a basic one," Gnat said derisively. "You don't want to install *that* in your secondary Class slot, not when you can fill it with an advanced Class. If I were you, I would hold out until you acquired a better Class."

I frowned. The skeletal bat's words had dashed my fantasies of sniping goblins from the dark, but... he was right. I couldn't be hasty in my choice of second Class, and at the moment, I was doing well enough with my current skill mix.

With a reluctant sigh, I stored the Class stone in my backpack. Turning my gaze upon the rest of the camp, I worked through it carefully until I had found everything usable.

You have acquired 2 goblin shortbows. Each item increases the damage you deal by 5%.

You have acquired 4 iron daggers. Each item increases the damage you deal by 8%.

You have acquired 2 sets of primitive goblin hide armor. Each set reduces the physical damage you sustain by 10%.

You have acquired a bedroll. This item increases the rate at which stamina, psi, and mana are replenished when sleeping.

I studied the fruits of my scavenging thoughtfully. I could fit everything in my backpack except the hide armor. They, unfortunately, were both too bulky and heavy to fit in my pack.

I will have to leave them behind, I decided and stored the rest of the items in my pack. Feeling too exposed in the circle of light cast by the campfire to dally there any longer, I stepped into the comforting darkness of the tunnel beyond.

Almost immediately, I noticed my night vision was better. The two additional points I'd invested in Perception had made a noticeable difference, and even in the darkest corners of the tunnel, I could make out the blurred outline of the shapes they contained. *Good,* I thought. My enhanced night vision could prove advantageous in future encounters.

I ventured only a few dozen yards down the corridor before stopping again. I was starving, and it was high time that I took a few moments to rest. Sinking down to the floor, I pulled out my water flask and rations, and sat down to a well-earned lunch—or supper.

Or whatever.

CHAPTER 27: TUNNELS

A single field ration assuaged my hunger and had me ready to forge on. Rising to my feet, I shrugged on my backpack—it was noticeably heavier now—and studied the darkness ahead.

Up ahead, in the far distance, I could make out a fork in the tunnel. I stifled a yawn. It felt like forever since I had entered this world, and I knew I would have to find somewhere safe to rest soon. But for now, the tunnel beckoned.

Dropping into a crouch, I concealed myself and advanced down the passage's rocky surface. I reached the fork without incident. Standing at the center of the three-way intersection, I stared down the depths of the unexplored paths to my left and right.

Both tunnels were of the same size and gave no hint of what they concealed. With a shrug, I entered the right corridor. After only another few minutes of walking, I came to another fork. This time, I didn't hesitate and ventured down the right fork without pause.

A few hundred yards later, the corridor branched again. Once more, I chose the tunnel to the right, realizing now that I had entered something of a maze. If I wasn't careful, I could quickly become lost. *Just keep taking the right fork, and you will be fine,* I told myself.

A hundred yards later, the tunnel ended in a dead-end. *Aaargh.* Filled only with large boulders, the cul-de-sac was barren of life.

Forced to backtrack, I decided to retreat all the way back to the tunnel network's first fork and chose the left passage from there. Unsurprisingly, I soon came to another branch. I went left again.

Three forks—and three left turns—later, I found myself at another dead end. With a sigh, I returned back to the starting tunnel and pondered my options.

It is a maze, I decided. Even in the darkness shrouding the tunnels, I could tell they were all of identical size and shape. I would not find my way through by trying to spot the difference between the tunnels. *Assuming there is a way out to find,* I thought morosely.

I dismissed that pessimistic thought. It was not as if I had a wealth of options at my fingertips. Either I found a way through the maze, or I turned back and faced the trolls or candidate gangs. And I didn't want to do either of those things.

So how do I do this? I wondered.

I could choose tunnels at random, but if the maze was a large one, that was certain to get me irretrievably lost. *Better to do this by a surer means, even if it is likely to take far longer than I like.*

I placed the palm of my right hand on the wall on the right side of the tunnel. As long as I kept my fingers in contact with the wall, no matter how much the tunnels twisted and turned, I would find my way out of their depths.

Eventually.

Entering the maze again, I began walking.

~ ~ ~

Two hours later, I was still walking.

I had circled cul-de-sac after dead end, navigated fork after fork, and still, there was no end to the maze in sight. My head had begun to droop, and the urge to rest was becoming more persistent.

Soon, I knew I wouldn't be able to resist my body's needs. *Just a little while longer,* I thought. *This damnable maze must end soon.*

The tunnel I was in hadn't branched in a while, and I was sure it would do so soon. I couldn't afford to lose concentration now. Shaking off my stupor, I focused on my surroundings.

That was when I spotted the pit.

I stumbled to a halt. A black maw of darkness yawned open less than three feet in front of me. Six yards in length and extending the width of the passage, the pit was unavoidable. Edging nearer, I peered within and predictably found its bottom decorated with sharpened stakes.

The sudden appearance of the trap was not the most surprising thing, however. What caused my eyebrows to shoot up and my forehead to crinkle in confusion was the thin wooden pole stretched across the pit. Someone had already crossed this way and left behind the means to do so again.

Unless it's a trap too.

The pole was a sliver of wood, only a few inches thick. Kneeling down, I inspected the near end of the pole. Deep bolts had been driven into the ground, and a pole had been wedged between them, presumably to secure it in place.

Placing a foot on the near end of the plank, I pressed down gently. The wood flexed beneath me as a sapling would but did not creak. I pressed harder, and still, the pole did not give any indication it would crack. It seemed sturdy enough to bear my weight. Letting my eyes unfocus, I studied the surroundings again. I could spot nothing else that appeared out of place, or that screamed of danger.

With no further reason to delay, I stepped fully onto the pole and took a second to clear my mind for the task ahead. Very deliberately, I did not wonder if I was acrobatic enough to manage the feat. If I began questioning my ability, I knew I would fail.

Slowly, I stretched out my arms. It would help balance my weight. Expelling a careful breath, I raised my right leg and blocked out everything else but the simple motion of swinging it forward and placing my foot with deliberate care in the precise center of the pole. Then, transferring my weight to that leg, I restarted the process with my left leg.

Step by step, I made my way across the pit. The farther I ventured from the edge, the more the pole bowed beneath my weight. By the time I reached the halfway mark, the pole had sagged nearly three feet beneath ground level.

But it did not break. Nor did my concentration.

My world had narrowed to my feet. Nothing else mattered but placing one foot in front of the other. No matter how much my muscles trembled, no matter the dripping sweat blurring my eyes, I let nothing impinge on my awareness and kept walking.

An eternity later, I touched down on the far end of the pit.

To my surprise, I had managed the crossing without incident. Despite the lack of discernable threats nearby, I had half-expected to be attacked at some point. Thoughtfully, I placed my right palm against the tunnel wall and resumed my journey through the maze.

Thirty minutes later, I came across another oddity. A few yards ahead of me, the tunnel broadened into a chamber. It was the first cavern I had encountered since entering the maze. And that was not the only startling thing.

Arrayed on the flat cavern floor in the shape of a square were sixteen granite flagstones. The flagstones were themselves squares, and carved on the surface of each was a luminous archaic symbol. Some of the symbols glowed golden, some shone red, and others were colored blue.

Standing on the chamber's threshold and not daring to enter, I studied its interior intently. To my suspicious mind, the chamber screamed of one thing only: a trapped room.

Except for the flagstones themselves, the chamber was empty. On the opposite end of the room, I spied another exit, but to get there, I would have to cross over the flagstones, which I was leery of doing just yet. My eyes darted from one to the other of the chamber's smooth stone walls and found three of them to be bare. The fourth one, though, the one to my right, contained strange markings, that on first glance, seemed indecipherable text.

Ignoring the scrawled writing, for now, I lifted my gaze upwards. My eyes narrowed. Covering the entirety of the roof arching overhead were small dark holes. My eyes flitted between the murder holes in the ceiling and the flagstones beneath. It was not hard to imagine how the trap worked: step on the wrong flagstone and be skewered or boiled alive from whatever rained down from the roof.

I turned back to the text on the right wall. They seemed to have been haphazardly drawn in chalk by someone who was in a hurry. Though no matter how hard I stared at them, I couldn't figure out what they meant.

"Gnat," I whispered finally, "what are those markings?"

The undead bat peered where I pointed and studied the text in silence for a moment. "Goblin writing," he pronounced at last.

My mouth dropped open. "Goblin? Are you sure?"

"Of course I am," Gnat snapped waspishly.

I scratched my head. It was a surprise to find out that goblins could write, much less to discover that they had a written language of their own. But beyond that, what troubled me further, was wondering what they had written here. "Can you read it?" I asked.

Instead of answering, the skeletal bat glided off my shoulder and towards the right wall. Hovering before the writing, he read out aloud, "Red is dead. Gold hurts. Blue is safe."

I blinked. "Really?" I murmured, my eyes flying back to the flagstones. Assuming the stones bearing blue symbols were safe, there was a clear path across. The real question, though, was: *can I trust what the goblins have written?*

My thought drifted back to the two archers. Before this, it had not occurred to me to wonder *how* the two goblins had come to be where I had found them. There was no evidence that they had crossed the trapped trench, which ruled out them arriving from the dungeon's third leg.

But what if the pair had originated from *beyond* the maze?

It would mean that the goblins, too, would have had to traverse the maze — only in the reverse direction from me. It would also explain the pole across the pit. I frowned. *Still, why would the goblins leave behind a means for others to overcome the maze's traps?*

But then again, how many of my fellows would have spotted the pole, much less managed the crossing? And could the goblins have predicted that my familiar would have been able to read their writing?

I sighed. There was only one way to be certain. And that was to step onto the flagstones.

CHAPTER 28: TRAPS

My foot crunched down on the flagstone. With bated breath and my eyes glued to the murder holes riddling the ceiling, I waited for a reaction.

When, after long moments, nothing happened, I relaxed muscles rigid with tension. I glanced down at the flagstone beneath me. The sigil inscribed on it had begun to pulse, waxing and waning through different shades of blue. Not wanting to wait and see if that boded ill, I stepped forward onto the next blue flagstone.

Still, no trap activated.

Growing more confident, I stepped to my left, then forward, and left again before taking the final two steps forward required to clear the flagstones.

I was through. I exhaled a relieved breath and resumed my way down the next tunnel.

My journey through the maze continued without incident for another two hours. During that time, I encountered four more traps—a stretch of passageway seeded with snares, a deadfall, a trapped room filled with whirling blades, and a collapsing tunnel. Each time, I saw some sign that someone else had been that way, and I grew increasingly convinced it had been the goblins. Which only made me wonder what lay beyond the maze.

Was it a tribe of goblins? I wondered. The chief, the two archers had spoken of? I wasn't certain, but I knew whatever it was, I would find a way around the challenge.

As the hours passed, despite my determination to stay alert, the day's excitement and exertions began to claim its toll, and I was lulled into a half-daze by the increasing familiarity and sameness of the maze's surroundings.

Which was why I was caught off-guard when I exited the maze. One moment, I had been brushing the wall to my right with my fingertips. The next, I felt nothing but air beneath my searching hands.

The sudden emptiness shocked me alert. Grounding to a halt, I took stock of my surroundings. I was standing on a high ledge. A few feet away, on all sides of me, the ground dropped away suddenly. I was no longer in a tunnel, I realized. I was in a cavernous natural-rock chamber.

My surroundings had brightened considerably too, I saw, and tinges of red-orange shot through the darkness. There was no light source within my line of sight, and I deduced that whatever the source of light, it came from below.

Sinking into a crouch, I crept to the edge of the ledge and peered warily down. A hundred feet below, I spied a rickety wooden table with two oil lamps resting in its center. The rest of the table was strewn with odd bits of junk and food.

Three goblins sat around the table, too, with their heads resting on its surface. From the loud snores emanating from the trio, I guessed they were asleep.

Directly behind the goblins was a grilled-metal gate, and mounted on the wall next to it was a large bronze bell. The cavern below was being used as a guard station, I deduced, and the three goblins were guards if poorly-trained ones.

I turned my attention to the ledge itself. A rope ladder leading to the room below had been conveniently fastened to its edge. My gaze flitted from the guards to the ladder. Assuming the goblins really were asleep, I could make the journey down unseen.

Moving slowly, I swung myself onto the rope ladder. On my shoulder, Gnat fluttered his wings once but did not break the silence. I lowered myself down the rungs of the ladder and touched down onto the cavern's floor without incident. I dropped into a crouch.

You and your familiar are hidden.

The rhythm of the goblins' snores was still unchanged. Padding softly through the cavern in a wide arc to avoid the brightly-lit center, I repositioned myself behind the three goblins.

Unlike the two archers, the trio was armed with small axes, and their hide armor appeared heavier. *Close combatants, then.* I drew one of my blades and moved right up to the closest goblin. With his head resting on the table, the back of his neck was exposed. I licked suddenly dry lips, readying myself for what I knew I must do.

I had to kill the three guards, and I had to do it quietly.

The bell behind me was evidence enough that somewhere beyond the grilled-metal gate, there were more goblins waiting to respond to whatever emergency arose. I couldn't let that happen, or I would be swamped.

Raising my sword, I positioned it a few inches from the back of the goblin's neck and deliberately relaxed tense muscles. *Do it,* I thought. My blade flashed downwards, point first, and pierced vulnerable flesh.

For a fraction of a second, my victim tensed. His snores cut off abruptly, and I felt a shriek build within him. But before the goblin could give voice to his pain, his life fled away, and with a gentle sigh, his body sagged against the table.

You have killed a level 13 goblin warrior and have gained experience.

With my blade still buried in the goblin, I stood motionless, poised to flee or fight. Killing someone without any betraying slip of noise was much harder than I expected, and I was on edge. For a drawn-out moment, I watched the other two goblins, waiting to see if they would react in any way to their companion's demise.

They snored on, oblivious.

I sagged slightly in relief. Placing my left hand against the dead warrior's head, I extracted my bloody blade from his neck. Then I crept behind my next target and repeated the deed.

You have killed a level 10 goblin warrior and have gained experience. You have reached level 9!

Once more, I pulled off my assassination without a hitch. *One last time,* I thought and drove my blade through the last guard.

You have killed a level 11 goblin warrior and have gained experience. Your shortswords has increased to level 21. Your sneaking has increased to level 24.

I stumbled backward from the three corpses and coming up against the cavern wall, slid downwards. The killings left a bad taste in my mouth, but I knew they had been necessary. If the three guards had been awake and alert, my chances of surviving the encounter would have been slim, at best.

A flicker of motion on the table caught my attention. A wooden chest had materialized there. I pushed myself to my feet again.

Upwards and onwards, Michael.

CHAPTER 29: COMPLICATIONS

The chest contained only four items.

You have acquired 2 moderate health potions. Each item restores your health by 30%.

You have acquired a basic skillbook: heavy shields. This skill is incompatible with your slotted Classes and may not be learned. The skillbook is a single-use item.

You have acquired a pack of six field rations. This item can be consumed to replenish stamina slowly over time.

I grimaced as I saw the loot. The potions and rations would come in handy, but the main item was, again, one I couldn't use. Still, I stored it in my inventory.

The goblins, I did not search—or loot. In fact, I did my best to leave them as undisturbed as possible and even went so far as to wipe away as much of their blood spatter as I could. Considering the presence of the guard station and the alarm bell, this section of the dungeon was obviously well-populated and, by all appearances, under the control of the goblins.

I assumed that at some point, other goblins would come to relieve the three, and not knowing how long I would be stuck in the area, I wanted to delay the discovery of the guards' fate as long as I could.

There was one last thing I had to do before moving on. Closing my eyes, I communicated with the game.

Your Dexterity has increased to rank 4.

With my chores in the room done, I moved to the cavern's only exit. Through the grilled-metal gate's iron bars, I could see that a darkened tunnel lay beyond. The corridor was empty and formed of the same ubiquitous grey rocks I'd found everywhere else.

It seemed like the tunnel network had not ended as I'd hoped when I had exited the maze. In fact, if not for the guard station itself and the presence of the alarm bell, I could almost believe I was still in the maze. I looked down at the grilled gate. Its hinges had been well-oiled, and there was no lock. Swinging open the gate, I slipped into the corridor.

I shut the gate behind me and ducked down into the tunnel. I listened intently for a few moments but heard no signs of movement. The fact that I had found the guards asleep suggested that the goblins were in the middle of their sleep cycle, but I knew it was too early to make that assumption yet.

I padded cautiously down the tunnel and presently arrived at a four-way intersection. I scanned all three other passages but spotted nothing of interest in any of them. The corridor directly in front of me bent out of sight after only five yards, while the ones to my right and left continued unerringly straight for a few dozen yards.

I was still debating which way to go when I heard the tread of footsteps. My head turned slowly to the right. Listening intently, I thought I made out the sound of two sets of footsteps. They were heading my way but were still out of sight.

A faint orange tinge began to seep into the intersection. I cursed softly. The ones approaching had to be carrying torches. There was nowhere to hide in the intersection, and even a cursory inspection under torchlight would reveal me.

Which way to flee? I wondered. *Left, forward, or back?* I wasn't willing to entangle with two unknown entities in the open tunnel, not until I knew what other enemies were nearby.

Out of time, I dashed forward into the tunnel directly opposite me. The wiser course would have been to flee back to the guard station, but I wanted to observe whoever approached, and it was my thought that I could do that around while concealed behind the corridor's bend.

Of course, I was assuming that the two who approached wouldn't turn in my direction, but that was a risk I was willing to take. I crossed the five yards to the corner and rounded the bend. After only a hurried glimpse to confirm that the tunnel stretching in front of me was empty, I spun around and dropped into a crouch.

Then waited.

The footsteps grew louder. From their tread, they sounded unhurried and relaxed. The pair did not talk, nor did they slow as they reached the intersection. Instead, they continued onwards, oblivious of my nearby presence.

I waited until I was sure the two had cleared the intersection before ducking around the bend and padding back to the intersection. Warily, I peered around.

As I had suspected, the unknown entities were goblins. I studied the backs of the retreating pair. Each was dressed in hide armor and carried a spear in one hand and a torch in the other. *A patrol?* I wondered, biting my lip worriedly. *Has to be.*

That complicates things. Attacking the pair was out of the question. I *might* win in a confrontation against the two, but there was no way I was doing that before they raised the alarm. I could only see two options. Either I tried to exit the area before my presence was discovered, or I took the fight to the goblins... on my own terms.

I chewed the inside of my lip. But before I could decide on my approach, I needed to explore the tunnel network I found myself in more. I glanced at the disappearing patrol. And I didn't have much time to do it.

Spinning on my heel, I headed around the bend and continued down the corridor with renewed urgency dogging my footsteps. Less than a minute later, I stopped short as a shadow of blackness appeared on the corridor's right wall. A tunnel opening.

I drew up cautiously to the entrance and peered within. The tunnel opened up into another cavern. Although it was shrouded in darkness, I could make out the outline of five large tables and twice as many benches. I frowned worriedly. The cavern appeared to be a dining area, one sized to hold a large gathering.

Just how many goblins are in this tunnel network? I wondered. Going by the size of the dining area, there could be upward of fifty goblins nearby. I hurried onwards but stopped again only a little later.

Just up ahead, there was another cavern opening on the tunnel's left wall. I wrinkled my nose in disgust. The smells emanating from it were revolting. Breathing through my mouth, I moved to study the room.

It was a kitchen. Well, not really.

It was perhaps more accurate to say the cavern was a food-preparation area. There were three open fire-pits, each filled with coals glowing a sullen red. Hooks had been inset all around the chamber's walls. Hanging off them were strips of meat of dubious origin and, from the smell, somewhat rancid.

A handful of goblins slept on the floor. Unlike the other goblins I had seen recently, the five were unarmed and unarmored and also smaller in stature. *Worker goblins,* I realized.

I was tempted to enter the cavern and slay the creatures, but with every passing minute, my anxiety was growing. I needed to quickly find my way out of this dungeon section. It was clear to me now that this tunnel network contained the goblins' living quarters, and if the alarm was given while I was still in it, then my chances of survival were minimal at best.

Leaving behind the kitchen, I pressed onwards into the tunnel. Presently, I came to another cavern. I paused only long enough to ascertain the chamber—a training room, if I had to guess—was empty before hurrying on.

I passed another half dozen openings on my left and right but didn't stop to investigate. The corridor I was in appeared to be the tunnel network's main passage, and I was hoping that, sooner or later, it would lead me to the area's exit.

Five minutes later, I noticed the bright orange glow of torches up ahead. My steps slowed, and I dropped deeper into my crouch as I crept closer. An intersection lay just ahead. It was the first branch in the tunnel I had come across since running into the patrol at the other crossing.

Beyond the intersection, the main passage continued for only a few more yards before ending abruptly in a thick metal door. The bright orange glow that I had spotted came from the torches affixed on either side of the door. Lounging in front of the door were six goblin guards.

I had found the tunnel network's exit.

But to my disappointment, it was guarded and with greater care than the maze's exit had been. While the goblin squad standing guard outside the door appeared slovenly and rumpled, they were unfortunately very much awake.

Worse yet, there was also a bell mounted on the wall behind the goblins. If I attempted a head-on assault, the guards were sure to raise the alarm.

Resting on my haunches, I considered the problem. Luckily, while the area near the door was well-lit, the torchlight did not extend far, and both the intersection and the passageway in which I crouched were shrouded in shadows.

I have to lure the guards away from the door, I decided. *But how?* In whatever manner I did it, it would have to be innocuous enough not to rouse the guards' suspicions. *Perhaps, if I—*

A deep clanging sounded from behind me. I froze. In front of me, the goblin squad tensed suddenly and set hands to weapons. The clanging rose in pitch, and its call was taken up by another.

My pulse quickening, I drew further back into the shadows. I knew what had happened.

I had been discovered.

CHAPTER 30: DISCOVERIES

I lurked in the shadows a few heartbeats longer and waited to see what the door guards would do. But other than whispering to one another and scanning their surroundings suspiciously, the six goblins did nothing else.

I sighed. I wouldn't be getting out through the metal door. The door guards, it seemed, were too well-trained to abandon their post. Feeling the press of time and a sense of danger drawing closer at my back, I turned around and raced back the way I had come.

While I padded through the passage, my eyes scanned the darkness for danger. The bell was still clanging, and the sleeping goblins were surely rousing. *They will begin hunting me now.* Soon, I expected the passage would be flooded with goblins.

I had no concrete plan—yet. But I knew I had to get out of the main tunnel. My first thought had been to head back to the maze, but after only a second's consideration, I realized how foolish that would be.

The alarm must have been raised when one of the patrols discovered the guards I had slain. Even now, more goblins were surely massing at the guard station to block off my retreat into the maze. Heading to the guard station would be suicide—as would attacking the door guards.

With the only two exits I knew of sealed and guarded, I had few options remaining. *There is only one surefire way I'm getting out of this*, I thought. *And that's killing all the goblins.*

New sounds began filling the air: the thud of feet and the cries of goblins hollering to one another as they tried to figure out what was going on. As yet, the ruckus still sounded far off, and I couldn't spy the tell-tale glow of approaching torches.

I calmed my racing thoughts and slowed my steps. I had some time yet. This was not the time to get careless or let an errant goblin surprise me. I drew my swords from their sheaths. Then with my senses extended, I padded forward again.

I reached the first side room leading from the passage without incident. Sidling up to the wall next to the entrance, I listened intently. I heard no signs of movement from within. Cautiously, I ducked my head around the opening and studied the interior.

The room was empty and cluttered with junk. It appeared to be a storeroom of sorts. But more importantly, it was only a few yards in diameter. *Too small to hide in*, I thought. If the goblins searched the room, it would not take them long to spot me.

Moving away from the room, I crept to the next opening in the passage. It was only a few yards ahead. Placing myself next to the entrance, I strained my ears again. This time, my sharp hearing picked up a rumble of sound too indistinct to identify. I frowned. *Is that whispering?*

I peered around the edge of the wall. The room was large. Its walls extended off into the distance, and in the darkness, I couldn't make out their far ends. What I could see of the interior was filled with sturdy wooden tables. On each were piles of leather and blood-stained furs.

My gaze flitted across the room, trying to pinpoint the source of the sounds I'd heard. But whatever the source, it had fallen silent. I hesitated. The room was certainly large enough to hide in, but the noises worried me.

I glanced down the passage. The ruckus was getting louder. There was no guarantee that I would find a better place to conceal myself, and every moment longer I dallied, the odds of me being spotted in the passage increased.

Decided, I slipped into the opening.

Staying on the edges of the room, I walked clockwise through it. All along the left wall, I found a set of large metal racks. Pieces of hide were stretched out on them. Seeing the skins, I realized the room's purpose. *This is a tannery.*

I continued my slow circuit of the room. The back wall was stacked from floor to ceiling with rows of wooden cages. Most were empty, but two were filled. And their occupants were glaring at me with pale, yellow eyes.

Two hostile entities have detected you! You are no longer hidden.

I bit off a curse and took a few hurried steps away, hoping to conceal myself again from the piercing gazes of the imprisoned beasts. But it was no use.

You have failed to conceal yourself.

Despite me being shrouded in the room's deepest shadows, two sets of hate-filled eyes tracked me unerringly. "Damnit," I muttered. This would not do. Not at all. If any goblin entered the room, I was in deep trouble.

The noise I had heard earlier had started up again too. This time I recognized it for what it was: growling.

I returned the beasts' glares with one of my own. They had both risen to their feet and were pacing the confines of their cages. The creatures looked like wolves, but I hesitated to label them as such. For one, they were unnaturally large. The smaller of the pair was four feet tall, and the larger topped my own height.

For another, their gazes bore an uncanny intelligence. While the menace in beasts' eyes was obvious, their gazes bore something else, too, something much harder to identify. They stared unblinkingly at me, almost as if considering the threat I posed and finding me wanting.

I shuddered. I didn't want to entangle with the beasts, whatever they were. *Best to leave while I can,* I thought and began retreating from the room.

On my shoulder, I heard Gnat mumble something that I didn't quite catch.

I paused. "What did you say?" I whispered.

"I said," Gnat repeated, "smart choice. You don't want to tangle with dire wolves."

"Dire wolves," I mused. "What rank creatures are they?"

"Rank one," Gnat answered. "Those doggies are not just large and mean. They're smart too."

My eyes narrowed. "Smart? How smart exactly?"

"Not as smart as me. Obviously," Gnat said, preening slightly, "but intelligent enough to judge a threat and know when to flee." The familiar paused. "It's a wonder, really, that the goblins managed to capture a whole pack of them."

My gaze flitted between the hides stretched out on the racks and the caged dire wolves. It was clear that the goblins were using the beasts to create their hide armor, and after having been forced to watch their packmates being skinned, I didn't doubt the two still-living wolves hated the goblins.

But what about me? Would they associate me with their tormentors? "Are they clever enough to tell friend from foe?" I murmured.

Gnat cocked his head to the side. "You want to free them, don't you?" The bat snorted derisively. "That would be foolish. Dire wolves are dangerous. If given half a chance, those doggies will eat you alive."

"Just answer the damn question, Gnat!" I snapped, out of patience with my familiar as I felt the press of passing time. Soon the goblins would be here. Whatever I decided to do, I had to do it quickly. "Can I trust them to tell me apart from the goblins?"

Possibly," Gnat said grudgingly. "But don't count on them sparing you even if they do," he warned.

I bit my lip as I considered what I contemplated. Killing all the goblins on my own was a tall order, and I could do with some help, but how much aid could the two wolves provide? After all, they were only rank one creatures.

Pensively, I studied the creatures again. They were still staring at me. Both beasts' ribs poked through black coats matted with blood, and now that I looked more closely, I could see the limp in the gait of the smaller. *They're injured and half-starved.*

Gnat was right. Mad with hunger, there was no telling what the wolves would do if I freed them. *It isn't worth the gamble,* I decided. *Better to find somewhere else to hide.*

Resuming my retreat, I headed towards the exit.

CHAPTER 31: A GAMBLE REFUSED

I was about to duck out of the room when I heard the tread of marching feet. *Bloody hell!* I swore, stilling instantly.

From the echoes of the footfalls, it sounded like an entire squad of goblins was on the move. They sounded a way off still but were drawing closer with every second. Drawing up to the opening, I risked a quick peek into the passage and noticed the glow from about a dozen burning torches from further up the passage.

I ducked back inside the room and cursed myself for a fool. *Why did I delay so long in this damnable room?* I should have left when I had the chance. Now it was too late.

Hurrying to the left corner of the room, I dropped down next to the metal racks and tried to hide.

You have failed to conceal yourself from the nearby entities.

Muttering imprecations under my breath, I stared venomously at the two dire wolves. They look back placidly.

"You three!" barked a goblin in the passage. "Search the armory. And you two, the pantry."

With no small measure of relief, I listened to the sound of six sets of boots hurrying away—no doubt to search other nearby rooms. Unfortunately, the rest of the squad didn't wait on them. Instead, they kept advancing down the passage. Their footfalls echoed ominously louder as they drew closer.

I was doomed, I knew. The goblins were obviously searching the tunnel network room by room. And with me unable to conceal myself, the moment the guards entered this room, the alarm would be raised, and the goblins would converge on my position.

Still, I would not go cheaply. My hands tightened around my bared blades. The goblin squad was nearly at the entrance of the room where I hid. *Almost time now.*

"You three check the workshop," the officious-sounding goblin squad leader ordered. Three sets of steps approached the darkened entrance while the rest of the goblin squad marched onwards.

The goblin trio paused on the threshold. The one in front bore a torch in one hand and a sword in the other. The two behind him both carried spears. At the moment, the obstructing tables blocked me from the goblins' sight. Peering from under the table, I could see them, but they couldn't see me. But as soon as any one of them walked to the left side of the room, I would be spotted.

To retain the element of surprise, I would have to act before then. I slowed my breathing and bounced lightly on my haunches, readying myself to spring into action. A game message dropped into my mind.

You and your familiar are hidden.

Biting back a start of surprise, I swung back around to the caged beasts. The two wolves were slouched down on the ground. Their heads were resting on their paws, and their eyes were closed.

I stared at the beasts disbelievingly. Was it chance that just as the goblins entered the room, the two had closed their eyes and oh-so-coincidently let my sneaking skill conceal my presence?

I didn't believe it, but I wasn't about to look a gift horse in the mouth. Settling back down, I prepared myself to wait and see what the goblins did before acting.

"Search room," the torchbearer ordered, sounding bored. "I wait here."

"You not boss!" sneered one of the spear-wielders. "*You* search. I guard door."

The torchbearer swung on him and raised his sword threateningly. I smiled, unable to believe my luck. It would be just perfect if the two started fighting.

But it was not to be. "Quiet, you idiots!" said the second spear-wielder. "We fight. Chief will have us heads!"

The other two goblins grumbled but lowered their weapons. "What we do then?" the torchbearer asked.

"We check together," the second spear-wielder said. He pointed to the left side of the room where I hid. "Starting there."

I swallowed a groan. Why 'o why did they have to pick this side of the room to start with? The three goblins turned my way and started forward. But before the trio could take more than a few steps, a loud threatening rumble filled the room.

"What that?!" the torchbearer whispered, spinning around in a circle. His eyes had grown large, and the whites were showing.

"Relax, fool," laughed one of the spear-wielders. "It only wolves."

The torchbearer scowled. His gaze swung toward the direction of the cages. Mine too. With their eyes closed, the wolves were growling again.

My brows drew down. This time, I was sure the beasts were trying to help me. The timing of their pair's sudden growls was too coincidental to be anything else.

"You two got spears. Go check them," the torchbearer commanded.

The first spear-wielder opened his mouth to protest the order, but his companion yanked on his arm and pulled him toward the cages before he could start another argument.

The two goblins moved towards the far end of the room, leaving the torchbearer standing alone near the door and with all his attention fixed on his two companions.

I smiled. *Perfect.* Padding forward, I crept up on the oblivious goblin.

A hostile entity has failed to detect you! Your sneaking has increased to level 25.

I made it all the way behind the torchbearer without being detected. I paused for a second to take stock before acting. In the passageway, the echo of the marching goblin squad had faded away. Wherever they were, they were too far to interfere.

Up ahead, the other two goblins were poking their spears into wolves' cages, trying to get them to stop their growling. The beasts, however, ignored the prodding spear tips and refused to quieten.

It was time to act.

I sheathed the sword in my left hand. Then sprang upwards. My left hand grabbed the raised torch in the goblin's hand—stopping him from dropping it—while the blade in my right hand simultaneously sheared through the goblin's unprotected neck.

You have killed a level 11 goblin warrior and have gained experience. You have reached level 10!

Congratulations, Michael! You are now a rank 1 player. Your experience gains have decreased. Experience gains are inversely proportionally to your rank and will decrease at each new rank you attain.

For achieving rank 1, you have been awarded one additional attribute point. You have 2 attribute points available.

The dead goblin's lopped-off head bounced alarmingly loud—to my ears at least—on the rocky floor. But beneath the sound of the wolves' growls, the noise went unnoticed by the other two goblins.

Gingerly, I set down the torch on a nearby table and advanced on the remaining goblins.

Two hostile entities have failed to detect you! Your sneaking has increased to level 26.

It was only a few yards to the pair, and I was almost within striking distance when my luck ran out. The torch, which I had no choice but to leave resting on its side on the table, flickered as its flame sputtered and nearly died out.

One of the goblins glanced back, and his eyes widened as he saw me.

A hostile entity has detected you! You are no longer hidden.

Hurling myself forward, I thrust out with both my swords. The goblin tried to raise his spear to block my attacks, but he was too slow. Both my blades pierced his hide armor and thrust deep within his torso.

The goblin fell backward. And I went down with him, straddling his body as I bore him to the ground. Keeping the goblin pinned down with my left blade, I withdrew my right sword and hacked into him again.

You have killed a level 12 goblin warrior and have gained experience. Your shortswords has increased to level 22. Your two weapon fighting has increased to level 15.

I rolled off the corpse, expecting to be attacked by the third goblin. But no blows fell on my unprotected back. Rising to my knees, I glanced up. But for the wolves and me, the room was empty.

The last goblin was gone.

CHAPTER 32: ONE GOOD DEED DESERVES ANOTHER

"God damnit," I growled. I had no doubt the third goblin would return soon and with help too. I rose to my feet and swung around to the wolves. Both had stopped growling and were staring impassively at me.

"I know what you're thinking," Gnat warned. "Don't do it. Those dogs aren't friendly."

Ignoring my familiar's advice, I didn't hesitate. My sword flashed downwards and slashed free the rope holding the doors of their cages shut.

The beasts dashed out and straight towards me, looming ominously large, and for one horrible second, I thought I had made a horrible mistake. I squeezed my eyes shut, but the beasts only passed me harmlessly by with their mangled coats brushing my bare arms.

Opening my eyes, I swung around to watch the pair. The two were heading straight for the room's exit, but the smaller one—a female, I thought—was limping badly, and the larger male was forced to slow his steps for her.

"Wait!" I called.

The beasts stilled, and as one, two heads swung my way—their gazes both questioning and imperious.

"Gnat," I asked urgently, "will the healing potions work on the wolves?"

"Yes," the familiar replied, looking at me strangely, but not adding anything further.

It was all the confirmation I needed. The dire wolves had helped me far more than they had needed to in that encounter, even going so far as allowing the goblins to prod them with their spear tips. And even though I knew time was in short supply, I had to repay my debt.

I took a tentative step forward toward the beasts. The large dire wolf bared his teeth and growled. A warning, I thought.

"Easy," I murmured. "I mean no harm." Holding my palms out to show I held no weapons, I removed a moderate healing potion from my bag and knelt before the female wolf. The male watched me suspiciously all the while, but he stopped growling.

Moving slowly, I unstoppered the potion and held it before the injured wolf. She sniffed the flask and, seeming to understand my intention, sat down on her haunches and opened her mouth. Gingerly, I upended the flask's contents into the wolf's waiting mouth.

You have restored 30% of a level 14 dire wolf's lost health with a moderate healing potion. A dire wolf is no longer crippled. A dire wolf's health is now at 100%.

The wolf's open wounds closed as the last of the magical potion disappeared down her throat. Smacking her lips, the beast rose to her feet and tested her restored leg. It bore her weight without buckling.

A cry of alarm sounded in the passage. Both the wolves' gazes snapped toward the entrance. The escaped goblin had found help. We were out of time.

"Go," I hissed to the beasts. Nearly too fast to track, the wolves spun around and flowed out of the room. I cast a quick glance around the room but spotted no loot chest. I frowned, wondering why none had appeared but had no time to consider the matter further. I would question Gnat on the subject later.

Rising to my feet, I followed after the wolves.

~ ~ ~

By the time I reached the entrance, the wolves were nearly out of sight. I managed only a half-caught of their hindquarters and tail as they headed *towards* the yelling goblins.

I paused for a second on the room's threshold to consider my own options. The goblins were not yet visible, but their shouts were coming from further up the passage, in the direction of the maze guard station.

As yet, I heard no cries of alarm from further down the passage. But I hesitated before fleeing that way. There were no rooms in which to hide in that direction, and both the goblin squad that had recently passed by and the door guards lay that way too. If they spotted me, I would be quickly overcome.

Better to help the wolves and then find another room to conceal myself, I decided. Choosing speed over stealth, I made no effort to conceal myself as I raced up the passage.

As I ran, I heard new sounds fill the air, and the goblins' yells became intermingled with cries of pain and growls of anger. I smiled grimly. The wolves had engaged the enemy. I hurried on for a few more yards before stopping short.

A little further up the corridor, multiple shadowy forms battled one another. The two wolves, lithe and sure-footed, weaved between what looked like six goblins. I couldn't make out the goblins' numbers clearly—the squad the wolves had ambushed had either carried no torches or had lost them in the ruckus somehow.

The wolves clearly were unhampered by the dimness of the surroundings. The goblins, on the other hand, were obviously struggling. My own sight in the dark was good enough to make out the battling figures, but I hesitated to trust it entirely to track the goblins' blows in the dark.

I need to see better, I thought and willed my choice to the Game.

Your Perception has increased to rank 8.

Immediately, my vision sharpened, and the somewhat-blurred forms of the goblins snapped into focus. There were seven of them, I saw.

Drawing my blades, I moved to engage the closest goblin. The warrior had his back turned to me, and distracted by the wolves raging within his squad's ranks, he failed to notice me as I advanced on him. Without hesitation or remorse, I plunged my blades into his defenseless back.

You have killed a level 11 goblin warrior and have gained experience. Your two weapon fighting has increased to level 16.

The goblin stiffened momentarily before dropping, slumping lifelessly. Withdrawing my swords, I moved to engage the next warrior.

I was not so lucky with my next foe. Whether he spotted his companion's demise or heard my movement, as I raised my blades to strike, the goblin swung around and parried away my descending blades with his spear.

A level 12 goblin warrior has evaded your attacks.

Grimly, I raised my swords to strike again. But before I could do so, the goblin jumped back and shouted, "He's here! The player is here! Kill him!"

Immediately, two other goblins broke away from the wolves and turned to confront me. Faced suddenly with three opponents, I broke off my attack and danced backward.

The goblins closed quickly, not letting me retreat. The one to my right thrust out with his spear, but with his sight marred by the darkness, the blow was ill-timed and hesitant, and I easily sidestepped the attack.

You have evaded a level 10 goblin warrior's attack. Your dodging has increased to level 15.

Nearly simultaneously, two other blows descended upon me: another thrust spear from the front and a slashing sword from my left. I did my best to avoid both.

You have evaded a goblin warrior's attack. A goblin warrior has injured you.

I fended away the spear but wasn't able to dodge the third goblin's attack and was struck a glancing blow. I flinched at the new line of red that appeared on my bare arm.

Buoyed by their success, the trio crowded me again. Knowing that simultaneously trading blows with all three goblins was a losing proposition, I dropped to the floor and rolled out from between them.

With their poor night vision, the goblins struggled to track my sudden motion. Caught flat-footed by the maneuver, the trio swung their heads frantically in an effort to relocate me. But the darkness hampered their efforts, enough so that I rose to my knees on the sword wielder's left flank. Before the goblin could react, I shoved my blades under the warrior's hide armor.

The goblin shrieked as my swords buried themselves deep within his ribcage. Feebly, he swung around to strike at me. But his life was fast escaping, and the blow carried no force behind it.

I leaped back to my feet as the dying goblin's companions retaliated. A spear was thrust at my face. I beat it away with my left sword.

Another spear was shoved toward my hip. I swayed to the side and chopped down on the wooden shaft with my second blade. The force of my blow momentarily unbalanced the goblin wielding the spear, and he stumbled forward. As quick as a flash, I lunged forward and rammed the blade in my left hand through his throat.

More by instinct than anything else, I sensed the last goblin thrust toward my exposed back. I swung around, knowing I was too late already.

But the blow was poorly aimed. Instead of running me through, the goblin's spear bounced off my shoulder, gouging my skin, but not penetrating much further.

Before the warrior could recover his stance, I pushed forward and struck from up high with my left blade. To my surprise, the goblin dropped hold of his spear and grabbed onto my left arm with both hands.

Mid-motion, my blow was stopped. Gritting my teeth, I tried to force the weapon downwards, but the goblin was too strong, and my blade traveled not an inch further. Seeing me straining fruitlessly, the goblin grinned triumphantly.

His pleasure was short-lived, though. With the attack of my first weapon blocked, I brought the second into play and thrust it brutally forward.

The goblin's eyes grew round, and his smile turned bloody as the blade in my right-hand tore through his innards. A moment later, the warrior's eyes glazed over, and he slipped lifelessly to the floor.

You have reached level 11! Your two weapon fighting has increased to level 18. Your dodging has increased to level 16. Your shortswords has increased to level 23.

I swung around, ready to do battle with my next foe. But none of the other goblins remained standing. The dire wolf pair had finished off the other three warriors.

Both wolves' muzzles were bloody, and new scratches marked their faces, but otherwise, the beasts appeared unharmed. Seeing that I was finished with my own opponent, the wolves bobbed their heads in my direction and wagged their tails once before turning on their heels and sprinting off into the darkness.

I frowned. Had the wolves just said goodbye?

CHAPTER 33: GOING HUNTING

Finding myself alone in the passage, I surveyed the battlefield. I could hear no other goblin cries nearby, and the alarm bells had stopped clanging, but I knew that sooner rather than later, more goblins would turn up.

And before that happened, I had to be gone.

I didn't think I had time to search any of the dead goblins, and once more, no loot chest had appeared. Wiping my blades clean on a corpse, I sheathed my swords and dropped into a crouch.

You and your familiar are hidden.

Padding stealthily through the passage, I put some distance between myself and the recent scene of carnage. Once I was sure I was far enough away that I wouldn't be immediately uncovered by a search, I ducked into the closest suitable room to take stock and plan my next move.

The room I entered was empty. From the lumps of furs evenly spaced about the floor, I assumed the cavern served as the sleeping quarters of about a dozen goblins. The room was unlit, and I immediately crept to its darkest corner. Placing my back against the cold rock, I slumped to the ground.

The last hour or so had been frenetic. Danger had dogged my heels every step of the way. And now I could feel weariness settle in. I needed rest, real rest, and soon.

But not just yet. I was still in danger. *How many goblins still remain?* I wondered. *And how do I defeat them all?*

I could follow in the dire wolves' footsteps, but I doubted I would be able to keep up with the two beasts. Besides, I had gotten the distinct impression that the pair didn't want me tagging along. Whatever they were about, they didn't want—or need—my help.

I was on my own. I glanced at the bat resting on my shoulder. Well, except for my familiar. My gaze flicked to the room's entrance. I still didn't hear the tread of approaching feet. Whatever the dire wolves were doing, they seemed to have drawn attention away from this section of the passage. I had time, I thought, to risk a short conversation with the familiar.

"Gnat, why didn't any loot chests appear?" I asked in a low-voiced tone. The mystery was still bugging me. Given the number of enemies in the area, I was hoping that I would be able to fill out my skill list and perhaps even obtain my second and third Classes with all the loot I would collect.

"I told you, training was over," Gnat grumbled. "Loot chests will not appear as often or as regularly as they did in the first phase."

"But the Game granted me loot chests on both my previous encounters," I protested. "After I ambushed the archers *and* killed the guards. Why stop now?"

"Hmpf," Gnat sniffed. "Those were distinct and contained conflicts. Consider the battle you are in now, one big encounter. It may be drawn out, but it won't end until all the goblins are dead—or you are." The bat paused. "But given the odds, you are facing, it is probable the Game will reward you—and handsomely too—once you complete this challenge."

My eyes narrowed in consideration. I wasn't sure if I believed Gnat, but the evidence before my eyes was undeniable: I had been rewarded with no loot chests thus far. And I couldn't bank on getting any more soon.

So either I get a whole treasure trove when I finish clearing out these tunnels, or I get nothing.

Still, it didn't change what I knew I needed to do: hunt down all the goblins. It was the surest means of securing my escape, and despite the lack of loot chests, each kill I made would only make me stronger.

But first, I must prepare.

Closing my eyes, I willed the Game to display my player data. It had been a while since I had looked at it.

Player Profile: Michael

Level: 11. Rank: 1. Current Health: 100%.

Stamina: 40%. Mana: 100%. Psi: 100%.

Species: Human. Lives Remaining: 3.

Attributes

Available: 1 point.

Strength: 0. Constitution: 0. Dexterity: 4. Perception: 8. Mind: 0. Magic: 0. and Faith: 0.

Classes

Primary Class: Scout (basic).

Secondary Class: None.

Tertiary Class: None.

Traits

Undead familiar: +1 to necromancy rank.

Nimble: +2 Dexterity.

Skills

Available skill slots: 2.

Dodging (current: 16. max: 40. Dexterity, basic).

Sneaking (current: 26. max: 40. Dexterity, basic).

Shortswords (current: 23. max: 40. Dexterity, basic).

Two weapon fighting (current: 18. max: 40. Dexterity, advanced).

Abilities

None.

Equipped

1 common thief's cloak (+3 sneaking).

2 basic steel shortswords (+10% damage each).

Backpack Contents

11 x field rations.

1 x flask of water.

3 x used poison darts.

2 x unused poison darts.

5 x empty potion flasks.

1 x summon lesser wight spellbook.

3 x minor healing potions.

1 x archer Class stone.

2 x goblin shortbows.

4 x iron daggers.

1 x bedroll.

1 x heavy shields skillbook.

1 x moderate healing potions.

My stamina was low, I saw and restoring it was my first priority. Pulling out a field ration, I unwrapped it and popped a piece in my mouth while I studied the rest of my player profile.

I frowned as I chewed, less than pleased with my advancement. My skills were progressing slowly, I was still badly underequipped, and I had yet no abilities to speak of.

Even worse, I was unhappily aware that my attributes were skewed. Despite my high investment in Perception, I had *no* perception-based skills yet. It didn't matter that circumstances—and my dire need to improve my night vision—had forced my choices in that respect. In the long run, further investment in Perception would hamper my future development.

I can see well enough in the dark now, I decided. It was time to stop improving my Perception. *But what do I invest in now?* I rubbed my chin as I considered how to spend my single remaining attribute point.

Dexterity was the obvious choice, but the latest encounter with the goblins had made clear that if I was going to keep throwing myself in melee combat, I would need to make at least some improvements to my Strength. The last goblin I had fought had overpowered me too easily.

But I also needed Constitution to be able to soak up more damage. And it was still my hope to obtain a magic Class at some point, which made the Magic attribute important as well. Faith and Mind, I wasn't too sure about yet, but they could also be necessary. I sighed. *Too many options and not enough points.*

I pondered my choices a while longer before reaching a decision. *For now, it makes the most sense to play to my strengths,* I concluded. Investment in other attributes could wait until I at least obtained some useable skills for them. I willed my choice to the Game.

Your Dexterity has increased to rank 5.

There was one other matter I needed to consider before moving on: the archer Class stone. It was the only other Class option available to me at the moment, and despite it being only a basic Class, I needed to at least deliberate on its potential benefits once more. I willed the Adjudicator to display the Class properties again.

The archer is a basic Class that confers a player with three skills: light armor, daggers, and a ranged weapon skill of the player's choice. This Class also permanently boosts your Perception attribute by +1 and your Constitution attribute by +1.

Should I acquire the Class? I wondered. Archery itself was useless to me at the moment. I couldn't see well enough in the tunnels' poor light to shoot over any meaningful distance. In that respect, the Class was of little worth to me in my current predicament.

But becoming an archer would also give me access to the all-important light armor skill. The goblins' hide armor was crude, but it would give me at least a modicum of protection.

Still, I had only two Class slots remaining, and taking up another basic Class was not the smart choice in the long run. *Don't forget Michael, you have three lives,* I told myself. *If you die, you die.*

I grimaced. It was a fatalistic attitude to adopt. But I knew I could not escape taking some measure of risk. And as much as I didn't want to experience death, I couldn't shrink from it.

I will play the long game, I decided. *The archer Class is not for me.*

I rose to my feet. I was as ready as I could be and settled in my mind as to what needed to be done. Finishing my field ration, I tossed away the wrapper.

It was time to go hunting.

CHAPTER 34: A ROLL OF THE DICE

I slipped back into the passage, alert and ready for danger, but detected no hostiles in the vicinity.

Tilting my head to the side, I strained my hearing. Further up the passage, I thought I heard guttural voices, but the sounds were too faint for me to be certain. Padding along the wall, I crept towards the half-heard sounds. As I drew closer, they became more distinct. Another guard squad was up ahead.

The goblins were not yet in sight, but I could hear them clearly now. Pausing, I listened. They were noisy and loud and making no effort to be quiet. Some of the goblins were yelling, others moaned in pain, while yet others muttered nonsense.

I smiled. The squad was in disarray. *Was this the dire wolves doing?* I wondered. *Likely.* I drew closer. Rounding a slight bend in the corridor, I finally caught sight of the goblins. There were eight of them.

Four huddled in the small circle of light cast by a dying torch. Bellowing loudly to each other, the goblins were in the midst of a heated argument. Every so often, one of them would scan the surrounding darkness. The goblins were afraid and uncertain of what to do next. They had obviously been attacked recently. I scanned the darkness myself but could spot no sign of the dire wolves. The beasts had moved on.

My gaze flitted to the other four goblins. The nearest two were lying slumped on the ground, outside the light cast by the torch. Both appeared gravely injured.

The last pair were on the far side of the four goblins and looked to have been placed to guard their fellows. The wolves must have last been spotted on that side, I thought. The two goblins were doing a poor job of patrolling, though. Nearly petrified to be outside the torchlight, they seemed more intent on whispering feverishly to each other than watching the passage.

I inched forward, intent on finishing what the wolves had started.

Eight hostile entities have failed to detect you! Your sneaking has increased to level 27.

I crept up unseen on the two injured goblins. Both were nearly senseless with pain. I edged up to the first. Clamping a hand down across the goblin's mouth, I rammed my sword through his open wound.

With a final whimper, the goblin died. The second goblin was none the wiser. Dropping to his side, I pressed my hand against his mouth.

But I had miscalculated.

A hostile entity has detected you! You are no longer hidden.

Despite his writhing, my target was not as far gone as I had thought. The moment my hand clamped down on him, the goblin's eyes snapped open, and he shrieked.

Or tried to.

The resulting sound was muffled by my hand but not entirely cut off. A low moan escaped the warrior. The four goblins in the torchlight—already on edge—noticed immediately. "What that?" whispered one, setting his hands to his axe.

Biting down a curse, I pressed my left hand down harder on the goblin until no further sound escaped him and rammed the blade in my right hand through his throat.

The warrior did not die immediately. His limbs thrashed wildly, and blood spurted all over me. Ignoring my target's dying throes, I shoved my blade deeper until he stilled entirely.

You have killed a level 13 goblin warrior.

"Who there?" a second goblin yelled. Squinting his eyes, he was peering intently in my direction.

Still kneeling over my slain foe, I tensed. I was fully expecting the goblins to discover me and was ready to flee the moment they did. But much to my surprise, the goblin's eyes passed over me sightlessly.

You are hidden once more.

Given the goblins' failure to detect me, I was unsurprised by the Game message.

"Shuddup, you fool!" a third goblin hissed to the one who had yelled. "It be the beasts. They back."

"Enough yacking!" ordered the last. "Go find them!" But despite the command, neither the four goblins nor the two beyond them made any move in my direction. Fear had them petrified.

Six hostile entities have failed to detect you! Your sneaking has increased to level 28.

The moments ticked by, and I relaxed from my tense pose. Inch by inch, I withdrew my blade from the corpse and rose warily to a crouch. My stealth held, and I smiled grimly. It seemed that my sneaking skill had improved to the point that even after I took hostile action, the goblins had trouble finding me. At least while I was cloaked in darkness.

I backed away from the two dead goblins and warily circled around the light cast by the torch. Its flame was sputtering. From the splatter of oil on the floor, I assumed the goblins had dropped the torch during the wolves' ambush, and I expected it would not be much longer before the torch died entirely. Until then, the four goblins were safe from me.

Not so, the two on the far end.

I successfully maneuvered myself to the far side of the four goblins without being detected. Crouching down, I took a second to study my next two targets. Both had their backs to me.

Like the four goblins safe in the light, the pair were staring fixedly in the direction of their recently deceased fellows and were oblivious of the danger at their back.

Perfect.

Padding forward, I crept up on the pair. Neither noticed me right up until the moment I yanked back the head of the first and plunged my blade through his throat.

Only then did the second react. Jumping back in fright, he scrambled to lift his sword. But it was too late. Dancing forward, I batted aside his weapon with one of my blades and skewered him with my second before he could fully register my presence.

You have killed a level 11 goblin warrior. You have reached level 12! Your dodging has increased to level 17. Your two weapon fighting has increased to level 19.

At the clang of blades and the wet gurgle of my two dying victims, the four remaining goblins spun around, their weapons raised. Refusing to budge from their position, they scanned the darkness fruitlessly.

Four hostile entities have failed to detect you! Your sneaking has increased to level 29.

"How beasts get around so quickly?" whispered one of the goblins.

"Those dogs be demons!" another exclaimed.

"Chief stoopid to try tame them," agreed the first.

"Chief not stupid! Chief smart," objected the third. "Wolves strong. Good mounts!"

The fourth goblin grunted. "Chief is fool. We goblins. We ride worgs. Not wolves. Now we pay price for chief's mistake."

I smiled in grim amusement. The goblins were not smart. Despite the audible clash of weapons, they still seemed to believe it was the dire wolves that had slain their fellows. Which, given the four's visible fear of the beasts, I wasn't going to complain about.

It would make killing them easier.

I tiptoed silently away from my latest victims and placed myself to the remaining goblins' rear. With surprise on my side, I would back myself to triumph against the four even after being exposed by the torch, but there was no need to take any foolish risks.

So, crouching down on my haunches, I waited for the torchlight to expire. While I did, I idly pondered what had possessed the goblin chief to try taming the dire wolves. From my brief interaction with the beasts, I knew they were too intelligent and independent to be domesticated.

More importantly, where was this goblin chief I kept hearing off? *He must be somewhere in this tunnel complex,* I decided.

The torch flickered and died.

The goblins' eyes grew round, and they yelped in sudden fear as the encroaching darkness swallowed them. Muttering prayers to dark gods, they hastily repositioned themselves so that they stood with their backs to each other.

I almost snorted. *That is not going to save them.* Padding forward, I stopped until I was less than a yard away from the huddled figures. I was so close I could see the whites of the goblins' eyes.

Bending down, I picked up a few loose stones in one hand. Then flung it beyond the goblins. The stones ricocheted loudly in the silence.

Nearly as one, the four spun around and whispered nervously to each other as they tried to pick out the menace that stalked them from the darkness—albeit in the wrong direction.

I drew one of my blades and dashed forward.

My first target was the goblin on the far left. Yanking on his arm, I pulled him off balance and away from his fellows. With a shriek of alarm, the goblin stumbled and fell. Plunging both my blade into the goblin's chest, I silenced his cry abruptly and rolled away from the corpse.

The other three goblins were in an uproar. They still couldn't see me, but they knew I was close. One shouted meaningless orders while the other two swiped blindly at the darkness with their weapons. Cloaked in shadows, I circled the trio until I was on their opposite flank.

Then darted forward again.

Ducking under the goblin on the right's wild slashes with his axe, I thrust my blades from below and ripped them upwards, tearing open his torso from hip to sternum. I spun away before the weapons of the other goblins could find me. But the surviving pair had had enough. Throwing down their weapons, they fled.

Or tried to.

In his blind panic, the first ran full tilt into the passage wall and staggered back in a daze. Ignoring him for now, I chased after the other.

Weighed down by both his armor and poor vision, the second goblin was easy to catch. Flying across the ground, I dove onto the fleeing goblin and bore him to the ground before plunging my swords through his exposed back.

I rose to my feet and searched for my last target. He was sitting on the floor, lips working soundlessly and eyes staring sightlessly. I strode closer and stood over the goblin. He didn't look up. The blow the warrior had taken to the head must have been harder than I thought.

"I'm sorry," I murmured to the senseless goblin. "Mercy is a luxury I can ill afford." Raising my blades, I buried them in the defenseless goblin.

CHAPTER 35: CLEAN UP

You have reached level 13! Your dodging has increased to level 19. Your two weapon fighting has increased to level 20. Congratulations, Michael! Your skill with two weapon fighting has reached rank 2. Your shortswords has increased to level 24.

I dismissed the Game message with a weary sigh, unable to muster enough enthusiasm for a smile. My skills were advancing much more rapidly now, but surveying the carnage around me, I couldn't help but wonder if it was worth it.

"Well done, Michael," Gnat said with an appreciative chuckle. "You are a truly magnificent killer, aren't you?"

I eyed the skeletal bat sourly. "You think you can fly ahead and keep watch while I loot these corpses?" I asked brusquely. I was not in the mood for the familiar's macabre humor and wanted to be alone.

Gnat opened his mouth to protest.

I cut him off. "Go," I ordered. "It's not combat, so it won't conflict with your Pact. Return to me if you see any goblins approach." I turned away from the bat, not waiting for his response, and after a momentary pause, I felt him glide off my shoulder to do my bidding.

Leaning over the first corpse, I began to search it.

~ ~ ~

It didn't take me long to loot the dead. It was a distasteful—but necessary—task.

While there were plentiful weapons and armor to be had, none were better than my twin blades, and there was little enough else of value. With my pack already weighed down, I was hesitant to add further unnecessary items to it.

Still, I did recover a few smaller objects that seemed as if they would prove useful in future.

You have acquired a coin pouch.
You have acquired 10 copper coins.
You have acquired one flask filled with water.

When I was done with the goblins, I glanced up and down the passage. Things were quiet in both directions, which I found strange. Surely by now, all the goblins in the complex must know the dire wolves were loose. Why weren't they searching for the beasts?

Unless they know where the wolves are already and are mustering there.

I frowned, feeling a touch of concern for my erstwhile allies. But the beasts had shown themselves capable of taking care of themselves, and I knew if I rushed to their aid, I would likely only endanger myself.

It was better to continue my cautious approach up the passage, I decided, and trust that wherever the dire wolves were, they hadn't fallen prey to the goblins yet.

Before moving to rejoin Gnat, I took a moment to spend my new attribute points.

Your Dexterity has increased to rank 7.

With the last of my tasks seen to, I melded into the darkness and continued on. A dozen yards later, Gnat dropped wordlessly onto my shoulder, and we resumed our careful exploration.

I hadn't progressed much farther before strange noises attracted my attention. It was coming from a chamber on my right. I peered in. Three goblin fighters were in the room—all in various states of distress. One was trying to bandage his torn arm, another clutched at his ripped-open torso, while the third's right leg was gnawed to the bone.

But for the three goblins, no one else was in the room. I studied the three's wounds again. They had all been made by tooth and claw. The dire wolves had done this.

Slipping into the room quietly and without fuss, I put an end to the three fighters. Then, I resumed my journey. Not much later, I stopped again. Two goblin workers were crawling across the passage, leaving bloody streaks behind them. The pair were mewling pitifully and nearly senseless with pain. They too had been mauled by the wolves. Bending down, I took their lives.

The dire wolves' tactics were becoming clearer: hit and run. The beasts were doing just enough damage to disable their foes but were not bothering to finish off their kills. In this manner, they kept one step ahead of the goblins and stopped themselves from being bogged down and ambushed.

Perhaps that is why they didn't want me to join them. I had neither the speed nor the ability to meld as completely into the darkness as the beasts, and I would only have hampered their efforts.

Instead, I had been relegated to clean-up duty. *Not that I am complaining,* I thought wryly. The pair had still left plenty of goblins for me to kill.

For the next few minutes, I followed the trail of injured goblins as I retraced my path back up the passage. In only a few cases did I find the enemy hale enough to put up a fight. In every instance, I paused and slew the goblins. I was not about to leave a live enemy behind me.

By the time I reached the crossroads near the maze guard station, I had dozens of goblin kills under my belt. Weirdly enough, I gained no player levels from my grim work. The Adjudicator, I realized, had to be factoring in the circumstances of each of my kills and not just my opponents' levels when calculating my experience gains.

My lack of advancement did not bother me much, though. Despite the number of goblins I slew, they were too *few*, given the size of the tunnel complex and the facilities I spotted. It was becoming increasingly obvious to me that somewhere up ahead, I would find a large force of goblins.

I did stop long enough to loot all my kills. Realizing the goblins carried little of value besides the arms and armor, I only bothered to riffle through their coin pouches. If I lived long enough to secure the tunnel complex, I would come back and search the corpses more thoroughly. But for now, my efforts yielded a tiny sum of money.

You have acquired 123 copper coins. This has a monetary value of 1 gold, 2 silvers, and 3 coppers.

Standing at the crossroads, I studied the three options that lay before me. Up ahead was the way to the maze, which given the chaos wreaked by the wolves, was likely not guarded anymore.

The left passage was dark and quiet, with not the least hint of sound emerging from its depths. In the far distance of the right tunnel, though, I spotted a glimmer of light, and when I strained my ears, I caught the faint echoes of shouts and yells.

I considered my choices. Undoubtedly, retreating back to the maze was the safest course, but the maze itself was a dead end. Heading back there made little sense.

The left tunnel was more promising. If I explored its depths, I might just find a way out of the tunnel complex that wasn't guarded. But there was no guarantee I wouldn't run up against another dead-end either.

Going right... venturing that way was fraught with peril. I was sure that the remaining goblins in the tunnel complex were gathered somewhere down the right passage. And likely the wolves too. If I headed in that direction, I would be running straight into conflict.

Though if I had to face off against the goblins, I preferred to do it with allies at my back. *Better to face the goblins now while there is still a chance the dire wolves are alive.*

To battle, I decided and headed right.

CHAPTER 36: CHIEFLY MATTERS

As I padded down the right tunnel, the din steadily increased in volume. So too, did the orange-yellow tinge of torchlight. Somewhere up ahead, there were a great many goblins.

Fifty yards later, the corridor ended in an arch broad enough for an entire squad of goblins to walk abreast. With my back braced against the passage wall and doing my best to remain out of sight, I edged up to the arch and peered through.

Beyond the arch was an enormous cavern. Torches were dotted all along the chamber's rim. More torches were affixed on wooden stakes at regular intervals along the floor as well, but the cavern was so large that, despite the many torches, it was gloomy and full of dancing shadows.

Most of the floor space was taken up by long rows of tables, many more than I had seen in the other room that I had mistaken for the goblins' main dining room. *This is a great hall,* I decided.

No goblins were seated at the tables, though. But neither was the chamber empty.

Gathered against the cavern's far end was a crowd of some fifty-odd goblins. My heart sank upon catching sight of their numbers. *So many,* I despaired. *How am I going to defeat them all?*

The creatures were pressed up against a large wooden dais, hollering and cheering while watching the spectacle playing out on the stage with avid interest. What I had first mistaken for yells of panic were actually jeers of laughter.

Fearing the worst, I lifted my gaze upwards to ascertain the source of the goblins' amusement. An oversized chair—a throne, really—had been placed on the dais and, standing before it, was the largest goblin I had yet seen.

Without a doubt, he was the chief I had heard the other goblins talk of. Nearly twice my own height, the chief towered over every other creature in the room. Facing off against him were the two dire wolves. With raised hackles and bared fangs, both beasts circled the goblin. The two wolves sported a host of cuts and bruises, while the chief's spiked hide armor was spotless.

I bit my lip worriedly. What was going on here? It was clear from the chief's languid stance and the negligent manner in which he swung the greatclub in his hands that he felt not the least bit threatened by the beasts. Nor did the spectating goblins seem to believe their leader in any threat.

But if that was the case... why were the dire wolves squaring off against the goblin chief in a direct confrontation? The wolves were smart enough to size up the odds. Why abandon their hit-and-run tactics?

A blur of movement in the shadows cast by the throne attracted my attention. Narrowing my gaze, I focused on a half-seen figure. It was a pup. No, not one, but *three* dire wolf pups. Each was chained by an iron collar to the throne and was straining at their leashes to get free.

"Ah," I breathed. Now the adult dire wolves' actions made sense—both the urgency that drove them and the imperative that forced them to confront the chief.

They are trying to save their pups. Still, the manner in which they sought to do so was foolish. The dire wolves could not triumph.

A pup whined. Another yelped. Seemingly in response to her pups' distress, the dire wolf mother darted forward to nip at the chief's heels. But the goblin had been anticipating the attack. His club swept towards her in a brutal arc and smashed into her midriff.

With a yelp of pain, the dire wolf mother was sent flying through the air before crashing back onto the floor in a boneless heap. The whines of the three pups turned to angry barks and growls.

I bit off my own cry of anger and stopped my first reckless impulse to draw my blades and charge into the chamber. I could no more prevail against the goblins in direction confrontation than the dire wolves.

Forcing myself to patience, I studied the fallen beast. She was still and unmoving, but from this distance, I could not tell if she was unconscious or dead. *Either way, there is nothing I can do to help her yet.*

I turned my gaze to the dire wolf sire. He was pacing in a wary circle just outside the range of the chieftain's club. But he made no move to attack. He was either wiser than his mate or less driven by rage. The chieftain twirled his club and watched the beast with a sneer pasted on his face.

I tore my gaze away from the pair. Their confrontation could only end in one way, and if I wanted to help the dire wolves, I needed to figure out a means to do so while the goblins were still distracted.

I scanned the rest of the cavern. On the right side of the chamber were two large black cauldrons laid over two open fire pits. Near the pots were four goblin workers. They were the only goblins in the chamber not gathered near the stage, yet their gazes were just as transfixed by the goings-on on the dais as their fellows.

A cream-grey goo was bubbling inside the cauldrons. Raising my head, I took a cautious sniff. It smelt like some sort of gruel. *Has the night passed?* I wondered. Was that why the goblins had gathered here? For breakfast? I wasn't sure, but it was clear the goblins intended on eating soon.

My thoughts whirled, and a bold—if risky—plan took shape. My gaze flitted between the cooks and the stage. I didn't know how much longer the goblins would remain distracted. If I was going to act, it had to be now.

Go, Michael.

Banishing my doubts, I retrieved a handful of items from my backpack, then crept into the room.

~ ~ ~

Slipping from shadow to shadow, I made my way toward the two cooking pots as fast as I dared.

Out of the corner of my eye, I saw the dire wolf sire was still patiently circling the chieftain. I didn't know if the beast had a plan, but I silently willed him *not* to attack. The longer the contest between goblin and wolf dragged on, the more time I had to enact my plan.

For now, both the crowd of goblins and cooks remained mesmerized by the spectacle on the stage, making my task of sneaking through the cavern's jumble of shadows easier.

Multiple hostile entities have failed to detect you! Your sneaking has increased to level 30. Your skill in sneaking has reached rank 3.

I made it to within a few yards of the bubbling cauldrons undetected. Crouched down under a table, I considered my next move.

Only a few feet separated the four cooks from the two pots, and the area between was, unfortunately, well-lit. But the goblin workers had their backs turned to me and the cauldrons. I *could* reach the pots unseen, *provided* none of the cooks turned around.

If that happened, it was game over.

I licked my lips nervously and got going. Ducking out of the shelter of the table, I moved forward, one cautious step at a time.

I judged it was ten steps to the cauldrons. I took the first step, then waited with bated breath. No reaction.

I placed my next foot forward. Still no reaction.

Another step. A cry rose from the dais. I stilled. A roar followed from the crowd. I didn't turn to look. It would only waste valuable time. My concentration absolute, I placed another foot forward, then another.

A pup howled. The sound was forlorn and grief-stricken. My heart sank. Was the dire wolf sire dead? I stepped forward again, my eyes fixed on my destination.

The crowd bellowed again, drowning out the pup's cries. I stepped forward. I feared I was out of time, but I was committed now. Turning around was no longer an option.

Another step. Two more steps, and I would reach the cauldrons.

"GOBLINS!" a voice shouted suddenly. I froze.

"LOOK at these pathetic dogs!" the speaker continued. "Is THIS what you've been afraid of?" It was the chief speaking, I realized, but I didn't dare turn around to look.

"WHY?" he thundered. "They are nothing more than pitiful beasts!" The chief's words reverberated throughout the cavern, and as their echoes died, the watching goblins' yelling died down.

I closed my eyes, then, screwing up the courage, took another step forward, trusting that none of the goblins' attention would waver from their leader.

"With me as your chief, you need fear NOTHING! Do you hear me, goblins?"

"AYE!" fifty voices roared in response.

I stepped forward again. I was at the cauldrons finally. Moving with deliberate haste, I unwound the poisoned darts from the cloth protecting them and dropped them into the cooking pots.

You have lost 3 used poison darts and 2 unused poison darts.

With my deed done, I turned a slow circle. The chieftain, I finally saw, was still on the stage with his eyes turned downwards and directly upon the crowd of goblins gazing adoringly at him.

"We will KILL all the players," the chieftain screamed. "We will earn the Master's reward. WE. And only we will do this. Our tribe."

"AYE," echoed the goblins.

I began my careful journey back to shadows, with half an ear on the chief's words. It had not escaped my notice that the goblin leader was not only larger than his fellows but that his speech was smoother and more cultured too. *He will be a dangerous foe*, I thought.

"And then," the chief continued, "we will return to the surface and RULE. We, the Fangtooths, will stand above all other goblins. We and no other."

"LONG LIVE FANGTOOTH. LONG LIVE CHIEF," the goblins sang.

I reached my table without mishap and ducked under. The table was wide, and the shadows beneath it were deep enough that unless a goblin looked directly under I wouldn't be spotted. I was safe—for now. Heaving a relieved sigh, I turned my gaze upon the stage again.

"These dogs will serve us," the chief said. Bending down, he picked one of the squirming dire wolf pups in his hands. "Fangtooths will ride wolves—not worgs. They will be a symbol of our supremacy. Dire wolves will bow to Fangtooths. How say you, my goblins?"

"CHIEF, CHIEF, CHIEF," the goblins bellowed, shouting each word louder than the last until their utterances blended together in an unintelligible and deafening wall of sound.

I clamped my hands against my ears, wincing at the painful noise. *Blimey. These goblins are fanatical. Good thing they won't be around for much longer.* Making myself comfortable under the table, I settled down to wait.

CHAPTER 37: A BROKEN BREAKFAST

It was a full ten minutes before the ruckus settled down, and the goblin crowd dispersed from the stage. Chatting animatedly, the goblin warriors slowly took their seats at the tables while the workers returned to ministering the pots.

No goblins seated themselves at my own table. The hall was, at best half-filled, and wanting to be closer to their chief, all the warriors jostled together for places at the tables nearest to the stage.

The chief, of course, seated himself regally on his throne and, with his nose stuck in the air, watched his followers from above.

From beneath my table, I watched it all absently. My gaze was fixed on the two felled dire wolves. Both remained on the stage. The sire, I saw with relief, was moving—if feebly—but I couldn't tell what the female's condition was.

The pups had somehow managed to extend the range of their iron chains and reach their mother. Gamboling around her, they frantically licked and sniffed at her snout, but the dire wolf mother still did not stir.

Just as I began to wonder if the beasts would be left untended, the chief gestured imperiously, and two older, and scarred goblins ascended the stage. Bending over the wolves, they began to lather *both* with some pale green paste.

I blew out a relieved breath. It seemed the chief intended to keep the creatures alive and that the female was not yet dead. Whatever was in the paste, it had to be a form of healing ointment.

Movement on my left drew my gaze. Dipping huge ladles into the cauldron, two workers were filling wooden bowls while the other pair, with a bowl in each hand, began making their way towards the tables.

Breakfast was being served.

Renewed anxiety filled me. I was about to find out if my plan had any merit. Of course, I had no idea of the potency of the darts' toxins or what effect—if any—they would have on the goblins.

I was gambling, though, that they would have some effect. Considering how quickly a single dart had felled the young slime, I was willing to bet the poison would cause *some* adverse reaction in the goblins. How severe that reaction was would determine the further actions I took.

I wanted to save the dire wolf pups. I wanted to help their sire and mother, but I could not risk it if the poisons didn't in some way incapacitate the goblins in the hall.

I watched the two workers bearing the dosed bowls of gruel ascend the stage. It seemed that the chief was to be served first. As the workers neared him, the chief grabbed a bowl and, without ceremony, began stuffing huge gobfuls of the creamy goo into his mouth.

I observed the chief with keen interest, searching for the least hint that the goblin realized something was amiss with his food. But in an astonishingly short space of time, the chief flung away his empty bowl and grabbed another from the waiting workers, and started eating again.

I smiled. The poison had gone undetected and the chief was none the wiser. Of course, it could also be that the toxin had been too diluted in the cauldrons' contents to retain any potency, but I refused to believe that.

The poisons *had* to work.

The chief ate through all four bowls the two workers held out for him before he slouched back on his throne with his hunger sated. Rubbing his hands over his stomach, the goblin sighed and closed his eyes. I scratched my chin. Was the poison working? I couldn't tell.

The workers descended the dais and began serving the warriors. On the stage, I spied one of the pups approach the chief's empty bowls, but after a cautious sniff, the pup wrinkled his nose and backed away. *That at least is a good sign,* I thought hopefully.

I turned my attention back to the warriors at the tables. They were eating with gusto and, like their leader, showed no sign of noticing anything amiss.

How long would it be before I knew if the toxins were working? There was no way to tell. Stretching out flat on the floor, I rested my head on my hands and schooled myself to patience. I would find out soon enough.

~ ~ ~

With a start, I jerked awake.

Amazingly, I had fallen asleep. *Damn, I'm tired. I can't keep going on like this. I need rest.* How long had I been unconscious? I wasn't sure. Blinking my eyes rapidly to shake off the clinging tendrils of sleep, I looked around warily.

Something had awoken me... but what?

I was still under the table and unnoticed. The cavern remained murky and poorly lit but had grown silent. Deathly silent. *Are all the goblins dead?* I wondered hopefully.

A snore erupted. Then another.

Guess not.

More sounds filled the air: stifled groans, wheezing moans, and wretched puking. I rose to my haunches. At least some of the goblins were still alive, but from the sounds of it, they weren't doing too well.

"C-c-cooks, what have you done!" bellowed a voice, with both fury and pain choking his words. "Report! At ONCE!" It was the chief.

Damnit. I had been hopeful that the goblin leader at least wouldn't have survived the darts' toxins, but if anything, he sounded haler than his followers.

My gaze drifted to the cauldrons. The four goblin workers were on the floor there, writhing in silent agony. It seemed like they, too, had partaken of breakfast.

I slipped out from under the table.

Multiple hostile entities have failed to detect you!

"COOKS! Where are you!" the chief shouted again, his words half-muffled. "Come here NOW!"

Silence was his only response. I drew my blades and raised my eyes to the dais. The two adult dire wolves had been chained to the throne. Iron collars draped the necks of both. Lying on their sides, with their eyes closed, both appeared unconscious. I would get no help from them. The goblin leader was curled over on his throne, with his head bowed in his hands.

The chief was vulnerable.

Instinct urged me to strike at him while he was distracted. I bit back the impulse. The stage was the most brightly-lit portion of the cavern. Even if I did manage to sneak up on the goblin leader and slay him before he detected me—which was unlikely—the other goblins could not fail to notice me thereafter.

My gaze dropped from the dais to rove over the rest of the hall. The warriors had scattered all over the cavern, seeking solitude to vent their suffering. I wrinkled my nose. The air was rancid with vomit and... worse things. *Urgh.* All the goblins had been afflicted, but not all of them were equally ill.

Despite their violent retching and sickened groans, many of the goblins were not senseless. I was sure they would act once I was revealed, and if I was not careful, they would overwhelm me with numbers alone.

Best to improve the odds before tackling the chief, I thought, *and see to the demise of the weakest first.* My gaze drifted to the four goblin workers. *Starting with them.*

CHAPTER 38: ASSASSIN

You have killed a goblin worker!
You have killed a goblin worker!
You have killed a goblin worker!
You have killed a goblin worker!

Slaying the four duped cooks went off without a hitch. None of the goblin warriors so much as glanced in my direction.

Leaving the blood of the four to stain the ground, I crept through the shadows and behind the nearest sick goblin. Vomit liberally spattered his armor, and his head lay flat on the table. He was snoring. The warrior had fallen unconscious, and I thrust my blade through his exposed neck without regret.

You have killed a goblin warrior!

Once more, my actions went unnoticed.

Slipping away from the corpse, I began hunting my next victim. The chieftain had not stopped his bellowing. Even though all his repeated calls went unanswered, he kept at it. *Perhaps, it gives him comfort,* I thought idly.

Setting aside my speculation over the chief's behavior, I focused on the task at hand and over the next few minutes, carried out my grim work with ruthless efficiency.

You have killed a goblin warrior!
Your sneaking has increased to level 31.
You have reached level 14!
You have killed a goblin warrior!
...

...
You have killed a goblin warrior!
Your sneaking has increased to level 32.
You have killed a goblin warrior!
Your shortswords has increased to level 25.

Halfway through my slaughter, my luck ran out, and one of the sick warriors noticed that his fellow—whom he had first mistaken for being asleep—was, in fact, sitting in a widening pool of blood.

Even half-senseless with pain, the warrior retained enough awareness to realize that something was amiss, and he raised the alarm. "Ware! Intruder! Knorl is dead!"

As if awakening from a daze, the chieftain raised his head, took in the hall, and after a stunned moment, seemed to realize that over a score of his followers were dead. His head whipped around to the back of the throne but seeing the five dire wolves were still chained there he turned back to his warriors. "RISE, you fools!" he roared. "There is a foe amongst you." Following his own orders, the goblin leader rose unsteadily to his feet and grabbed his greatclub.

I was on my way to my next target, but at the chieftain's rallying cry, I aborted my maneuver and slipped deeper into the nearest shadow, where I trusted to my skill in sneaking to hide me.

Rousing themselves out of their various states of distress, the nearly two dozen remaining goblin warriors shambled and stumbled to their feet, crying in alarm or disgust as they slipped over vomit, blood, and excrement. Urged on by their leader, they began half-heartedly searching for me.

My eyes glinted coldly. There was neither order nor discipline to the warriors' search, and if they continued in this manner, there was little chance of them finding me. In fact, the goblin leader's commands had made my own task easier by dispersing his followers even further apart in clumps of ones and twos.

To my disappointment, the chief himself did not budge from his place on the stage. I had been hoping he would descend into the cavern's shadows, where I had a much better chance of striking at him unseen. But for now, I would have to content myself with killing his followers.

A warrior staggered past me, cursing foully as he stubbed his toe on a nearby table leg. After a quick glance around to ascertain none of his fellows were nearby, I rose from my half-crouch and dashed two steps forward. Coming up behind the oblivious warrior, I wrenched back his head and slit his throat.

You have killed a goblin warrior! Multiple hostile entities have failed to detect you!

The kill was not spotted, and I dropped back into hiding unseen. Tiptoeing through the shadows, I repositioned myself and took a moment to observe the goblins' movements.

Two warriors, who were weaving unsteadily between the tables, would pass close by my hiding spot if they stayed on their current course. The first's stomach was heaving convulsively, while the second was coughing incessantly. Both were preoccupied with their ailments.

I hesitated, torn between ambushing the pair and letting them pass unmolested. While neither appeared particularly aware of their surroundings, trying to take down both quietly was risky.

My hands tightened on my blades. *The goblins know I am here already.* Even if I was caught in the act of slaying the pair, I would not be surrendering much of an advantage. Decided, I waited for the two warriors to draw closer.

Two hostile entities have failed to detect you!

The pair passed within a few feet yet still didn't see me. When the goblins were two steps beyond me, I leaped upwards from my crouch and raised my blades up high. In a flash, I brought both down simultaneously.

You have killed a goblin warrior!
Your attack against a goblin warrior has been deflected!

The first goblin died instantly as the sword in my right hand plunged into his back and squarely through his heart. My attack against the second goblin did not fare as well. The point of the sword in my left hand was slightly off-kilter, and instead of penetrating the warrior's hide armor, the blade skittered off.

The goblin spun around wildly and, even in his ill-disposed state, spotted me immediately.

A hostile entity has detected you! You are no longer hidden.

My foe's eyes widened, and he fumbled for the still-sheathed sword at his side. Biting off a curse, I lunged forwards. The goblin was not nearly quick enough to stop me, and I struck high and low simultaneously.

You have critically injured a goblin warrior!
You have critically injured a goblin warrior!

Unfortunately, neither blow was instantly fatal, and a painful howl escaped the warrior. I spun around. Delaying neither to finish my opponent—he'd die soon enough from his wounds anyway—nor to observe the rest of the goblins' reactions, I scurried into the deepest shadows I could find.

CHAPTER 39: DEATH LURKS IN THE SHADOWS

Of course, as soon as the other goblins heard their fellow's death throes, they converged on his location.

But even before the warriors had reorientated themselves, I was long gone from the vicinity. Ducking from shadow to shadow, I wove an erratic path toward the cavern's exit. My plan was to flee the chamber in the event that any of the goblins spotted me.

Though after only a dozen yards, I realized my precautions were unnecessary as I slipped entirely from the goblins' sights again.

Multiple hostile entities have failed to detect you! You are hidden once more.

Well, well, I murmured. It seemed that given my relatively high stealth and the goblins' debilitated state, I had an even greater advantage in the darkness than I first realized. Reversing direction, I headed back to the converging goblins and searched for a straggler.

My escape into darkness had not gone unnoticed by the goblin leader. "FIND HIM!" he roared, but he still made no move to take up the search himself. Ignoring the chief, I found another target and plunged my shortsword through his neck.

You have killed a goblin warrior!

With the deed done, I slipped away to find another mark.

~ ~ ~

I was methodical. Systematic.

One by one, I ran down lone goblins and dispatched them quickly and silently. Meanwhile, the chief ranted and raved from the stage. I was content to let him do so. Every one of his warriors that I slew was one less who would be around to aid him once we finally clashed.

It took the warriors a while to grasp that death was stalking them from behind. The realization galvanized them into some semblance of order, and the survivors formed into two large groups to hunt me.

It was too little, too late.

By then, I had felled a dozen more of their number, and only ten remained. Concealed in the near center of the room, I studied the two bands of roving goblins while I decided which to attack first. The warriors were mostly recovered from the effects of the darts' poisons and already looked more alert and dangerous.

All the same, I felt confident of my ability to defeat their two five-man squads—as long as I managed to meet each separately and their leader didn't intervene. I glanced up at the stage. Leaning forward on his throne, the goblin leader was still spitting furious orders to his followers. At least there didn't appear to be any danger of him interfering soon.

Behind the throne, I saw that the two adult dire wolves had finally roused. Restrained by their chains, the beasts lay on all fours and panted heavily as they observed the chaos below them.

The many deaths I had dealt in the hall had honed my skills, and now I felt measurably stronger. Turning my gaze inwards, I reviewed the changes to myself and invested my new attribute points.

You have reached level 15! You have 2 attribute points available.
Your sneaking has increased to level 34.
Your shortswords has increased to level 27.
Your dodging has increased to level 21.
Your two weapon fighting has increased to level 23.
Your Dexterity has increased to rank 9.

Returning my attention to the two goblin squads, I waited until they were on nearly opposite ends of the hall before creeping through the shadows towards the nearer group.

It's time to end this.

~ ~ ~

You have killed a goblin warrior!

I killed the trailing goblin of the five-man team before the others realized battle was upon them. Stepping past the corpse, I engaged the next warrior in the squad.

But the heavy thud of his fellow's lifeless body had alerted my target, and he spun around, sweeping his axe before him.

I dodged under the weapon's arc. In the same motion, I slashed out with my twin blades. The swords were a dark blur as they severed the warrior's tendons both below and above his knees.

You have crippled a goblin warrior!

The warrior crumpled to the ground. Clutching his now useless legs, he shrieked in agony. Knowing I was out of time, I didn't leap back to my feet. Instead, with my opening gambit completed, I dropped straight into a roll and retreated swiftly, deftly avoiding the thrust sword and spears of the other three goblins in the process.

A few yards away, I bounced back to my feet. At my back, I heard the shouts of the other squad. They were racing to my position. Up ahead, the three remaining warriors from the first squad were closing fast too. I had only a second before they were on me.

Setting my stance, I waited.

The three goblins were hollering, forgetting all semblance of discipline in their eagerness to get at their elusive prey. Reaching me, the three attacked in an uncoordinated and messy fashion.

The goblin on the left thrust out his spear. I spun away, dodging the weapon to place myself on the trio's left flank. The swordsman—in the middle and a step ahead of the others—slashed out with his blade but fouled his strike on his companion's spear. The goblin on the right tried to lunge past the others to get at me and predictably crashed into them, sending both stumbling.

I didn't allow the goblins to recover. Nipping forward, I plunged my right blade into the first spearman's torso, before slipping behind the still unbalanced swordsman and skewering him with the sword in my left hand.

The last goblin swung around. Dropping his weapon, he stared at me with wide and fearful eyes. Mercilessly, I thrust both my blades through his heart.

You have killed 3 goblin warriors!

I stepped back from the corpses and looked up. The battle with the goblins had lasted just a few seconds, and the second squad were still only halfway across the room.

Feeling another's gaze burning into me, I turned towards the stage. The chief was glaring hatefully at me. Pasting a mocking smile on my face, I raised my bloody weapons in salute to him.

The goblin leader's face turned purple with rage. With a roar of anger, he rose from his throne and stomped forward.

Hahaha, that's done it, I thought with a more genuine smile. Spinning around and leaving the chief with no target for his fury, I disappeared into the darkness.

CHAPTER 40: DANCING WITH DEATH

Concealing myself from the remaining warrior squad was laughably easy. My skill at sneaking had advanced to the point that even the cavern's least shadows were enough to hide me from the goblins' poor night vision.

You are hidden once more.

The moment I faded from sight, the five-man team skidded to a halt, but not for long. At the chief's bellowing call, they reversed direction and hurried to the stage.

Crouching in the darkness, I watched the goblin leader descend from the dais. After observing the massive figure's stride for only a few seconds, I realized why he had not joined his followers earlier.

The chief was slow and cumbersome, at least in his steps.

Despite the goblin leader's oversized limbs and the undoubted power contained in his large frame, his smaller followers were more nimble. I smiled. In the cavern's murky depths, the chief would make for easy prey.

After the goblin leader stomped to the side of the five remaining warriors, the goblin squad resumed their search for me, though this time, their pace was notably slower.

"Where are you, puny HUMAN!" the chief bellowed. "Show yourself and face me!"

Ignoring the goblin's taunts, I ducked through the shadows and circled around the squad to place myself at their rear. The chief himself strode behind the five warriors. I was not sure if that was because the larger goblin was guarding the formation's rear, or if it was because the warriors out front were shielding *him* from *me*.

Either way, it conveniently left my most dangerous foe exposed to a sneak attack from behind. With drawn blades, I scampered forward and closed the distance to my mark.

"There is NO ESCAPE for you," the goblin leader shouted, unaware of the approaching danger.

Almost within striking distance, I unbent from my crouch and raised my blades.

"I alone," he continued, "hold the keys—"

A hostile entity has detected you! You are no longer hidden.

I was less than three feet from the chief and already darting forward with my blades, when the Game message dropped in my mind. I was startled, but pressed on with my attack anyway, thinking that it was surely too late for the leader to respond.

I was wrong.

Reacting instantly—almost as if he had expected the attack—the chief spun around. The goblin leader might have been slow at covering ground, but there was nothing wrong with his reflexes. The broad head of his greatclub swung around.

It was too late to change the angle of my attack, and my twin blades glanced harmlessly off the stout wood.

A level 41 goblin goliath has blocked your attacks.

I bit off a strangled yelp of surprise. *Level forty-one?* How? Why? Momentarily stunned, it took me a second to realize the chief was bringing his weapon around in an attack of his own.

The greatclub was swinging upwards from the goblin's feet and towards me in a sweeping backhand blow. There was no time to dodge. Acting on instinct, I crossed my swords and held them before me to ward off the attack.

In hindsight, I chose poorly.

Given the chief's prodigious strength and the weight of his weapon, my thin blades stood no chance of stopping his weapon. The greatclub collided with my swords and, with barely a hitch, kept going.

You have failed to block a goblin goliath's attack. A goblin goliath has critically injured you! Your health is at 50%.

Stout wood met unprotected flesh, and flesh yielded. Blood vessels ruptured, and bones broke. My ribs cracked, and the organs beneath were punctured. Even my body was unable to fully absorb the greatclub's momentum, and I went sailing backward through the air.

Yet the chief miscalculated. He had struck too hard. I flew almost a dozen feet before crashing back to the ground again.

And out of his reach.

"HAHA, stupid human," the chieftain crowed. "You cannot sneak up on ME!"

The wind had been knocked out of me, and I was half-dazed and near-senseless with pain. My vision was blurred with tears, and blood dribbled from my mouth. My agony demanded to be given voice, and a scream was forcing its way up my throat.

Somehow, I choked it back.

One thought was foremost in my thoughts: *hide. I have to hide now!* The imperative for self-preservation overrode even the pain riddling my body and drove me to roll over onto my stomach.

The chieftain, seemingly certain I was no longer a threat, was still roaring with laughter. From beyond him, I heard his warriors snickering, too, if somewhat less confidently. Ignoring the goblins, I blinked my eyes clear of swimming tears and searched frantically for the shadows—only to find I was already squarely within one.

My relief was so palpable I almost broke down crying. Swallowing back the desire, I willed myself to meld into the darkness.

You have successfully evaded detection by six hostile entities! You are hidden once more.

Giving thanks to whatever god looked over fools and madmen in this world, I rested for a second on the cool stone underfoot.

A moment later, I picked my head up and eyed the surroundings. I was not safe yet. The goblins knew where I was, and as soon as they neared my position, I would be revealed.

Move Michael. Planting my elbows on the ground, I dragged myself forward. I stifled a whimper. Moving was torture, but I had no choice. It was that or die here.

"Boss..." I heard one of the warriors say tentatively.

Foot by foot, I dragged myself across the ground, moving further away with every second. My body cried for me to down a healing potion, but I knew I couldn't afford to take the time to search my pack for one yet. *Get to safety first,* I told myself. *Then heal.*

"Chief," the same warrior said louder.

The goblin leader's laughter subsided. "What?" he growled.

"The human," the warrior said, sounding worried. "He's gone."

There was a stunned quality to the silence for a moment. Then the chief erupted once more. "What are you fools waiting for? GO! Find him!"

I gritted my teeth against the pain and tried to scamper away faster. I thought I was far enough away that the goblins wouldn't find me immediately. But I knew the warriors would expand their search quickly.

Ignoring the ominous tread of approaching feet, I crawled faster through the shadows.

CHAPTER 41: A BETTER PLAN

The next few minutes passed in heavy silence. Even the chief had stopped his incessant bellowing and had joined the five warriors in stalking the darkness.

But after the first minute had elapsed and the goblins had not found me, I knew I was safe, and my own tension faded.

Six hostile entities have failed to detect you! Your sneaking has increased to level 35.

Still, I did not stop moving until I was safely concealed under a table far from their search area. Only then did I drink a few healing potions.

You have restored 30% of your lost health with a moderate healing potion.
You have restored 10% of your lost health with a minor healing potion.
You have restored 10% of your lost health with a minor healing potion.
Your health is now at 100%.

The relief was instantaneous as bruised skin healed and broken ribs were mended. I smiled in silent gratitude as the pain was washed away. "That's better," I murmured.

I rose to a seated position and turned to the almost-forgotten skeletal bat on my shoulder. I was still perturbed by the chieftain's level and decided to risk a conversation with the familiar.

"Gnat," I whispered, "why is that chief so damn high-leveled?"

He shrugged nonchalantly. "He must be a sector boss."

I eyed the bat skeptically. "But still, rank four? How am I supposed to defeat him alone?"

Gnat chuckled quietly. "You're not, Michael. Bosses are challenges meant for a full party."

I frowned. I certainly didn't have one of those handy. Turning my head, I glanced at the goblin goliath. He was a few dozen yards away and still stomping around the area where I had vanished. Beyond him, the five warriors searched in a more lackluster fashion. It was as if the chief refused to believe that I had recovered from his blow and escaped.

The goblin leader was stubborn and arrogant, and it had made him complacent. My lips turned down. *But he is not the only one guilty of complacency.*

I had underestimated the chief. Grown used to success, I had not considered the possibility that the goblin leader could see through my stealth. He was slow and overconfident but not stupid.

The chief is too powerful for me to defeat. In a straight-up fight, anyway.

But I wasn't ready to walk away yet. *How do I kill him?* I wondered. I studied the goliath's tall figure, looking for weaknesses.

He was dressed from head to foot in spiked hide armor that looked more heavily reinforced than an ordinary warrior's, and I worried that my lack of Strength would prevent me from penetrating its defensive layers. Even the chief's head was well-protected, with only his eyes and mouth showing through his helm.

I will have to strike between the joins. I winced, not fancying my chances of doing that in open combat. A glint of metal on the chief's belt caught my attention, and I studied the small clanging shapes.

Now, what are those?

My gaze narrowed as I realized what the chief was carrying. I rose to my haunches. I knew what I had to do.

Creeping forward, I slipped through the darkness to do battle with the goliath again.

~ ~ ~

On my way to the chief, I paused to fill a discarded breakfast bowl with blood from one of the goblin corpses. It was an unpleasant but necessary task. I needed a distraction.

Reaching the center of the cavern where the chief roamed, I paused to study the nearby warriors. A dozen yards separated the closest from the chief. *Far enough,* I thought, *to enact my plan.*

With the bloody bowl in one hand and sword in the other, I snuck closer toward the chief's broad back. I was tense and alert and ready for anything.

When I closed to within three feet of my target, the expected happened.

A hostile entity has detected you! You are no longer hidden.

The chief pivoted, greatclub lashing out. This time the goblin's response did not catch me flatfooted. I ducked under the whistling club, and before my opponent could recover, I flung the bowl's contents into his face.

You have evaded a goblin goliath's attack.

Dark, sticky blood splashed onto the goblin's helm, flooding his eyes and filling his mouth. With a half-choked-off cry, the chief staggered back.

You have blinded a goblin goliath for 2 seconds.

Good enough, I thought. I lunged forward as the goblin leader shook his head and blinked his eyes, trying to clear them of the obscuring muck. The sword in my left hand flashed out and cut clean through the chief's leather belt. At the same time, my right hand darted forward and wrenched free the item that had been dangling upon it.

You have stolen a goblin goliath's keyring!

Yes!

Belatedly, the chief seemed to realize my intentions. Forgetting his eyes, he struck out blindly with the greatclub. But with my prize clutched in my hands, I was already rolling away.

You have evaded a goblin goliath's attack.

Not pausing or bothering to hide, I sprinted toward the stage.

"GET HIM," the chief roared.

The five warriors took off after me immediately. But they had been caught flatfooted by my attack, and I was faster than them. Every second, the lead opened up further, and I reached the stage well in front.

Seeing me hurtling towards them, the two dire wolf adults rose to their feet. Both looked poised, and I fancied I could see eagerness glint in their eyes. Around their feet, the three pups yapped excitedly.

Not bothering to deviate right or left towards the stage's stairs, I threw myself directly at the elevated dais and scampered quickly up its six-foot-tall sidewall. I dashed towards the throne, then paused.

Now comes the tricky part, I thought, looking down at the keyring in my hand.

There were eight keys on it, two of them shining with a faint blue aura that suggested they were magical in nature. I discarded them from the equation immediately. There didn't appear to be anything magical about the locks holding the dire wolves collared.

That still left me six keys to try in five locks. *Aargh*. I glanced downwards. The goblin squad was closing rapidly, but thankfully the chief was still many yards distant.

I had two chances—or at best three—to match a key to a lock. I knelt down beside the dire wolf sire. He was fully recovered from his earlier ordeal. Whatever the green paste was that the goblins had used on the wolf earlier, it appeared to have done the job of healing the beast.

The pups, each no more than ankle-high, rushed forward to lick and nip at my heels, but at a growl from their mother, they returned to her side, tails wagging furiously. "Don't worry," I murmured to them, "we're all going to get out of this."

I picked one of the six keys at random, and seeming to understand my intent, the dire wolf sire sat on his haunches and obligingly stuck out his neck, exposing the lock on his metal collar.

I fit key to lock. It didn't turn. *Urgh*.

I tried another. It, too, failed to work.

I glanced over my shoulder. The goblins were almost at the steps to the dais. I had one more try. If this didn't work, I would have to take care of the squad before freeing the wolves.

I fitted the next key.

It turned all the way, and the lock sprang open. The sire rose to all fours and shook himself.

"Go!" I ordered. "Hold them at the steps if you can while I free the others."

The beast didn't need to be told twice. With an agreeable growl, he bounded forward to engage the goblins.

Returning my attention to the rest of the pack, I picked out another key. The dire wolf mother stepped forward and bared her neck. It took me only two tries to free her. Pausing only to lick my face in thanks, the beast raced away to help her mate.

I studied the melee raging on the dais steps for a second. The dire wolf sire was holding his own. One of the goblin warriors was down already, and on the narrow steps, the others could only have a go at him two at a time. The chief was still too far to aid his followers, but that didn't stop him from shouting out pointless instructions. Things were going to plan so far.

I turned back to the pups. "Right, time to free you three," I said, and the trio gamboled eagerly forward.

CHAPTER 42: TAKING DOWN A GOLIATH

Freeing the pups was easier than trying to restrain them.

The moment the first was uncollared, he tried bolting towards his parents. Luckily, I caught him before he got far. Clutching him to my chest, I set about freeing the other two. The second one was just as daring and made a dash for it too.

"Stop!" I hissed, out of patience with the unruly hounds. Surprisingly, it worked, and the two lay meekly on the floor. After freeing the last pup, I rose to my feet and turned to the battle.

Three of the five warriors were dead, throats torn open, and the other two appeared reluctant to engage the wolves further. But the chief was nearly at the stage.

"Back," I yelled to the two adult wolves. They were no match for the chief on their own, especially in a head-on confrontation.

The dire wolf sire raised a bloody muzzle in my direction and growled in protest.

"Now," I barked. I didn't free them, only so they could die. Besides, I had a plan for dealing with the chief already, but I would need the wolves' help.

The sire whined but didn't protest the order again. Turning tail, the two beasts abandoned their posts at the steps and hurried to my side.

"GET THEM," the chief roared. Left with no choice, the two remaining warriors bounded up the steps.

Drawing my swords, I rushed forward to meet the pair. I had to kill them fast, before the goblin leader reached us. Focusing on the warrior on the left, I parried away his axe with one blade, and rammed my other sword through his gut.

You have killed a goblin warrior!

The hammer of the second goblin was already racing towards me. But pivoting with my attack, I dragged the dying goblin—still pinned on my sword—into the path of the oncoming weapon and successfully foiled the blow.

The warrior growled in disgust and raised his weapon to strike again, but before he could do so, the dire wolf sire blurred through the air and ripped out his throat from behind.

"Thanks," I panted absently. My gaze darted to the chief. He was ascending the steps. I swung back to the wolves. "Go!" I hissed, pointing to the other steps. "Retreat to the cavern's center. We will face him there!"

Five wolves stared at me expressionlessly for a moment, then, as one, leaped in the direction I pointed. *Damn, those beasts are smart,* I thought as I watched them go.

I hurried to the back of the throne and unclipped one of the chains that had kept the two adult wolves imprisoned. I judged it large enough for my purpose.

You have acquired an iron chain and collar set.

With the item in hand, I began my own retreat. Keeping a wary eye on the chief, I backstepped towards the stairs at the far end of the stage.

The goblin leader's face turned purple with rage as he saw me flee. He knew he was too slow to stop me. "Running again, human?" he growled. "Some player you are!"

I smiled at the chief's attempt at goading. I had no intention of fleeing, but I would only fight him on my terms. "Oh, I don't plan on running," I said. "I've killed all your followers, and I intend on slaying you too." I pointed to the center of the cavern. "Come face me there. If you dare."

The chief's gaze narrowed, and he stomped forward menacingly, but he didn't respond immediately. His gaze flitted between me, the wolves, and the spot I gestured to. Finally, he snorted. "Even together, you three are no match for me!"

I shrugged. "Let's find out, shall we?" I said and hurried down the steps.

~ ~ ~

Despite his bold words, the chief did not follow immediately after. With his arms folded and chest heaving, the goliath eyed us furiously from the stage.

While we waited for the goblin leader to make up his mind, the dire wolf mother ushered her pups to a far corner of the room, where from her stern growls and barks, I assumed she was instructing them to stay put.

Sitting down cross-legged on the floor, I eyed the chief with studied nonchalance. The dire wolf sire sat beside me. I unwrapped two field rations, handing one to the sire. He wrinkled his nose but didn't reject my offering.

"You really think this plan of yours is going to work?" Gnat asked curiously.

I shrugged, "It does, or it doesn't." My plan was simple, and I had already explained it to both dire wolves with furtive gestures and whispered words. Both beasts seemed to understand the part they were to play, but with our communication as limited as it was, I couldn't be sure. *Time will tell.*

The dire wolf mother rejoined us, and I handed her a field ration too. After long minutes, the sight of us sitting unconcernedly in the center of his hall grew too much for the chief, and he trudged down the stage, shouting, "I will rend the flesh from your bones, you impudent wretches!"

I rolled my eyes. The chief liked the sound of his own voice a little too much, I thought. To signal our contempt, the two wolves and I remained seated while the goblin leader approached—although it was mostly pretense designed to enrage the goblin further.

The truth was I was uncertain about our chances of success, but the plan was the best one I had been able to come up with. It was either go with it or retreat.

And neither the wolves nor I were willing to walk away. In fact, from the beasts' burning gazes and murderous growls, I could tell both were keen to wreak vengeance on their tormentor. I wondered how many of their pack they had lost to the goblins. *Too many,* I thought sadly, thinking of all the hides I had seen in the leather workshop.

The chief was only ten yards away now. I stood up.

It was time.

~ ~ ~

The dire wolves rose their feet with me, and as planned, they circled warily around the goblin leader until we had him surrounded on all sides.

The chief eyed the circling beasts contemptuously. "This is your plan?" he laughed.

My lips thinned, but I said nothing.

The dire wolf mother darted forward suddenly. The goliath whirled in her direction, and his club flashed out, but the beast's attack had been a feint only, and she aborted her attack before falling within the range of the goblin's club.

I reached into my backpack and pulled out the iron collar and chain. Bouncing on the balls of my feet, I readied myself. It was nearly time to act. I eyed the goliath's eleven-foot-tall figure and planned my approach.

The wolf sire rushed forward. The chief spun his way and lashed out with his club again. It was time. I kicked off, sprinting towards the goblin.

The sire didn't break off his attack. Slipping under the chief's weapon—barely—he nipped at the gigantic figure's heels. The goliath raised his weapon to strike at the wolf chewing on his armored leg.

I was less than two feet from the chief now. Launching myself into the air, I flung myself forward and crashed into the goblin's broad back.

"WHA—?" the chief yelled in outrage.

The impact barely staggered the goliath, but the sudden addition of my weight pulled the chief off-balance and foiled his aim, and the dire wolf sire dashed away as the goblin's weapon crashed into empty ground beside him.

"What are you doing, worm?" the chief roared, swinging his head around as he tried to catch sight of me.

I didn't bother to reply. Using the spikes on the chief's armor as handholds, I scampered up his tall frame, leaving a bloody trail in my wake as other spikes dug into my bare flesh.

Realizing that I was up to no good, the goblin let his greatclub fall to the floor and reached up with both hands. "I will squash—" he began.

The wolf mother leaped.

Her aim was true, and her jaws clamped shut around one of the goliath's hands, and for one fateful second, the chief was delayed in his attempt to remove me.

I pulled the metal collar free from where I had secured it on my sword belt and clamped it shut around the chief's neck. Only a few inches from the goliath's face, I saw his eyes widen in surprise—and bewilderment.

I smiled at his confusion and threw the attached chain to the dire wolf sire. "Now!"

The beast leaped in the air and twisted to catch the end in his mouth. Her job done, the dire wolf mother released the chief's hand and retreated swiftly.

The chief's hands continued upwards, and his face contorted in fury. "Impudent wretch," he screamed.

I flung my arms around goliath's neck. I only had to hold on for a little while longer. Assuming my plan worked, of course. If it didn't, well, I was likely dead then.

The wolf sire landed back on solid ground and yanked on the chain. Its length snapped taut, and the collar wrenched on its captive's neck.

The goblin chief teetered. His eyes grew round, and I saw the dawning comprehension on his face as he finally understood our plan. A heartbeat later, his eyes narrowed and fixed on me. "Die worm!" he spat.

The goblin's hands clamped down on me and heaved. I hung on for dear life, but already I could feel myself slipping. *Bloody hell, he is going to toss me!*

But before that happened, the wolf mother joined her mate and added her efforts to his. The goliath jerked sideways as both wolves yanked on the chain.

Gritting his teeth, the chief wrenched back on the chain, pitting his strength against the wolves, but he lacked the leverage the beasts had.

The two wolves tugged again, and this time the chief stumbled, one foot lifting off the ground entirely.

That was the beginning of the end.

The wolves heaved again, and the goliath fell forward, arms windmilling outwards as he tried fruitlessly to halt his fall. I squeezed my eyes shut and braced myself for the crash.

The chief and I hit the ground with bone-jarring impact.

My bones felt bruised, and my teeth rattled, but with my fall cushioned by the goblin beneath me, I suffered no lasting injuries. Alas, the chief suffered no great harm either. But I hadn't expected him to.

Freeing my arms, I straddled the goblin's neck and drew my blades. The wolves abandoned the chain and, joining me, added their weight to the goblin's back.

"GET OFF ME!" the chief screamed in outrage when he recovered from his momentary daze. He tried to roll over, but with all three of us pinning him down, he was unable to regain his feet.

I raised my swords up high, then hacked down.

You have injured a goblin goliath!
You have injured a goblin goliath!

Both blades slipped between gorget and helm, and bit into the goblin's bare skin below. But surprisingly, neither penetrated deeply. The chief's skin was itself toughened and resistant to damage. *Damn, this is going to take some time.*

I plunged my blades downwards again.

You have injured a goblin goliath!
You have injured a goblin goliath!

The chief's screams transformed into shrieks of pain, but I didn't relent. I kept hacking, and bit by bit, the goblin leader's life bled away.

CHAPTER 43: FINISHING UP

It took the goblin chief a long five minutes to die.

But finally, the deed was done. Drenched in gore, I rolled off the corpse and onto the ground. Heaving in deep breaths, I spat out the blood that had spurted into my mouth and tried futilely to clean the ichor off my face. *God, what I wouldn't do for a bath now.*

The five wolves padded over and licked my face. Closing my eyes, I let them while I perused the avalanche of Game messages awaiting my attention.

You have killed a level 41 goblin goliath.
You have reached level 16!
You have reached level 17!
You have reached level 18!
You have 3 attribute points available.

Your shortswords has increased to level 29. Your dodging has increased to level 23. Your two weapon fighting has increased to level 25.

You have accomplished the feat: <u>Solo your First Boss</u>! Requirement: slay a dungeon boss while not in a party. As only the 1037th rank 1 solo player to defeat a sector boss, you have been awarded the trait: <u>Beast tongue</u>. This rare trait is normally reserved for rank 3 druids and allows you to converse with any beastkin capable of speech. Note, the traits you earn from feats are based on the circumstances and manner of your achievement.

You have completed the hidden task: <u>Free the wolves</u>! Tasks are special missions that can be allocated to you by either one of the Powers or the Game itself. In certain instances—and only at the Adjudicator's behest—the nature of a task will be hidden until completed. Be wary of which tasks you fulfill. All tasks will have consequences and a bearing on your standing with the Game's factions.

You have accomplished the feat: <u>Play the Game</u>! Requirement: complete your first task or reach rank 2. You have been awarded the trait: <u>Marked</u>. This is a generic trait that all players eventually receive.

Congratulations, Michael! You have joined the ranks of the Marked! As a Marked, you can now see the spirit signatures of other Marked and determine their allegiance to Shadow, Light, and Dark. Beware, other Marked can similarly read your own Mark, and it may affect their interactions with you.

Your actions during the execution of your first task have shown a mix of ruthlessness, good intentions, and cunning and have influenced the Marks you've been allocated. Marks are not fixed and will grow or diminish based on your future actions.

Your spirit signature has been etched with 3 new Marks! You have acquired the Mark: <u>Lesser Light</u>, and have begun to tread the ways of Light.

You have acquired the Mark: <u>Lesser Shadow</u>, and have begun to tread the ways of Shadow. Your deeds have also attracted the notice of Loken and Artem, Powers of Shadow and members of the Shadow Coalition.

You have acquired the Mark: <u>Wolf-friend</u>. You have proven yourself an ally to wolfkind, making them less inclined to attack you in future. Only wolves will see this Mark on you.

My head was spinning after reading all the notices. *Marks? Feats? Powers?* It was a lot to digest, and to try and make sense of it all, I worked slowly through the messages again. But much of it, I still didn't understand. Suddenly, the Game seemed a lot more complicated. I needed help. *Time to have another long conversation with Gnat.*

But not right now. Later. After I had time to savor my victory—and the rewards.

I opened my eyes. The wolves had stepped back and were sitting on their haunches in front of me. Feeling a little less dipped in blood, I sat up and addressed the patiently waiting wolves.

"It is done," I said gravely to the wolf mother and sire. I could scarce believe it. It was no mean feat we had accomplished, and I still felt energized by our success.

"Thank you."

I blinked. Someone had just spoken to me. And in my mind. My gaze flitted between the two wolves. Lowering herself to all fours, the wolf mother opened her mouth, tongue lolling out.

She was laughing at me, I was sure.

"I am Aira. My mate is Oursk."

It *was* the dire wolf talking to me, I realized in stupefied awe. Only then did I belatedly remember the trait I had earned: beast tongue. Tentatively, I tried responding through whatever mental communication channel we were using and spoke directly into Aira's mind. *"I'M MICHAEL."*

Aira whined and lowered her head. *"It's a pleasure to finally speak to you, Michael. Only... try not to shout."*

I lowered my head, abashed. *"Sorry,"* I mumbled.

Another voice laughed in my head. *"Do not feel bad, human. Youngsters are always loud and brash,"* Oursk said. He nipped at one of the pups tugging on his coat. *"These three young idiots are Shadetooth, Stormdark, and Moonstalker,"* he said fondly.

"Hello there," I greeted the pups and waited expectantly.

All three turned my way but remained silent.

"They are still too young for speech," Aira said.

Of course, I thought, reddening slightly at my own foolishness. *"How did your pack end—"*

I broke off as Gnat flapped down from the darkness. "Wow, Michael! You actually killed the big bugger. I can't believe it."

I smiled wryly. "Me neither. You won't believe—"

"Don't trust him," Aira said.

I turned to stare at the dire wolf mother. *"Who? Gnat?"*

"He serves the Dark," Oursk said, fixing the skeletal bat with a predatory gaze.

"Oh, I know that," I said. *"He is the Master's creature, but is bonded to me through—"*

"Something wrong?" Gnat interrupted.

"Uhm," I said, wondering how to explain.

"Trust him if you must," Oursk said, rising to his feet. *"But don't tell him you can speak to us."*

At the dire wolf's movement, Gnat flapped his wings. I glanced at the bat. He was eyeing the wolves sideways and almost seemed... nervous.

I frowned.

Had the familiar always been this wary around the wolves and I just didn't notice before? I couldn't remember. But he had disliked the beasts from the very beginning, I recalled, and had advised me against freeing them from their cages. *He is as mistrustful of them as they are of him.*

"Yes?" Gnat prodded, still waiting for my answer.

I rose to my feet myself. "Nothing," I said, not yet certain how to handle the matter, and deciding to put it off for now. Looking for a distraction, I searched for the loot chest. Surely one must appear this time?

But there was no wooden box next to the chief's corpse.

God damn, I cursed. *What do I need to do to earn…*

My internal monologue trailed to a stop, and my eyes grew round as I saw what was on the stage.

It wasn't one chest.

It was six.

Chapter 44: Just Desserts

"Damn," I murmured, still not quite able to believe my eyes as I studied the chests in front of me.

Gnat, the five wolves, and I were on the dais. Arranged in a neat line in front of the throne were five wooden loot chests—and one bronze one.

"Why is that chest bronze?" I asked Gnat, slightly breathless at the possibility of what it contained.

The familiar cackled. "It's your lucky day, Michael. Bronze metal chests carry better loot than plain old wooden ones, and not many earn them. The Adjudicator must have judged your performance exemplary for you to get one."

"Bronze," I mused. "Does that mean there are higher-order chests too?"

Gnat laughed. "Heh, already dreaming of bigger things, are we? The short answer to your question is yes. But to earn anything better than bronze, you have to perform truly *extraordinary* feats." The skeletal bat's amusement faded abruptly as something seemed to occur to him. "You mentioned rewards earlier. Did the Game award you with anything unusual?"

"No," I replied, not looking away from the chests.

I wasn't sure why I lied. Perhaps it was because of the seed of doubt planted by the wolves, or perhaps it was because of my own recent misgivings regarding the Master, but whatever it was, I realized there were some things I wasn't willing to share with the familiar yet.

"Really?" Gnat pressed. "You got nothing strange at all? You sounded so excited."

"Well..." I said, struggling not to let my expression slip, "I did gain in nearly all my skills and advance *three* whole levels. Which far surpassed my expectations." I paused. "But I wouldn't call any of that strange."

"Oh," Gnat said.

I wrinkled my brows and finally turned to look at him. "Why do you ask? Did you expect the Game to reward me with something... different?"

Gnat shifted uncomfortably on my shoulder. "No," he replied. "I just thought the Adjudicator might have provided you with some explanation for the bronze chest."

"Explanations!" I snorted. "Those would be nice."

I glanced away so that the skeletal bat wouldn't see my troubled expression. I was sure now that Gnat was lying to me—or at least not being entirely forthcoming.

What I didn't know was why.

I turned back to the chests again, and only with considerable effort did I stop myself from rubbing my hands in glee. I had an abundance of loot in front of me and didn't really want to deal with Gnat at the moment.

I had six chests to open.

I stepped closer but still maintained a healthy distance to the chests. They had to be boobytrapped, of course. I rubbed my chin. The question was: would I be able to detect the traps' nature?

I sighed. *Only one way to find out,* I thought and got to work probing the chests.

~ ~ ~

The five dire wolves watched curiously as I first threw pieces of armor at the chests, then poked them from afar with a spear, and finally banged their sides with a goblin hammer. None of these tests revealed any traps, but I was only getting started.

Gnat flew off, pleading boredom and no doubt realizing it would be some while yet before I risked raising the lid of any of the chests.

No sooner had the bat vanished into the cavern's depths than Aira addressed me again. *"Why don't you just open them?"* she asked, tilting her head to the side.

I had joined the wolves' former chains together and looped a portion of its length around one of the chests. Fearing a hidden pressure plate or some such, I was slowly dragging the chest out of position. *"They might be trapped,"* I replied, not looking away from what I was doing. *"In one of the earlier dungeon legs, I found—"*

"They're not trapped," Oursk interrupted.

I glanced at him with one eyebrow raised in polite disbelief. *"You can't be certain of that."*

"I am sure," he said with complete assurance.

When I still didn't look convinced, the dire wolf growled in frustration. *"Look here, human, we are wasting time. Any moment, more goblins may arrive. We have to leave the dungeon."*

I paused, letting the chain in my hand go slack. *"Leave? You know the way out?"*

"We know the route to the surface," Aira confirmed. *"And my mate is correct. Time is not on our side. We must get our pups to safety. Will you come with us?"*

"Of course," I replied. I turned back to the chests. *"As soon as I open these. It will only take another hour or two,"* I assured the wolves.

My response, however, was not to the wolves' liking. Before I could stop him, Oursk dashed forward and shoved his nose under the lid of the first chest.

"Wait! Stop, it could be—"

It was too late.

With a flick of his head, the dire wolf flung back the lid, and it yawned open. I froze.

But no trap was sprung.

"I told you," Oursk said, padding casually to the next chest. *"They're not trapped. Now loot them, and let's be on our way."*

~ ~ ~

I took Oursk at his word and flipped open the lids of the other five chests in quick order. Still, I couldn't help but wince each time I did. The dire wolves' confidence proved well-founded, though.

None of the chests were trapped.

It was confusing.

If any of the chests in a dungeon were going to be boobytrapped, surely they would be the ones revealed after the boss was killed? I found the Game's choice not to trap these chests confounding, but overcome by my eagerness to see the items I had earned, I let the matter lie.

I looted the five wooden chests first, saving the best for last.

You have acquired 6 moderate healing potions, 3 full healing potions, and 4 packs of field rations.

You have acquired a basic fire-starting kit. This item contains all the items necessary to start a campfire.

You have acquired a moonstone lamp. This item contains a gem enchanted to provide 3 hours of white light. The enchantment can be replenished with mana.

You have acquired a common fighter's sash. This item increases all known weapon skills by +3.

You have acquired a basic ability tome: crippling blow. You have the necessary skill: any weapon skill rank 2, to learn this ability. The ability tome is a single-use item.

You have acquired a basic Class stone. This stone contains the path of: a rogue. The rogue is a basic Class that confers a player with three skills: sneaking, daggers, and poisoning. This Class also permanently boosts your Dexterity attribute by +2.

The items from the five wooden chests were… interesting—especially the ability tome—yet still less than I hoped for. I studied the book in my hands. Reading it would provide me with my first ability, and without hesitation, I set about it.

The pages of the tome were filled with lines of bronze script, and I absorbed its knowledge too fast for conscious thought to follow.

You have acquired the basic ability: crippling blow. This is a touch-based ability that simulates a debilitating attack by locking a foe's limb in a stasis field. The targeted limb is disabled for 3 seconds. This ability can only be activated by physical contact—either directly or through a weapon.

The effects of this ability may be overcome by physical resistance. This ability consumes stamina and its activation time is near-instantaneous.

Crippling blow may occupy any Dexterity or Strength ability slot and has been installed in one of your available Dexterity slots.

I smiled as understanding of the ability filled me. In battle, it would prove enormously beneficial. I turned my attention to the other items. The path of the rogue, I didn't even consider adopting. The Class was only a basic one, and I already had one of the Class' skills.

The sash I draped about my waist and immediately felt a small but perceptible increase in my shortswords skill. I stored the remaining items in my backpack and finally turned my attention to the bronze chest.

I flexed my fingers in anticipation. *Now, let's hope this contains something better,* I thought and reached inside.

You have acquired a lesser attribute gem. This item grants you one attribute point.

You have acquired an advanced Class stone. This stone contains the path of: a psionic. The psionic is an advanced Class that confers a player with four skills: telepathy, telekinesis, chi, and meditation. This Class also permanently boosts your Mind attribute by +4.

You have acquired a basic ability tome: simple charm. You cannot learn this ability. You do not have the necessary skill: telepathy, or slots available in the required attribute: Mind. The ability tome is a single-use item.

I sat down in stunned shock as I studied the items in my hand. All three items were valuable. The lesser attribute gem alone was worth one free level. The other two items seemed to have been paired together: an advanced Class *and* a basic ability for one of its skills. I stared at the marble in my hand. Unlike the other Class stones I had seen, this one was solid silver.

Psi, I mused. *Magic of the mind.*

It was not the more traditional magic I had envisioned myself wielding, but judging from the skills listed in the class description, the psionic Class did have a magic of sorts, and possibly quite strong magic too.

Did I wait for a better Class to come along? But how long could I wait? If I died before absorbing the Class, I would likely lose the opportunity to do so forever. A Game window opened in my mind.

You have two available Class slots. Do you wish to acquire the psionic Class?

It makes no sense to wait, I concluded and made my decision.

CHAPTER 45: A MAGIC OF SORTS

I felt the silver marble in my palm turn warm. Just like with the previous Class stone I had absorbed, it melted into my skin. Words appeared in my mind.

You have acquired the psionic Class. The psionic is a versatile psi Class, providing you with equal opportunities for growth in any Mind skill. It comes with neither the restrictions nor benefits of more specialized psi Classes.

You have gained the base trait: metamind. This trait increases your Mind by +4 ranks. Your level cap for mind-based skills has increased to 40.

You have gained one basic skill: meditation and three advanced skills: chi, telekinesis, and telepathy.

Meditation replenishes a player's store of psi, while chi uses the power of the mind to perform extraordinary physical feats. Telepathy allows a caster to subliminally influence others, and telekinesis is used to move objects with the mind.

I closed my eyes and tasted the new knowledge filling my consciousness. The psi skills I had obtained were strangely different from the physical ones I had acquired earlier. Bowing my head, I rubbed at my temples. My mind felt different too.

Fuller. Clearer. Sharp. And full of psi.

I had gained access to a new source of energy, one eager and waiting to be used. I pulled out the charm spellbook and flipped through it.

You have acquired the basic ability: simple charm. This is a mind spell that temporarily overrides the target's consciousness, forcing them to serve the caster for 10 seconds. This ability can only be activated through direct line of sight.

The effects of this ability may be overcome by mental resistance. Beware, taking hostile action against your bespelled minion will break the charm. This ability consumes psi, and can be upgraded. Its activation time is average.

You have 3 of 4 Mind ability slots remaining.

I smiled to myself. That was two new abilities I had now, and already I could imagine a dozen different ways to employ them. *Clearing out this complex would have been a lot easier if I had them to begin with.*

I opened my eyes to find Aira and Oursk staring at me. "Almost done," I murmured. Focusing on the last item, I willed my desire to the Game.

Lesser attribute gem used. You have gained 1 attribute point.

One last thing to do, I thought and willed open my player profile.

<u>Player Profile: Michael</u>
Level: 18. Rank: 1. Current Health: 95%.
Stamina: 30%. Mana: 100%. Psi: 100%.
Species: Human. Lives Remaining: 3.
Marks: Wolf-friend, Lesser Shadow, Lesser Light.
<u>Attributes</u>
Available: 4 points.
Strength: 0. Constitution: 0. Dexterity: 9. Perception: 8. Mind: 4. Magic: 0. and Faith: 0.

<u>Classes</u>
Primary Class: Scout (basic).
Secondary Class: Psionic (advanced).
Tertiary Class: None.

Traits

Undead familiar: +1 to necromancy rank.
Nimble: +2 Dexterity.
Beast tongue: can speak to beastkin.
Metamind: +4 Mind.
Marked: can see spirit signatures.

Skills

Available skill slots: 4.
Dodging (current: 23. max: 90. Dexterity, basic).
Sneaking (current: 35. max: 90. Dexterity, basic).
Shortswords (current: 29. max: 90. Dexterity, basic).
Two weapon fighting (current: 25. max: 90. Dexterity, advanced).
Chi (current: 1. max: 40. Mind, advanced).
Meditation (current: 1. max: 40. Mind, basic).
Telekinesis (current: 1. max: 40. Mind, advanced).
Telepathy (current: 1. max: 40. Mind, advanced).

Abilities

Crippling blow (Dexterity, basic).
Simple charm (Mind, basic).

Equipped

1 common thief's cloak (+3 sneaking).
2 basic steel shortswords (+10% damage each).
1 common fighter's sash (+3 shortswords).

Backpack Contents

<u>Money</u>: 1 gold, 3 silvers, and 3 coppers.
31 x field rations.
2 x flask of water.
8 x empty potion flasks.
1 x summon lesser wight spellbook.
1 x minor healing potions.
1 x archer Class stone.
2 x goblin shortbows.
4 x iron daggers.
1 x bedroll.
1 x heavy shields skillbook.
6 x moderate healing potions.
1 x coin pouch.
1 x keyring.
3 x full healing potions.
1 x basic fire-starting kit.
1 x moonstone lamp.
1 x rogue Class stone.

"Excellent," I murmured to myself. I had four attributes to spare, but given my recent growth in power, I saw no need to spend them yet. *Perhaps, it is time I started banking my attributes.* I had evolved rapidly on my first day in the Game—*has it only been one day?*—and I felt capable of taking on any foe I had encountered thus far, even the trolls. *Perhaps I should return to their lair and—*

I broke off the thought. Now was not the time to fall prey to overconfidence. The dire wolves had a way out of the dungeon, and the least I should do before throwing myself in danger again was to investigate what lay beyond.

I rose to my feet and turned to the waiting wolves. *"Let's go."*

~ ~ ~

We did not leave the cavern immediately, of course.

There were still fifty-odd goblin corpses in the hall that I had yet to loot them. But with Aira and Oursk impatient to get going, I limited my search of the dead to their coin pouches. Besides, I didn't have nearly enough space in my backpack to carry much else.

You have acquired 4 gold and 240 copper coins. Total money carried: 7 gold, 7 silvers, and 3 coppers.

It was only the goblin leader's corpse that I took the time to inspect more fully. He had carried the bulk of the money I had found: four golds, and it led me to anticipate finding other stuff of value on him. But unfortunately, other than his spiked hide armor and greatclub, the chief carried nothing else of worth. With lots of cursing and tugging, I managed to remove the goliath's helm. Holding it in my hand, I considered its game data.

This is a rank 1 spiked hide armor helm. This item decreases the damage you sustain by 20%. This item requires a minimum Constitution of 4 to equip.

My brows drew down. The helm's properties were different from other items I had encountered. It had a rank of its own and a prerequisite to equip. Thoughtfully, I turned my attention to the greatclub.

This is a rank 2 greatclub, +1. This item increases the damage you deal by 40% and has been enchanted to increase the wielder's two-handed club skill by +1 rank (10 skill points). This item requires a minimum Strength of 8 to wield.

My frown deepened. Like the helm, the chief's weapon also had a rank and prerequisite to use.

"What's troubling you now?"

I looked up. Gnat was back. "Hmm?" I murmured absently.

"You're scrunching up your face again," he said. "Why?"

I gestured to the greatclub resting on the floor. The darn thing was so heavy I could barely hold one end aloft. "This item needs eight Strength to wield."

"Oh," the bat said. "That's normal. Nearly all equipment will have restrictions."

I glanced at him. "But the equipment sold by the vendors in the Master's domain didn't," I pointed out.

Gnat snorted. "That's because those were newbie items meant for rank zero players."

"I see," I muttered.

"Don't worry," Gnat said. "You'll find items more suited to your current rank and Class in the safe zone," he said. "There are vendors there."

My gaze sharpened. "This is the first I'm hearing of it," I said. "Why didn't you mention them before?"

Gnat shrugged. "There was no need. You would've found out soon enough once you got there."

"How far away is the safe zone?" I asked. "And what are my chances of reaching it alive?"

"I don't know," Gnat admitted.

I sighed. The safe zone and its vendors might as well be on the other end of the world for all the use they were to me now. It would have been nice, though, to be able to spend the gold in my pouch. "Where did you go?" I asked suddenly.

"Why?" The bat looked me over carefully. "Don't tell me you were worried?" He laughed as if the whole thing was amusing.

"Of course, I was," I replied, my own response devoid of emotion. Gnat hadn't answered my question, but I didn't push the matter.

I turned back to the chief's gear. Both armor and weapon were too heavy for me to carry away, and I had no choice but to leave them behind. *What a waste.*

I turned to Aira. "Alright," I said aloud for Gnat's benefit. "Lead on." *And let's find this exit.*

CHAPTER 46: THE LOCKED GATE

The five dire wolves led the way out of the great hall. It felt like I had been inside its cavernous depths for an eternity, and being back in the lightless passages felt strange again.

"Where are we going?" Gnat asked.

"I don't know," I lied, not turning to look at him. There was no way I could explain my knowing our destination without explaining how the wolves and I were communicating. "The beasts seem to want us to follow them."

Gnat grunted unhappily. "You shouldn't trust them."

Ignoring the bat's comment, I followed after the dire wolves. Oursk led our small party back to the first crossroad I had come across in the goblin complex and turned down the left fork. It was the only tunnel I had yet to explore.

Since leaving the hall, we had not encountered any goblins, but I was still wary at the thought of venturing down an unexplored tunnel.

My gaze flitted between the dire wolf mother and Gnat, wondering if I dared reach out to her with my mind while the bat was around. I had not failed to notice that the wolves had only spoken to me when the skeletal bat wasn't about. *Can Gnat sense our mindspeech?* I wondered. While I might have grown suspicious of the familiar, I didn't want him to catch me out in a lie. That would risk a confrontation, and I wasn't ready for that yet.

"Do not fear. The dead thing cannot overhear us," Aira said suddenly, somehow divining my thoughts.

My stride stuttered, and I nearly missed a step. The wolf mother had startled me. Recovering my balanced, I let my gaze slide to Gnat. He seemed oblivious of her words. *"How did you know what I was thinking?"*

"Your mind shouted out your thoughts to the world," she said. *"I suspect you gained the telepathy skill since opening the Game's chest."*

"I did," I admitted.

Aira tilted her gaze upwards to stare at me with a solemn gaze. *"Telepathy is a powerful gift, but a dangerous one too. It has opened your consciousness to new possibilities, but it has also stripped your mind of its natural defenses. To protect yourself, you will have to consciously will your mind closed and learn to control your thoughts. Think too loudly, and other telepaths may overhear you."*

"I see," I said. I instinctively knew what she meant. Marshaling my thoughts, I willed a barrier around my mind.

"Better," the dire wolf said approvingly. *"Your mental defenses are weak and flimsy, and even a week-old pup could shred through them, but as your skill grows, it will strengthen."*

"Thank you," I said before returning to the matter of her original words. *"How can you be certain Gnat can't hear us? I got the impression that you and Oursk were afraid of speaking around him."*

"We were," Oursk said, joining the conversation. *"During the fight with the chief, the creature left your side. When he returned, I detected a hint of psi flowing around him. Aira and I were afraid he might be a telepath himself, but since then, I have probed him carefully and am sure now that he doesn't bear the skill."*

I frowned, disturbed by the wolf's words. I couldn't recall seeing Gnat during the fight with the chief, but then I frequently lost track of the skeletal bat during battles. Since he couldn't involve himself directly, I had always assumed he flew off to observe from a safe distance. *"Where did he go?"*

"We don't know," Aira said. *"But he returned with a psi shield around his mind. That is what Oursk first sensed. Someone has shielded the creature from mental attacks."*

I digested that in silence. It was troubling news and raised more questions than I had answers for. *I will have to keep a closer eye on Gnat from now onwards,* I decided.

My foot landed in an unexpected dip in the ground, and I nearly slipped. Looking around, I was reminded that we were in an unexplored passage. It recalled me to my original reason for wanting to speak to the wolves. *"Aira, the way ahead might not be safe. You and the pups should move to the rear."*

I heard her chuckle. *"Do not fear. We will smell any goblins long before we see them or they, us. Besides, we have been this way before. This passage is barren, and the only goblins to be found are the ones at the guard station at its end."*

Trusting her judgment, I didn't say anything further and followed silently in the wolves' wake. But I struggled to stay focused on my surroundings. My thoughts kept returning to the problem of my familiar and how to deal with him.

~ ~ ~

Aira was right.

The tunnel was empty, with neither rooms nor caverns leading off from it. What was more, as we tramped down its length, I felt the ground slope gradually upwards, which boded well. And despite my tiredness, I felt reenergized at the thought of finally escaping the dungeon.

After ten minutes of uneventful walking, Oursk stopped. *"What is it?"* I asked Aira.

"We've reached the exit," she said. *"Goblins still guard it."* Raising her snout, she sniffed delicately. *"There are three of them."*

Only three, I thought. It should be no great matter to deal with them, and it would also afford me an opportunity to test one of my new abilities. *"Alright,"* I said. *"You stay back with the pups. Oursk and I will deal with them."*

I slipped into stealth and crept forward, with the big dire wolf sire following behind. After a hundred more yards, I spotted the red-orange tinge of torchlight in the distance: the guard station.

Three goblin warriors were sitting with their backs to the gate, alert and awake. Beyond the guards were a grilled-metal gate and a large bronze bell. The guard station's configuration was nearly identical to that at the maze entrance and banished any doubts I had that we had found another exit.

I turned to Oursk. *"We take out the guards at the end first. I'll take the warrior on the right, you the one on the left."*

"As you wish," he replied.

We crept forward, two patches of blackness nearly indistinguishable from the darkness in the tunnel.

Three hostile entities have failed to detect you! Your sneaking has increased to level 36.

I paused just outside the circle of light cast by the torches blazing at the goblins' backs. I didn't think I would remain hidden once I entered the light, but there were only three goblins. Readying myself, I dashed forward.

Three hostile entities have detected you! You are no longer hidden.

Two steps into the light, I was spotted. Pushing back their chairs, the warriors rushed to their feet. "There be two!" the goblin in the middle yelled.

I closed in on my target. He rushed forward to meet me, swinging his axe. Out of the corner of my eye, I saw the other two warriors converge on Oursk. The goblins had reacted quicker than I expected, and I adjusted my own tactics accordingly.

I ducked out of the way of my foe's flailing axe, and instead of continuing the engagement, I touched one of my swords to his arm while simultaneously channeling stamina through the blade.

A level 14 goblin warrior has failed a physical resistance check! You have crippled your target's right arm for 3 seconds. Your shortswords has increased to level 30.

Energy gushed out of me, rushing from my center, through my palm, out the tip of my blade, and into the goblin. The warrior's right arm went abruptly slack, and the two-handed axe in his hands sagged down.

Startled, the goblin dropped his axe.

It was the perfect moment for me to strike, but a strange weakness was afflicting me. Finding myself suddenly lightheaded, I almost stumbled and fell.

I swore, realizing what had happened. *How much stamina did the ability drain?* Too much from the feel of it. I had been careless and distracted and hadn't thought to replenish my stamina before the battle or question the energy cost of my new abilities.

Not a mistake I'll be making again.

I staggered past the crippled goblin and, pulling together my concentration, fought off the weakness plaguing me. My gaze snapped back into focus, and I thrust my blade into the back of one of the goblins attacking Oursk.

You have critically injured a goblin warrior.

The warrior collapsed, and his companion turned to strike at me, but he foolishly left himself open to attack from the dire wolf. Oursk seized the opportunity and, leaping forward, bore the goblin to the ground.

I left the pair for the dire wolf to finish and spun around to my original opponent. His arm was functional again. Leaning over, he picked up his axe.

I lunged forward and struck at the goblin while he was still off-balance. He parried away my blade, but I struck again with my other blade too quickly for him to block again.

You have injured a goblin warrior.

My blade bit through the goblin's hide armor and drew a line down his torso. The warrior yelped and tried to retreat. I didn't let him. Stepping inside the arc of his axe, I buried both my blades in his belly.

You have killed a goblin warrior!

I turned around to see Oursk finishing the last goblin. I sat down on one of the vacant chairs. *"Call the others,"* I said with a weary smile and rested my head on the table.

~ ~ ~

Five minutes later, after munching through two field rations, the sudden weariness that had afflicted me during the skirmish faded away.

I was still tired and needed proper rest, but I felt as if I could go on a while longer. Aira and the pups had rejoined us. Pushing myself to my feet and I went to inspect the grilled-metal gate and surprisingly found it locked.

Setting a hand on the gate, I pushed, but it refused to budge.

"What's wrong?" Oursk asked.

"The gate is locked," I answered.

"That is strange," he replied. *"When the goblins brought us into the dungeon, it was open."*

I studied the wolf curiously. *"You were captured outside the dungeon?"* I asked, realizing I didn't know how the dire wolves had come to be in the dungeon. I had assumed that, like the goblins, they had been brought in by the Master.

"Yes," he replied. *"The valley this tunnel leads to is our pack's hunting grounds. When the goblin tribe came, they stumbled onto our lair while most of the pack was absent. Those of us that were present fought, but many were captured."* Oursk sighed. *"Even more died."*

"I'm sorry," I said, unable to think of anything more comforting to say. *"Why did the goblins invade the valley?"*

"To enter this dungeon." Oursk bowed his head sadly. *"Somehow, the Dark managed to tunnel an entrance to the Endless Dungeon from our home without us realizing it. They've been using it to funnel resources into their sectors for years."*

I nodded thoughtfully, realizing there was still much of this world that I didn't understand, not least of which was what purpose the many dungeon sectors served.

Leaving the wolf alone with his memories, I leaned down and inspected the lock. It had a faint bluish tinge to it. Understanding dawned. I had the means to open the gate already. I retrieved the chief's keyring from my pack and tried the first of its magical keys. It worked, and the lock turned easily.

Pushing open the gate, I walked through.

CHAPTER 47: THE WAY OUT

Oursk and Aira took the lead again, with the pups following behind. There was new energy to the beasts' steps, and I imagined they were eager to return to their pack.

The ground began to slope more steeply upwards, and it was not long before I noticed the passage had begun to brighten. Squinting, I peered down the tunnel. In the far distance, I made out a bright source of light. White light. *The exit,* I thought. I hurried my steps, feeling a measure of excitement too. A minute later, I reached the source of light.

My face fell as I realized what it was. It was not daylight as I'd first thought, but rather a shimmering curtain of bright white that stretched across the entirety of the tunnel.

The dire wolves were standing in front of the energy field. Aira looked back at me. *"The field is harmless,"* she said. *"We can cross."* So saying, she and the other wolves passed through, proving the truth of her words. *"Come,"* the dire wolf mother called from the other side. I couldn't see her anymore, but her words carried to me clearly.

I stepped forward and tentatively held out the palm of my hand an inch from the field. It gave off no heat that I could sense, and was fully opaque, which made me slightly hesitant. Who knew what lay beyond?

Still, the shimmering curtain was not unlike the portal I had used to enter the dungeon, and that was what I took it to be. *It must be safe. The dire wolves have passed through,* I thought and stepped into the field.

Congratulations, Michael, you have discovered an exit from the Endless Dungeon. This portal leads directly from sector 14,913 to the surface of the Forever Kingdom. This location is a key point and has been added to your Logs.

Transfer through portal commencing...
...
...
Passage denied!

This exit is controlled by the faction: Awakened Dead. Only players sworn to the faction's Powers or Marked by the Dark are permitted to use this portal.

Your task: <u>Escape the Dungeon</u> has been updated. You have discovered the location of the sector's exit portal without fulfilling the original objectives. However, you've found your way blocked. Revised objective: Find a means of using the sector 14,913 exit portal.

You have been allocated a new task: <u>Find your own way out</u>! Your attempt to use the sector 14,913 exit portal has been unexpectedly stymied, and the Adjudicator has seen fit to grant you an alternate task. Your new objective is to discover another way out of the sector. This task and the task: Escape the Dungeon are mutually exclusive. Only one of the two can be completed.

I bounced back from the portal. My face and foot stung from the shock the energy field had dealt them, but I barely noticed.

"What the hell is this, Gnat?" I snarled.

"Hmm?" the skeletal bat asked, his attention on the portal.

"I can't use the exit! What's going on?"

The familiar looked at me silently for a moment. "What did the Game say?"

"That I've been denied passage," I growled.

"Did it say why?"

My eyes narrowed. He seemed to be evading my question. "The Game informed me," I said between gritted teeth, "that it's because I'm not sworn to the Master and don't bear a Mark of the Dark."

Gnat ducked his head, not meeting my eyes. "That's unfortunate," he muttered.

"What is?" I asked sharply.

Gnat hesitated before answering. "I suspect you've gone about the Master's task the wrong way. If you obtained your Classes before coming here, you probably wouldn't have noticed or, uhm, been stopped by the portal."

"That's a non-answer, Gnat," I said, staring at him hard-eyed. "How do I use it now?"

The skeletal bat blew out a breath. "I'm not sure," he admitted. "But perhaps if you explore the other dungeon sections, you might find an answer there."

I bit off a curse. "What's a Mark of the Dark?" I asked, trying another tack.

"Nothing you need worry about," Gnat assured me. "When you complete your first task, you'll find out all you need to know about it."

I opened my mouth. It was on the tip of my tongue to tell him I'd already completed a task, but I closed it with a snap as I came to my senses. That was not information I wanted to share with Gnat, especially not given these latest developments. Seething in silence, I glared at the skeletal bat. What the Game had told me about Marks did not lead me to believe I should take them lightly, despite Gnat's words to the contrary.

"You know, you still haven't told me about the boss' loot," Gnat said suddenly.

"What's that?"

"Did you find a Class in the loot chests?" the bat asked. "A master Class one, by any chance?"

I stared mutely at the bat for a drawn-out moment before answering grudgingly. "No, but I found an advanced one. I'm a psionic now."

Now that I knew I was going to be stuck in the dungeon longer, I saw no reason to hide my new Class from the familiar. It would only make him suspicious, and besides, once Gnat saw me use simple charm in battle, he was sure to figure out my Class anyway.

"Ah, only a standard Class," Gnat replied. "That's unfortunate."

Oursk emerged through the curtain of white, interrupting further conversation. *"What's wrong, Michael? Why do you not follow?"*

At the dire wolf's reappearance, I felt relief wash over me. I had been worried about them. *"The portal isn't allowing me to pass,"* I said, which raised an interesting point.

I turned back to Gnat. "Why did the portal stop me and not the wolves? Do they belong to the Master's faction?"

The familiar snorted. "Of course not. The portal is configured to interrogate players only. Most beasts and other creatures can pass through unaffected. The wolves are—"

Gnat broke off as Aira and the pups also reappeared. A strange gleam entered the bat's eyes as his gaze slid from the wolves to me. "I think... I think I know how you may get through the portal."

I just stared at the familiar, waiting for him to go on.

Gnat slid across my shoulder and placed his mouth next to my ear. "Killing the wolves may just do the trick and earn you the Mark you need," he whispered.

I jerked back my head and stared at the skeletal bat in disgust. "No," I said.

"If you want to escape, it's the easiest way."

"No," I repeated firmly again.

"But—" the bat protested.

I shoved Gnat off my shoulder, not willing to listen to anything further he had to say on the matter. "Go away," I ordered.

Muttering angrily, the bat flapped away. Aira watched the familiar vanish down the tunnel. *"What did the Dark creature say?"*

"Nothing of importance," I said. Changing the subject, I explained my predicament.

Aira fell silent, but on the fringes of my mind, I sensed telepathic sendings pass between her and her mate. *"Oursk and I have talked over the matter,"* she said finally. *"He will accompany you while you search for another exit."*

I shook my head. *"Thank you for the offer,"* I said gravelly to Oursk, *"but I must decline. You have your pack to take care of."*

The dire wolves gazed at me searchingly. *"Are you sure?"*

"I am," I said. *"The dungeon is dangerous but less so for me than you. I can be reborn. You cannot. Go, return to your pack."*

The wolf sire bowed his head, acknowledging my decision. The pups rushed forward to lick my hands and say goodbye.

"Take care, human," Aira said in farewell. *"And if you ever escape this dungeon, seek out our pack. You will be received as a friend."*

I nodded my thanks and, after watching the dire wolves leave, turned away and headed back into the dungeon.

CHAPTER 48: MAKING NEW CHOICES

As I retraced my steps through the tunnel, I wondered if I had made the right decision in rejecting Oursk's offer and Gnat's 'suggestion.'

But even after considering the matter as coldly and rationally as I could, I couldn't stomach the thought of killing the wolves. Betraying my allies was not something I thought I would ever be comfortable with, no matter how much it benefited me personally.

I do not betray my friends.

The thought resonated with me, and it felt as if I had rediscovered a core tenet of who I had been. A small smile stole on my face at the realization.

My thoughts drifted to the dire wolves. But even after giving the issue considerable thought, I was convinced I had made the right decision in rejecting Oursk's offer.

Everything I had told the wolf was true. He had his pack to care for, and unlike me, he couldn't be reborn, but more than that, I feared what could happen to the wolf in a sector controlled by the Awakened Dead. If it came to it, I wasn't sure that I could protect Oursk from the Master's minions, other candidates, or even... Gnat.

The more I learned about the Game and myself, the less I believed that the Master's interest and my own were aligned. I was no longer certain I trusted Gnat. And of the Master, I was even more suspicious. I feared I was being manipulated, but to what end? That I still didn't know.

Even worse, I worried if I pushed too hard against the tide, if I questioned the direction I was being driven in too much, then the Master's minion would turn on me. And I couldn't in good conscience put Oursk in the center of all that. The wolves had suffered enough at the Master's hands.

So, what do I do now?

Keep my ears open and plod onward, I decided, *and hope that somewhere along the line, I figure out what game the Master is playing and find a way of escaping his reach.*

Returning my thoughts to the dungeon, I considered where to head next. There were still three avenues open for me to explore: the cavern occupied by Saben's gang, the passage blocked by the trolls, and the metal door at the end of this tunnel complex.

So, where to start? *The metal door,* I concluded. It was closest, and with most—if not all—the nearby goblins killed, it was the least risky of my three options.

With a destination in mind and a plan—of sorts—my steps firmed. Reaching the crossroads, I turned down the main passage and headed towards the door at its end.

~ ~ ~

Halfway down the main passage, Gnat rejoined me. "Are the wolves gone?" he asked.

I nodded. He didn't say any more on the subject, and neither did I. I had decided to let matters lie between the familiar and me. For now, anyway. I wouldn't act until I understood his game better. Until then, I planned on learning what I could from the bat.

Nearing the end of the passage, I saw torches were still burning up ahead. Despite the chaos that had raged in the rest of the tunnel complex, it looked like the guards at the metal door hadn't abandoned their post. I faded into the surroundings and crept onwards.

A little while later, I finally spotted the guards. The six appeared tense and alert. As I drew closer, I idly wondered what the guards had made of the new silence filling the tunnels. It perhaps explained the anxiety I saw on their faces. Reaching the very edge of the torchlight, I came to a stop and crouched down fully.

I checked my reserves of stamina first. It was at a healthy seventy percent and still slowly ticking upward from the food I had eaten earlier. *Good enough,* I thought. Returning my attention to the guard station, I scrutinized its layout and planned my attack.

My stealth would not serve me in this battle. The glare from the torches was too bright. But I *did* have a new means of tilting the odds in my favor. Loosening my swords in their scabbards, I got to work.

I reached into the pool of psi at the center of my consciousness and sent tendrils of will reaching out to my target—the largest and meanest looking of the goblins. The warrior was oblivious as I slipped into his mind. Instinctively, I knew what to do. Superimposing my will over the targets, I forced my wishes—*my* needs and *my* desires—upon his.

A level 14 goblin warrior has passed a mental resistance check! You have failed to charm your target. Your mental intrusion has gone undetected! Your telepathy has increased to level 2.

I bit off a curse. I was unhappy at the failure but also relieved at the goblin's continued ignorance of my presence. The skill gain, too, was not to be sniffed at. I could only assume that my telepathy had advanced because my attempted intrusion had evaded detection.

Readying myself, I tried again.

And failed once more.

Your mental intrusion has gone undetected! Your telepathy has increased to level 3.

I ground my teeth in frustration, but I wasn't ready to give up, not yet. *Again,* I told myself and sent my will reaching toward the goblin once more.

A level 14 goblin warrior has failed a mental resistance check! You have charmed your target for 10 seconds. Your telepathy has increased to level 5.

I heaved a sigh of relief. *Finally.*

I had complete control over the goblin, but the spell I had employed lacked subtlety. With it, I had wielded my will like a hammer—not the most precise of instruments—and while my domination of the goblin was absolute, I was only able to issue him with the most basic of commands.

The other warriors hadn't been alerted as to their companion's subversion. Aware that the clock was running down, I sent my order pulsing through my newly-forged mental link with the goblin, *"Attack."*

Obedience was instant. The charmed warrior drew his axe. In the same motion, I raced out of the shadows.

Five hostile entities have detected you!

Shouting warnings to each other—and still unaware of the danger in their midst—the other goblins drew their weapons and stepped toward me. Without even the least flicker of hesitation, the charmed warrior brought his axe down and caved in the skull of a smaller goblin in front of him before swinging around to slash at another on his right.

Your minion has killed two level 13 goblin warriors.

Surprised and shocked faces whipped around. "What are you—" a third goblin managed to get out before he, too, felt the bite of the bewitched warrior's axe.

Your minion has critically injured a goblin warrior.

Almost cleaved in half, the goblin crumpled to the ground. The other two warriors cursed their betrayer and spun around to attack him, leaving me forgotten behind them.

I sped forward, flying across the ground. Before I could reach the battling trio, though, the two hostiles buried their spears in the charmed warrior. An instant later, my spell lapsed, and the mental link tethering the axeman to my will snapped.

You have lost control over a level 14 goblin warrior.

But it was too late for the impaled goblin. His eyes grew round, and his mouth dropped open as he tried to say something. Before he could get the words out, the light in his eyes flickered out.

A goblin warrior has died.

The spearmen ripped out their spears and began turning around. But I was already amongst them. In a series of lightning attacks, I chopped left, then right, before thrusting out simultaneously with both my blades and skewering the pair.

You have killed a goblin warrior.
You have killed a goblin warrior.
Your shortswords has increased to level 31.
Your two weapon fighting has increased to level 26.

It was over quicker than I expected.

Panting slightly from adrenaline and exertion, I studied the aftermath. Only one goblin remained alive—the second warrior struck by the axeman. Blood gurgled out of his mouth, and he was panting frantically. I knelt beside the warrior.

"It's over," I said. Quietening his struggles, I slipped my blade under his armor and watched his life drain away.

You have killed a goblin warrior.

"You've come a long way," Gnat said from where he sat, almost forgotten on my shoulder.

I nodded wearily. I had. Killing was becoming second nature. My mind flew back to my first fumbling battle with the slime. It was hard to believe that it had been less than a day ago.

I was no longer that person. I was changed.

Evolved.

A killer.

I do what I must, I thought wearily as I levered myself back to my feet. Ignoring the bodies scattered on the ground, I moved to study the door.

It was locked.

Like the gate at the sector's exit, a bluish tinge covered its lock too. I pulled out the chief's keyring and tried the second magical key in the door. It fit perfectly.

But I didn't turn the lock. Not yet.

I was sure I had slain the last of the goblins in this tunnel complex, and I was safe, or as safe as I could be in a dungeon.

Before I moved on, it was time to give my body what it craved most—rest.

CHAPTER 49: MARKETS AND MORE

I didn't go to sleep immediately. First, I searched the tunnel complex from end to end again, making certain that I had indeed eliminated every last goblin.

Then I had a bath.

Finding a storeroom full of water barrels, I couldn't resist the desire to wash. I was covered in filth and grime, and while I had done my best to ignore my disgusting state, I stank. Dreadfully. Making extravagant use of the water, I scrubbed myself from head to foot and cleaned my bedraggled and torn—but still somehow whole—clothes.

I still didn't sleep after that.

Feeling somewhat human again, I decided to spend a few minutes meditating. Meditation was one of the skills I had learned with the psionic Class, and it was critical to restoring my reserves of psi.

Sinking down into a cross-legged stance, I closed my eyes and stilled my mind. Blocking out my awareness of everything and stopping my conscious musings, I focused only on the simple process of breathing. My thoughts drifted, and the pool of psi that lay in the pit of my subconsciousness stirred.

You have replenished 1% of your psi. Your psi is now at 71%. Your meditation has increased to level 2.

Psi flowed out of me and then in again. Over and over, in an endless loop. And ever-so-slowly, with every breath, the body of psi within me increased.

You have replenished 1% of your psi. Your meditation has increased to level 3.

Psi was... different. Energy of the mind, simply the act of relinquishing conscious thought and letting the mind rein free was enough to replenish it. In a way, the process was similar to sleeping, but mediation of the sort I undertook was more focused in its intent and thus worked far faster to restore my psi.

You have replenished 1% of your psi. Your meditation has increased to level 4.

Meditating was a strangely passive act, though, and one I struggled to perform initially, but once I fell into a rhythm of easy breathing, it became more natural, and my psi began replenishing faster.

Your meditation has increased to level 5.
...
...
Your meditation has increased to level 10.
Congratulations, Michael! Your skill in meditation has reached rank 1, increasing your psi recovery rate and decreasing the skill learning rate.
...
...
Your meditation has increased to level 15.
Your psi is now at 100%.

I opened my eyes. My reserves of psi were at full capacity again. "Excellent," I murmured.

I found it curious that I had not yet found any stamina or mana potions, or for that matter, psi ones. I had assumed at first that was because they were rarer than health potions, but now after experiencing meditation, I wondered if it was because they were simply unnecessary.

I turned to the bat sitting beside me. "Gnat, why haven't I found other types of potions?"

The familiar glanced at me. "Like what?"

"Ones to restore energy. A mana potion, for instance."

Gnat snorted. "Those are always in high demand and almost always bought out by the high-ranked players and merchants as soon as they are placed for auction on the markets. As a newbie, you won't come by them easily."

I rubbed my chin consideringly. "Are you saying health potions aren't as valued?"

Gnat chuckled. "Think about where you are."

"Huh?"

"You're in a sector of the Endless Dungeon controlled by the Awakened Dead."

The skeletal bat's response was unenlightening and I stared back at him blankly.

Seeing my look, Gnat laughed, then added, "The *dead* don't need health potions."

I frowned, trying to make sense of his words. "I don't understand what you're getting at. What difference does it make in which sector of the dungeon I am in? And for that matter, what do markets and auctions have to do with game-generated loot?"

Gnat sighed. "Sometimes I forgot how clueless you newbies are," he muttered. Before I could protest this insult, he continued, "The items in loot chests are *not* created by the Game."

I blinked. "They're not?"

Gnat shook his head. "The Adjudicator buys the items through the global auction and determines their value based on local markets."

My brows drew together as I tried to wrap my mind around the idea of the Game—or Adjudicator—buying items. I found the concept strange but set aside the matter as I puzzled out the rest of Gnat's explanation. "Are you saying that the only reason I've been finding healing potions is because they are *unwanted* in the local markets?"

"Correct."

"So... when I leave the Awakened Dead's territory, healing potions won't be as easy to come by?"

Gnat snickered. "*If* you leave. But again, correct."

I thought about that for a bit. If what Gnat said was true, I would have to be more sparing with my healing potions than I had been so far. It did lead me to wonder about my other finds, though. Had the Game only been rewarding me with trash loot all along? "The other things I've found in the chests... are they also considered less desirable items?"

The familiar laughed. "You're catching on now. Wooden loot chests rarely contain much of value."

"Really?" I asked. "You expect me to believe skillbooks are worthless? And Class stones too?"

"They're not *entirely* worthless," Gnat replied, "but their value is certainly limited. The overall demand for skillbooks, Class stones, and ability tomes is far lower than consumables. Players will only ever use a particular type of skillbook once, but the same player could use hundreds, if not thousands of potions in his lifetime."

I nodded slowly, seeing Gnat's point. But what the bat was saying only held true if potion ingredients—and perhaps even alchemists themselves—were rare. I didn't dwell further on this aspect, though, and instead turned to the other matter that had piqued my interest. "Tell me about the auction and the markets. Where are they?"

"The global auction is a place called the Nexus," Gnat said. "It can be remotely accessed, but only by players with the merchant Class, and even they must pay a surcharge for the privilege. All other players must physically visit the Nexus to access the auction."

I nodded, understanding the gist, if not all, of the bat's explanation. "And what are the local markets?"

"They're just that," Gnat replied. "Marketplaces in individual sectors where merchants congregate. Usually, they're to be found in a safe zone, and every sector, be it in a dungeon or a region on the surface, has safe zones."

"Thank you, Gnat," I said, grateful for his explanations. While I had grown suspicious of the familiar's intentions, he was still my only source of information, and I was forced to depend on his Game expertise.

Rubbing my chin, I turned over what Gnat had said. It seemed that the Game had an intricate economic system. And if I was to make a home in this world, sooner or later, I would have to understand it more fully.

I yawned. But not right now.

Now it is time to sleep, I thought. Closing my eyes, I laid down on my bedroll and let unconsciousness claim me.

~ ~ ~

You have slept 10 hours. Stamina, mana, and psi reserves have been fully restored.

My eyes opened slowly. Sitting upright, I stretched. My body felt sore, and my muscles ached, but otherwise, I felt fully rested and reinvigorated.

The rest has done me good, I thought. I looked around. It was pitch black in the small and out-of-the-way room I had chosen to sleep in. I had not bothered trying to light the area. Torches would only attract unnecessary attention, and besides, I had long since grown comfortable with the dark.

I rose to my feet and strapped on my backpack. There was no use delaying. It was time to see what lay behind the metal door.

CHAPTER 50: BEHIND THE LOCKED DOOR

Opening the door was anticlimactic.

Turning the key in the lock, I pushed the door open and dropped into a crouch. Hidden in darkness —I had extinguished all the nearby torches—I waited for a reaction.

Nothing jumped out at me. All that lay on the other side of the door was more grey rock and dank air, at least as far as I could see. Leaving the door unlocked behind me, I cautiously ventured into the new passage. It was empty. Feeling more secure, I increased my pace as I slipped down the length of the tunnel.

Two hundred yards later, I stopped in surprise. The tunnel had come to an end, terminating in another metal door that was a near replica of the one I had just opened. With renewed caution, I crept up to the door and tried the handle.

It was locked.

Urgh, I despaired. *Have I wasted all this time on a dead end?*

I bent down and inspected the lock. It bore a bluish tinge. *Hmm... I wonder.* Pulling out the chief's keyring, I tried the same key I had on the previous door.

The lock turned smoothly.

Yes!

Smiling, I stepped through the door. Expecting to see only more dank tunnel, I nearly fell back in shock at the sight that greeted me.

I was in another large cavern. This one was different, though. Less than ten yards in front of me, it looked like the rocky ground had been sheared off, causing the floor to fall sharply away. It was the same all along the rim of the cavern. It was as if some giant hand had hollowed out the center of the cavern to form a bowl-shaped crater— one large enough to house a small village.

More surprisingly, the cavern was filled with soft light. The crater was carpeted with glowing mushrooms, and the ceiling was dotted with thousands of luminous crystals, making it brighter in the crater than a star-filled night sky. Yet it was neither the cavern's design nor the lighting that had me amazed.

It was the noise.

The crater was full of people, painted stalls, and tents. I spotted elves, dwarves, humans, gnomes, and undead. A low buzz of conversation hung over the sparse crowd moving through the stalls, and on the far end, I saw pavilions and marquees of all sizes and shapes.

"What is this place," I murmured under my breath, not expecting a response.

"It must be the safe zone," Gnat said.

I glanced at him. "The safe zone?"

He nodded. "It can't be anything else."

I turned back towards the crater with a stupefied look. *So close.* I couldn't believe it. All this time, I had been so close to safety and never knew it. *But I am here now. I've made it.* I ran my gaze over the people in the crater below. Most were dressed in white cotton shorts and shirts and were clearly candidates.

It seems like I am not the only one to reach this place.

But how had the other candidates made it here? They had obviously not ventured through the goblin complex. I searched the rim of the cavern with more care. The cavern's edges were the least well-lit area, and while I didn't spy another obvious entrance directly opposite me, I spotted a patch of blackness that *looked* like it could be a tunnel mouth.

My fascination with the cavern faded, and caution reasserted itself. Safe zone or not, I was not necessarily safe here. My fellow candidates could prove as dangerous as the goblins, if not more so.

I thought of Saben and his ilk. *If any of them are here...*

I glanced at the open door behind me. Thankfully, both it and I were shrouded in darkness, and it didn't look like my entry into the cavern had been observed. I realized, too, that a treasure trove lay behind me, one that I had largely been unable to loot because of weight limitations. But if there were merchants in the safe zone... I smiled. I could make a tidy sum selling all the goblins' weapons and armor—as long as the other players didn't realize where I was getting them from.

I need to keep my manner of entry a secret, I thought and locked the door behind me. *For as long as possible.* I turned back to the crater.

Now, how do I get down?

~ ~ ~

After further investigations, I discovered two ramps led into the crater, one on the left side of the cavern and the other on the right. At all other points, the walls of the crater appeared unscalable.

I didn't immediately proceed to either of the ramps, though. Staying hidden, I navigated a full circuit along the rim and confirmed that my initial assessment was correct—there was indeed only one other entrance into the safe zone, the passage opposite the metal door.

Standing in the tunnel mouth, I let my concealment fade. If anyone was watching, they would assume I had arrived through the passage. I was perhaps being overly cautious with my approach, but I wasn't about to take any unnecessary risks at this stage. With a relaxed stride, I made my way toward one of the crater's entrances.

The moment I set foot on the top of the ramp, a Game message opened in my mind.

Congratulations, Michael. You have discovered the safe zone of sector 14,913. This location is a key point and has been added to your Logs.

Safe zones are regions of the Game where players are prevented from taking hostile action against one another. Only players and Powers may enter a safe zone.

The regulations in the safe zone are strictly enforced by the Game. Do not attempt to harm another player. You will be given only one warning. Thereafter punishment will be swift and merciless.

Enjoy your stay!

I paused in my step and reread the message. *There is that mention of Powers again...* I opened my mouth to question Gnat about it, but the skeletal bat was flapping away. I glanced at him in surprise. "What's going on?"

The familiar circled my head. "I cannot enter the safe zone. I will join my brethren above and rejoin you when you leave."

Not waiting for my response, the skeletal bat shot up into the darkness. I tracked him with my gaze and saw him alight on the cavern roof and perch upside down on it. Besides Gnat, I made out the blur of other white shapes. My eyes narrowed. The small forms were others of Gnat's kind, more undead bats.

The familiar's departure, while something of a surprise, made sense given the Adjudicator's message. I turned back to the safe zone and smiled.

It seemed that I was on my own.

CHAPTER 51: THE RICH AND THE POOR

I resumed walking down the ramp, feeling a greater measure of trepidation now that I was alone. For all that I had begun to question Gnat's motives, I had grown used to his constant presence at my side, and suddenly bereft of it, I felt slightly lost.

Stop being foolish, Michael, I scolded myself. *You're not alone.* There were plenty of other candidates around to speak to. And more importantly, in the safe zone, I would finally have an opportunity to allay my fears regarding Gnat's motives—or confirm them.

I studied the safe zone more closely. The ramp led down into a wide central avenue. Market booths encroached on either side of the road. Some of the stalls were little more than open wagons parked next to the road; others were elaborate wooden constructions with roofs and walls, but without fail, all the booths were boldly painted and covered with symbols.

Every stall was manned too, by merchants of all shapes, sizes, and species—each and every one of whom was presently staring at me.

My brows crinkled. *Why are they looking at me like that?* My eyes drifted to the figures dressed in shorts and shirts walking between the booths, and my frown deepened. Something about the candidates struck me as off, but I couldn't put my finger on it. Their gazes, too, were fixed on me.

Alright... I thought, realizing that I had erred in some way and that my arrival was not going to be as unnoticed as I'd assumed. I took a cautious step off the ramp and onto the road.

No one moved. No one spoke. My thoughts churned. What was going on here? *What does everyone find so fascinating about me? The merchants have already met other candidates, so it can't be that. Why then—*

My thoughts ground to a halt as I finally realized what my brain was trying to tell me: none of the candidates had any gear. They were all in their starter kits: pristine white shorts and shirts.

Where is their armor? Their weapons? Now that I had noticed the candidates' lack of dress, I identified the emotion I saw in their eyes: avarice. Hungry gazes roved over the twin swords hanging on my hip, the pack on my back, and the cloak draped over my shoulders. I gulped. *That's not creepy at all. They look like a pack of starving dogs that have spotted supper.*

If this was anywhere but a safe zone, I would've run. But I needed information and gear, and had gold to burn. *I'm safe here,* I told myself firmly, quenching the urge to flee.

Steadfastly ignoring the many eyes upon me, I approached the nearest market stall. It was one of the more elaborate ones. Its roof and side walls were painted black and embellished with pictures of a bird. *A crow,* I realized as I got closer. The front of the booth was a wooden countertop resting on a half-wall.

Two cloaked and hooded figures were behind the counter, manning the stall. I couldn't see their faces, but I could feel their eyes on me. I noticed something else too. There was a haze to the air around the two merchants, almost like an aura, a feeling of death and... rot.

What in the world—? I stopped suddenly. Narrowing my eyes, I studied the shimmer around the pair. It was indistinct, and I couldn't really be sure I was actually seeing anything. *Am I imagining things?* A Game message opened in my mind.

This entity bears a Mark of Minor Dark.
This entity bears a Mark of Greater Dark.

Both merchants were Marked, I realized, and I was seeing their spirit signatures. Which also meant they were seeing mine. Did that account for their stares? *Perhaps.* But with everyone else staring at me as well, there was no way to tell.

Given everything else I had learned of the Dark so far, I was wary of entangling myself further with those associated with it, but I *was* in the middle of a sector controlled by a Dark faction and couldn't reasonably expect to avoid the Dark's minions altogether. I sighed and resumed my approach toward the merchants.

Just as I got to the stall, I saw a flicker of movement further up the avenue. Two candidates were hurrying away, whispering furiously to each other as they headed deeper into the safe zone. The other candidates followed more slowly after the pair, and soon the road was empty but for me and the many merchants in their booths. I frowned.

Now, what is that all about?

"Well, isn't this a surprise," a voice rasped. "A live one, finally."

I turned back to the stall. The merchants were inspecting me. From under their hoods, two sets of burning red eyes studied me as if considering a curious insect.

"And Marked too," the second noted.

"But what pathetic Marks they are," said the first merchant.

"Should we serve him?" his companion asked.

"Hmm," mused the first. "His Marks are lesser ones only. He can be redeemed yet."

"But does he deserve redemption?" the second asked.

Tired of being ignored and listening to their one-sided conversation, I intervened before the other merchant could respond. "Who are you?" I asked brusquely.

There was a moment of silence as if the pair were startled by my rudeness or temerity. "We are merchants of the Awakened Dead faction," the first said. "I am Vomer, and my companion is Velath."

"We serve the Master, boy," Velath added. "So you best be careful in how you address us."

I ignored the implicit threat in his tone and shifted my gaze to the pictures covering their stall. "Is the Master's insignia a crow?" I asked, recalling that the glass chips I had been given so long ago had also borne the symbol of a crow.

"It is," Vomer said.

I studied the pair again. "Where are your familiars?" I asked.

Velath snickered. "We don't have any. Only foolish candidates need them."

It was on the tip of my tongue to ask why, but I bit back the question in time. These two served the Master, I reminded myself, and it was not likely they would be forthcoming on the matter of the familiars. *Better not to rouse their suspicions unnecessarily.*

"You can see my Marks," I said, stating the obvious.

"We can," Velath said. He leaned over the counter and sniffed. "And they stink. You will do well to rid yourself of both. The Master will not take kindly to them."

I stepped back. I was not the only one who bore a stench.

Before I could respond to Velath, Vomer reached down beneath the counter and pulled out a package swathed in black silk. "But that is why we are here: to help you find your way." Placing the package on the counter, he unwrapped its silk covering to reveal six gold marbles. "Feast your eyes on these, candidate. "I guarantee you won't find better in the Sector," he finished with a trace of amusement.

My gaze dropped to the gold marbles, instantly mesmerized by the sight of them. They were Class stones.

Master Class stones.

CHAPTER 52: MASTERFUL BAIT

I reached out involuntarily to the Class stones but stopped myself before I could touch them. I glanced up at the merchants. "May I?" I asked, licking my lips.

Vomer chuckled. "Go ahead and inspect them."

"And don't even think of stealing them," Velath added. "The Game will consider any attempted theft a hostile action."

Good to know, I thought absently and willed the Game to reveal more about the objects before me.

This stone contains the path of: a pestilence druid. It is a master Class that confers a player with four skills: dark magic, necromancy, earth magic, and light armor. This Class also permanently boosts your Magic attribute by +3 and your Faith attribute by +3. This is a Dark Class.

Master Classes grant you a free Class ability, and their skills start at rank 1. Classes attuned to a specific Force—Light, Dark, or Shadow—contain alignment restrictions. All traits of a Force Class will increase in strength as your Mark advances.

A Dark Class will Mark you as a follower of the Dark and will prevent you from wielding purely shadow-based or light-based abilities.

This stone contains the path of: a nether wizard. It is a master Class that confers a player with four skills: dark magic, necromancy, fire magic, and air magic. This Class also permanently boosts your Magic attribute by +3 and your Faith attribute by +3. This is a Dark Class.

This stone contains the path of: a death cleric. It is a master Class that confers a player with four skills: dark magic, necromancy, medium armor, and a medium weapon skill of the player's choice. This Class also permanently boosts your Faith attribute by +3 and your Constitution attribute by +3. This is a Dark Class.

This stone contains the path of: a dark paladin. It is a master Class that confers a player with four skills: dark magic, heavy shields, heavy armor, and a heavy weapon skill of the player's choice. This Class also permanently boosts your Faith attribute by +2, your Strength by +2, and your Constitution attribute by +2. This is a Dark Class.

This stone contains the path of: a vile monk. It is a master Class that confers a player with four skills: dark magic, necromancy, chi, and telekinesis. This Class also permanently boosts your Faith attribute by +3 and your Mind attribute by +3. This is a Dark Class.

This stone contains the path of: a cult assassin. It is a master Class that confers a player with four skills: dark magic, necromancy, poisoning, and thieving. This Class also permanently boosts your Faith attribute by +3 and your Dexterity attribute by +3. This is a Dark Class.

I whistled soundlessly as I digested the information provided by the Game. All six Classes provided a host of benefits. In particular, the skills provided by the path of the pestilence druid, nether wizard, and cult assassin appealed to me.

Any one of the three Classes would nicely complement my existing skills, and ordinarily, I would not have hesitated to purchase them—if not for the Classes other so-called 'benefits.'

The common thread running between the six Classes had not escaped my notice. All were considered Dark Classes. I read the line that had given me pause again: '*A Dark Class will Mark you as a follower of the Dark.*' It made me wonder about the true purpose behind the merchants' offerings.

Before I could question them further on it, though, another Game message opened in my mind.

Your task: <u>Escape the Dungeon</u> has been updated. You have discovered a means of using the sector 14,913 exit portal. Revised objective: Adopt a Dark Class or otherwise use the sector 14,913 exit portal. This task and the task: <u>Find your own way out</u>, are mutually exclusive.

So, I thought, ruminating over the latest Game message. It made clear that by adopting a Dark Class, I would become Marked by the Dark. I glanced up at the Vomer. "Are these the only Classes you have?"

"Yes," he said simply.

I had suspected that to be the case. "How much are they?"

"One gold each," the merchant replied.

My eyes widened. *Only one gold?* I couldn't claim to be an expert on prices in the Forever Kingdom, but that sounded dirt cheap for a master Class stone, and it only heightened my suspicions.

Mistaking my expression, Vomer added hastily, "Our prices are open to negotiation, of course. If you don't have that much, perhaps we can come to some other agreement."

Velath scrutinized me closely. "How much *do* you have? We aren't running a charity here."

I stayed silent. I was tempted by the merchants' offer. With any of the six Classes, I could fill my one open Class slot, obtain the magic I desired, *and* obtain the Mark of the Dark I needed to escape the dungeon.

But I was too wary of doing that, not without further investigations. "I'm not yet ready to buy," I said to Vomer, making no attempt to disguise the regret in my voice. "Perhaps later."

"Of course," the merchant replied, sweeping the Class stones off the counter. "Browse the other merchants' wares if you wish. I promise none of them will have anything comparable."

My heart sank. Somehow, I didn't think Vomer was lying.

"Junk," Velath growled. "That's all you will find at the rabbles' stalls."

Ignoring Velath's interjection, I ran my gaze over the rest of their stock. There were multiple other objects stored on the shelves. I turned back to Vomer. "What else do you have for sale?"

"Unfortunately," the merchant replied, following my gaze, "those items are only available for those sworn to the Dark. Perhaps if you purchase a Class stone, we can be persuaded to sell you something else." He paused. "A discount wouldn't be out of the question either."

I coughed to cover my reaction. Vomer was doing a good job of sweetening the bait. *I better get out of here before I give way to temptation,* I thought. "I'll consider it," I promised the merchant and turned away, but paused halfway as something else occurred to me.

"What are you?" I asked, swinging back to the merchant.

"What do you mean?" Vomer asked, sounding confused.

"I mean, what species are you?" I gestured to his hood. "I can't tell with that hiding your face."

"Ah," the merchant replied and pulled back his hood to reveal a corpse-pale face, red eyes, and a pair of elongated fangs in a grinning mouth. "We are vampires, of course."

I beat a hasty retreat after that.

Standing in the center of the avenue, I studied the other stalls. The merchants at them were all watching me, but none beckoned to me or attempted to attract my attention in any manner. *Strange sort of merchants,* I thought.

No candidates were in sight either. Wherever they had disappeared to, none had returned. I considered the stalls again. Most were painted black, and a small number were colored in various shades of grey. Nearly half of the booths proudly displayed the symbol of a crow. All those that did were black-colored, I noted.

Do the colors signify anything? I wondered.

Perhaps it indicated the alignment of the stall owners. The more I learned about the Game, the more I realized the importance of its three driving Forces: Light, Dark, and Shadow. The Adjudicator, I recalled, had mentioned the Forces during my welcome message, but since then, I had barely encountered any mention of them—that is until I obtained my Marks. Now I saw their influence everywhere.

Reminded of my Marks, I looked more closely at the vendors themselves. The air around each shimmered suggestively as I focused on them. *They are all Marked,* I realized.

One by one, I read the Marks of each merchant, and quickly reached the conclusion that my surmise had been correct: the colors of the booths *did* indicate their owner's allegiance. Of the ten merchants I could see, nine bore a Mark of Dark. A few—those with grey-colored stalls—also carried a Mark of Shadow.

No merchant bore a Mark of Light.

And only one vendor didn't carry any Marks of Dark at all. Following some half-understood instinct, I made my way to the merchant in question's stall.

CHAPTER 53: THE NATURE OF FORCES

The merchant I approached was elven, a swarthy male with silver hair and storm-grey eyes. *A dark elf?* His hair was neatly plaited and reached down to his waist. He was dressed in a tailored suit, with each piece dyed a different shade of grey. As I drew closer, I studied his Marks again.

This entity bears a Mark of Greater Shadow, and the Mark of an Under-dweller.

The first Mark was easy enough to interpret. The second was less so, but it didn't obviously denote allegiance to the Dark, and for the time being, I was assuming the merchant was not allied with the Master.

The dark elf's booth was also the smallest. It was a wagon with boarded-up sides and top, and a single tiny window from which the merchant looked out. When it became clear I was heading his way, the dark elf disappeared from the window frame and a second later stood outside his wagon to greet me.

"Greetings player," the merchant said, executing an elaborate bow. "Welcome to the central branch of the Hamish and Spuren Trading Company. How may Hamish serve you today?" His eyes twinkled merrily and his face was split in a broad grin.

I paused, taken aback by the elf's extravagant welcome. Since entering the Game, I had not encountered such a... jubilant and merry individual, and in this bleak underworld, I had a hard time believing that he was truly what he appeared to be.

"Uh... uhm, are you Hamish?" I asked, not sure if he had introduced himself in the third person or whether he was referring to someone else.

"I am, indeed," he said, beaming. "And if I may, what is your name, my splendid fellow?"

"Michael," I said. "And I am not a player. Not yet, anyway."

"Oh, but—" Hamish broke off, his eyes darting momentarily sideways. The other merchants were watching closely, I saw. "It is a pleasure to meet you, my friend," the dark elf continued blithely, making no attempt to explain his bitten-off words. "What can I do for you?"

"You are a merchant?"

"Of course! Would you like to see my wares?"

"Please."

"Then come around, fine sir. I assure you I stock only goods of the best quality."

Uh-huh, I thought, not buying his whole salesman spiel. Hamish led me around the other side of his wagon, and coincidently out of sight of the other merchants. Was that deliberate?

But there was no change in the merchant's demeanor as he addressed me again. "Now, what may I interest you in?" Hamish asked, eagerly rubbing his hands together.

The wooden panels on this side of the wagon had been taken down, exposing the shelves inside. They were stacked to the brim with an assortment of objects: weapons, armor, jewelry, and books. A bedroll had been spread out on the floor of the wagon, and I spied a small traveling stove too. It appeared that not only was the wagon Hamish's shop, but it was also his living quarters as well.

"Can I see the Class stones you have available?" I asked.

Hamish hung his head. "Alas, I can't sell you any Class stones."

"Why not?" I asked, more sharply than I intended.

The dark elf winced. "Only merchants from Ere— uhm... I mean, the Master's faction are permitted to sell Class stones in this sector."

I stared at him in consternation. "But isn't this a safe zone? How can the Master—or anyone for that matter—stop you from selling what you want?"

The merchant chuckled weakly. "Ah, to be young again and ignorant in the ways of the world." Seeing my frown, he added, "Technically, you are correct, young man. I can sell whatever I wish, but I—and every other merchant—must still travel between the safe zones to peddle our wares. If I sell you a Class stone or break any of the Master's other rules, I will earn his ire." He shuddered. "And I assure you, you don't want the Master for an enemy."

I sighed, better understanding Vomer's earlier certainty now. I thought for a second before speaking again. "Alright, maybe you can't sell me any Class stones, but perhaps you can answer a question about them?"

Hamish bit his lips but didn't reply.

"Surely answering a question doesn't break any of the Master's rules?"

Still the merchant hesitated.

"I promise to buy something from you if you do," I said, a wheedling tone entering my voice.

The dark elf finally wavered. "Go ahead then. Ask your question."

I smiled in relief. "What does it mean for a Class to be aligned with a Force?"

Hamish drew his brows together. "I'm not sure I take your meaning."

I looked around furtively. No one was nearby, but I still lowered my voice. "What I want to know is why are the Master's merchants so eager to sell me a Dark Class."

"Ah," Hamish said, his expression falling. "Answering that question comes perilously close to breaking one of the Master's rules." He sighed heavily. "But you *did* promise to buy something." He paused, glancing at me suspiciously.

"I will," I confirmed.

"Nothing cheap?" he pushed.

"Nothing cheap," I promised, even though I had no idea what constituted cheap.

Hamish sighed again, but didn't back out of our deal. "Very well. Force Classes come with a host of both restrictions and benefits over standard Classes, although it is widely believed that the benefits outweigh their restrictions." Hamish paused. "The one characteristic that all Force Classes have in common is that over time they increase the player's affinity with his chosen Force to the detriment of his other Marks. It is why they are popular."

I rubbed at my chin as I considered the merchant's words. "So, if I adopt a Dark aligned Class, it will reduce my affinity for Light and Shadow?

Hamish nodded. "Correct. Not only that, but over time the Dark Mark will erase the other Marks from you altogether. This is the primary reason why players take on an aligned Class: to keep their allegiance to their chosen Force true and unsullied. If you choose a dark-aligned Class it doesn't necessarily guarantee that you will become sworn to the Dark, but to rise in the ranks of any other Force will be incredibly hard— if not impossible."

My brows crinkled in thought. "But why would anyone want to join any of the Forces? Why not remain neutral?"

"Ah, that is a much larger question," Hamish said with a chuckle. "And one I am not well-placed to answer. Suffice to say that to stand aside from the Forces is impossible." The merchant's smile returned and he clapped his hands together. "Now I have kept my end of the bargain. Will you keep yours?"

Reluctantly, I nodded.

CHAPTER 54: THE GREY MERCHANT'S WARES

I spent a moment considering what to spend my money on: equipment, consumables, skills, or abilities.

Skills are my first priority, I decided. They required time to train and, unlike consumables and equipment, couldn't be lost if I died. Next would be abilities. Only once I had a good mix of both would I turn to my gear.

"Show me your skillbooks," I said.

"Coming right up," Hamish said and scurried back into the wagon. He returned almost immediately and held out his finds to me, bobbing excitedly up and down as I inspected them.

I took the proffered skillbooks. Disappointingly, there were only three. They covered the skills of light armor, longswords, and air magic.

"These are the only ones you have?" I asked. Of the three, only light armor was useable to me, and I had four skill slots to fill. I had been hoping for better.

Unaware of the unhappy direction of my thoughts, Hamish simply nodded in response. Dejected, I bowed my head to consider the skillbooks again.

"Of course," Hamish added after a moment, "these three are only samples. I can get whatever you want."

I lifted my head to stare blankly at him. "Huh?"

"I am a merchant, you know," Hamish said with a twinkle in his eyes. I still didn't take his meaning.

The dark elf's smile faded. "You *do* know what being a merchant means, don't you?"

I shook my head mutely.

"How did you manage to get to level eighteen and still not know these things?" Hamish asked disbelievingly.

I blinked. "You know my level?"

"Of course, I do!" he exclaimed. "I analyzed you."

Something else occurred to me. "Hamish," I asked slowly, "are you a player?"

The merchant looked at me strangely. "Did you not get a message when you entered the safe zone? Only players and Powers may enter its borders."

"Uh, right," I said, my face reddening. I recognized the look Hamish was giving me now. *He thinks I'm an idiot.* With good cause too. I shouldn't have forgotten something so simple.

I sighed. "I'm sorry, Hamish. Please excuse my ignorance. I should have realized you and the other merchants are players. If you don't mind, can you explain how you will get more skillbooks?"

The dark elf grinned. "Of course, anything for a customer!"

I smiled wanly. "Thanks."

"I have the merchant Class," Hamish began, "which means I can access the sector containing the Nexus from anywhere in the Forever Kingdom." He paused. "Do you know what the Nexus is?"

I nodded, relieved that I wasn't *wholly* ignorant.

"Good," he replied. "That makes the explanation easier. Simply put, I contact my partner in the Nexus. He buys what I need and sends it back to me."

"How though?" I asked, intrigued.

"Aether magic," he replied simply.

"Aether magic?"

"It's a form of non-combative magic used primarily for long-distance communications and transporting goods and people across the aether," Hamish explained. "Only a few Classes have access to the skill."

"Interesting," I murmured. "How long does it take to send something through the aether?"

"The transfer itself is instantaneous. The only delay experienced is a result of the spell casting time," Hamish answered. "Which depending on the distance involved and the mass being moved, can be anywhere between five minutes and one day."

"Huh," I said, impressed. "So you can get any item I need?" I asked, getting back to the matter of the skillbooks.

"Well... I might have exaggerated slightly," Hamish said, looking sheepish, "but I can certainly source anything *within reason*."

I smiled at the merchant's qualification. The dark elf looked at me expectantly. "So what do you want?"

I scratched at my chin. When it came right down to it, I really didn't know enough to make a choice from an unknown set of options. I had been assuming I would be presented with a limited range to choose from. "I'm not sure," I said. "Can you take me through the options?"

Hamish's face did not show the slightest concern, despite the scale of my request. "Of course, anything for a customer!"

~ ~ ~

Things worked out simpler than I expected.

Hamish had a slim leather-bound book, proudly titled: 'Hamish and Spuren Trading Company Catalog of Skills and Abilities.' The catalog laid out every skill and ability Hamish and his partner were able to provide. The moment my eyes fell on the book in the merchant's hands, I couldn't stop myself from grabbing it and burying my nose in its pages.

The catalog was a treasure trove of information. While the book did not contain detailed descriptions, it provided me with what I desperately sought: an understanding of the bigger picture, at least as it related to skills and abilities. For a newbie like me, the slim volume was worth its weight in gold.

"How much for the catalog?" I asked, tearing my gaze away from the book for a second.

Hamish stared at me, his face a comical mix of humor and disbelief. "You're serious, aren't you?"

I nodded.

"It's free." He paused. "For paying customers."

"Thanks!" With a pleased smile, I dived back into the book and scanned through the catalog, which was admirably sorted and cross-indexed. Picking a few items at random, I perused their information in more detail.

Water magic skillbook. Governing attribute: Magic. Tier: advanced. Cost: 5 gold.
Focus skillbook. Governing attribute: Constitution. Tier: basic. Cost: 2 gold.
Poison dart spellbook. Governing attribute: Mind. Tier: basic. Cost: 5 gold. Requirement: rank 0 earth magic.
Fireball spellbook. Governing attribute: Magic. Tier: advanced. Cost: 10 gold. Requirement: rank 5 fire magic.

The prices caused some of my good humor to evaporate, but I didn't stop flipping through the catalog.

It turned out that what Hamish actually meant by 'within reason' were primarily basic and advanced tier skills and abilities. The catalog did contain a few master tier ones, but for the most part, the cost put them out of reach. It did make me curious, though, about their grading.

"What separates master tier skills from basic and advanced ones?" I asked.

"When it comes to skills, rarity is the differentiator," Hamish replied. "Master tier skills are not necessarily better than basic ones, but they are harder to find."

"And abilities?"

"Abilities are a different matter entirely. A higher tier ability is *always* better than a lower one, but they come with higher skill requirements. But for a new player like yourself that is all immaterial. You will only be able to use basic abilities."

I nodded thoughtfully. Something else was puzzling me. "Why are abilities so much more expensive than skills? Considering skills are more valuable, I would have expected the reverse."

Hamish chuckled. "You would think so, wouldn't you? But it's all about supply and demand. Players are *always* searching for more abilities—even basic ones—but conversely, once their class configurations are completed, players almost never need new skills."

"I see," I murmured and returned to scanning through the catalog. One other thing quickly became clear: I did not have nearly enough money to buy all the skills and abilities I desired. I needed more money, and there was only one way to get it.

I closed the book with a snap and turned back to the merchant. "Before we go any further, I must know: do you buy as well as sell?"

Hamish grinned. "Of course. I will take any trinkets you do not need of your hands."

"Perfect," I said. Emptying my backpack, I laid all the items I was willing to part with on the floor. "So how much will you give me for these?"

CHAPTER 55: BUYING AND SELLING

We haggled for what felt like hours but in reality was no more than a few minutes. Despite his genial manner, Hamish was relentless when it came to pricing, and in spite of every argument I made, he was only willing to buy my items at fifty percent of the selling prices.

In the end, I sold my superfluous items for more than I expected, but less than I had hoped.

<u>Items sold</u>
1 summon lesser wight spellbook for 5 gold,
1 heavy shields skillbook for 1 gold,
1 archer Class stone for 1 gold,
1 rogue Class stone for 1 gold,
2 goblin shortbows for 1 silver each,
2 iron daggers for 1 silver each, and
8 empty potion flasks for 1 copper each.

You have received: 8 gold, 4 silvers, and 8 coppers. Total money carried: 16 gold, 2 silvers, and 1 copper.

I was unsurprised to find that Hamish valued my two basic Class stones at the same price as skillbooks of the same tier. It was to be expected given that demand for them would be low.

I was more surprised to find that Gnat's information on potions proved accurate. The merchant was almost comically eager to get his hands on my healing potions, offering me as much as two golds for the least of them, which I guessed put their relative value in perspective. I refused, of course. At this stage, the potions were too critical to my survival.

With my items sold, came the next step: deciding what to buy. This was a *considerably* more difficult task. I had about sixteen golds in my pocket, and by my rough estimate, I could gain at least fifteen more by selling the arms and armor of the seventy or so corpses in the goblin tunnel complex—and that was ignoring what the chief's own equipment would bring in.

So, I have at least thirty-one gold to play with. What should I get?

~ ~ ~

I spent the next hour picking Hamish's brain on a range of skills and abilities. After seeing my gold, the merchant didn't seem to mind my questions and answered each with a smile.

In the end, I shortlisted four skills for further consideration.

Insight skillbook. Governing attribute: Perception. Tier: basic. Cost: 2 gold.
Light armor skillbook. Governing attribute: Constitution. Tier: basic. Cost: 2 gold.
Thieving skillbook. Governing attribute: Dexterity. Tier: basic. Cost: 2 gold.
Deception skillbook. Governing attribute: Perception. Tier: master. Cost: 20 gold.

Light armor was necessary for defense, something which I had been sorely lacking up to this point. Thieving and insight were primarily non-combat skills, however, both were essential if I was going to spend more time in the dungeon.

Thieving was required to disarm those pesky traps, while insight was necessary to spot them in the first place. Not to mention that once I leveled up insight sufficiently, it would allow me to identify weaknesses in my foes *before* engaging them.

Deception was the outlier. It was not a skill essential to my survival in the immediate future, but in the long term, I was guessing it would prove invaluable. The skill was a mirror of the insight skill and allowed me to conceal my own weaknesses from others. My only concern with it was related to its cost. A master tier skill, it was expensive.

Before deciding on my skills, I created a similar shortlist of the abilities I desired. This was even harder than I expected. There were many abilities and spells I could do with, but I simply didn't have the money for them.

There was another important consideration when it came to spells: their somatic and verbal components. Many spells seemed to require some sort of hand gesture or chant, and while I did not entirely rule out such spells, for obvious reasons I was reluctant to purchase them at this stage.

In battle, my hands would not be free for spellcasting, nor would I be able to chant spells when hidden. In hindsight, I realized, I had been fortunate that my one and only spell, simple charm, had no somatic or vocal components.

But even after stripping down the list to the bare minimum—to abilities I felt I simply couldn't do without and that suited my combat style—there were still seven on my shortlist.

Minor backstab ability tome. Governing attribute: Dexterity. Tier: basic. Cost: 5 gold. Requirement: rank 1 sneaking and light weapon skill.

Basic analyze ability tome. Governing attribute: Perception. Tier: basic. Cost: 5 gold. Requirement: rank 0 insight.

One-step spellbook. Governing attribute: Mind. Tier: basic. Cost: 5 gold. Requirement: rank 0 telekinesis.

Stunning slap spellbook. Governing attribute: Mind. Tier: basic. Cost: 5 gold. Requirement: rank 0 chi.

Lesser trap detect ability tome. Governing attribute: Perception. Tier: basic. Cost: 5 gold. Requirement: rank 1 insight.

Basic trap disarm ability tome. Governing attribute: Dexterity. Tier: basic. Cost: 5 gold. Requirement: rank 0 thieving.

Simple lockpicking ability tome. Governing attribute: Dexterity. Tier: basic. Cost: 5 gold. Requirement: rank 0 thieving.

It turned out that the biggest disadvantage of Magic, Mind, and Faith skills was that most of them couldn't be trained with simple physical actions—like wielding a sword, for instance. Instead, the skills had to be advanced by casting spells. This made their training slower, more difficult—and of course, more expensive.

To improve my telekinesis and chi skills, I had to have an ability from each of their skill trees, though, my choices were limited to those with rank zero skill requirements.

My need for the trap detect, lockpicking, and trap disarm abilities was obvious: they were required for safely opening loot chests. And given my penchant for sneaking up on my foes, backstab was an essential combat ability.

All this left me in a quandary.

Even after going through my shortlist for a second and third time, I was certain I needed *all* seven abilities. But I didn't have nearly enough money for that. To purchase the seven abilities and four skills, I needed sixty-one golds. Even if I reluctantly left out the deception skill, I still needed a whopping forty-one golds.

That's still way out of my reach.

Should I sell my health potions? No, that wasn't a good option. Bowing my head, I wracked my mind for a solution.

Seeing me agonizing over my options, Hamish interrupted me tentatively. "I don't normally like interfering with a customer's choices, but you seem in need of assistance. Can I help in any way?"

I raised my head and studied the merchant. So far, he had been more helpful than I had any right to expect, and I had no hesitation in explaining my dilemma to him.

Hamish listened patiently. But when I was done, rather than speak his mind, the merchant bit his lip and refrained from saying anything.

I frowned. "You have something to say, I can tell. What is it?"

Hamish pressed his hands together. "It's not my place—"

"Share your thoughts. Please," I said, interrupting him. "I could do with the advice."

Hamish sighed. "Alright. It seems to me from everything you've told me that the two thieving abilities are unnecessary."

"Really?" I asked, my brows shooting upwards. "How will I disarm and unlock loot chests then?"

It was Hamish's turn to evince surprise. "Loot chests are never locked." He paused. "Or trapped."

I gaped at him. "Are you sure?"

"I am," he said without the slightest hesitation. "Loot chests are direct rewards from the Adjudicator for something you've *already* done. In terms of the Game's rules, it makes no sense to boobytrap them."

"But-but..." I was confused, and despite the dark elf's obvious conviction, I was uncertain how far to believe him. "Are you saying chests in a dungeon are never trapped?"

"I did not say that," he said primly. "*Loot chests* are never boobytrapped, but other chests you find may be." Seeing me about to protest, he held up a hand for patience. "I know what you are about to ask: how do you tell a loot chest from an ordinary one?"

I nodded.

"The general rule of thumb for dungeoneers is if you see a chest before an encounter, it's been placed there either by the faction controlling the sector, or the denizens of the dungeon itself, in which case you *should* assume the worst. But if you notice a chest appear only after an encounter, then it is the doing of the Adjudicator, and you need not fear any traps."

"I see," I said quietly. Having listened to Hamish's patient explanation, I no longer doubted him. It fit with what I knew. It had struck me as odd that of all the many chests I had run across thus far, only one had been boobytrapped. Now I knew why. That chest had likely been placed there by the Master as part of his challenge.

Something Gnat must have known.

Which meant my familiar had lied to me. Or at the very least, he hadn't been completely truthful about the nature of the dungeon's traps. It was not a big lie. But it was an untruth and added more weight to the words Aira had whispered to me: *Don't trust him.*

"Michael?" Hamish interrupted. "Is everything all right?"

I shook my head to clear it of my worries. I would have to deal with the issue of Gnat later. "It is," I said, turning back to the merchant. "Thank you for the advice."

Closing my eyes, I considered the matter of my skills and abilities again. If I left out both thieving abilities and the deception skill, I should have enough money to purchase the rest of the skills and abilities I needed, buying half now, and the rest after I hauled the goblin loot back to Hamish.

I opened my eyes. "I'm ready to make my purchases now."

CHAPTER 56: THE NIGHTSTALKER

My first priority was acquiring the skills I needed and they were cheap—mostly. I still thought the thieving skill was necessary to my build despite not urgently needing the trap disarm and lockpicking abilities, and I didn't hesitate in purchasing it along with the other skillbooks I required.

You have bought an insight skillbook, light armor skillbook, and thieving skillbook.

The basic analyze ability was a priority, and I didn't have to think too hard about buying it. For my second ability tome, it was a toss-up between one of the two spells required to train my psi skills. In the end, I went with stunning slap because it was more directly combat-orientated than one-step.

You have bought a basic analyze ability tome, and a stunning slap spellbook.
You have lost: 16 golds. Total money carried: 0 golds, 2 silvers, and 1 copper.

"Excellent!" Hamish said, rubbing his hands in glee once our transaction was complete. "You've been a fantastic customer. Now is there anything else I can do for you?"

I chuckled. "I plan on being back again soon to complete my purchases, but first—" I looked eagerly at the books in my hands—"I have to learn all this."

Opening the first skillbook, I began reading.

You have acquired the basic skill: insight. This skill allows you to analyze your environment and opponents, to detect anomalies and weaknesses. You have 1 of 6 psionic Class skill slots remaining.

I blinked, allowing the new knowledge to soak into me before turning to the next skillbook: light armor. However, light armor was a constitution-based skill, and I needed to increase the attribute to at least the first rank before learning the skill.

Your Constitution has increased to rank 1. Your level cap for constitution-based skills has increased to 10.
You have acquired the basic skill: light armor. You may now use light armor during combat. All armor penalizes Magic and Dexterity. As you increase your skill, the penalties you incur will be reduced. You have 1 of 6 scout Class skill slots remaining.

The skill settled into me, and I opened the last skillbook.

You have acquired the basic skill: thieving. Thieving is a non-combat skill that increases your ability to perform nefarious activities such as lockpicking, pickpocketing, and setting and disarming traps. You have 0 of 6 scout Class skill slots remaining.

About to open one of the ability tomes, I paused as another Game message unfurled in my mind.

Congratulations, Michael! You have fully configured your first Class. Based on your choice of skills, acquired traits, and actions to this point, you have the option to evolve your scout Class.
Do you wish to change this Class to that of a nightstalker? Note, none of your existing skills, or characteristics will be lost through your Class evolution.

"Wow!" I exclaimed, nearly stumbling back and dropping the ability tomes still in my hands at the surprising Game message.

"What's wrong?" Hamish asked anxiously. "Was there something wrong with the skillbooks?"

Excitement overrode my caution, and before I could think to stop myself, I said, "No, nothing like that. I've been offered a Class evolution!"

Hamish's stance relaxed. "Ah, congratulations are in order then." He looked around to confirm no one else was nearby and lowered his voice. "But be careful to whom you say that. It may earn you unwanted attention."

My face reddened, embarrassed by my loose tongue. Then what the dark elf said penetrated. "What do you mean by that? And did you know that was going to happen?"

The merchant shook his head. "Class evolutions are a known phenomenon, but they are rare." He clapped a hand on my shoulder. "Well done. You're one of the lucky few to experience it."

"So... it's a good thing?"

"Definitely," the merchant said with a vigorous nod of his head. "But," he admitted a moment later, "it will attract the notice of high-level players. Class evolutions have been a mystery that even after millennia, no one has been able to crack. There is no rhyme or reason to them, at least not that anyone has been able to figure out. They just seem to happen according to the Adjudicator's whim. That hasn't stopped hordes of players from trying to evolve their Classes, though. If one of them hears about your evolution, believe me, they won't stop pestering you."

I scratched my head, perturbed and more than a little bewildered by Hamish's response. I certainly didn't want to attract the attention of high-leveled players—nothing good could come of that, I knew— but...

But how can I reject a rare chance to evolve my Class?

All this assumed the merchant was being truthful with me, of course. But I had no reason to doubt him. Still, I wished there was someone else I could ask about this. I smiled wryly. Even Gnat would be welcome right now.

I reread the message, looking for some clue as to what a Class evolution would entail. *A nightstalker,* I mused. *What sort of Class is that?* The Game message didn't give away much, other than the Adjudicator's offer seemed to be related to my past actions. *Hmm...*

I glanced at the patiently waiting merchant. This time, I knew better than to reveal any more to Hamish. If Class evolutions were rare, then knowledge of my new Class was not something I wanted to spread about.

Closing my eyes, I pinched the bridge of my nose and pondered my choice for a moment. Besides the potential danger of attracting attention, I could see no downside to acquiring the new Class. The Game message did say I would retain all my existing skills.

Shrugging, I willed my response to the Game.

Your Class has evolved! You are now a nightstalker!

The nightstalker is a path that can only be walked by those with an affinity for the night and who are gifted with a Wolf Mark. The Class bestows you with lupine traits that further enhance your ability to function in the dark and hunt your prey. This Class will deepen your Wolf Mark.

Your Class base trait has changed from nimble to wolven. The path of the nightstalker is closely intertwined with that of wolfkind. By virtue of the path you have chosen to walk, the wolf blood running in your veins has begun to stir. The further you advance in this Class, the more wolflike you will become. Your Dexterity is increased by +2 ranks, and your Strength by +2 ranks.

Your evolved Class has granted you the trait: nocturnal. The nightstalker lives and breathes in the dark. It is his natural habitat. Your sight has been adapted to suit your new calling. You can see perfectly in the dark now.

I took my time processing the avalanche of Game information prompted by my Class evolution. Once I was sure I understood everything, I opened my player profile.

My brows drew down in consternation. Except for the changes to my traits, little had changed about my player data. Well, my Class sounded much cooler now, my strength had been boosted a little, and I could see perfectly in the dark.

But besides that? Nothing.

While my new night vision was great, I couldn't see it being something veteran players would get excited about. *Why all the fuss over evolutions, then?* I wondered. But the Game messages did hint that other benefits would be received further down the line. *Perhaps, that's it.* Setting aside the mystery, I turned back to Hamish. "Thank you."

"No problem. Now, why don't you go ahead and learn those spells? I can see you are eager to do so."

I grinned, reminded of the books still in my hand. Flipping open the first, I did as Hamish bade.

You have acquired the basic ability: basic analyze. This ability allows you to inspect your foes for strengths and weaknesses. Beware, some targets may sense when this ability is used upon them. The success of this ability is determined by the target's level and deception skill. This ability consumes no energy and can be upgraded. Its activation time is near-instantaneous. You have 7 of 8 Perception ability slots remaining.

You have acquired the basic spell: stunning slap. This is a touch-based ability that stuns your foe for 1 second. This ability can only be activated when your hand is in physical contact with the target. The effects of this ability may be overcome by physical resistance. This ability consumes psi. Its activation time is fast. You have 2 of 4 Mind ability slots remaining.

Knowledge of the two abilities seeped into my mind. Stunning slap excited me especially. From what Hamish had told me, the ability was a staple of monks and other unarmed fighters.

A one-second stun didn't sound like much, but it would let me get off at least one hit unopposed on my target, and once I could perform coordinated maneuvers between stunning slap and backstab...

I could stun-lock a target while dealing huge swaths of damage. Of course, I would have to fight single-handed when using the ability, and the stamina drain was said to be significant, but some pitfalls couldn't be avoided.

"All done?" Hamish.

"All done," I confirmed. I shook the dark elf's hand. "Thank you for everything. Now, I must be off, but I expect to return shortly. Will you still be here?"

"I will be here for the next couple of days at least," Hamish said. "I can't afford to leave yet. Business has been slow—who am I kidding?—business has been atrocious. You are my first customer in this sector."

About to walk away, I paused. "Really?"

The merchant nodded glumly. "I assure you it's not because of any lack on my part. My goods are of the finest quality."

I pursed my lips. "I only counted nine other merchants here. Surely at least some of the candidates must have visited you before this?"

Hamish wrangled his hands as some of his distress leaked through. "There are aplenty players around. Sadly though, you are the first player to arrive in the safe zone with money in his pocket. If things keep up like this, I fear I will have to return home in abject failure." His smile brightened slightly. "But you've given me renewed hope that things will turn around."

"Glad to help," I murmured and bade him farewell. Turning around, I walked slowly away. I found Hamish's news both concerning and puzzling, and a frown marred my face.

What did it mean, I wondered, that no other players had made it to the safe zone alive? *And if they only reached here through resurrection, why would they choose to remain?*

CHAPTER 57: AN ARMY OF NOOBS

My head was bowed and my thoughts were preoccupied with the news Hamish had just shared, which was why I didn't notice the obstacle in front of me until too late.

I bounced into something hard and not very pliable. *Ooof.* I staggered backward and regained my balance.

"Look at me, scum," someone ordered.

I raised my head. I was surrounded, encircled by a ring of candidates. There were lots more than I had seen earlier too. An easy five dozen of them in a close-knit mob around me.

I pivoted in a slow circle, scrutinizing the candidates carefully. Every single one of them was in newbie gear. *Hamish was right. No way this bunch has more than a copper between them.*

"Hey! I'm talking to you."

I ignored the speaker again, and took in the crowd's measure. They seemed angry. Fists were clenched. Some were scowling. Others muttered. The candidates were ready to commit violence. I frowned. *But this is a safe zone. What would make them attempt that?*

A massive hand dropped onto my shoulder and spun me around. "Don't ignore me little man, or you'll regret it," the voice growled.

I followed the hand upwards to the owner, finally giving the speaker my attention. "Oh?" I said carelessly. "And why is that?"

My response appeared to momentarily confound the candidate who had addressed me. She was a giant. Literally. Twice my own height, she had to hunch over to even set her palm on my shoulder. Her skin was tinged orange, and her hair appeared to be strands of burnished gold. Altogether she made for a striking figure.

Like the others, the giantess was dressed only in a white cotton shirt and shorts. On her, they looked laughably tiny and bulged at the seams. *Looks like someone issued her one size too small.*

"Because I will crush you, little worm!" she sputtered.

"No, you won't," I said lightly. "This is a safe zone, remember?"

It was the wrong thing to say, and I could see the giantess' confidence grow before my eyes. She hunched over further and placed her face an inch from mine, a wide grin splitting her face.

I didn't back away. From this close, I could see that flecks of gold danced in the pupils of her brown eyes.

"Ah, but you can't stay here forever, can you?" the giantess said, her tone silky. "You will have to leave sometime. Then you will be mine, you treacherous dog."

She had a point, but I was damned if I was going to acknowledge it.

I wrinkled my nose at the less-than-pleasant odor wafting over my face from the giantess' breath, but my reaction didn't seem to faze her. "You will have to catch me first," I quipped.

The giantess' smile widened. "Oh, we'll catch you. Never fear."

Her certainty was daunting. *Alright Michael, you've poked this particular bear enough. How about you try to get some real information?*

"Where's all your equipment?" I asked suddenly.

Her brows drew down. "What?"

"Why are you lot all in newbie gear?" I asked, gesturing to the crowd. "Have you people just entered the Game?"

The giantess' nostrils flared wide, and the mutters in the crowd grew in volume. "Don't play the fool, *Michael*," she growled. "Some amongst us recognized your face. We know you started in the Master's domain too."

Huh? How does she know my name? Did —

Of course. She used analyze.

Remembering that I had the ability myself, I reached out to the giantess with my mind and probed her. The air around her large form began to shimmer with strange translucent symbols. Instinctively, I knew they contained data about my target. I drew in the information, and my mind automatically decoded its meaning.

The target is Decalthiya, a level 8 sun half-giant. This entity is a player. You have failed to advance your insight: skills cannot be gained in this area.

Ah, so she wasn't quite a giant then, but my guess had been close enough. The haze that had formed around Decalthiya reminded me of something else: I hadn't seen any Marks around her. I glanced at the crowd of candidates behind her. None of them were Marked either.

"What's wrong, Michael? Nothing more to say No more denials of what you are?"

Decalthiya's words drew my attention back to her. *She has no Marks and is still rank zero.* The half-giant *was* a newbie, but she had managed to gain some levels, so she hadn't just entered the Game. Which meant there was only one explanation for why she and her fellows were standing in front of me without gear.

She must have died. They all must have.

That realization made me more sympathetic to their plight, but it still didn't explain their hostility towards me. It couldn't simply be jealousy, could it?

"So. You don't deny it," Decalthiya said, taking my silence to signify agreement. "You admit to being one of Saben's crew."

"What? No! Of course not!" I replied, indignant. "Why would you think that?"

Decalthiya leaned back, stretching to her full height. "Don't lie, little man. Your arrival was observed. You were *seen* entering from the north tunnel. Saben's men wouldn't let any but one of their own through."

Ah. Perhaps my attempted deception hadn't been such a good idea after all. I was beginning to get an inkling that matters here were more complex than I'd initially realized. "I'm not a member of that gang of thugs," I insisted.

Decalthiya folded her arms. "Then how did you get here?"

I stayed silent. I wasn't willing to share the secret of the goblin complex.

A scarred elf pushed through the crowd and stepped up to the half-giant's side. He was a tall, wiry individual with a greenish cast to his skin, slitted upturned eyes, and peaked ears. I cast analyze over him.

The target is Tantor, a level 7 high elf. This entity is a player.

I frowned. Hmm, the elf was also rank zero. Was everyone in the safe zone's level this low?

"Bring the human to Morin," the elf said, addressing Decalthiya and ignoring me altogether. "She wants to speak to him."

"And if I have no desire to speak with this person?" I interjected.

Tantor's eyes slid my way. "Would you prefer we hunt you down when you leave the safe zone?"

My lips tightened at the threat, but I didn't respond to it. Bowing mockingly, I stretched out my arm. "Lead on then."

CHAPTER 58: THE PAINTED WOMAN

Tantor and Decalthiya led me back to the central avenue of the safe zone, with the other candidates following in our wake. As one large mob, we traipsed down the road. The merchants watched us keenly but said nothing.

Beyond the merchant stalls, the avenue led to the marques and pavilions I had seen from afar. Their entrance flaps were closed, and I couldn't see inside, but I didn't think they were more shops.

"What's in there?" I asked, not expecting an answer but hoping for one.

The high elf eyed me sideways. "Sleeping quarters," he said laconically.

The answer surprised me. It suggested the candidates were staying in the safe zone. *But why?* I wondered. Were they scared to leave? Or was something else at play here? Whatever was going on, it was clearly tied to the thugs I had observed yesterday.

Perhaps I will learn more from this Morin. Hers was the name I heard repeated mention of from Saben's gang.

We turned off the road and headed into the gathering of tents. The road, I noticed, continued onwards and ended at the crater's western entrance. Between the tents, I saw more candidates in the fields of mushrooms. Some were gathering the glowing fungi; others were chewing on them.

My eyebrows flew up. "You eat the mushrooms?" I couldn't imagine doing any such thing. "They must taste horrible."

Tantor frowned at me but didn't say anything.

Decalthiya growled in anger. "You dare mock us, worm?"

Before I could react, her large hand clamped down on my cloak, and she hoisted me effortlessly into the air, leaving my feet dangling a few feet off the ground. I didn't draw my swords. I wasn't ready to escalate matters. Not yet. Instead, I struck at her arm with my fists. To no avail; her grip was like iron.

"This is all your glorious leader's fault!" the half-giant raged. "With no gear or money and confined to this purgatory, what other choices do you think we have but to eat the damned mushrooms and beg the merchants for scraps?"

Violation of safe zone protocols detected. Player Decalthiya has taken hostile action against you. Do you wish her punished?

My offended dignity screamed 'yes,' but the rational part of my mind knew that would be a mistake. I realized I had unwittingly stumbled onto a conflict between two groups of candidates, and one faction—the losing one seemingly—appeared to have mistaken me for a member of the opposing gang.

Allowing the Game to punish the half-giant—while gratifying—would increase the resentment Morin's people bore towards me, and that would only make extracting myself from the mess I had found myself in harder. *Better to find out more before I act,* I thought.

"Let me go," I hissed, holding the half-giant's stare. I knew she was angry, but I didn't think she truly meant me harm. Lost to her rage, the half-giant didn't respond immediately.

"Decalthiya," Tantor said warningly. "We can't afford this. You're on your last life." Some of the fury clouding the half-giant's eyes cleared at that, but still, she hesitated. "Do it!" he snapped.

The half-giant opened her hands, and I dropped to the floor. Nimbly finding my footing, I waved away the Game's query.

The high elf studied me curiously, no doubt wondering why I had saved his companion from punishment. "Thank you," he said grudgingly after a moment.

He didn't elaborate, but I took his meaning. I glanced at Decalthiya. She folded her arms and glared at me, remaining tight-lipped.

I rolled my eyes and swung back to Tantor. "Well, what are we waiting for? Take me to this Morin, and let's get this over with."

The sooner I can get this conversation over with, the sooner I can leave.

~ ~ ~

The half-giant and half-elf led me into a whitewashed leather tent. None of the other candidates followed us inside.

Three people in newbie gear were waiting for us: two humans and one dwarf. Four feet tall, the dwarf was squat and built low to the ground. He was older than most of the other candidates I had seen, and his bushy-black beard was speckled with grey.

One of the humans was male. Blonde-haired, blue-eyed, and with a square jaw, he was solidly built. The last figure, an athletic-looking woman whose height matched my own, was the most interesting and... strange. From head to foot, every inch of the woman's skin that I could see was painted. And I had no trouble imagining the same applied to the bits of her covered by her white shirt and shorts.

What would possess someone to paint themselves in such a manner? I wondered.

But as I looked closer, I realized that it wasn't paint but tattoos that covered the woman—tattoos formed of solid squares of brown and green laid out in a checkered pattern to cover her entire body. *Weird*, I thought, and cast analyze over the three.

The target is Bornholm, a level 7 dwarf. This entity is a player.
The target is Sigmar, a level 9 human. This entity is a player.
The target is Morin, a level 10 painted human. This entity is a player.

I frowned. Again, their levels were much lower than I expected. I couldn't understand it. *And what the hell is a painted human?* Everything about Morin appeared disturbing. It also hadn't escaped my attention that she was the highest-leveled candidate I'd encountered in the safe zone.

I fixed my gaze on her. The woman's eyes were a startling shade of green, and her long hair was colored in the same shades of brown and green as her skin. She and her two companions stared at me, no doubt studying me as intently I was them.

"Well?" I demanded after the silence had drawn out long enough. "Why am I here?"

"Show some respect!" Decalthiya snarled from behind me. Almost automatically her arm swung forward to cuff me.

I deftly ducked the blow. Grown wise to the half-giant's temper, I had been keeping a wary eye on her. *She really has no sense of self-preservation,* I thought in passing.

The half-giant's eyes narrowed as her palm failed to connect. She took a threatening step forward.

"Enough," Morin said softly.

Mid-motion, Decalthiya froze and swung to face the painted woman. "Sorry boss," she mumbled.

Morin's eyes flicked to Tantor. Reading the command in her gaze, he began speaking. "He's spoken to three people only: the Master's two pets and Hamish. My people are questioning the vampires now—" the elf made a face—"but you know how they are. I don't expect to get much information out of them."

Morin nodded. "And what did he and the grey merchant speak about?"

Tantor frowned, and his gaze flicked sideways to me. "The dark elf won't say, which is odd, considering how garrulous the damn idiot is."

"Hamish told you nothing? Really?" the human Sigmar asked.

"Nothing except that he would never betray a customer's secrets," Tantor said, sounding disgruntled.

I couldn't help chuckling at that, my liking for the cheerful merchant growing. It seemed that I owed him another good turn.

Morin didn't even spare me a glance and continued her questioning as if I hadn't interrupted. "So he bought something from the merchant?"

"Bought *and* sold," Tantor said.

The dwarf's eyes narrowed at that. "What did he sell?" Bornholm asked, his voice a deep rumble. "Player gear?"

The elf shook his head. "Nothing that we could definitively identify as having belonged to any of our people," Tantor said. "He didn't sell much. Only two goblin bows, a pair of crude daggers, some books, and two Class stones."

"All of that was loot I collected myself," I declared loudly. My interjection was ignored by everyone except Decalthiya, who glared at me venomously.

"What idiot sells Class stones?" Sigmar asked, speaking over me.

"This idiot, that's who," I growled, beginning to get annoyed. It was obvious these people were suspicious of me, but it was equally clear that they couldn't do much to act on those suspicions. And I was done playing their games.

"He bought a bunch—" Tantor began, continuing his report as if I had not spoken.

"Enough!" I barked. "I've humored you, people, long enough, and I've just about run out of patience. Tell me what you want, or I leave now."

Bornholm bellowed. "Who do you think—"

Morin waved him to silence and stepped up to me. "How did you get here?" she asked, her face an expressionless mask.

I held the green-eyed woman's gaze for a moment, then shrugged. "I see no reason to tell you that."

"Isn't it obvious?" Sigmar scoffed. "He was seen at the north tunnel mouth. Saben's people let him through. Either he is part of their gang or an accomplice."

"He hasn't come from Saben," Morin said, not looking away from me.

Tantor frowned. "How can you be sure of that?" My own gaze turned curious. I was wondering the same thing.

"Look at his level," the painted woman instructed. "He is level eighteen."

"That's another mark against him," Sigmar said. "How can his level be so high? He must be the Master's spy."

Me, a spy? I glared at the human, ready to deny his words, but no one was paying his accusation much heed, so I kept my own mouth shut.

Bornholm tugged at his beard. "His level is high, true, but how is that relevant?"

Morin started circling me. "Saben is only level twelve. He would never tolerate a player of higher rank than himself in his gang. And he especially wouldn't allow such a player into the safe zone to buy better gear. No, however, he got here, it was not with Saben's permission."

"That's pretty thin, boss," Sigmar said. "If he is not the Master's spy, he must be Saben's. Or he could be a—"

Morin pinned him with a stare. "He isn't. I'm sure."

Decalthiya tugged at her hair, not doubting her leader. "So if Saben didn't send him, who did?" she asked.

Morin swung back to me. "That's the question, isn't it?"

CHAPTER 59: A GAME WITHIN A GAME

"No one sent me," I said into the silence that had formed around me.

"Why should we believe you?" Bornholm asked suspiciously.

I cast him an exasperated look. "I don't *care* if you believe me. I want nothing from you people. Just leave me alone."

"We can't do that," Morin said.

I swung back to her. "Why not?" I demanded.

The painted woman lowered her gaze. "Because our straits are dire," she said softly. "And we need your help."

I laughed. "Help? You want *my* help?" She had to be joking. "Is this—" I gestured to the five of them clustered around me—"how you ask for help? Through interrogation?"

Morin sighed. "I apologize. Trust is in short supply these days."

I stared at her. Her attitude had softened remarkably from a few moments ago. What's more, her request appeared genuine. *She really is asking for my help.*

"What are you doing, Morin?" Sigmar hissed. "We don't need his aid. And we can't trust him!"

"We have no choice," Morin said. "The longer we stay here, the more precarious our position becomes. Saben's people grow stronger while we don't. One way or the other, if we do nothing, he will wipe us out." She turned back to me. "Will you help us?"

I folded my arms and held her gaze. "I won't agree to anything, not until I know what's going on." I hesitated. I didn't like the way I had been treated, but I couldn't forget the glimpse I had caught of the captives in Saben's camp. "But I am prepared to listen to what you have to say."

Morin smiled. The expression transformed her tattooed face, making it appear less alien. "Fair enough," she said and gestured to the floor. "Why don't you have a seat. The explanations may take a while."

~ ~ ~

A few minutes later, the six of us were seated in a circle. From what I'd gathered so far, Morin was the leader of the candidates in the safe zone, and the other four were part of her inner circle.

"Where to begin," Morin murmured, running a hand through her hair. She closed her eyes and thought for a moment before glancing at me. "You were the last of the Master's candidates to arrive, weren't you?"

I nodded.

"That's why some of my people recognized you." Morin smiled. "You cut quite a memorable figure entering the room with the Master."

I looked at her quizzically.

Tantor chuckled, and I glanced at him.

"You were the only candidate to be personally greeted by the Master," he explained. "The rest of us were *welcomed* by Stayne. The first time we heard the Master speak was during his speech."

"Like you, we also entered this world with no memory of our past," Morin said. "Unlike you, the rest of us had weeks to acclimatize to this world."

"Weeks?" I asked, startled.

"Weeks," she confirmed. "We spent the time learning what we could of this world, the Game, and—" she glanced at her companions—"forming friendships."

I nodded slowly. It explained why the other candidates had seemed so easy with each other. "So you knew what we were getting into before entering the dungeon?"

Morin shook her head. "Not for certain. The Master's people kept us isolated, but some of the undead let things slip." She shrugged. "We only had rumors and random bits of information to work with. Still, it was enough for most of us to guess what was going on."

Sigmar snorted. "A few were further *blessed*."

I stared at him. "What do you mean?"

"Some of the Master's lieutenants took candidates under their wing," he explained. "They fed them information and provided advice."

"And the Master let all this happen?" I asked.

"The Master doesn't care," Tantor said. He lifted his arms, gesturing to the surrounding dungeon. "All of this is a game to him. A game within the Game." He gave a lopsided grin. "I suspect he finds all this amusing."

I could well believe that.

"Which brings us to Saben," Morin said.

I quirked one eyebrow. "Meaning?"

"Stayne mentored Saben personally," Morin said. "And Stayne is no ordinary undead. He is a player."

"A player?" I asked. "Are you sure?"

Morin shook her head. "Sure? No. It was by his own admission after all, and none of us had the analyze ability at that time."

I frowned. "Why would Stayne bother with helping a candidate though? What's in it for him?"

"Tantor has a theory," she replied and nodded for the elf to explain.

"The Master wants players to join his faction, but he does not care how that happens," the high elf said. "There is a hierarchy amongst the Awakened Dead too, and Stayne is near the top. By taking Saben under his wing, he is acting to strengthen his position."

My brows crinkled. "How?"

"What do you know of Saben?" Morin asked me.

I shrugged. "I know he is not the finest of individuals. I've never met him, but I've seen his gang and the prisoners they've taken."

Bornholm leaned forward. "You have? Tell me, lad, how are they faring?"

I glanced at the dwarf. His face was animated as he eagerly waited on my words. "They were... not good," I said, deciding not to elaborate further.

Bornholm slumped back, and Morin laid a comforting hand on his knee.

Sigmar was studying me with slitted eyes. "What were you doing in Saben's camp?"

Before I could tell him I was never in the camp, Morin chopped her arm down in irritation. "Hold your questions for later, Sigmar. Let Tantor finish." She gestured for the elf to go on.

"Saben is not like the other candidates," Tantor said. "He isn't interested in the dungeon or loot. While the rest of us were racing through the dungeon, killing goblins and claiming loot, Saben and his thugs were doing something entirely different."

"What?" I asked.

"They were capturing candidates and pressing them into service—Saben's service," the elf replied.

I frowned.

"I believe," Tantor continued, "that Saben has sworn allegiance to Stayne and that he has been tasked with gathering more followers for the undead player."

"That sounds... diabolical," I said, scratching my chin in thought. "But how can Saben force candidates into doing something they don't want to? Sure, they'd risk death by denying him, but we all have three lives, don't we?"

Tantor smiled grimly. "Not anymore. "We've all died at least once." He nodded to Decalthiya. "And some of us more than once."

"It is more than that, though," Morin said. "When we die, we are reborn here—in the safe zone."

"Which you would think is a good thing," Tantor continued, "but there is only one passage leading into and out of this area—or only one that we have been able to access anyway."

"Ah," I said, realizing their predicament now. "And Saben has blockaded the exit?"

"Correct," Tantor said. "His gang is camped about a hundred yards down the north tunnel."

"But you knew that already, didn't you?" Sigmar interjected.

Tantor waved him to silence and continued, "Saben is refusing to let anyone who does not join his gang leave the safe zone."

"We've tried twice to break through," Bornholm added sadly. "But without weapons and equipment, we failed miserably both times."

Morin leaned forward. "You can see now why we need your help." She pinned me with her emerald green eyes. "Will you tell us how you slipped past Saben's gang? If you do that, I promise we will ask nothing more of you—" she glanced at Sigmar— "nor will we pass judgment on you for anything you may have done. Tell us please, and give us a chance to escape this hellhole."

An expectant hush fell over the tent.

Breaking away from Morin's piercing gaze, I studied each of her companions in turn. The hope in their gazes was almost painful. Even doubting Sigmar and the angry half-giant seemed eager to hear what I had to say. *What do I tell them?* I wondered.

And how far dare I trust them?

CHAPTER 60: A QUESTION OF TRUST

I took my time.

Bowing my head, I considered the options before me. Having listened to Morin's people's tale, I knew I had nothing to fear from them. They might or might not be trustworthy, but they were certainly no threat. Even if the candidates did their damnedest, given their levels, they could not stop me from sneaking away if I wished.

Saben's gang was a danger, though. But with Morin's people serving as a distraction, the gang likely wouldn't budge from their encamped position for some time yet.

So running away and leaving the two groups to sort out their mess was an option. *And a good one,* the cautious part of me emphasized.

A second option would be to help, but only minimally. I could open the locked doors and let the trapped candidates escape Saben's blockade that way. It had the advantage of keeping me out of danger while at the same time ensuring my own conscience remained clean. The biggest risk I'd face would be losing all the loot still sitting in the goblin tunnel complex.

But option two was a half-measure only. While Morin's people didn't know it yet, escaping through the locked door was not going to do them much good.

There were other considerations, too.

Like, where did I go from here? By my recollection, there was only one area of the dungeon I still had to explore: the tunnel with the trolls. According to Gnat, the creatures were at least of the second rank, which made them a threat to be reckoned with. I *could* attempt to sneak past the trolls, but I didn't relish leaving the creatures alive behind me, and without any magic of my own, I could see no way to kill them.

Then there was information. It was something I sorely lacked. It had not escaped my notice that Morin and her people seemed to understand more of this world's workings than I did. After all, they had been here for many weeks longer.

The safe zone itself was another consideration. If I ran but needed to return, I did not want to find a hostile and powerful force—like Saben's—in control.

Lastly, there was the gang itself. While I was skeptical of some parts of Morin and Tantor's tale, I had witnessed the behavior of Saben's crew with my own eyes. My mind replayed the memory of the prisoners being beaten. Whatever doubts I might harbor about Morin's people, I was certain Saben was a menace. And I could not ignore the fact that the gang must have amassed a fortune by now. *The plunder will be rich.*

So. Securing magical aid. Safeguarding the safe zone. Information. Rescuing the prisoners. And loot. *Five good reasons to do more.*

I sighed, realizing what I was contemplating. There was a third option: not just giving Morin's people a way out but helping them defeat Saben.

Option three would not be without risks of its own, though.

I knew very little of Morin's people. Their attitude up to this point left much to be desired, and while I could chalk up most of their anger and rudeness to fear and suspicion, I did not know enough about them to judge who they really were beneath their prickly exterior.

They could attempt to betray me the first opportunity they got. They could be as evil as the Master claimed. But I put little stock in the Master's words anymore, and I backed myself to escape any attempted treachery.

I raised my head and met Morin's gaze. Her eyes had never left me. I considered all the ramifications of what I was planning again. I was certain it could be done, but much would depend on the painted woman's people.

I don't need to trust them. I only need to be able to work with them.

I reached a decision. "I did not slip past Saben's people."

"I knew it! He is one of them," Sigmar crowed. He glanced at Morin. "Let me question him. I'll get the truth out of him."

The painted woman waved him to silence. "You know the Game won't allow that, not in the safe zone."

Sigmar's remarks and his particular emphasis on questioning disturbed me, but I ignored him and kept my gaze fixed on Morin. "I entered the safe zone through the opposite tunnel—the one behind the barred metal gate."

Sigmar sputtered. "Impossible," he finally managed to get out. "The door is locked. You're lying!"

Tantor gave a sad shake of his head. "My people checked the door again after you were spotted. It remains locked. Sigmar is right. You aren't telling us the truth."

Morin said nothing. With her hands folded in her lap, she waited patiently for my explanation.

I reached into my backpack. "It's locked," I agreed, "because I locked it behind me." I held out the magical key. "With this."

In stunned shock, five pairs of eyes fixed on the key in my hands.

"Where did you get that?" Morin whispered, sounding breathless.

"From the goblin chief," I said.

She stared at me blankly.

I waved away the matter. "I'll explain later. The important thing is that the sector's exit portal lies beyond the metal door, but I don't advise using it because—"

"You've found the sector exit?" Morin asked disbelievingly. "Do you realize what this means?"

"Err..." I frowned. "No?"

The others had also sat up, new excitement shining on their faces. "The goblin chief you mentioned," Tantor asked abruptly, "was he by any chance, the sector boss?"

"Uhm, I think so," I said, not sure what had gotten them so worked up. I hadn't even gotten to the most important part of what I wanted to tell them.

"I don't believe it! The lad has cleared the sector," Bornholm bellowed.

"Impossible," Sigmar muttered again.

I looked at them, mystified. "I don't understand."

"Every dungeon sector has a single boss," Morin explained. She was smiling, I saw, and tears glistened in her eyes. "Defeating the boss is always the final challenge." She paused. "You've opened the way for the rest of us to exit the dungeon, Michael. Thank you."

Seeing that my face remained furrowed in confusion, she asked gently, "Did your familiar not tell you?"

"No," I murmured. "He did not."

"Let's not get excited just yet," Sigmar muttered sourly. "After all, he may be lying."

"Why would he lie?" Bornholm demanded. "And besides, he has the bloody key!"

"How did he get the key without buying it from the damned merchant?" Sigmar countered.

My eyes shot to Morin, looking for an explanation for Sigmar's puzzling statement.

"We all recognize the key in your hand because there is an identical one for sale at one of the merchants," she said. "We've known for some time now that the locked door leads to the next stage of the sector, but even collectively, we haven't been able to come up with enough money to purchase the key."

I nodded. "How much does it cost?"

"Twenty gold," she replied.

I winced.

"How did you get to the region beyond the door?" Morin asked.

I glanced at her. There was no hint of suspicion on her face. She was asking out of simple curiosity. I shrugged. Seeing no reason to lie, I explained how I reached the goblin's tunnel complex.

"He found a backdoor," Tantor marveled.

"Sounds like it," Bornholm agreed.

"What happened to your team?" Decalthiya asked. It was the first words she had spoken in a while.

I stared at her. "My team?"

She nodded. "Did the goblin chief kill them?" When I didn't answer immediately, her gaze sharpened. "Or did you abandon them?"

I shook my head. "I have no team. I've made my way through the dungeon alone."

Another hush descended at my words, and even Morin looked startled.

"Yeah, right," Sigmar scoffed, breaking the silence.

"It's true," I said, holding his gaze.

"You expect us to believe you killed the sector boss and a few dozen goblins—all on your own?" he asked, his words dripping with skepticism.

"It was seventy."

"What?" he asked, baffled.

"There were seventy goblins in the tunnel complex, give or take a few."

"And you claim to have killed all of them?" Tantor asked quietly.

"I do," I said.

The conviction in my words, more than anything else, seemed to sway them—everyone except Sigmar, of course.

"Then the way to the surface is open," Decalthiya said, her eyes shining. "We're free."

I shook my head. "No, you're not."

CHAPTER 61: A BOLD PROPOSITION

The half-giant turned slowly to face me. "Why not," she demanded.

"I wasn't able to use the exit portal. None of you will be able to do so either without a Dark Mark," I said. I explained what had happened when I had attempted to pass through and the way the Marks worked, managing to do so *without* making any mention of the wolves or the fact that I myself was Marked. "I'm sorry, but you're stuck here," I concluded. "We all are."

"Damn the Master," Bornholm cursed. "I knew it! He has rigged the bloody game."

Morin closed her eyes and squeezed her hands together to hide the faint tremor to them. "So, now we know his end game," she murmured to herself.

Decalthiya was frowning. "I don't get it."

"If what Michael says is true, the only sure way for any of us to get a Dark Mark is to adopt a Dark Class," Tantor explained. "To leave the dungeon, we must forgo the other paths. The Master is trying to force us to follow *only* the Dark," he concluded.

I didn't say anything, but I had reached much the same conclusion myself. In hindsight, it seemed obvious that the Master had been manipulating us ever since we entered the Game. First, with all his talk of us being evil, and then with how he had pitted the candidates against each other.

It was equally clear that the Master's minions—Gnat and Stayne included—were also part of the scheme. I wasn't certain how I was going to deal with my familiar yet, but I was sure of one thing: I would not fall prey to the Master's ploy. I was determined not to give him the satisfaction. One way or the other, I would escape the dungeon without becoming sworn to the Dark.

What I still had to figure out, though, was how I was going to eventually escape.

Morin opened her eyes. She seemed to have regained her equilibrium. "All is not lost," she said, studying each one of her companions in turn. "We have a chance now. We can make our way through the goblin tunnel complex and to the trolls' lair. Beyond them, perhaps we can find another exit from the sector." Despite her words, Morin did not sound very optimistic.

"You should do that," I agreed. "I plan on doing the same myself." I breathed in deeply. "But before we go down that path, I propose we try something different first."

Morin looked at me questioningly.

"We take out Saben's gang," I declared.

The others did not react as I expected. Sigmar laughed, Decalthiya bowed her head, Morin refused to meet my gaze, and Tantor shook his head.

"We cannot, lad," Bornholm said sadly. "No one wants to end Saben's brutal reign more than me. But the bastard has a core of two dozen hardened warriors and wizards, his so-called 'elites.' They're all at rank one and armed to the teeth. Even though our numbers are greater, to attack them without any gear is suicide."

I smiled. "Who said anything about doing this without equipment?"

Five pairs of eyes jerked towards me, equally startled.

"There are some seventy dead goblins in the tunnel complex," I said. "All wearing hide armor and carrying weapons of one sort or the other. Not perfect equipment, I admit, but I dare say, good enough to outfit most of you for an assault?"

The despair filling the tent gave way to something else: hope.

Bornholm rose to his feet, his eyes wide and his nostrils flaring. "Don't toy with me, lad," he breathed. "Are you serious? You will share your loot with us?"

I nodded.

The dwarf studied my face for a wordless moment. Finding whatever he searched for, he threw back his head and roared, "Then, by god, let's do this!" Not waiting for his companions, he stomped out of the tent, bellowing for the other candidates to gather.

After an astonished second, Decalthiya clamped a hand on my shoulder and whispered in my ear, "Thank you, little man." Then she, too, rose to her feet and ducked out of the tent.

~ ~ ~

The rest of Morin's inner circle, including Morin herself, took more convincing.

In the end, the trio agreed to withhold judgment until they saw the loot I spoke of themselves. I expected nothing less from Sigmar, and Tantor seemed the cautious type, but I was surprised by Morin's reticence. I thought she would've jumped at the opportunity I presented.

Perhaps she has already lost hope, or what I offer seems too good to be true.

But despite her doubts, Morin was quick to act. "Tantor, set a squad to guard the north tunnel entrance," she ordered as the four of us left the tent. "I suspect Bornholm had been less than discrete with whom he has chosen to share Michael's information."

"On it," Tantor said and hurried away.

I looked at Morin curiously.

Catching my gaze, she said, "Saben's people periodically conduct forays into the safe zone." She made a face. "And some of our people have also been known to... switch sides. On the two previous occasions we assaulted his camp, Saben caught wind of our plans early and was ready and waiting for us. We can't risk that happening this time. Whether we flee or attack, Saben must not know what we are about."

I nodded, appreciating her caution.

"Why are you doing this?" Morin asked suddenly.

I glanced at her. "What do you mean?"

"Pointing the way out to us is one thing, but to give us all your loot?" She eyed me speculatively. "You don't seem the altruistic type."

"Firstly, I'm not giving you *all* my loot. I've already taken the best bits," I said. "Secondly, I expect what I'll gain in return from Saben's gang will be well worth it." I spread my arms wide to encompass the gathering candidates, "All of this, arming your people, call it an investment."

"So it's all about the loot?" she asked, a note of disappointment creeping into her voice.

"Of course," I said lightly. I wasn't ready to divulge all my reasons to her yet. "What else is there?"

The painted woman only shook her head. Turning around to Sigmar, she said, "Gather everyone at the locked door."

"Everyone? Are you sure?" Sigmar asked.

"I am," she said.

"Alright," he replied and strode away, but not before muttering under his breath. "I hope you know what you're doing."

Morin smiled—a trifle sadly, I thought. "I hope so, too," she said, before turning back to me. "Come, let's head towards the gate. The others will meet us there."

I fell into step with the painted woman, and for a moment, we walked in silence. Passing candidates recognized Morin and saluted or nodded respectfully.

"Why do they follow you?" I asked eventually, gesturing to the candidates around us.

Morin shrugged. "I don't know. I never set out to lead them. It just happened. My own group was one of the few to have had any success against Saben's thugs. After we fought off his gang's initial attempts to capture us, other candidates joined us, seeking safety in numbers." She sighed. "But Saben was always one step ahead, and eventually, we, too, fell victim to his gang and ended up here."

I frowned. "But how did Saben get so strong that he managed to overcome so many?"

"That's the question, isn't it?" Morn murmured. "Some think he must've found an overpowered item."

I noticed her choice of phrasing. "But you don't believe that?"

"Saben has abilities that no other candidate possesses. He rarely fights himself, but when he does, the effect is devastating. I think he has a master Class."

I whistled appreciatively. "A master Class? Found one early on, did he?"

Morin shook her head. "You mistake me. I'm sure he entered the dungeon *with* the Class."

I looked at her sharply. "How?"

"I think Stayne gave it to him," she said.

I narrowed my eyes, considering the implications. If what Morin suspected was true, then Stayne and the Master had fixed the game even more than I'd expected.

Am I doing the right thing? I wondered. If Stayne had gone to all the trouble to give Saben a master Class, then I didn't think he would have stopped there. What other surprises would the gang leader have up his sleeves?

It begged the question: was attacking Saben's camp wise? *Perhaps not*, I admitted, *but it will upset the Master's plans.* It was another reason for venturing down the path I had chosen and one that only occurred to me now. Everything else aside, I realized that I relished the idea of spoiling the Master's plans.

I had been manipulated. And I hated it.

And it was time I got back a little of my own.

CHAPTER 62: OUTFITTING AN ARMY

You have left a safe zone.

The moment Morin and I exited the crater, two small white figures dropped out of the darkness to alight on our shoulders.

I turned to look at my familiar. "Welcome back," I said and left it at that.

Gnat bobbed his head. "Making friends, are we?" he asked, gesturing towards the painted woman.

I shrugged and didn't say anything. I glanced at Morin and saw that her familiar was whispering in her ear. I wondered what it was that he was telling her. I hadn't yet discussed the matter of the familiars with the other candidates, and I wasn't sure yet how far Morin trusted her own.

When we drew closer to the locked metal door, I saw Decalthiya and Bornholm standing outside it with a dozen candidates. They congregated around the entrance and looked up at our approach. Morin muttered something under her breath about hasty half-giants and impatient dwarves and hurried ahead. I followed more slowly in her wake.

As I reached the door, a sheepish-looking Decalthiya and Bornholm began ordering the waiting candidates into disciplined ranks.

"Go ahead," Morin said, gesturing me to the door. Setting the key in the lock, I turned it and pushed open the door.

"Urgh, that smells awful," someone said from behind.

I wrinkled my own nose. Whoever had spoken was right. I hadn't noticed it before, but the smell of death hung heavy in the air. I stepped over the threshold and, without pause, hurried down the passage. "Follow me," I called over my shoulder to the others.

Reaching the second door, I glanced around. Everything was exactly as I had left it. Spotting the bodies of the six guards I had slain, I picked one whose armor appeared mostly intact and knelt by his side.

Morin and the others hadn't reached the door yet. "Come on in," I yelled and began tugging the goblin's armor off. It smelled horrible and was covered in gore, but it appeared usable.

I had just managed to remove the goblin's gloves when I heard the approach of tentative footsteps. Looking up, I saw it was Morin. "You see," I said, gesturing to the corpses. "I wasn't lying. Six sets of armor and weapons right at the door, and there's plenty more farther in."

Morin didn't say anything.

"What?" I asked, sensing her unease.

"I can barely see a thing," she said. "How can you?"

"What do you mean, it's—"

I broke off. To my sight, the passage was brightly lit as if under a noon-day sun. But it wasn't, I realized. My new nightstalker trait was enhancing my vision. It worked so seamlessly I hadn't even perceived any difference in the lighting between the safe zone and this passage.

But how will I be able to find shadows to hide in if I can't see them? Triggered by the thought, my vision darkened, restoring the passage's familiar murkiness.

Nocturnal sight has been disabled.

Remarkable, I thought and reactivated the trait. At a muttered oath from behind, I turned around. Decalthiya had stubbed her toe on an outcropping—much to Bornholm's amusement.

The dwarf was the only one in the group besides me that was not struggling to see. I glanced at Morin again. She was still looking expectantly in my direction. Instead of answering her, I reached into my backpack and withdrew the magic lamp.

Moonstone lamp activated. Three hours of light remaining.

White light flooded the passage, and the others gasped in relief. A chortling Bornholm walked up to me. "You must have a bit of dwarf in you to see so well in the dark, lad," he said. There was a twinkle in his eyes, but there was also a hint of a question in his tone too.

I shrugged and turned back to the goblin, using it as an excuse to avoid discussing the matter. I was prepared to work with the other candidates, but I wasn't yet ready to share all my secrets. Stripping off the creature's armor, I cleaned and equipped it.

You have equipped a set of primitive goblin hide armor. This item set reduces the physical damage you sustain by 10% and penalizes your Magic and Dexterity by 50%.

Note, each rank you achieve in the light armor skill will reduce the penalty incurred by 5%. Current modifiers: -5 ranks in Dexterity. Dexterity skills and abilities have been limited to rank 4.

I grimaced. My Dexterity had been halved. It was a good thing my dexterity-based skills were still too low to be affected, but I felt notably clumsier. The meager ten percent physical damage reduction was not worth the penalties, but I didn't remove the armor. I needed to train my light armor skill, and the only way I could do that was by wearing the armor.

I looked around. Bornholm and Decalthiya were supervising the other candidates while they looted the five remaining corpses, and Morin was watching me. "I owe you an apology," she said.

I frowned. "What for?"

"This," Morin said, gesturing to the corpses. "I thought, at best, you were stretching the truth, or at worst, leading us into a trap." She bent down and picked up a fallen spear. "I see now that you weren't."

I looked at her curiously. "How can you be sure there isn't an ambush waiting for you around the next corner?"

"Saben has been hankering to get his hands on me for ages." She smiled. "It's why I accompanied you personally. If he was lying in wait nearby, he wouldn't have been able to resist the chance to grab me. His trap would have sprung by now." She twirled the spear in her hand. "Besides, whatever else Saben is, he is not careless. He wouldn't let my people arm themselves before attacking."

I blinked, processing her response. "So... you used yourself as bait?"

She laughed. "You could say that."

I nodded slowly. I would do well not to underestimate Morin, I realized. She appeared to be a canny leader. *And one not averse to taking risks.* "Then do we go ahead with the attack?"

The painted woman studied me a moment. "We do," she affirmed, then glanced down the passage. "How many chambers are there in this section?"

"A few dozen," I answered. "Including a great hall at the far end."

"Hmm, it will take us awhile to loot everything," Morin said. "What do you wish to keep for yourself?"

I hesitated, feeling a momentary twinge of regret for all the loot I was handing over. But I knew it was necessary to better our chances in the coming conflict. *Besides,* I consoled myself, *anything I sacrifice here, I am sure to make up once we defeat Saben.* "Nothing," I said.

Morin's eyes widened slightly. "Nothing? You're sure?"

"Nothing except the goblin chief's equipment," I said firmly. "The rest is yours."

"Thank you," Morin said gravely. "I know we have been less than gracious to you so far."

I smiled wryly. That was an understatement, but I didn't say anything.

"Perhaps it is this world, or perhaps it is just the Master's realm," Morin continued. "After weeks amongst the followers of the Dark, all of us have learned to harden our hearts and be wary of strangers." She held my gaze. "It's no excuse, I know, but don't judge us too harshly. Whatever happens from here on out, know that I will not forget your generosity," she promised.

I waved off her words, slightly ashamed. My motives in doing this weren't all that pure. "I do have two conditions, though."

Morin raised a questioning eyebrow.

"Your people trade with Hamish for any items they wish to sell or buy," I said. "I owe him a favor."

Morin nodded. "That we can certainly do. What's your second condition?"

"I need someone to help me haul the chief's gear back to the safe zone." My eyes roved over the candidates before coming to rest on the half-giant. "Will you lend me Decalthiya for the task?"

Morin chuckled. "That will please her to no end, I'm sure."

~ ~ ~

A little later, Decalthiya and I left the others behind and made our way to the great hall.

As Morin had guessed, the half-giant was not best pleased to be used as my mule. I let her sputtered protests wash over me. After all, it was only the mildest of rebukes for her earlier behavior.

We entered the great hall, and Decalthiya broke off midstream as she surveyed the carnage revealed by the moonstone lamp. She looked at me with new respect. "You did all this?"

I nodded mutely, shocked myself as, for the first time, I beheld the full scope of the destruction I had waged in the chamber. Almost, I turned off my nocturnal vision at the sight.

Shaking off my impulse, I tugged the half-giant forward. "Come on, the chief is this way."

We stopped at the fallen boss' side, and Decalthiya circled the corpse. "Big bugger, isn't he?" she remarked.

He was, but then again, so was the half-giant. In fact, the two were nearly of matching size. "You think you can carry all his gear?"

Decalthiya nodded. "I can." She made a face. "But removing everything will be messy work." Her eyes fell on the greatclub. Picking it up, she whipped it idly through the air. "Nice weapon," she grunted.

I eyed the half-giant twirl the massive weapon as if it weighed nothing. I had barely been able to pick it up, I recalled. "Uhm, you have the greatclub weapon skill?" I asked, unable to keep the surprise from my voice.

Decalthiya grinned at me. "Nope."

"Then, how—"

She chuckled. "I'm an armsmaster."

I stared at her blankly.

"It is a melee specialist Class," the half-giant explained. "It comes with a trait that allows me to wield any melee weapon or equip any armor, but at a significant skill penalty."

My mouth dropped open. "Wow. Is that a master Class?"

Decalthiya threw back her head and laughed. "No, it's a blended Class," she said when her humor subsided.

I frowned. "A what?"

"You don't know?" she asked, surprised. Her gaze flitted to the familiar on my shoulder. "Tell him," she ordered.

Gnat glared at the half-giant but didn't object to her request. "Classes aren't static in the Game. They can meld or evolve, although the latter rarely occurs," the skeletal bat said. "Melding happens when a candidate finishes configuring at least two of his Classes. If synergies exist between the paths in question, the Game will offer the candidate a blended Class to replace the original ones. And before you ask," Gnat said, seeing the question on my face, "a blended Class is always superior to the originals."

"That's right," Decalthiya agreed. "Bi-blends are common. The *real* trick to Class selection, though, is achieving a tri-blend: a meld of three synergistic paths. While tri-blends are not exactly rare, they are said to be difficult to achieve."

"I see," I said, digesting this sudden wealth of information. I glanced at Gnat. "Why didn't I know all this?"

He snickered. "You didn't ask?"

I scowled at him before turning back to the half-giant. On impulse, I analyzed her again.

The target is Decalthiya, a level 8 sun half-giant. This entity is a player. Your insight has increased to level 2.

Once again, the Game revealed no information as to her Class, but at least I had gained a level in the insight skill this time. I chewed my lip in consideration. "So, you can use the greatclub?" I asked Decalthiya.

She nodded.

"What about the armor? Can you use it, too?"

The half-giant eyed the chief's frame. "It looks to be the right size."

I sighed. I had been so looking forward to finding out how much Hamish would give me for the gear, but alas, it was not to be.

"Then, they're all yours," I said.

CHAPTER 63: PREPARING FOR WAR

Decalthiya didn't believe me, not the first time or the second time. She kept waiting for the other shoe to drop or for me to retract my offer.

I had to repeat myself a whole five times before she finally took me at my word. It was sad, really, and made me think harder about what Morin had said earlier. Perhaps the weeks spent living amongst self-declared followers of evil had affected the candidates more than I'd thought.

Once Decalthiya got over her shock, though, she wasted no time in equipping the items. While I waited for her, I closed my eyes and attended to my player growth. It had been a while since I'd seen to my player profile.

I had three unspent attribute points, and given the penalties, I incurred from my armor, I decided to advance my Dexterity one rank. The remaining two points, I used to increase my Constitution.

Your Dexterity has increased to rank 10. Current modifiers: -5 ranks in Dexterity. Dexterity skills and abilities have been limited to rank 5.
Your Constitution has increased to rank 3.

It had become clear to me that I would have to start investing more heavily in Constitution. Not only would it allow me to withstand more blows in combat, but given the prerequisites I now knew some items had, I needed to make sure that if I did come across any better light armor, I was in a position to use it.

After the changes were made, I reviewed my player data.

Player Profile: Michael

Level: 18. Rank: 1. Current Health: 100%.
Stamina: 100%. Mana: 100%. Psi: 100%.
Species: Human. Lives Remaining: 3.
Marks: Wolf-friend, Lesser Shadow, Lesser Light.

Attributes

Available: 0 points.
Strength: 2. Constitution: 3. Dexterity: 10. Perception: 8. Mind: 4. Magic: 0. and Faith: 0.

Classes

Primary Class: Nightstalker (advanced).
Secondary Class: Psionic (advanced).
Tertiary Class: None.

Traits

Undead familiar: +1 to necromancy rank.
Wolven: +2 Dexterity, +2 Strength.
Beast tongue: can speak to beastkin.
Metamind: +4 Mind.
Marked: can see spirit signatures.
Nocturnal: perfect night vision.

Skills

Available skill slots: 1.
Dodging (current: 23. max: 100. Dexterity, basic).
Sneaking (current: 36. max: 100. Dexterity, basic).

Shortswords (current: 31. max: 100. Dexterity, basic).
Two weapon fighting (current: 26. max: 100. Dexterity, advanced).
Light armor (current: 1. max: 30. Constitution, basic).
Thieving (current: 1. max: 100. Dexterity, basic).
Chi (current: 1. max: 40. Mind, advanced).
Meditation (current: 15. max: 40. Mind, basic).
Telekinesis (current: 1. max: 40. Mind, advanced).
Telepathy (current: 5. max: 40. Mind, advanced).
Insight (current: 2. max: 80. Perception, basic).

Abilities

Crippling blow (Dexterity, basic).
Simple charm (Mind, basic).
Stunning slap (Mind, basic).
Basic analyze (Perception, basic).

Known Key Points

Sector 14,913 exit portal and safe zone.

Equipped

1 common thief's cloak (+3 sneaking).
2 basic steel shortswords (+10% damage each).
1 common fighter's sash (+3 shortswords).
goblin hide armor set (+10% damage reduction, -50% Dexterity and Magic).

Backpack Contents

Money: 0 gold, 2 silvers, and 1 copper.
29 x field rations.
2 x flask of water.
1 x minor healing potions.
2 x iron daggers.
1 x bedroll.
6 x moderate healing potions.
1 x coin pouch.
1 x keyring.
3 x full healing potions.
1 x basic fire-starting kit.
1 x moonstone lamp.
1 x Catalog of Skills and Abilities.

I rubbed at my chin as I reviewed my Classes and skills. In light of what Decalthiya had explained, I couldn't help but worry that I might have erred in absorbing the psionic Class. *Synergies*, I mused. It was a fairly cryptic requirement. Would the Game see any synergies between my two existing Classes? I had no idea.

I sighed. My selection of primary and secondary Classes had been completed, and they either melded together when I chose my final psionic Class skill—or they didn't. There wasn't much I could do to alter my path with respect to them now.

How do I choose my final Class, though?

What path did I need to follow to ensure that it synergized with my existing ones? And how important was achieving a tri-blend anyway?

I sighed again. There was still so much about the Game that I didn't understand. Hamish and Morin's people could perhaps help me fill in the gaps in my knowledge. But first, I had to ascertain if I could trust them. *When we are done with this war, I* thought, *then, I will see what more I can learn about the Game's Classing system.*

I opened my eyes. Decalthiya was dressed and waiting. Beholding the half-giant, I knew I had made the right choice in gifting her the chief's equipment. In the spiked half armor and wielding the greatclub, Decalthiya looked downright scary.

I rose to my feet. "Care to spar?"

Decalthiya snorted. "You're not thinking of increasing your light armor skill that way, are you?"

That was exactly what I'd been hoping to do, but seeing her expression, my face fell. "It won't work?"

She shook her head. "Most combat skills only increase when you are in actual danger. Somehow the Game always seems to know when that is."

"Ah well," I said, disappointed. "Let's go see how the others are doing then."

~ ~ ~

When we got to the main passage, we found that Sigmar and the rest of the candidates had arrived. Morin had formed them up into a chain that stretched all the way back to the grey merchant.

Much to my amazement, the candidates were stripping the goblin tunnel complex bare—not just of armor and weapons but of *everything* not bolted down, including hides, cages, chairs, furs, and utensils. It was a more mammoth endeavor than I expected, but Morin had the people to do it.

On catching sight of Decalthiya's new gear, Morin nodded approvingly at me but was too busy directing the looting operation to join us.

The painted woman, I saw, was dressed in hide armor and wielding a goblin spear. Sigmar was similarly dressed but carried a longsword. Bornholm had no armor, though he had a warhammer strapped across his back.

"What is Bornholm's Class?" I asked Decalthiya.

"He's a steadfast defender," she answered. "It's a bi-blend Class focused on defense." She paused. "Poor Bornholm. He is lost without his shield and armor."

I winced. Decalthiya was right. Without the correct gear, the dwarf would be of limited use in the upcoming battle. Something else was bothering me, though. "How have you and Bornholm managed to fill your skill slots so quickly?"

Decalthiya's brows crinkled. "What do you mean?"

"I've barely managed to loot enough skillbooks to complete a single Class, but from the sounds of it, you and Bornholm have fully configured *two* of your Classes."

Decalthiya chuckled. "Oh, it's not just Bornholm and me. I'd reckon about half the candidates in the safe zone have twelve or more skills already."

My eyes grew round. "Really? How—"

"It's because of the loot we found in the first three legs of the dungeon," the half-giant said. "The chests in those stages were overflowing with skillbooks and, to a lesser extent, Class stones." Her humor faded. "A lot of candidates got themselves needlessly killed fighting over the books." She fell silent for a moment before continuing. "Anyway, early on skillbooks were not in short supply, and by one means or the other, most of us were able to get the ones we needed."

"I see," I said. It seemed that delaying my own entrance into the dungeon had cost me more than I'd realized.

"Don't feel bad," Decalthiya said, seeing the glum look on my face. "You may have missed out on the skillbooks, but you got something else even more precious."

I looked at her in surprise.

"Experience," she said. "I couldn't figure it out at first, but after seeing the corpses in the great hall, I've realized why you are so much higher leveled than the rest of us: you've gone at it alone." The half-giant leaned forward. "Early on in the dungeon, there were so many candidates about that I could barely get a blow in edgewise. Kills were hard to come by, and my skills barely advanced. Matters improved the farther we ventured, but it was always a struggle to keep other candidates from encroaching on our kills."

She met my gaze. "You may have fewer skills than the rest of us, but you've clearly gained levels faster, and I suspect the skills you do have, are much higher ranked than mine."

I nodded thoughtfully. What Decalthiya said made sense. I had underestimated the big fighter, it seemed. She was more perceptive than I had realized. "What about the others?" I asked. "What are their Classes?"

"Morin is a druid, Tantor a battlemage, and Sigmar, an inquisitor," the half-giant said, seeming to have no qualms about sharing the information.

My brows flew up. "An inquisitor?" Of the three, I found Sigmar's Class to be the most surprising. I studied Morin's human lieutenant again. "Isn't that some sort of priest Class? Does that mean he has a god to whom he is beholden?"

Decalthiya shook her head. "Not yet. Sigmar says he has to find a shrine first. Only then can he dedicate himself to one of the Powers." She scratched her head. "Although from what I've heard, binding yourself to any of the Powers is not necessary to be a priest. Those who employ Faith can wield the Forces directly." She shrugged. "I don't rightly understand any of it myself."

My curiosity was piqued by her mention of Powers and Forces, but before I could question Decalthiya further about them, Morin summoned the half-giant.

I pursed my lips as I watched the big fighter walk away. She had given me a lot to think about. If all the candidates had Classes as impressive-sounding as Decalthiya's own, it meant that despite their comparatively-low levels, I shouldn't underestimate any of them.

And to stay ahead of the pack, it was all the more important that I kept my own skills advancing. With nothing better to do, I sat down on the floor and began analyzing the other candidates.

The target is Morin, a level 10 painted human. This entity is a player. Your insight has increased to level 3.
The target is ...

I kept at it, determined not to stop until I had analyzed every candidate. Insight, at least, was one skill I could train outside of combat.

The target is ...
...
...
Your insight has increased to level 21.

~ ~ ~

It took a whole three hours to salvage everything of worth from the goblin tunnel complex. During that time, I finished analyzing all of Morin's people and raised my insight to rank two in the process. Unfortunately, even at that rank, the analyze ability did not reveal a target's Class.

I took the time to count the candidates too. Morin had nearly one hundred and fifty followers, and from what I had been told, that was nearly double the size of Saben's crew. But given that the gang was better armed and higher-leveled, I wasn't sure how much our numerical superiority would count for.

With the looting operation completed, outfitting the army was continuing apace in the safe zone. Leaving Morin and the other leaders to it, I joined Tantor's squad at the mouth of the north tunnel. My own preparations were complete, and I had volunteered to scout out the enemy. Unsurprisingly, I was the best scout we had.

"Michael, Morin wants you."

I broke off from my discussion with Tantor to turn around. The candidate who had addressed me was standing a few feet away and was waiting for my response.

"Can't it wait?" I asked.

"No," the messenger replied. "She wants to see you before you set out."

With a sigh, I turned away from the tunnel mouth and followed the candidate back into the safe zone.

I found Morin in her 'command' tent. Candidates buzzed around her, and messengers ran to and fro. The mood amongst the painted woman's followers had changed from just a few hours ago. Now, they were tense and eager, ready for the fight.

Morin turned at my approach. "Good, I caught you in time." She held out her hand. "This is for you."

I looked at her open palm. Five gold coins rested on it. "What's this?"

"What's left of the loot we sold after equipping everyone," she said. "Don't argue. Take it. Some of the goblins' goods turned out to be more valuable than expected—the furs in the leather workshop especially—and Hamish didn't stint us in his trades."

I looked at her silently for a moment, then did as she bade. "Thank you," I said.

You have received: 5 golds. Total money carried: 5 golds, 2 silvers, and 1 copper.

Morin smiled. "Buy whatever you need, then head out," she said.

I bobbed my head in wry acknowledgment of the half-order. "Yes, ma'am."

CHAPTER 64: FIRST CONTACT

Hamish was pleased to see me again. My status had been upgraded from 'only' customer to 'best' customer. The merchant was quite profuse in his thanks for the trade I had brought in, but despite his desire to talk, I didn't spend much time at his stall. My mind was too focused on the forthcoming confrontation. Apologizing for my haste, I bought what I needed and hurried away.

You have bought a minor backstab ability tome. You have acquired the basic ability: minor backstab. This is a weapon-based ability that allows you to deal up to 1.5x more damage with a single blow. This ability can only be used when the target is unaware of your presence or is incapacitated.
The effects of this ability may be overcome by physical resistance. This ability consumes stamina and can be upgraded. Its activation time is near-instantaneous. You have 8 of 10 Dexterity ability slots remaining.

Given that I could expect combat in the next few hours, the backstab ability seemed the perfect choice, and I had no compunction about acquiring it. With knowledge of my new ability safely embedded in my mind, I hurried to rejoin Tantor and his squad. The battlemage had a sword strapped to his side and wore a black robe. The five candidates accompanying him all wore hide armor and carried short-bladed weapons. *They have to be primarily scouts and rogues,* I thought.

"We still good to go?" I asked as I approached the group.

Tantor nodded. "No one has gone down this way. We haven't spotted any of Saben's goons coming up the passage either."

I stepped past the elf. "Alright, I'll be on my way then."

He placed a hand on my shoulder, stopping me. I turned around to face him. "You sure you don't want to take Cyrus with you?" Tantor asked. "His sneaking skill is fairly high."

I glanced at the candidate in question. He looked competent enough, but for this initial foray, I preferred to go at it alone. "No," I assured Tantor. "I'll be fine."

He hesitated, then nodded. "Go ahead then," he said. "And remember, you're only scouting for now."

"Of course," I said and slipped into the passage.

~ ~ ~

You and your familiar are hidden.

My shoulders relaxed as the tunnel's darkness enfolded me. I hadn't realized it, but all the time I had been with Morin's people, I had been slightly on edge and unconsciously craving solitude. *It's good to be alone again,* I thought as I padded through the empty passage.

According to the information Morin and Tantor had provided, Saben's gang had erected a guard post midway between the safe zone and their camp. My immediate objective was to confirm the guards' numbers. Once Morin's people were ready to move, the guards would have to be taken down quickly and quietly to ensure that we retained the element of surprise when we hit the camp proper.

I reached the guard post without incident. At this point, the passage was fairly narrow, a natural chokepoint only two yards across. Beyond the guard post, the tunnel was said to widen, eventually expanding into the cavern in which the gang had made their home.

It explained why the guards had been stationed so far forward—almost fifty yards from the camp. At the guard post, a small force, especially one well-armed, would have no trouble holding a larger one at bay. Staying hidden in the shadows, some ten yards from the makeshift guard post, I studied its layout.

A low wall, nearly three-feet-tall and formed from loot chests piled atop one another, had been constructed across the width of the passage. Rocks and gravel had been piled against the far side of the wall to brace the structure. Still, it didn't look entirely sturdy to me, and someone like Decalthiya would have no trouble breaking through.

But that would take time. Time the guards would use to rouse the camp and summon reinforcements.

Beyond the wall, six guards sat on wooden crates arranged in a circle. The candidates were not focused on the barricade they were supposedly guarding but on whatever lay at their feet. Hearing the clink of coins and the low rumble of laughter, I realized they were gambling.

Drawing on my will, I analyzed each in turn.

The target is Mersey, a level 8 human.
The target is Norton, a level 7 human.
The target is Tutti, a level 9 lizardman.
The target is Shael, a level 7 elf.
The target is Forsa, a level 8 dwarf.
The target is Tern, a level 7 gnome.
Your insight has increased to level 22.

One of the humans and the dwarf were in plate mail and definitely fighters of some sort. The gnome and other humans were in leather armor and carrying bows: archers. I wasn't sure about the elf and lizardman's Classes. Both wore robes and were definitely spellcasters of some sort, but whether they wielded Mind, Magic, or Faith, I couldn't tell.

The good thing, though was that all six guards were low-leveled. I pursed my lips as I considered the problem of capturing the guard post. Scaling the wall would be easy enough, but could I do so undetected?

Torches had been affixed on both of the passage's sidewalls, and the immediate area around the barricade was brightly lit.

I frowned. Considering the guards' distraction, sneaking over the wall might be feasible, yet it was too risky. If I was spotted, there was no way I could subdue all six before they raised the alarm.

Speed will serve me—us—better, I realized. For this battle, I would not be alone. With a handful of lightly armored combatants, moving fast, we could kill the guards before they raised the alarm.

It's doable, I concluded.

~ ~ ~

Morin and the rest of her inner circle were at the tunnel mouth when I reported back.

"What did you find?" Tantor asked.

"Six guards, two fighters, two archers, and a pair of spellcasters," I said before going on to describe the details.

"What level were the guards?" Morin asked.

"All were below level ten," I answered.

Tantor frowned.

"What's wrong?" I asked, seeing his look.

"Their levels, they're too low," he explained. "It means none of Saben's elites are there. Strange," he mused. "One of his lieutenants normally commands the guard post."

"Still, it's a good thing that none of them are present," Sigmar said. "We'll have more chance of overcoming the guards quietly this way."

Tantor nodded, but his expression remained troubled.

"What's the plan, lass?" Bornholm asked, turning to Morin.

I wanted to share my own plan but waited to hear Morin out first. The druid knew her own people's abilities better than I did.

The painted woman thought for a moment before glancing at me. "Do you think you can sneak close enough to charm one of them?"

I nodded. I had told her of my abilities earlier, deciding she needed to know at least some of my capabilities if we were going to work together.

Morin turned to the others. "Michael will distract the guards, giving the rest of us time to move in. Once the guards are in disarray, Tantor and I will advance and cast our disables. Then Bornholm and Decalthiya will charge in with a squad of fighters and finish them off. Questions?"

I scratched my chin but didn't say anything. The plan sounded a trifle complicated but workable. *We'll try it her way.*

"What about me?" Sigmar asked.

Morin pointed to the ranks of candidates assembling outside the tunnel mouth. "You're in command of the main force. Follow on our heels. If we fail to kill the guards before they raise the alarm, you charge straight through and assault the camp."

Sigmar inclined his head in acknowledgment of the order.

Morin surveyed the rest of the faces around her. Seeing that there were no more questions, she said, "Then let's get to it, people. Remember, this is our last chance. So let's make it count."

CHAPTER 65: MAYHEM BEFORE MAGIC

Morin put a mixed squad of rogues and scouts under my command. At first, I was reluctant to assume responsibility for them but then I realized that the more blades I had backing me up when I attempted my distraction, the less chance there was of something going horribly wrong.

My ten-man squad dropped into hiding and tiptoed down the corridor. I had made certain to confirm that each of them had a sneaking skill of at least rank one. The few that didn't I rejected and sent back to Morin.

But scouts and rogue though they might be, the other candidates in my squad weren't as comfortable in the dark as I was. None of them had a Perception as high as mine nor a trait for night vision.

Twenty yards from the guard post, I brought my squad to a halt and, out of earshot from the guards, issued my final orders. "Everyone clear on what you need to do?" I asked in a low-voiced whisper when I was done.

The nine candidates nodded, and I crept forward. Eight candidates followed on my heels, while the ninth stayed back. His job was to call in the waiting spellcasters when it was time.

Ten yards from the barricade, I stopped again. Everything beyond the low wall remained the same, and the six guards were still immersed in whatever game they were playing. I waved to my squad to remain in position. This was as far as they would go until I acted.

I inched closer, torturously slow.

Six hostile entities have failed to detect you!
Six hostile entities have failed to detect you!
Your sneaking has increased to level 37.

Ever so carefully, I worked myself towards the barricade. The low wall was actually working to my benefit, shielding me from the guards' direct line of sight.

When I was as close as I dared go, I reached into the pool of psi in my mind and began spellcasting. I picked the human fighter as my target. Neither the pair of spellcasters nor the lightly armored scouts were as big a threat to me as the two heavily armored fighters, and besides, out of all six guards, the two fighters were probably the ones with the lowest mental resistance.

Slipping threads of psi into the target's mind, I overlaid my will upon his.

Norton has passed a mental resistance check! You have failed to charm your target. Your mental intrusion has gone undetected! Your telepathy has increased to level 6.

Not unexpectedly, I failed my first attempt, but as on the previous occasion I used the ability, my target failed to sense the assault. Grimly, I tried again.

You have failed to charm Norton. Your mental intrusion has gone undetected! Your telepathy has increased to level 7.

And again. And again.

You have failed to charm Norton. Your mental intrusion has gone undetected! Your telepathy has increased to level 8.
You have failed to charm Norton. Your mental intrusion has been detected!

My heart nearly stopped at the Game's message. Beyond the barricade, the fighter bit off a shriek and bowed his head.

"Norton, what's wrong?" the dwarf asked.

The human fighter clutched at his head. "I don't know—" He broke off and moaned again.

Behind me, my squad tensed. I raised a hand to hold them in place while my mind raced. The other guards began questioning Norton, but none of them seemed to grasp what the source of the fighter's sudden pain was.

One more try, I decided.

I reached out with my mind again and attempted anew to forcibly bind the fighter's will to my own.

Norton has failed a mental resistance check! You have charmed your target for 10 seconds. Your telepathy has increased to level 10.

Congratulations, Michael! Your skill in telepathy has reached rank 1, increasing your chance of succeeding with telepathic abilities.

I had no time to spare for relief. Dropping my hand, I signaled my squad to advance while dashing forward myself. *"Attack,"* I whispered through the mental leash I held around the human fighter's mind.

Norton surged out of his chair and unsheathed his two-handed sword. His companions, who were clustered around him in concern, drew back in alarm.

In two steps, I reached the wall and, in a single bound, leaped atop it.

Five hostile entities have failed to detect you!

Before any of the other guards could draw their own weapons, Norton lopped off the lizardman's arm, transforming his cry of outrage into a shriek of pain.

Your minion has critically injured Tutti.

Realizing something was wrong, Norton's companions closed around the bespelled fighter again, this time with weapons drawn. The elf glanced upwards and spotted me leaping down from the barricade.

A hostile entity has detected you! You are no longer hidden.

"Forsa, lookout! Behind you!" the elf screamed.

The dwarf spun around and raised his hammer and shield defensively. With a grim smile, I raced around the fighter in a wide arc and didn't attempt to engage him. Stepping forward, the dwarf made to chase me down, but he had left the bespelled fighter at his rear unattended for too long.

Ignoring the attempts of the elf and two archers to stop him, Norton ran his big two-handed blade through the dwarf's exposed back.

Your minion has killed Forsa.

The dying guard's eyes widened in momentary shock before the light in them faded entirely. The elf and the gnome, realizing that half of the number had been felled or disabled in just a handful of seconds, turned around and fled.

They didn't get far, though.

My squad had reached the barricade. Going down on bended knees on top of the wall, three scouts let fly with their arrows. At such short range and with their targets clearly illuminated, it was impossible for them to miss.

All three projectiles found their marks. The first arrow thudded into the unarmored spellcaster's chest while the other two buried themselves in the gnome's shoulder and neck.

Shael has died.
Tern has died.

Of the original six guards, only the two humans—archer and bespelled fighter—were still standing. The archer was backing away from Norton and drawing his bow.

"Take out the second archer!" I shouted and altered my own heading towards Norton. My spell was about to wear off.

Two arrows thudded into Mersey, ending the archer's life just as he raised his own bow into firing position. But with my attention fixed on Norton, I paid the archer's death no heed. Slipping behind the fighter, I waited for my charm spell to lapse. Behind me, the archers reloaded and loosed again, putting an end to the lizardman's cries.

You have lost control over Norton.

My left hand snaked out and wrapped around the fighter's arm. Before Norton had a chance to react, I channeled stamina.

Norton has failed a physical resistance check! You have crippled your target's left arm for 3 seconds.

Energy rushed out of my palm, and the fighter's arm went slack. Norton began turning around.

Too slowly, though, far too slowly.

While Norton's other hand was still reaching for me, I flung up the disabled appendage and shoved my blade into the revealed armor joint under the fighter's armpit.

You have critically injured Norton!

Norton cried out and fell to his knees. Holding onto his arm, I thrust my blade again into him. And then once and twice more before the fighter slumped to the floor with a sad sigh.

You have killed Norton. You have reached level 19!
Your shortswords has increased to level 32.
Your light armor has increased to level 3.

Dropping the dead fighter's arm, my eyes flew to the tunnel ahead. I could hear no cry of alarm nor see any approaching guards. The tension eased out of me. We had succeeded. The guards had been contained without alerting the camp.

Motion drew my eye to the barricade, and my head whipped around. Morin and Tantor had arrived and were staring down in shock at the slain guards.

I sheathed my still-bloody blade and smiled wolfishly. "You're late."

CHAPTER 66: ON TO THE MAIN COURSE

"But did you really have to poke such a big hole through it, lad?"

I rolled my eyes at Bornholm's whining. The two of us were bent over the dead dwarven guard and trying to tug free his armor. "Next time, I'll make a special effort not to," I murmured.

"See that you do," the dwarf grunted, seemingly oblivious to my tone.

We were still at the captured guard post. Sigmar and the main force hadn't arrived yet. Up ahead, Morin, Tantor, and half the scout squad kept watch for the enemy while the rest were stripping the dead guards of their gear.

"You better hurry and get dressed, Bornholm," Decalthiya said. "Sigmar is nearly here, and you know he won't wait on you."

The dwarf didn't say anything, but he held off on further grumbling and began equipping himself faster. Leaving him to it, I sat down and took a moment to spend my new attribute point.

Your Constitution has increased to rank 4.

Then I closed my eyes. Trusting my heightened senses to warn me of approaching danger, I blanked my mind and let the pool of psi in my subconsciousness replenish.

You have replenished 2% of your psi. Your psi is now at 62%.

...

With every breath, my reserves of psi slowly regenerated. After reading Hamish's catalog, I had discovered there were skills similar to meditation for restoring stamina and mana, and while the idea of having them was nice, I didn't have enough skill slots to accommodate them.

A hand clamped down on my shoulder, jolting my mind back to the present.

Meditation interrupted! Your psi is now at 80%. Your meditation has increased to level 19.

I looked up. It was Bornholm, fully dressed in his new armor. "The others are here," he said.

I rose to my feet. Looking around, I saw that the candidates of the main column stood at the ready less than five yards away. I had been so absorbed in my meditation I hadn't heard their footfalls or the low murmur of their voices.

"What were you doing?" Bornholm asked curiously.

"Meditating," I replied absently, searching for the rest of Morin's inner circle. "Where's Sigmar?"

"Gone ahead to join Morin and Tantor," he replied. "Let's go join them."

~ ~ ~

We found Morin and the others twenty yards ahead and in animated discussion.

"... still don't like it," Tantor whispered.

"But where can they be?" Decalthiya asked, her voice sounding hoarse as she tried to speak softly.

"I don't know," Tantor replied. "And that's what worries me."

"Does it matter?" Sigmar asked. "This is our chance to take the camp. I say we take it."

At our approach, Morin looked back, and the others fell silent.

"Problems?" I asked, directing my question at the painted woman.

"Not exactly," Morin said, with a glance at Sigmar and Tantor. "The scouts have returned from reconnoitering the camp. The gang still isn't aware of our presence, but there is no sign of Saben's elites anywhere."

"Which may not mean anything," Sigmar said.

"But it does affect our plans," Tantor added.

I nodded, understanding their dilemma. The original plan had called for us to focus the assault on Saben's core group. We had agreed that defeating the elites was the key to winning the battle. To that end, Morin had divided our forces into squads and tasked some with hunting down the gang's lieutenants and leader. But with none of our primary targets visible, those plans had been thrown in disarray.

"It doesn't matter where they are," Bornholm said abruptly. "If we sit on our arses here much longer, we're going to be spotted. Whatever we decide, we must act quickly."

Morin glanced at the dwarf. "Bornholm is right. We've delayed long enough." She rose to her feet. "Sigmar, bring up the column. It's time to attack."

~ ~ ~

With Morin, Decalthiya, and Bornholm at the fore, the column of one hundred and fifty candidates jogged the last fifty yards to the camp. No one spoke, no one shouted, and no one broke ranks. The calm was impressive—and unnerving.

As the tunnel widened, the column spread out and formed into silent ranks. At first, our presence went unnoticed. That didn't last, though. But even after the alarm was sounded, Morin's people retained their discipline. Sticking to their orders and ignoring the growing chaos in the camp, they formed a battle line.

Positioned in the center of the line, I glanced at the candidates on either side of me. There was a quiet intensity to Morin's people, one that underscored the rage I saw simmering in their fierce gazes and clenched fists. The candidates were ready for this battle. No, they were more than ready, I realized. They were quivering with eagerness and thirsted for blood.

This was their chance to finally hit back, and they knew it.

"Go ahead, Decalthiya," Morin ordered.

I swung my gaze forward again. Morin was standing six steps ahead of the rest of the line, with Bornholm and Decalthiya on either side of her.

The half-giant breathed in deeply. "CANDIDATES," she bellowed, "The time has come to depose your vile leader! Throw down your weapons, and you won't be harmed. FIGHT, AND YOU DIE."

I wasn't particularly fond of this part of the plan and thought it foolish to surrender the advantage of surprise in this manner. But Morin had been adamant. She believed that, given a chance, many of Saben's people would abandon his cause. The painted woman had argued that if we presented the gang with a forcible-enough ultimatum and robbed Saben of the opportunity to properly intimidate his people beforehand, many would swap sides. And the others had agreed with her.

I was more doubtful myself but deferred to their knowledge of the candidates. They had known many of these people for weeks. I knew some of the candidates had been coerced into joining the gang. Even so, I didn't know how far I would trust former gang members, especially in the heat of battle. Scanning the enemy, I watched for their reaction.

There were only fifty or so candidates in the camp. We outnumbered them three to one, and they seemed to have realized that too. Nearly a minute had passed since we had entered the cavern, but the candidates in the camp were still milling about.

I frowned. *Where are their leaders? And where are all the undead I saw the first time around?* Sure, the candidates' familiars were present, but no other type of undead was in evidence.

I glanced at our right flank, where Tantor was commanding the spellcasters. His expression was worried. My own concern grew, and I began to fear that the battlemage's suspicions were warranted. Something was amiss.

At the clash of weapons, my head whipped around. A fight had broken out amongst some of the enemy, between a handful who were disarming and those nearby. Scanning the camp, I saw that nearly half of the gang members were throwing down their weapons.

Morin was right. I shook my head in bemusement and felt my worries ease. If enough of the enemy surrendered, then the battle would be won already, and it didn't matter where Saben and his elites had disappeared to. *Perhaps, they've run.*

Another fight broke out.

Then another.

I realized that despite Morin's good intentions, the candidates whose lives she was trying to save might just die anyway—at the hands of their fellow gang members.

Coming to the same realization, Morin gestured the waiting ranks forward. "Fighters, attack!" she ordered, "Spare those who surrender and capture as many alive as you can."

I let the line advance around me but stayed back myself. My blade was not needed. Given the disparity in size between the two forces, and the disarray among the gang members, I thought they would be quickly subdued.

On the right and left flanks, our mages and archers—about half our total force— stood idly by. Morin had not ordered them into play, and I could understand why. If the archers and mages joined the attack, keeping the casualties down would be next to impossible. After the ranks of fighters passed me, I strode towards the huddle forming around Morin.

"Where are the prisoners?" Bornholm asked, his voice quivering with anger and perhaps fear. "Why aren't they in the center of the camp. That's where that bastard has always kept them displayed!"

"I don't know," Morin said, "but we will find out soon enough. Sigmar has gone to question one of the gang members." Morin laid a comforting hand on the dwarf. "Cena will be fine," she added gently.

Bornholm's chest heaved rapidly, and his breath came out ragged, but at Morin's calm, measured tone, he quietened. I felt a spurt of sympathy for the dwarf. I had suspected earlier that he had recently lost someone to Saben's gang, and this confirmed that.

My gaze slid to Sigmar. A squad of fighters had managed to extract three thugs who had lain down their weapons from amidst the melee raging in the camp, and the inquisitor was questioning one of them.

I stopped at Tantor's side. "Do we know where Saben is?"

The high elf shook his head, his eyes also on the inquisitor. "Not yet, but Sigmar will find out," he said with grim certainty.

Nodding, I folded my arms and set myself to wait.

Chapter 67: Running down Prey

While I waited for the inquisitor to return with news, I observed the battle—such as it was. Individual squads of our fighters were moving swiftly to surround and quell isolated groups of enemies. The fighting had not subsided yet, but matters were proceeding well, and shortly I suspected, the camp would be fully subdued.

Sigmar's questioning finished sooner than I expected. Either the former gang member had been exceedingly cooperative, or the inquisitor had some sort of interrogation ability—which given his Class, he might very well have.

"Saben and his men are gone," Sigmar said, slightly breathless, as he ran up to Morin's side.

"Where?" she asked sharply.

Sigmar gestured to the right and left sides of the cavern. There were tunnel entrances on both ends, I noted. "Our timing was fortuitous. We caught Saben unprepared and with none of his elites present. The moment we hit the camp, he fled to his chambers on the western side. That way is a dead end. He's holed up there now." Sigmar's eyes glinted. "Trapped and alone."

"That doesn't make sense," I said. I glanced at the captive. He was still kneeling and hunched over. Whatever Sigmar had done to him had left the former gang member shaken and exhausted. "You're sure your informant is telling you the truth? Why would Saben flee to his chambers if there is no way out?

Sigmar's eyes narrowed. "I'm sure. They *always* tell the truth, and as for Saben... perhaps he panicked."

I frowned, not as certain as Sigmar. I glanced at the others, but there was no flicker of doubt on any of their faces, not even Tantor's. They all appeared certain of the veracity of Sigmar's information. *That must be some ability the inquisitor has.*

"What about the prisoners?" Bornholm asked anxiously.

The inquisitor threw the dwarf a sympathetic look. "Ten minutes before our attack, they were marched off into the eastern tunnel network by the elites."

"*All* the elites escorted them?" Morin asked.

Sigmar nodded.

Tantor frowned. "Why, though? Saben's people have surely cleared that section of the dungeon already?"

Sigmar shrugged. "My subject didn't know. Only the elites have ever been allowed to venture into those tunnels." He paused. "But the rumor in the camp is that the tunnel network beyond the eastern entrance is quite extensive. Squads of elites have been known to disappear there for hours at—"

"We have to go after the prisoners," Bornholm interjected.

"We do," Morin agreed, "but we also have to see to Saben." Her gaze flickered over the faces of her inner circle before resting on me for a moment.

I nodded in response, suspecting what she wanted me to do. I feared, though, that Saben was already out of reach. Despite the captive's tale, I thought it likely that the gang leader had a secret way out of his chambers.

"Right," Morin said, coming to a decision. "Bornholm, take the spellcasters and archers. Go find our people." Her emerald eyes turned cold. "And kill any elites you find."

"Aye, aye, lass," the dwarf said, not hiding his eagerness for the task. Hurrying away, he began yelling out orders to the squads Morin had assigned to him.

Morin watched him for a second before turning back to us. "As for the rest of us, we capture Saben." She glanced at Sigmar. "You're certain Saben's chambers are a dead-end?"

He nodded. "Yes, I made sure to question my subject closely about that. The western exit leads to a tunnel that loops about for about two hundred yards before ending in a large cavern. It used to be the lair of a giant spider. After the gang slew it, Saben claimed the chamber for his own. We have him trapped."

"Good," Morin said. Her gaze darted back towards the battle in the camp. "Matters appear to be in order here, but one of us will still need to stay behind and mop up things." Her eyes fell on Tantor.

"I'll do it," Sigmar volunteered.

Morin turned to him in surprise.

"It'll give me a chance to question more of the gang and see if I can pinpoint the prisoners' whereabouts," Sigmar said. "When things have settled down here, I'll send reinforcements your way." He grinned and glanced at me. "Not that you'll need it with this fellow backing you up."

One of my eyebrows rose. I was surprised by Sigmar's sudden show of faith in me. I had gotten the distinct impression that he didn't like me. I felt much the same way about him too.

"Excellent idea," Morin said, agreeing with his reasoning. "The more you can find out, the quicker we can recover our captured people." She turned back to Decalthiya, Tantor, and me. "We ready?"

The three of us nodded.

"Then let's finish this," the druid said. Spinning on her heel, she made for the western tunnel, with the rest of us following in her wake.

"Good hunting," Sigmar called from behind.

~ ~ ~

Sigmar was right about the winding nature of the western tunnel. Less than a dozen yards after the four of us entered the passage, it turned sharply left before curving right again.

Given the convoluted nature of the tunnel, the sounds of the battle still raging in the main cavern faded quickly, leaving the four of us walking in tense silence.

"I should take the lead," Decalthiya declared after a moment. The tunnel was wide enough for our party to walk four abreast, but at Morin's instructions, we were proceeding in a single file.

I was in the lead and, at the half-giant's words, stopped and turned around. The light in the tunnel was fading rapidly, and Decalthiya was eyeing the encroaching darkness nervously. Still, it had not stopped her from volunteering to go first.

I snorted. The half-giant, I was coming to realize, had an overly protective instinct, and at times it made her rash and reckless. But it was less Decalthiya's words that disturbed me than the worsening light. I turned to the others who had halted with me. "I'm guessing none of you see very well in the dark?"

They shook their heads.

I bit my lip, hesitating, then pulled out the moonstone lamp and handed it to Morin. "We'll have to risk a light then. It'll forewarn Saben of our approach, but it beats being ambushed."

The painted woman nodded in agreement.

"I'll be leaving you here as well," I added.

"Why?" Tantor asked sharply.

"My night vision is better than yours," I said, without venturing to explain just how much better, "I'll scout on ahead."

"Alone?" Decalthiya asked with a shiver of unease. "In the dark?"

I smiled. "Nothing I haven't done before," I murmured.

"It's a good idea," Morin said. "Go. We'll follow more slowly. Make sure to report back every five minutes. If you spot Saben, don't try engaging him on your own," she warned. "Despite his lower level, he is more than a match for you."

I doubted it but didn't argue. "I won't," I promised and slipped into the welcoming dark.

~ ~ ~

I hurried away from the others, quickly widening the gap between us. Only when the light from the moonstone lamp had faded to a distant blur did I slow down and slip into stealth.

You and your familiar are hidden.

"You know, at times, I can't figure out if you're smart or just stupidly brave," Gnat whispered in my ear. "You should've stayed with the others. It's safer."

"Shh," I hissed, not wanting to be distracted by the familiar now. Obligingly, Gnat fell silent and said no more.

The tunnel did not let up on its twisting and meandering nature, and soon I was unable to tell if I was still heading westwards. But true to Sigmar's words, no other branches or exits of any sort appeared. As I went farther, I began to notice near-translucent white strands running along the walls and ceiling of the tunnel.

The strands increased in concentration and soon began covering entire sections of the tunnel walls. *They're spiderwebs*, I realized.

I had to be getting close.

I slowed to a crawl. Given the many bends and twists to the passage, it was hard to estimate the distance I had covered already, but I judged the spider's lair could not be much further ahead. I continued onwards, my every sense extended and pausing between each carefully placed step to listen.

A dozen steps more, and the walls on either side of me turned white, draped with overlapping layers of silk. Pausing, I studied them intently but could detect nothing hidden within their depths. Fixing my gaze forward again, I kept going. I took one step, two, then another handful.

Then froze.

I heard noises from up ahead, the sounds of a whispered conversation. At this distance, the voices were too indistinct for me to pick out the individual words or identify the number of speakers, but if Saben was up ahead, it was clear he was not alone.

Damnit, I cursed, torn between wanting to find out more and informing the others. *Saben's not going anywhere,* I decided. *Best to warn Morin and get them to stay put, then come back and scout.* It was almost time to report back anyway. Pivoting on my heels, I reversed course.

A sliver of motion caught my attention. The web to my right was trembling minutely. My head whipped in that direction. A furtive figure was emerging from the webs.

A hidden entity has detected you! You are no longer hidden. You have detected a hidden entity. Saben is no longer hidden!
Your insight has increased to level 23.

My eyes widened.

I dashed forward, my hands dropping to my sheathed blades. Saben was a human male. I got a quick impression of manicured hands, black pin-straight long hair, delicate silk clothes, and a pale face that was fast transforming into a scowl as the gang leader realized he had been spotted. Then I stopped consciously seeing, and my reactions took over.

I was less than four steps away from Saben. I could end this here. My swords flew out, and I lunged forward.

The gang leader was prepared, though.

A cone-shaped wave of sickly green energy rushed out of Saben's hands and directly toward me. I sidestepped, attempting to dodge. But my own forward momentum betrayed me, and I was clipped by the edge of the waveform. My mouth opened in wordless horror as the green tendrils dug into my flesh, burrowing deep.

Saben has cast snare prey upon you.
You have failed to resist the spell! Saben has successfully drained your stores of energy. Your pools of stamina, psi, and mana have been emptied: -100%.

As if my strings had been cut, my blades fell from lifeless hands, and I collapsed in a heap.

CHAPTER 68: PREDATOR AND PREY

I lay on the ground, gasping. My limbs felt too heavy to move, and my thoughts were sluggish. I barely had the energy to slide my gaze upwards to the figure approaching me.

It was Saben.

He crouched down and peered at me. Judging by his attire alone, Saben was a wealthy courtier. A jewel-encrusted shortsword was belted at his hip. Soft leather gloves covered his hands, extravagant embroidery decorated his silk jacket, and his boots were polished to a high sheen.

His eyes, though, betrayed him. Storm grey, they spoke of death and suffering. There was something else about Saben that was different, too, something beyond the physical. Reaching out with my will, I cast analyze upon the gang leader.

The target is Saben, a level 14 human. This entity is a player and bears a Mark of Minor Dark and a Mark of Ishita.

Saben was higher leveled than Morin had said. Either he had gained the levels recently, or her information was bad. And if she was wrong about this... *what else is she wrong about?* Also, unlike every other candidate I had met, Saben was Marked. He had likely filled all three of his Class slots and completed the Master's task. *He will recognize my own Marks, too,* I realized.

The gang leader's painted black lips curved upwards in a thin smile as he studied me. "My, aren't you a slippery one," he murmured. "And Marked too already. Ishita will be most displeased."

My lips parted, and I attempted a rejoinder, but only a dry wheeze escaped me. Saben chuckled. "Oh, I wouldn't try talking," he said. "It's going to be a while yet before you have the energy for anything besides breathing."

You have detected two hidden entities. Goral and Markus are no longer hidden!

I sensed two figures emerge from the webs covering the wall behind me. "Sorry, boss," one said. "He moved too fast."

Saben glanced up at him, his face expressionless, but the speaker must have sensed something in the gang leader's face that I didn't because he stepped back hastily.

"We didn't think he'd—" he began, his voice shaking.

"Enough," Saben said, his voice mild but with the promise of pain to come. "You made me trigger the spell early. Do you know how rare that scroll was? Ishita will not give me another, and now we will have to capture the others the hard way." The gang leader shook his head in disgust. "Get him inside before the rest get here. I will deal with you two later." He paused. "And don't forget his weapons."

Goral and Markus picked me up by the feet and hands and hauled me off further down the passage. Still near-senseless, I was helpless to stop them. Swaying in the pair's grasp, I cast analyze on both.

The target is Goral, a level 11 human.
The target is Markus, a level 10 human.

After only a few yards, the tunnel opened into a cavern nearly thirty yards in diameter. Thick spiderwebs covered the entirety of the chamber's walls and roofs. A bed and table lay on the left side of the room, and on the right, nearly two dozen elites crouched down.

The two gang members dropped me carelessly in the center of the chamber. My gaze was fixed on the waiting elites, and I barely noticed. *So, it is a trap,* I thought, swallowing bile. The gang leader had known we were coming all along. *How though?*

"Not there!" Saben said. "Goral, hide him behind the web. Stay and watch over him. Markus, return to your position and report back as soon as you spot Morin's party."

With muttered replies of "Yes, boss," the pair hastened to comply with their leader's orders. Markus slipped out of the room again while Goral picked me up by the armpits and began dragging me back to the far end of the chamber. My mind raced, searching for a way out. I had to warn the others, and I had to escape Saben's clutches.

I glanced down at my empty scabbards. But how did I do that with neither stamina, psi, nor weapons? The simple answer was I couldn't. I had to figure out a way to regain all three if I was going to put up any meaningful resistance.

I surveyed the room again. The cavern was sparsely furnished, and nothing in it appeared of immediate use. I turned my attention to the room's occupants. Saben had swung around to face the entrance again and had his back turned to me. The other elites were not looking at me. In fact, they didn't appear to be looking at anything. Their eyes were curiously vacant.

As if they can't see.

The realization hit me swift and sharp. *Of course, it is pitch black in the cavern.* I cursed softly. I should have caught onto that fact sooner; my thoughts were still torpid. The only reason I could see was because of my nocturnal trait. My gaze slid back to Saben. Despite the dark, the gang leader, Goral, and Markus had had no trouble seeing me. *Which means... they must be able to see equally well in the dark.*

An inkling of an idea formed. I reached up with shaky arms to clutch at the straps of my backpack. Even that simple action required tremendous effort, but eventually, I managed it. Goral didn't notice. Huffing and puffing, he was too intent on getting me to where I needed to be. Inch by inch, I pushed the straps off my shoulders until they were nearly loose.

Then waited.

We reached the webs, and Goral pulled me through without pause. The silk strands parted easily for us, and without preamble, the elite dumped me onto the floor. I had been waiting for just this moment. As Goral released his hold on me, I pushed off my backpack's straps entirely so it fell to the floor, and twisted my body in an effort to fall atop it.

I succeeded only partially.

I landed on my side and next to the pack. The elite glanced down and saw the pack resting free near me, but didn't seem to care. Bending over, he hissed, "Now you be quiet, you hear? Any trouble from you and I'll slit your throat."

I stared at the thug for a moment. He had one of my swords hanging on his belt, I noticed. *Markus must have the other.*

"Well? Are you going to behave?" Goral growled, prodding me with his boot.

I bobbed my head obligingly. Satisfied that he had cowed me, Goral rose to his feet and peered forward again. I followed his gaze. The spiderweb lay between us and the rest of the chamber. Peering through it was like looking through thick gauze. I doubted anyone from outside would be able to spot Goral and me. It was how the trio had managed to hide from me in the first place.

I took in the rest of my new surroundings. The space between the webs and the cavern's walls was perhaps one yard across and but for me, Goral, and our two skeletal bats, it was empty.

Speaking of the familiars... the pair were hanging upside down from the ceiling and appeared to be whispering to each other. *Now, what could they be going on about?*

I glanced at the gang member again. With his gaze fixed on the cavern entrance, Goral was paying me no mind. I inched my left hand forward and under the flap of my backpack. By feel alone, I fished out a field ration and began unwrapping it.

"Where is your party?" Goral hissed suddenly. "They should have reached here by now."

In the act of drawing out the unwrapped ration, I paused and glanced up. Even though he addressed me, Goral didn't look my way. I resumed extracting my prize.

Morin, I realized, must've figured out something was wrong after I was late for my check-in. She would likely have stopped the party, and I imagined that even now, the trio was probably debating on whether or not to proceed. *I hope she returns to the main cavern for reinforcements.*

But whatever decision Morin made was out of my hands. I could only do my best to ensure I was ready to act when the time came.

My hand emerged from the backpack with the ration hidden in my palm. I slipped the morsel unseen into my mouth and chomped down.

After a tense few seconds, I felt a sliver of energy return to me. Holding in my relief, I kept chewing and swallowing. The food ration would not return nearly enough stamina to me in the time I suspected I had remaining, but it was a start.

I finished the ration and closed my eyes. I had done what I could for my stamina. Now I had to see to my psi.

Stilling my mind, I began meditating. It was risky blocking off awareness while I was so endangered, but I had no choice. There was no way I was getting out of the mess I was in with stamina alone.

I needed psi.

I could only hope that when Morin and the others entered the cavern, I retained enough awareness to sense their arrival—and act accordingly.

You have replenished 2% of your psi. Your psi is now at 2%.
You have replenished 2% of your psi. Your psi is now at 4%.
...
...

CHAPTER 69: STANDOFF

Meditation interrupted!

"... not go quietly!" The voice reverberated through the cavern, calm, measured, and undaunted.

Morin, I thought, my eyes snapping open. I checked my internal reserves, wondering how long I had been out.

Your stamina is at 12%, your psi at 36%, and your mana at 0%.

Judging by how far my reserves had replenished, only five or six minutes had passed.

Saben laughed, his languid tone in sharp contrast to Morin's. "And how will you do that?" he inquired mockingly. He gestured to the waiting elites. "You are outnumbered eight to one."

I peered into the cavern through the intervening silk strands. Morin, Tantor, and Decalthiya hovered near the entrance. The painted woman held the moonstone lamp aloft in one hand and her spear in the other. The half-giant's hands were clenched around the haft of the greatclub, and Tantor's eyes flitted around the room. Saben's elites had risen to their feet and had formed a half-circle at their leader's rear.

"Where is he?" Decalthiya demanded.

Saben tilted his head to the side with feigned interest. "Who?"

"Michael," the half-giant ground out. "Did he betray us?"

The gang leader chuckled. "Of course, my dear. Michael has always been one of mine. Who do you think forewarned me of your assault?"

Decalthiya's face turned red with rage, and my own lips tightened. Goral glanced down at me, the warning not to say anything clear on his face.

I stayed quiet, not because I was intimidated, but to play for time. The longer this dragged on, the greater the chance that Sigmar and the reinforcements would arrive in time to intervene. Hopefully, Morin realized the same. What I didn't know was why Saben was toying with the trio. Was it simply for pleasure? Or did he have some other game in mind?

Biding my time, I began analyzing each of Saben's followers while listening to the conversation with half an ear.

Morin laid a restraining hand on Decalthiya before addressing Saben again. "Enough of your games, Saben. We will not believe any of your lies."

There wasn't the slightest trace of doubt in the painted woman's voice, for which I was relieved.

"Surrender now," Morin continued, "and perhaps you will be spared."

The gang leader threw back his head and laughed uproariously. "Oh, this is too delicious," he said when his mirth subsided. "Tell me, Morin, why would I do that?"

"Because," she replied, unmoved by Saben's amusement, "the rest of the candidates are on their way here. All one hundred and fifty—each and every one baying for your blood." She paused. "The only one that can stop them is me. So, this is your last chance. Drop your weapons, and surrender."

I had to admit Morin was convincing, and I hoped what she said was true, but I doubted it. At best, Sigmar would only be able to bring three to four squads with him. Not counting those who had gone with Bornholm, the rest would be needed to guard the gang members that had surrendered. Nobody wanted them swapping sides again.

"Oh, I doubt that," Saben said, echoing my own thoughts.

Morin raised a questioning eyebrow. "And why is that?"

Saben chuckled. "Because I happen to know that only two dozen more of your troops are heading this way."

My own brows drew down. *Is Saben bluffing?* If he was, it was an oddly specific lie. I felt my trepidation rise. Something was amiss, but I couldn't figure out what.

"All the more reason to surrender now," Morin said, seemingly unphased by the gang leader's words. "The rest of my people will be following on their heels."

Saben shook his head with exaggerated sorrow. "No, Morin. I'm afraid you're wrong. No one else is coming after them." He cupped a hand around his ear. "And if I am not mistaken, here are your reinforcements now."

As if summoned by Saben's words, two squads of candidates appeared in the tunnel beyond the entrance, with Sigmar at their fore.

I saw Morin's stance relax minutely. Despite her brave front, the painted woman had been worried, I realized. I felt my own tension ease. With two dozen more candidates on our side, we had a chance now.

Sigmar, his face carefully neutral, entered the cavern and stepped up to Morin's side. The painted woman gave the inquisitor a welcoming smile before turning back to the gang leader. "Now, Saben, for the last time, surrender your—"

Morin broke off. Her eyes widening, she stared down at the bared sword at her throat.

It was Sigmar's blade.

Saben giggled. "Oops. I'm sorry. I misspoke earlier. Did I say 'your' troops?" He grinned. "I meant mine."

The silence in the chamber was deafening. Speechless with shock, Morin, Tantor, and Decalthiya stared at the still-impassive Sigmar.

"No," I whispered.

Saben clapped his hands. "Everyone, it is my pleasure to finally introduce to you my deputy, my right-hand man, and the most loyal of followers: Sigmar."

With a groan, I closed my eyes and bowed my head to the ground.

There was no getting out of this alive now.

~ ~ ~

"Is it true?"

At Morin's whispered words, I picked up my head. The druid's gaze was fixed on Sigmar, waiting for his answer. His lips pressed together in a grim line, the inquisitor didn't say anything.

While I waited for his response, I let my eyes rove past Sigmar to the candidates at his back. Now that I looked more closely at them, I realized none were part of the original warband that had set out from the safe zone. One I recognized as a gang member who had surrendered. Another was Markus.

I grimaced, realizing then how deep Sigmar's betrayal ran. He had played us from the very beginning.

Morin's words had broken the spell despair had cast over me, and after grasping the extent of Sigmar's treachery, my anger only grew. It didn't matter to me if I died here anymore, only that I sold my life dearly.

Gazing within, I took stock of my reserves. My stamina was still ticking upwards, but my psi remained at thirty-six percent—enough for three simple charm attempts, I judged.

"Don't keep the dear woman waiting," Saben said, seeming to finally run out of patience with his henchman's silence. "Answer her!"

Sigmar threw the gang leader a scowl before turning back to address Morin. "As with everything Saben utters," he said finally, "his words are a mixture of lies and half-truths." Sigmar's lips twitched upwards in a smile. "I'm not the zealot's follower. I'm his partner."

Morin's capacity for shock appeared exhausted, and she evinced no reaction. Not so, her companions. On the far side of Morin, Tantor's face drained of all color, while at Sigmar's back, Decalthiya's eyes burned with hate into the inquisitor.

"How long?" the painted woman asked.

"How long what?" Sigmar asked, looking confused.

"How long have you been betraying us."

"Ah," Sigmar said and fell silent for a moment. "Since before we entered the dungeon."

"I see," Morin said.

"This is all getting tedious," Saben said. "Can we get on with it, Sigmar?"

The inquisitor gave the gang leader a curt nod before turning to address the druid again. "Join us, Morin," he said. "The Dark is not all bad, and together we can curb Saben's excesses."

"Now, wait a moment," Saben protested. "This is not—"

"Shut up, Saben," Sigmar growled. He glanced at Tantor beyond Morin and Decalthiya standing on the other side of him. "We are still companions," he urged. "Take this chance. Please."

I don't know what Sigmar expected, but his words weren't reaching any of the trio. If anything, his words only appeared to infuriate his former companions further. Decalthiya, especially, seemed to be in the throes of an almost berserker rage, and I could see some of Saben's people edging away from her.

The half-giant's hands tightened suddenly around the haft of her club, and I knew she was about to lash out. I saw Tantor's eyes narrow as he came to the same realization. Morin was harder to read, but I thought I sensed a coiled readiness in her as well.

Sigmar, on the other hand, appeared oblivious of the danger at his back. I dipped into the pool of psi in my mind and prepared myself.

The time to act had come.

CHAPTER 70: DEATH AND MAYHEM

I was already halfway through my casting when Decalthiya's weapon hurtled forward.

Sigmar stood no chance.

In a single, mighty blow, the inquisitor's head was caved in, his hide armor helm proving no obstacle to the half-giant's greatclub.

Sigmar has died.

In the same instant, Morin's hand flashed downwards and sent the moonstone lamp crashing to the floor, destroying the cavern's only light source. The maneuver triggered Tantor's own action. The battlemage leaped backward, using the darkness to hide his movements. From his new position, he crouched down and began softly chanting the opening words of a spell while Morin stood tall and shouted out the words of her own casting.

With the object of her hatred dead, Decalthiya whirled about and charged into the candidates crowding the tunnel. She laid into them with abandon and, more importantly, stopped any of their numbers from entering the chamber.

The elites in the chamber were not caught entirely flatfooted. Despite being blinded, the fighters amongst them drew their weapons and charged Morin's position while the gang's mages and clerics began their own chants. Their voices were a soft counterpoint to the clash of steel and rising shouts of alarm.

Saben, too, was casting. But with my own spell preparation nearly done, I had no further attention to spare him or the others in the chamber.

Focusing on my target, I sent tendrils of psi reaching into his mind. Goral's back was rigid and his hand rested on the daggers on his belt, but despite his obvious tension, the thug made no move to join the fight in the cavern.

Goral has passed a mental resistance check! You have failed to charm your target. Your mental intrusion has gone undetected!

My first attempt failed, and without hesitation, I began anew. It grated on me to rely solely on psi for my opening attack but given Goral's night vision, and my lack of a useable weapon, I had no other option.

In the passage, Decalthiya was a force of destruction. With every blow, she maimed or crippled candidates while seeming to be immune from the blows she received in return. I saw Markus go down under her greatclub and couldn't help a small smile. That was one more threat I need not worry about.

Morin's spellcasting completed, and a circle of thorn vines rose out of the ground to snap at the fighters surrounding her. The gang's fighters fell back, but I saw that the druid was already bleeding from multiple cuts.

A flurry of ice and slurry roared out of Tantor's hands, flash-freezing everything in its path. But the darkness worked as much to the elf's detriment as the gang's, and he was forced to blindly target his spell. Unfortunately, only two enemy mages were caught out by the beam.

Then the gang's spellcasters' own castings came into effect.

Three globes of light arced to the ceiling and shone downwards to form a trio of overlapping cones of light. On the cavern's left, a zombie and six skeletons rose from the ground, and on the right, two wraiths materialized from the air. Shields of silver flickered into being around four mages, and a pair of magic missiles hissed toward Tantor.

My stomach clenched. The battle had already begun to turn. It was inevitable, of course, given the disparity in the numbers, but our party's opening salvo had given me cause to hope for better.

A gleam of obsidian drew my eye back to the cavern's center. Saben was releasing his spell. A black bubble of pulsating darkness grew from the gang leader's hands and bobbled towards the entrance. On a direct course for Morin.

My eyes widened in horror, and I nearly lost grasp on my own casting. Instinctively, I knew that whatever the bubble contained, Morin would not survive it. Tantor, rising out of his roll as he evaded the missiles heading his way, saw Saben's spellcasting, too, and managed to shout out a warning. Decalthiya's head whipped around and began swinging around.

Then my own spell completed, and my attention flew back to Goral. Wielding psi like a hammer, I forcibly crushed the gang member's will beneath my own.

Goral has failed a mental resistance check! You have charmed your target for 10 seconds.

At last, I breathed. I rose to my feet and, in a single motion, drew my sword from Goral's belt and plunged it through his throat.

You have taken hostile action against your minion! Control of target lost. You have killed Goral.

With night vision of his own, Goral had been too big a threat to let live. I let the corpse fall to my feet and slipped into hiding.

Multiple hostile entities have failed to detect you! You are hidden.

My gaze slid back to the cavern in time to see Decalthiya launch herself in front of Morin—and directly into the obsidian bubble that was still sailing slowly through the air.

As soon as she made contact with the pulsating orb, the half-giant collapsed as if her strings had been cut. The bubble was not done with her yet, though. It's cloying darkness seeped into her, causing her skin to ripple disturbingly.

Then Decalthiya began to shriek and writhe. Her limbs flailed, and her back arched as if her body was in the throes of some great agony.

"No!" Morin shouted and tried to reach the half-giant's side, but the moment the druid stepped outside the ring of her protective thorn vines, the fighters pushed her back.

A second later, the half-giant's cries cut off abruptly, and her body stilled.

Decalthiya has died.

Morin howled, and Tantor roared, giving vent to their anger and grief. Abandoning his spellcasting, Tantor drew his weapon and struck at his nearest foe. Green light bursting from her eyes and spear, Morin followed the high elf's lead and threw herself with reckless abandon at the fighters surrounding her.

For one drawn-out moment, I was shocked into stillness. *Damnit, Decalthiya, why?* I murmured. The half-giant had only a single life remaining, and she had sacrificed it to save Morin. *You should have run, you idiot.* The half-giant was nothing if not loyal, even unto the end.

My anger threatened to boil over, but I squashed it. I was still weak and nearly drained of energy. I had only one chance to act, and I couldn't afford anything but calculation to guide my blows.

My eyes locked on my target. Saben was casting again. Attempting simple charm on the gang leader was too chancy; the risk of failure too high. I would have to kill him up close. I took a moment to check my reserves.

Your stamina is at 21%, your psi at 16%, and your mana at 0%.

My stamina had recovered a little further, and I had enough for two abilities I judged. I would have to choose carefully which to use.

Brushing aside the silk strands, I stepped into the cavern proper with my bloodied blade in hand. Saben still had his back to me. Blocking out awareness of the rest of the fight, I slipped through the few pools of shadow left by the light cones beaming down from above.

Multiple hostile entities have failed to detect you!

My approach was unseen. None of the gang knew I had entered the battle, and their attention was wholly focused on Tantor and Morin.

Tantor has died.

At the Game's message, my steps faltered, and my focus momentarily wavered, but determinedly I wrenched my mind back to the task at hand. I was halfway to my target already and would not let myself fail now.

Multiple hostile entities have failed to detect you!

Another few steps. Saben was nearly within reach now.

Multiple hostile entities have failed to detect you!

I was less than two feet away. I had made it. Uncoiling from my crouch, I sprang upwards and channeled stamina. Energy flowed out of me and formed around my shortsword, reinforcing the weapon's physical damage.

Weakness assailed me at the sudden drain of energy, but this time knowing to expect it, I rode the backlash of its loss better and plunged the point of my blade through Saben's back without faltering.

Saben has failed a physical resistance check! You have backstabbed your target for 50% more damage! You have critically injured Saben.
You have interrupted your target's spellcasting. Saben's transformation was disrupted!
A hostile entity has detected you! You are no longer hidden.

Transformation? I wondered in bewilderment. *What spell was Saben casting?* I had no time to dwell on the confusing Game message, though, and I banished that errant thought almost as soon as it occurred.

My blade had slipped easily through the gang leader, and I was sure my blade had pierced his heart, but worryingly I received no death message.

Saben's head whipped around, and despite the agony, he had to be suffering, the gang leader managed to glare blackly at me and open his mouth.

Not waiting to hear whatever threat Saben no doubt intended on making, I withdrew my sword and slapped my left hand down onto his shoulder. Then I cast stunning slap.

Drawing psi from my mind, I sent it coursing through my muscles, out my hand, and directly into Saben's body. In an instant, the invasive energy flooded the gang leader's own muscles and froze him in place.

Saben has failed a physical resistance check! You have stunned your target for 1 second.

Quicker than thought, I plunged my sword through the gang leader again.

You have killed Saben. You have slain a priest of Ishita, earning her ire!

It was done. Or at least the most important part was. Paying the other more-ominous sounding part of the Game message no mind, I shoved aside the corpse and took in the room.

Most of the enemy were still focused on Morin, but a few of the gang members had spotted me beside their downed leader and, with cries of anger, were running my way. Ignoring them for now, I studied the battle raging around the painted woman.

Even though she was surrounded by a swarm of fighters and mages, remarkably, Morin was still alive. Dancing amongst her thorn vines, she struck at the fighters threatening her while deftly avoiding their blows.

Alive though she might be, the painted woman was struggling.

There was a hitch in her step, and blood flowed freely down her sides. Any moment, I knew, she could meet her end. I took a step towards her. But before I could get any closer, a broadsword cleaved through the druid's torso, hewing her nearly in two.

Morin has died.

I paused in my step and squeezed my eyes shut. The others were all dead, and I was alone, with nearly no stamina or psi.

I could not win.

Dying was all but a foregone conclusion. But that didn't mean my fight was done yet. My eyes snapped open. *Let's see how many of them I can take with me.*

CHAPTER 71: A RECKONING

"It's that damned rogue!"

"Get him!"

"He's killed Saben!"

With Morin dead, the attention of the remaining gang members turned my way. My gaze flicked left and right. Players were converging on me from all sides, and I saw no safe path to the exit or back to the spiderwebs lining the walls. Crouching down, I tried slipping into the shadows.

You have failed to conceal yourself from the nearby entities.

So be it, I thought. *I will make my stand here.* Bending over Saben's corpse, I removed his shortsword.

You have acquired the rank 1 shortsword: spider's bite. This item increases the damage you deal by 15% and bears the enchantment: webbed, which causes magical strands to appear beneath your opponent's feet on every successful hit. If the target fails a physical resistance check, it will be held for 1 second.

This item requires a minimum Dexterity of 4 to wield. The item's enchantments are presently fully charged and can be replenished with mana.

Huh. Nice sword, I thought, calm despite the screaming gang members rushing towards me. I pivoted to face the entrance and, armed with a blade in either hand, charged the candidates there.

~ ~ ~

A skeleton was at the fore of the group, three steps ahead of the others. I hurtled toward the undead. Sidestepping the creature at the last moment, I slashed at it in passing with Saben's sword.

You have critically injured a level 11 skeletal warrior. Webbed triggered! A skeletal warrior has failed a physical resistance check! You have immobilized your target for 1 second.

I moved on.

A warrior and mage were before me, with others crowding on either side of them. The warrior raised her shield defensively and smashed down with her mace while the mage pointed his wand at me.

I dodged to the right and out of the warrior's reach, and before the mage could release his spell, I sliced open his bare throat with my lefthanded blade.

You have killed Larsen.

A spearman to the mage's right was lunging at me with his weapon. I fended off the spear with my right blade and ripped open his torso with the one in my left.

You have killed Javelin.

Two blows struck my rear in quick succession.

A magic missile has injured you! A magic missile has injured you!

I was caught flatfooted by the impact and staggered forward. A warrior approaching on my right took the opportunity to swipe at me with his axe. I swayed left, barely dodging the blow, and fell against another spellcaster.

A priest, I thought. I shoved into my smaller foe and thrust one of my swords through her robes and into her heart.

You have killed Layla.

A sword struck me from behind, and a line of fire ripped down my shoulder. My back arched back involuntarily, and I shrieked.

An unknown assailant has injured you!

A dagger plunged into my thigh. Then another into my side. The end was near. Dizzy with pain, I pivoted on my heel. Or tried to. Instead, I barely managed a quarter turn. Still, the move put another foe in front of me, and without hesitation, I buried both my blades in his chest.

You have killed Declan. You have reached level 20!

I smiled a bloody grin and kept going. More blows rained down on me, but I didn't feel any of them—which I knew was not a good sign.

Throwing back my head, I howled.

I imagined it was a terrifying sound because, for one blessed second, the attacks stopped. Still cackling with glee, I let go of all semblance of control. Forgoing conscious thought entirely, I hacked blindly with both my blades, with neither plan nor consideration for who or what was in front of me.

For a few glorious seconds, I was invincible. It had to end, of course. Changing tactics suddenly, the gang members withdrew away from me like a receding tide.

That's when the first arrow struck my shoulder.

A second followed, thudding into my hip. A third glanced off my helm. The fourth buried itself in my chest. My vision went blurry, and my thoughts ground to a halt. I didn't stop trying to fight, though. Staggering blindly, I wafted my blades aimlessly.

Warning! Your health is dangerously low at 3%. Death is imminent.

"Enough!" I heard a voice roar.

But it didn't matter if they stopped now. I was too far gone. I swayed and crashed to the floor, managing only a half-caught glimpse of a pair of glowing red eyes before my consciousness fled entirely.

~ ~ ~

Awareness seeped back slowly. A second later, memory followed. My eyes slid open, and I found myself staring at a rock ceiling. Not moving, I took stock of myself. All my injuries had been healed, and I was blessedly free of pain.

Your health is now at 100%.

The Game message confirmed what my senses told me. *Is that what dying feels like?* I wondered. The experience hadn't been so bad after all.

Another sensation made itself known. Lethargy. My limbs felt sluggish. *As if my pools of energy are still low.* I frowned. If I had been reborn, my stamina should have been replenished.

"Look at me, boy."

My head creaked to the left, and I found a pair of red eyes glaring at me.

"Stayne," I muttered. His body was hidden in interlocking plates of armor formed from black glass, but his luminous eyes and grinning skull—left deliberately bare, I suspected—were unmistakable.

The undead grunted. "Why is it that I always find myself waiting for you to wake up?"

"Twice is hardly always," I growled and pushed myself up into a seated position. "What are—"

I broke off, finally seeing my arm. I was still wearing my hide leather armor.

"You haven't died if that is what you're wondering," Stayne said.

I raised my head again and took in my surroundings. I was in Saben's chambers, lying in the same spot where I had fallen. Bodies still littered the floor, and a few gang members moved quietly about in the background. Other than Stayne himself, no one else was paying me any attention.

Gnat glided down from the darkness to alight on my shoulder. I nodded to him before turning back to Stayne. "Why am I still alive?" I asked quietly.

The undead's eyes flickered momentarily to the bat before returning to me. "It's time we had a chat." He paused, looking at me expectantly.

Hearing a low chuckle and hushed voices, my gaze drifted beyond Stayne to the gang members bending over something on the ground. It was Decalthiya, I realized. The thugs were stripping her body and making obscene comments about her size.

Fury lashed through me. *Bastards. How dare they—*

With considerable effort, I wrestled my thoughts under control. Now was not the time. But soon, I promised myself, the wretches would pay. I turned back to Stayne. "Go on," I said evenly.

"You've been a busy boy," Stayne said. He waited for me to comment. When I said nothing, he went on. "Level twenty and two Marks already," he mused. "A pity that they are such weak ones, though." His glowing red orbs flared suddenly. "What task did you complete to get those Marks?"

My jaw tightened in the face of the undead's stare. *So this is an interrogation.* I remained silent, but Stayne's words reminded me of something else. Drawing on my will, I analyzed him.

The target is Stayne, an ascendant undead of indeterminant level. This entity is a player and bears a Mark of Supreme Dark, a Mark of Erebus, a Mark of Death, a Mark of...

Morin had been right. Stayne *was* a player. He carried a long list of Marks, too, many of them meaningless to me. *What is an ascendant undead?* I wondered.

"Answer me!" Stayne demanded.

I said nothing.

Gnat lowered his head and placed his mouth next to my ear. "You should tell him what he wants to know, Michael. Stayne is dangerous. Don't toy with him. "

My gaze slid sideways to the bat, but still, I remained silent.

"You should listen to the familiar," Stayne said. He leaned forward. "You want to get out of the dungeon, don't you?"

I glanced at the undead, my interest finally piqued. "I do," I said at last.

He leaned back. "Then tell me what I want to know. It's the only way you will leave this place alive. You understand?"

I nodded, deciding to play along.

"Good, now tell me about the dire wolves."

So he knows about them. "What about the wolves?"

"Don't be coy with me, boy. I know your task was related to them."

I stared at him for a long moment, internally debating what to say and what to try to keep hidden, then shrugged. "There's not much to tell. Freeing the wolves was a hidden task."

"And what rewards did the Adjudicator give you?"

"The Marks, obviously."

"Nothing else?"

I drew my brows down in feigned confusion. "Like what?"

Stayne's eyes narrowed, inspecting me the way a cat would a mouse, but he didn't question my response further. "Where are the wolves now?"

"They left through the sector exit."

"Why didn't you go with them?"

I glared at him. "You know why."

Stayne didn't bother pretending ignorance as to my meaning. "What? Don't tell me you thought the task the Master set you was going to be *fair*?" He chuckled. "Trust me when I say you will not escape the Master's clutches without proving your loyalty to the Dark. The sector portal is the only way out."

I didn't believe him. The Master might have an agenda, but I suspected the Adjudicator was—if not fair—at least impartial. The second task I had acquired was proof enough of that. But I would gain nothing by mentioning any of that to the undead. "Why are you here, Stayne?" I asked, attempting a question of my own.

To my surprise, he answered. "To issue you a warning."

"What warning?"

"Correct your ways, or perish," Stayne stated baldly. "You have strayed from the path the Master deems acceptable. Normally this would be of no concern, and you would be left to wither away. But for some reason, the Master has taken an interest in you." The undead's gaze pinned me again. "Do you know why?"

I shook my head mutely. I had an inkling, though. *My Class evolution... it has to be that.* What I didn't understand yet was why it would attract the Master's attention.

Stayne snorted, seeming to have no trouble believing my answer. "Well, however you have managed it, you have impressed the Master. I am here at his behest."

I struggled to keep any alarm from showing on my face. The Master's interest was the last thing I wanted. "And how am I expected to 'correct my ways?'" I asked carefully.

Stayne laughed. It was a hollow sound, stripped bare of any joy. "It's simple. Seal yourself to the Dark. You can do that by taking on a Dark Class or by swearing allegiance to the Master through me. The Master doesn't care which option you choose." The light in the undead's eyes intensified. "But naturally, I would prefer you take up the second choice."

"You want me to become your follower?" I asked, unable to stifle the note of disbelief in my voice.

"Technically, the Master's follower. But yes," Stayne replied. "I can make it worth your while, you know." He eyed my gear derisively. "For starters, I can see to it that you are much better equipped.

"What about Saben?"

"What about him?"

"Isn't he your follower? Won't me swearing allegiance to you anger him?"

"Saben isn't one of mine," Stayne said curtly. "The fool rejected what the Master offered him. Now, make your choice."

I frowned. If it wasn't Stayne or the Master who was helping Saben, who was it? After witnessing the gang leader's abilities for myself, it was clear that Tantor's and Morin's suspicion were correct. Someone was aiding him. There was no way he had gotten as strong as he had on his own.

"My time grows short," Stayne said, interrupting my musings. "What is your choice?"

I bit my lip, thinking. I didn't want to refuse the undead player outright. I suspected he wouldn't take rejection well, but how was I going to placate him? "Tell one more thing," I said, deciding to play for time, "what is Saben?"

"And why should I tell you that?" Stayne asked, his tone amused.

"Call it a gesture of good faith?" I tried.

The undead snorted but decided to humor me anyway. "Saben is a dark acolyte and sworn servant of Ishita."

"Ishita?" I asked sharply. "What is she? Another player?"

Stayne laughed. "You're clueless, aren't you? Ishita is as far beyond a player as I am from you." His eyes glinted. "Ishita is a Power of the Dark and another member of the Awakened Dead faction." He paused. "And for some reason, the spider goddess is interested in you, too. Saben had orders to capture you for her."

"Spider goddess?" I repeated. *Of course.* The transformation spell I'd interrupted. The spiderwebs. It all came together. "Sigmar lied about that too, didn't he? This was never a spider's lair. Saben is a shapeshifter. *He* is the spider."

"My, my, so you aren't as dumb as you look. You've got it in one. Now you've wasted enough of my time." Too quick to follow, Stayne slashed his blade across my throat.

Stayne has critically injured you. Warning! Your health is dangerously low at 2%. Death is imminent.

My eyes bulged, and my hands clutched at my neck in an attempt to stem the bleeding. "Why?" I managed to croak as my life drained away.

Stayne shook his head. "You may have promised, boy, but you don't know your place. Consider this your first lesson. You don't question me. *Ever.* Now you've got two more chances. Use them wisely, and don't disappoint the Master or me again."

Swinging around, Stayne walked away, leaving me to my fate. Death was not long in coming.

You have died.

CHAPTER 72: A NEW LIFE'S RESOLUTION

I returned to awareness with shocking suddenness. It was as if I had been dipped in an ice bath. I inhaled sharply as my memories returned in a rush.

With them came gut-wrenching agony.

I shuddered, and my limbs began convulsing. I was dying. Again. I knew it for a certainty. I could *feel* my lifeblood spilling away. The pain was excruciating. *No! I won't die like this!* Not again. My eyes snapped open, and my hands flew to my throat.

There was no gash.

My mind refused to believe it. Frantic fingers roved over my neck, probing every inch of skin for the source of the pain that I could still *feel*. That I *knew* was there. It was so real: the taste of the cold, cruel blade slicing through my throat, the flood of blood gurgling out of me, the waves of agony coursing through my veins, and the sense of fading self.

I shivered uncontrollably. My heart thumped in my chest, and sweat broke out across my brow.

No! I refuted. *It's not real. They're only memories!*

With difficulty, I wrenched my mind back to the present, grimly ignoring the vivid sensations that my mind insisted were real. They weren't. The evidence was undeniable. I was whole and uninjured.

But if only I could get my mind to accept that.

A Game message hovered before my eyes. Desperately, I sought refuge within it.

You have been reborn. Lives remaining: 2. Time lost during resurrection: 8 hours. Rebirth location: sector 14,913 safe zone.

Other notices were waiting for me. One by one, I perused them. Ignoring my body's tremors and my mind's panic, I studied the messages carefully and deliberately.

Your task: <u>Escape the Dungeon</u> has been updated. You have discovered a second means of using the sector 14,913 exit portal. Revised objective: Adopt a Dark Class, swear allegiance to the Master, or otherwise use the sector 14,913 exit portal. This task and the task: <u>Find your own way out</u> are mutually exclusive.

Your light armor has increased to level 18. Your skill in light armor has reached rank 1, decreasing your light armor penalty by 5%.

Your insight has increased to 25. Your chi has increased to level 3. Your meditation has increased to level 22. Your telepathy has increased to level 11. Your sneaking has increased to level 38. Your shortswords has increased to level 34. Your two weapon fighting has increased to level 29.

Congratulations, Michael! You are now a rank 2 player. Your experience gains have decreased further. For achieving rank 2, you have been awarded 1 additional attribute point and 1 Class point.

I went over each Game alert repeatedly until I fully understood the sense of their contents. Most of the messages were fairly mundane, but the one related to the Class point was intriguing enough to jolt my downward-spiraling thoughts back to the present. I wasn't certain, but I had a feeling the Class point was used to upgrade a Class.

Ignoring it for now—I needed to find out more about Class points before I spent it—I turned my attention to my attribute points. Seeing no reason to delay, I invested a point apiece in Constitution and Mind.

Your Constitution has increased to rank 5. Your Mind has increased to rank 5.

When I was done, I breathed out carefully. As I had hoped, dealing with familiar things had settled my mind. I was calmer now, and the shock of my death had passed. I was ready to face the world again.

I sat up.

I was lying in a shallow pool of strange liquid. Whatever it was, it was not water. My hands were bone dry. I looked downwards. And, of course, I was dressed in newbie clothes again. "Damn," I muttered.

I looked around. The rim of the pool was edged by a low stone wall inscribed with indecipherable runes. *This has to be the rebirth well Gnat mentioned.* The well itself was housed in a tent, and at the moment, I was its only occupant.

I rose to my feet and climbed over the stone wall. I could hear the murmur of voices outside the tent. Other candidates were in the safe zone. But before I stepped outside, I closed my eyes and took a moment to compose myself. A lot had happened in the moments before my death, and I had yet to process everything.

Sigmar's betrayal.

Stayne's ultimatum.

Saben's secret.

Decalthiya gone.

The last bit hurt surprisingly more than I expected. I had hardly known the half-giant, and for much of our short acquaintance, she had been poorly disposed towards me. Still, the big fighter had been slowly growing on me. And whatever else could be said of her, Decalthiya had been loyal. Steadfast.

And so cruelly betrayed.

She had deserved better. The Master, Sigmar, Saben, and Stayne—all of them had had a part to play in her demise. But if I was being honest, more than anything else, it was the injustice of the half-giant's death that ate at me.

And it was not only Decalthiya who had been wronged. Every candidate who had perished in this sector—going through what I had just experienced three times no less—was equally a victim and pawn in the Master's game.

Someone has to seek redress, I thought. *Someone has to seek justice on their behalf.*

Did it have to be me? No. But who else was there? Morin and Tantor were capable, but they couldn't do what I could.

I had been playing it safe with Gnat for fear of the Master's reprisals, and I had turned away from the plight of Saben's prisoners previously because the chance of success had been low. The odds were still weighed against me, even more so now with Stayne's involvement.

But this time, I could not—would not—look the other way.

Stayne and his offer be damned. I will not bow to the Master's demands. My path crystallized. I would hunt down the two directly responsible for Decalthiya's death. It was not an entirely rational decision, nor was it the smartest move.

But it was the right choice.

Stayne and the Master were out of my reach. For now. Not so, Saben and Sigmar. Despite having no gear and perhaps no allies, I resolved I would not leave this sector until I killed the pair.

Repeatedly if necessary.

Unbidden, a Game message popped into my mind.

You have been allocated a new task: <u>Vengeance for the Fallen</u>! Your determination to avenge your comrades has been noticed, and the Adjudicator has

granted you a task. Hunt down those directly responsible. Objective 1: Deal final death to Sigmar. Objective 2: Deal final death to Saben.

A grim smile lit my face at the message, but it never reached my eyes.

~ ~ ~

Exiting the tent, I found myself at the rear of a small crowd of about thirty. Most of the candidates had their backs turned to me and, by the sounds of it, were listening to a heated argument raging beyond my sight.

My appearance did not go unnoticed, and by ones and twos, the candidates fell silent and turned around to face me. Presently the crowd parted, and two figures approached me: Morin and Tantor.

I sighed. That the two were still here could not bode well. I had been hoping that by now, they had returned to the gang's camp, rounded up the survivors of our little army, and routed the remains of Saben's elites. That the pair had not done so could only mean matters were even worse than I suspected.

The two stopped before me, and Morin swung around to address the watching crowd. "Alright, everyone, go get some rest. We'll meet in another two hours. And by then, I promise we'll have a plan."

"Yeah, right," someone shouted.

"No way!" another screamed. "You're only going to get us killed again. This time for good!"

"Blasted human! We should never have trusted you in the first place," a third yelled.

But despite the anger expressed by the three hecklers, the mood of the rest of the candidates was more subdued. Scanning their faces, I saw only dull eyes, somber expressions, and lowered gazes. *They've lost hope,* I realized.

As the crowd began dispersing in a lackluster fashion, I turned back to Morin. "What's going on? Why haven't you rejoined the others at the camp? Where's Saben? Did you—"

Tantor held up his hand. "Not here," he said. "We can't be sure who may be listening. Let's speak in the tent."

I frowned. I didn't like the thought of delaying our exit from the safe zone any longer than necessary, but I realized the pair must have their reasons. Gesturing to Tantor to lead the way, I followed after.

~ ~ ~

"I can't say I'm pleased to see you," Morin said once the three of us were seated in her tent. "When you didn't appear immediately, we thought..." She sighed, her eyes heavy with sorrow. "It doesn't matter what we thought. We've failed." She bowed her head. "*I* failed. I was a fool to trust Sigmar."

"What's happened, Morin?" I asked, worry clouding my face.

The painted woman held up her arm for patience. "We'll get to that in a moment. Can you tell us first what happened after we died?"

I nodded and proceeded to tell the pair what they wanted to know. I told them about Stayne's appearance, the information I had gleaned from him, and the undead player's ultimatum. I didn't tell them about my tasks, though. It would not affect whatever decisions we needed to make, and after Sigmar's betrayal, I was resolved to play my cards closer.

"Ishita!" Tantor spat when I was done. "By all accounts, she is one of the foulest Powers in the Axis."

"That explains some things," Morin said. She shook her head. "But Saben a priest... that was the last thing I expected."

I frowned at the two. "I keep hearing mention of these Powers, but I still don't know what they are. Are they really gods?"

Tantor shrugged. "As far we can tell, they are. They seem to be the preeminent beings in this world, excluding the Adjudicator itself, of course. The Master is one of their number."

I had figured as much. I glanced at Morin. "A druid is a form of priest, right? Are you sworn to one of the Powers too?"

The painted woman shook her head. "No, I wield Force directly, as do all who have Faith. Those candidates who swear themselves to one of the Powers do so for reasons other than Faith."

Decalthiya had told me much the same thing, and while I would have liked to pursue the topic further, there were other more important matters to discuss, so I simply nodded in response.

"Do you know why the Master is interested in you?" Morin asked.

I hesitated. "I think so, but I rather not say at the moment."

"I understand," she said and didn't press me further.

"So, what's happened?" I asked. "Why are you still here?"

Tantor and Morin exchanged looks before the elf answered. "Sigmar prepared better for his betrayal than we expected," he said grimly. "It turned out that no few of those who surrendered to us when we invaded the gang's camp were actually gang loyalists. The moment our party entered the tunnel leading to Saben's chamber, Sigmar and his loyalist slaughtered our troops that remained behind." He sighed heavily. "I don't know how I failed to foresee Sigmar's treachery, but we have paid a hefty price for my blindness."

Morin squeezed the elf's shoulder. "I bear as much blame for Sigmar as you, Tantor." She turned to me. "The short of it is: we've lost our army."

I was as much to blame for Sigmar as the pair. Foolishly, I had chalked up my dislike for the inquisitor to his annoying habits and nothing deeper. And I had been reckless too. I hadn't feared betrayal because I had believed myself capable of escaping any trap. Still, I had learned my lesson. Candidates weren't goblins. Encounters with my fellows could be—and likely would be—wildly unpredictable.

My face hardened. The news was dire. "What about those who went with Bornholm?"

"Sigmar claims the gang is hunting them down as we speak," Morin said, "but none of Bornholm's people have reappeared in the safe zone, so there is some hope yet that they survive."

I bowed my head, thinking. "We should still head out," I said finally. "If we move fast, perhaps we can recapture the camp before the gang is ready for us."

Tantor shook his head. "We can't."

"Why not?" I demanded, my voice rising as I sensed more bad news coming.

Morin winced at my tone. "Saben's people have blockaded both ramps. There is no way out of the safe zone."

My eyes widened. "The gang is in the cavern?"

She nodded. "Some of them, at least. Sigmar and Saben had it all planned out. They used the battle as an opportunity to advance the blockade, and their people were in place before we could react. An hour before your rebirth, Saben revived. He took great pains to spell out his demands. None of us will leave the crater alive unless we swear ourselves to him."

"Some of our fighters must surely still be alive," I said stubbornly. "Even excluding those who went with Bornholm, we had about seventy fighters in the gang's camp. I only saw thirty in the crowd outside. Where are the rest?"

"The others are dead," Tantor said softly. "Like Decalthiya, they have gone to their final deaths. As far as Morin and I can tell, all those who had a remaining life have returned to the safe zone." He looked at me unhappily. "Thirty candidates is all we have left."

I lowered my head into my hands, finally understanding the true extent of our plight.

How am I going to get out of this now? I wondered.

CHAPTER 73: TRAPPED IN A BOWL

A few minutes later, I left the tent alone. The air of defeat about the camp was unmistakable this time around, and few of the candidates were willing to meet my gaze. I strode down the central avenue of the crater. All the merchants were still present. I spotted Hamish's wagon, too but didn't see the merchant himself.

As I reached the crater's exit, I saw what Morin meant. Lounging at the top of the ramp and just outside the boundary of the safe zone were twelve fully clad and heavily armed gang members.

Saben and Sigmar were with them. The gang leader was in all his old gear, including the shortsword I had taken from him—although his shirt appeared new. Sigmar's equipment was entirely different. His ill-fitting goblin hide armor was gone, replaced instead by sleek midnight-black leather armor and an ebony longsword.

It was an embarrassment of riches, and gazing up at them from the bottom of the ramp, clad only in my white shorts and shirt, I couldn't help but feel intimidated.

One of the gang members spotted me and called out a warning. Saben and Sigmar turned my way. A slow smile curved upwards on the gang leader's face. "Well, look who has come calling," he said. "And dressed so lovely, too," he added with a chuckle.

I remained tightlipped. Despite his death at my hands, Saben's arrogance had not dissipated. If anything, his confidence had grown. My gaze slid to Sigmar. The inquisitor was staring at me with loathing. His hand was tightly wrapped around the hilt of his sword, and he seemed poised to launch himself at me.

Saben noticed his companion's tense demeanor too. "Easy, Sigmar," he murmured.

"You're a dead man," the inquisitor growled.

"Well, technically, not anymore," I quipped.

Sigmar didn't get the joke. His chest heaving, the inquisitor glared back at me. "I will kill you slowly," he declared. "I will roast you alive over warm coals and feed you to the undead."

I stroked my chin. Sigmar seemed to be feeling more than the simple anger I expected. I had no idea what was driving the abnormal hatred he directed toward me, but I could use it. "Really?" I asked, arching one eyebrow. "How'd that go for you the first time? If I recall, Decalthiya made short work of you."

Color flushed the inquisitor's face, and he looked ready to explode.

I pretended to think. "By my account, you have only one life remaining. I'd say that in any contest between us, that puts the odds in my favor." I stared unblinkingly into Sigmar's eyes. "Your betrayal will not go unpunished."

The inquisitor quivered. Jerking forward, he took one step into the safe zone with his sword halfway unsheathed. But before he could go any further, Saben's hand shot out and restrained him. Sigmar's head whipped around to scowl at the gang leader, but he let himself be pulled back.

Ah well, I thought in disappointment. *It had been worth a try, at least.*

"As delightful as I find your threats, they are toothless," Saben said. He gestured languidly to the crater. "You are trapped in this bowl and will not get out without our permission."

Keeping my expression impassive, I folded my arms and played my next card. "You will oppose Stayne's wishes? He is my patron now." I was stretching the truth but hoped they didn't know better.

Saben grinned. "Technically, you aren't, not yet, anyway. And besides, I don't serve the Master, and I have no obligation to his dog." He drummed his fingers along the side of his face theatrically. "But seeing as Ishita and the Master are allied, I *could* be persuaded to let you make your pledge to the Master. If you are ready, please—" he bowed mockingly—"step up the ramp, and I will summon Stayne to take your oath."

When I made no move to comply, he laughed. "I thought not."

"Why did you two do it?" I asked abruptly.

Sigmar ignored my question entirely, and Saben only looked confused. "Do what?" the gang leader asked.

"Set such an elaborate trap in the first place," I said. "You had enough forewarning to assemble your entire gang in the camp and crush us there when we attacked. It would have been simpler and less risky."

"Ah," Saben said. "That's no mystery. Morin is too wily by far. She would have withdrawn if she saw that we were ready for her." He shook his head sadly. "Besides, I was growing bored and desired an end to our little siege."

I gaped at him. "So instead, you sacrificed the greater part of your followers to draw her out?"

The gang leader waved his hand dismissively. "It was no great loss, truly. Besides, it was an excellent opportunity to weed out the disloyal."

Saben's callousness left me speechless, and for a moment, I could only stare at him. "What about Bornholm," I asked eventually. "Where is he?"

At the mention of his former companion's name, Sigmar finally stirred. "Bornholm is no concern of yours," he sneered.

Wordlessly, I studied the inquisitor's face. Then I swung about and walked away. I had learned what I had come for.

~ ~ ~

I checked the crater's second exit next. But like the first one, it was guarded by twelve gang members. My observations only confirmed what Tantor and Morin had told me. Attempting to leave the safe zone by way of either ramp was a death sentence.

Which left only the crater walls.

Ignoring the hoots and jeers of the gang members as I retreated from the second ramp, I tread a slow circuit around the crater's base. Its sides were six yards of sheer vertical rockface. What few cracks and seams existed were too far apart to serve as handholds.

Still, there was no other way out that I could see, and I would have to attempt the climb. But before I did that, I needed to pay Hamish a visit.

The dark elf's wagon was boarded up, and it looked like he was preparing to depart. Banging on the sides, I called out, "Hamish, you in there?"

A head popped out from a window, and grey eyes peered at me. "Michael, is that you?"

I walked around so that he could see me clearly.

"Ah, it is," the grey merchant said softly. "So they got you too?"

I nodded.

"One second," he replied. The merchant ducked back inside and, a moment later, climbed out the wagon's rear to stand next to me.

"You're leaving?" I asked.

"I have no choice," Hamish said. "For a while there, business picked up—" he shot me a grateful look—"all thanks to you, but with what's happened now, it is sure to dry up again." He sighed. "I've wasted enough money on this venture, and time is money. I can't afford to remain here any longer."

"Oh," I said, disappointed.

"I'm sorry, Michael," the elf replied. He paused. "Did you need something?"

"I do," I said. "Information and a favor."

Hamish's face turned solemn. Straightening the front of his suit, the merchant folded his arms in front of him. "I can't promise anything," he said, almost gently, "but I'll hear you out."

"Thank you," I said gratefully. Much depended on his willingness to help me, and I hoped that I had established enough goodwill with Hamish for him to extend me a measure of trust—and credit. "Information first, then: what can you tell me about Class points?"

"Ah, an easy enough question to answer," the merchant replied, seemingly relieved by the simple nature of my query. "Players are awarded Class points at every second player rank and use them to upgrade their Classes. Each Class point can be used to upgrade a single Class by one rank."

I nodded. So I would gain more Class points in future as well. "What does upgrading entail?"

"As you no doubt already know, each Class comes with a base trait. When you upgrade a Class, its base trait will be improved as well. The Game will also give you the opportunity to select an additional trait or Class ability." Hamish shrugged. "It is impossible to know beforehand what traits or abilities the Adjudicator will offer you during the upgrade, only that they will be suited to your Class and work to enhance your Class features."

"I see," I said, wondering which of my two Classes I should spend my Class point on. Given my current predicament and the fact that my best skills were dexterity-based, it likely made more sense to upgrade my nightstalker Class.

Seeing my frown, Hamish said, "If I may offer a bit of advice?"

"Go ahead," I said.

The merchant shifted slightly. "I don't know what Classes you possess currently, but I am guessing at this stage, none of them have melded?"

"They haven't," I admitted.

"In that case, I suggest you wait before spending your Class point," Hamish said.

I was taken aback. "Wait, why?"

"You know about blended Classes?"

I nodded.

"Well, the most obvious benefit of a blended Class is that its base trait is a combination of its constituents. When you upgrade a blended Class it is the *combined trait* that improves, providing you with further benefits. Not to mention that the choices the Adjudicator offers when advancing blended Classes are invariably better than those for single Classes."

"Hmm," I mused. The base trait of my nightstalker Class was wolven, and that of my psionic Class was metamind. If the two traits combined together... then the benefits of waiting to spend my Class point were obvious. And that was discounting the additional benefits a tri-blend Class would bring.

All this hinged on the assumption that my Classes *would* meld, though, and I was unhappily aware that I would need every advantage I could manage in the upcoming fight. *But I still have two lives remaining.* I could afford to take a calculated risk on my next attempt against the gang. If I died again, then I would use my Class point.

"Thank you, Hamish. I see sense in what you suggest." I breathed in deeply. "Now for the favor."

The grey merchant bobbed his head gravely and gestured for me to go on.

"I was hoping you would extend me a line of credit," I began. Seeing Hamish's brows draw down in an unhappy frown, I finished in a rush. "Not a lot, only enough for one item."

The merchant opened his mouth. Paused, then closed it again. "One item?" he asked.

I bobbed my head.

"Which one?" he asked tersely.

"The one-step spellbook."

Hamish's frown deepened. "A spellbook?" he muttered. "I thought you were going to ask for something foolish like a sword." He eyed me sideways. "What are you going to do with the spellbook?"

"Escape the safe zone unnoticed."

Hamish's eyes flitted from me to the distant crater walls. He rubbed at his chin thoughtfully. "I see."

"If I make it out, I will return to repay you, of course," I promised.

"And if you don't make it out?"

"Then you will have lost five gold," I admitted.

The merchant studied me intently, weighing the risk no doubt. "Your request is an unusual one," he said at last, "and ordinarily not one I would entertain." Hamish sighed. "But I like you, Michael, and I can't say that about many people. I will accede to your request—on one condition."

"What's that?" I asked, bracing myself.

"Any further trading you do in this sector, you do through me."

I grinned. Hamish's terms were not nearly as onerous enough as I'd feared. "We have a deal, my friend."

CHAPTER 74: CONFRONTATION

You have acquired the basic spell: one-step. This is a psi ability that allows you to take a single step in the air as if it were solid ground. This ability consumes psi and can be upgraded. Its activation time is fast, and its cooldown time is average. You have 2 of 5 Mind ability slots remaining.

I wasted no time learning the spell, and after thanking Hamish profusely, I returned to Tantor and Morin.

"I have a plan," I said to the pair as I ducked into the tent and proceeded to explain the bare bones of what I had in mind while being deliberately sketchy on the details.

"It's risky," Morin said when I was done.

"But we don't have any other options," Tantor said quietly.

The painted woman nodded and glanced at me. "When you reach the top of the crater, let down a rope, and Tantor and I will join you."

I shook my head. "No offense, Morin, but this first part, I'm better off doing alone. Neither you nor Tantor has stealth, and—" I held her gaze—"you two are on your last lives."

She opened her mouth to protest, but I spoke over her. "Please. It's smarter this way. Have someone keep a lookout for my signal, and as soon as I judge it safe, I will rejoin you. Agreed?"

She nodded reluctantly. "Good luck then."

~ ~ ~

I chose the remotest section of the crater to enact my plan. It was about as far as I could get from both ramps. I was still within sight range—if barely—of the gang members on either end, but given how far I was from them, I didn't think I would have a problem concealing myself with sneaking.

Reaching the spot I had selected, I scanned the area. None of the candidates in the safe zone were close by. Tantor and Morin had seen to it that I would be undisturbed. Drawing on the shadows, I masked my presence.

You have successfully concealed yourself.

Now comes the hard part, I thought. Looking upwards, I eyed the handhold I had identified—a rock seam about four yards up and deep enough to grip, or so I hoped. It was too far to reach under normal circumstances, even with my high Dexterity, but with one-step to boost me, I thought I could manage it.

Here goes. I hurried towards the wall at a fast walk, not running because that would break my stealth. At the same time, I drew on my psi and began channeling. When I was about two yards away, I jumped while simultaneously casting one-step. Energy flowed from my mind and out of my leg, but instead of solidifying the air underfoot, the psi frittered away.

You have failed to one-step. You have failed to advance your telekinesis: skills cannot be gained in this area.

Unbalanced, I crashed to the ground face-first. Sitting up, I swore bitterly. The reason for the spell's failure was obvious. My telekinesis skill was too low. The only silver lining was that my concealment hadn't been broken.

With a sigh, I rose to my feet. *This may take a while.*

~ ~ ~

It took me five more attempts before I was successfully able to cast the spell. And then, predictably, I fouled the next maneuver and crashed face-first into the wall, scratching futilely for the seam that was only inches above my reaching fingers.

After another ten failed attempts—with a meditation break between to regain my psi—I was getting desperate. I was too stubborn to quit, but I was no longer certain I could defeat the wall.

Come on, Michael, you can do this.

Standing still, I breathed in deeply and took a minute to settle myself. I mapped out in my mind what I needed to do, picturing every step and movement in exacting detail.

Exhaling a slow, controlled breath, I launched myself forward again. Two yards from the wall and timing the move to perfection, I leaped upwards, channeling psi as I went.

You have successfully one-stepped.

The air underfoot hardened, and my left foot found solid ground. In the same motion, I sprang upwards again and flung up my hands.

For a heartbeat, I sailed through the air, then crashed into the hard rockface, but my body was braced for the impact, and my fingers blindly searched for purchase.

I found the seam.

Gravity yanked me downwards. My knuckles turned white with the strain, but to my relief, my grip held.

Yes! I exulted. I had done it, or the first part, anyway. I was hanging four yards up on the crater wall. Bending back my head, I spotted my next objective: a deep crack about a yard above the seam I clung to. I expected reaching it would be much easier.

Contorting my body weirdly and using one-step to temporarily anchor my feet as I worked, I pulled my body up the rockface inch by inch until finally, my toes rested on the seam, and my fingers dug into the crack. From there, scaling the remaining one yard to the crater's edge went off without a hitch.

You have left a safe zone.

Reaching the top, I rolled onto my back and breathed a sigh of relief. I had done it. I made it out of the safe zone alive.

~ ~ ~

My escape went unnoticed by the gang, and despite the cavern's soft light, my stealth was sufficient to conceal me as I crept to the closest cavern wall. Bracing myself against the wall, I took stock of the area again.

Saben and Sigmar were still with the gang squads on the west ramp. A few yards to my left, the door to the goblin complex lay open, and directly across me, on the opposite side of the cavern, was the tunnel leading to the gang's camp. Amongst the group guarding the east ramp, I thought I spotted Goral. He, like Saben, could see about as well as I could in the dark.

While I surveilled the chamber, Gnat glided down from the darkness to land on my shoulder. "Well done," he whispered in my ear.

I didn't reply as I considered my next move. My first priority was arming myself. Unfortunately, with both gang squads in the cavern alert and with candidates able to see in the dark, I could see no easy way to go do that. Which meant moving on to my next objective: finding Bornholm. There were two ways I could go about that.

One, retreat back through the goblin complex and maze and make my way around to the gang's camp from the other end. It would be a tortuously long journey but safe.

Two, make for the gang's camp more directly through the tunnel across me. It was likely guarded, and the risk of discovery would be greater.

I favored the second option. Time was of the essence. The gang was still hunting Bornholm's people, and the longer I took to reach them, the more of my allies would die. And besides, if the north tunnel was too well-guarded, I could always retreat and go the long way around through the maze.

The north tunnel it is, I decided. I glanced at the familiar on my shoulder. *But first, I have to deal with Gnat.*

With that in mind, I slipped back into the goblin complex. It was time for the skeletal bat and me to have a long-overdue discussion.

~ ~ ~

Ideally, I had wanted to have the conversation with Gnat while armed to the teeth and braced for anything. But given the recent events in Saben's chamber, I didn't think I could afford to put off my confrontation with the familiar any longer. And besides, if my suspicions were correct, I feared that if matters between the bat and I devolved into a fight, I was dead already.

Ducking into an empty chamber that was sufficiently far from the safe zone's cavern that we wouldn't be disturbed, I sat down cross-legged.

"Why have you come here?" Gnat asked.

I brushed the familiar off my shoulder and gestured him to a spot across me. He alighted on it obediently.

"We have to talk, Gnat," I said.

The skeletal bat tilted his head to the side and looked at me curiously. "Talk?"

I held his gaze squarely. "Yes, talk. About whom you serve and your true purpose in accompanying me."

"What nonsense is this?" Gnat asked, his tone dismissive. "I serve you, of course."

I shook my head. "No, you don't. How did Stayne find me?"

"You think *I* told him?" Gnat asked scornfully. "Preposterous! Saben must have informed him."

"Saben serves Ishita. He had no reason to inform Stayne of my whereabouts. Try again."

"Then it was Sigmar," Gnat said, disinterest lacing his voice.

"Possibly," I allowed. I still don't know if Sigmar was sworn to any amongst the Dark. He could very well have given his allegiance to Stayne. Letting the point be, I moved on. "How did Stayne know about the wolves?"

"I don't know." The bat feigned a yawn. "Enough with the questions. Can we get going now?"

I wasn't buying his pretense. "Not good enough, Gnat. Answer me."

Gnat scowled. "How should I know? Maybe he scryed you out from afar!"

"Unlikely. Why would he go to all that trouble for some random candidate?" I shook my head again. "I know you are lying to me, Gnat." I held up my hand to still his protest. "What I want to know is why." I stared at the bat coldly, making certain he saw my resolve. "If you don't come clean, then I will sever our Pact."

This, at last, seemed to shake Gnat. "You don't want to do that, Michael," he said softly.

I nodded. "I suspect you are right about that. But if you leave me no other choice, I will."

"Are you sure you want to know?" Gnat asked, the luminous orbs of his eyes glinting. "You will be turning down a dangerous path if you do this."

I smiled wryly. "There has been nothing safe—or easy—about my journey ever since I got to this world." My face hardened. "Tell me."

"Very well." Gnat sighed. "I did not tell Stayne about you or the wolves. I don't serve *him*. But," he allowed, "Stayne may have found out about you from the one I told."

"You informed the Master," I stated.

"I did," Gnat admitted. "I am bound to him by ties greater than the ones I have to you." He met my eyes. "It is my duty and that of every other familiar to report any unusual occurrences we observe."

"So the familiars are spies?"

"We are."

I had suspected as much, but I feared that spying was the least of their tasks. "That is not your only function, though, is it?"

Gnat did not try dodging the question this time. "It isn't. I'm also obliged to contact the Master's death squads when it is certain that a candidate has rejected the path he has set for them."

My eyes narrowed. "Contact how?"

"With an aether magic spell that sends a distress signal to them. They will then open a portal to my location and send through the kill team."

"I see. What happens if I break our Pact?"

"I contact the Master."

"And if I attack you?"

"I contact the Master," Gnat replied just as evenly.

I was unsurprised by the familiar's answers. It was what I had been afraid of all along. I thought for a moment. "Do you report to the Master through the aether too?"

"No. Such magic is too advanced for me. My reports are delivered personally." Gnat gestured upwards. "You cannot see it from here, but there is a small opening in the ceiling above that connects to a second tunnel network that overlays the dungeon itself. It leads directly to the Master's domain."

I glanced up but, true to Gnat's words, could see no opening. "How many times have you reported on me?"

"Thrice."

I winced. "Tell me about them."

"The first time was during your battle with the goblin chief. Once it—"

"Why did you report then?"

"Your interactions with the wolves were... unusual, and it was beginning to look like you might actually triumph against the boss. Both events were worthy of reporting."

"And what did the Master make of your report?"

"His interest was aroused," Gnat replied. "Before I returned to you, the Master cast a psionic shield over me."

"Why would he do that?"

Gnat shrugged. "To shield me from the dire wolves, I suspect. They are natural telepaths."

I nodded. "And the second time?"

"When the bronze chests appeared. The Master scryed you out himself after that."

I shuddered. "Why?"

"To make sure you didn't receive a Light or Shadow Class." Gnat looked at me solemnly. "If you had received a non-dark aligned Class, the Master would have acted immediately."

I didn't have to ask him *how* the Master would have acted. I could well imagine. "And when was the third time?"

Gnat fidgeted. "That wasn't at my behest," he said, sounding puzzled.

I looked at him sharply. "What do you mean?"

"Vomer, one of the merchants, slipped me a handwritten note to pass on to the Master. It was after the Master received the merchant's report that he sent Stayne to find you."

My eyes narrowed. "When exactly was this?"

"It was during your first visit to the grey merchant." Before I could ask, Gnat added, "I could see—but not hear—your conversation from above."

I rubbed my chin in consideration. "Can other players see my Classes, Gnat?"

"Only if their insight is high enough."

The pieces were falling into place. Vomer must have observed my Class evolve from scout to nightstalker and reported it. The Master's interest in me was troubling, but it perhaps gave me a bit of leeway to work with. *This is something I can use.*

I turned back to Gnat. "Thank you for your candor Gnat," I said gravely. "I assume that this conversation is something else you must report to the Master?"

The bat bobbed his head. "It is."

"Then I want you to carry a message of my own back to the Master."

Gnat looked startled, but he waited patiently to hear what I had to say.

I closed my eyes and took a moment to compose my thoughts. "Tell the Master that I will assume a Dark Mark if he wishes. But I ask that I be allowed to go about it in my own way. Request that he keep Stayne away. I intend on killing those who've betrayed me: Saben, Sigmar, and all that follow them, and I ask that the Master does not interfere. Let me go about my vengeance unimpeded." Opening my eyes, I glanced at Gnat. "Do you think that will satisfy the Master?"

The bat snorted. "It just might, assuming you can pull it off."

"Well, then," I said, rising to my feet. "I better get started."

CHAPTER 75: TURNING THE TABLES

I watched Gnat fly up to the ceiling and hoped I had done the right thing.

I knew I had no other choice. I had to pacify the Master in some manner and keep Stayne off my back. Direct confrontation with Gnat was ill-advised, which only left co-opting the Master's aid.

At least for now.

I needed time. Time to deal with Saben and Sigmar and time to find another way out of the damn sector. And then perhaps, I could risk the Master's wrath.

The familiar disappeared from sight. Slipping into the shadows, I made my way back to the safe zone cavern. Gnat had promised he would not be gone long and that on his return, he would find me. It seemed that our Pact allowed him to hone into my location from anywhere.

Back in the cavern, I saw that the position of the two gang squads had not changed. I found it curious that neither Saben nor Sigmar had joined in on the gang's hunt for Bornholm but was grateful nonetheless for their inactivity. Hugging the wall, I crept past the east ramp and the squad accompanied by Goral, and slipped into the north tunnel without incident.

The passage stretched out before me, as barren and as pitch-black as before. The tension in my shoulders eased. I still had a mammoth task ahead of me, but being enfolded by darkness made everything seem possible. I tiptoed through the tunnel with my senses extended, but encountered no obstacles, at least not until I reached the chokepoint.

The guard post was manned again.

There were four guards on watch, two mages, and a pair of fighters. While the guards were relaxed, there was no talking among them, and they appeared alert. The half-wall of loot chests had been removed too, and the illumination in the area increased. Magelights floated above both mages, supplementing the torches' light with magic. *So they are learning to fear the dark,* I thought. *Good.*

Neither of the fighters was heavily armed. Both were dressed in leather armor and bore swords or daggers on their hips. Reaching out with my will, I cast analyze.

The target is Darnell, a level 11 elf.
The target is Martin, a level 12 human.
The target is Susa, a level 11 lizardman.
The target is Cathar, a level 13 elf.

I bit at the inside of my lip, wondering if I should retreat. It was the safer course, but if I managed to charm one—or even two—guards and kill another in the process, I thought the encounter was winnable. Though even if my attack was a complete success, at some point, the guards would be missed and the gang alerted to my presence.

Still, the opportunity to rearm myself could not be ignored. *I might not get a better chance than this.*

It's worth the risk, I thought and slipped further back into the shadows, about as far back I could go while still retaining line of sight to the guards. Picking my target, I cast simple charm.

Darnell has failed a mental resistance check! You have charmed your target for 10 seconds.

I smiled as the spell worked on the first attempt, and the elven fighter fell under my control. *"Attack,"* I whispered, directing my new minion's efforts toward his fellow fighter—the human.

Darnell unsheathed his longsword and buried it into his target's torso. The human fighter screamed and stumbled away. The blow wasn't fatal, though.

"He's here," Martin gasped. He pressed one hand against his side, and with his other, he drew a shortsword. "Leave Darnell to me! You two find the bastard!"

I pursed my lips. My minion's initial attack had been less successful than I'd hoped. Still, despite the human fighter's brave words, I thought he was too badly injured to prevail against the charmed elf. Turning my attention to the mages, I began casting again.

The pair had spun about and were scanning the darkened passage, but I was too well hidden for them to spot. Unfortunately, that was not the only action they took. The two magelights, fixed above the spellcaster's position, bobbed forward to search the passage.

Two hostile entities have failed to detect you!

My trepidation increased as the magical orbs drew closer, brightening the shadows surrounding me, but I thought I had enough time to finish my spell and didn't break off from my casting.

A moment later, my preparations were completed, and I reached out with my mind to the lizardman, attempting to subvert his will.

You have failed to charm your target. You may not bewitch more than one target at a time with simple charm. Your mental intrusion has been detected!

I cursed under my breath. The spell's limitation caught me off guard, leaving my plan in tatters. With all four guards alive and with the magelights still advancing, I had no choice but to retreat. I rose to my feet and fled back down the tunnel.

Two hostile entities have failed to detect you!

The bobbing searchlights had drawn closer, but even in the tunnel's new half-light, my sneaking was high enough to remain undetected—at least for now. Another pair of Game messages dropped into my mind.

Your minion has been critically injured!
Your minion has killed Martin.

The unexpected report caused me to pause in my step. It changed the complexion of the encounter: one guard was down, and another was badly wounded. *Dare I go back?* I wondered.

Now that the guards were aware of my presence, retreating was just as dangerous as returning to the fight. If I kept fleeing, the mages would likely pursue me all the way back to the safe zone. If that happened, I would be in serious trouble.

Better to face the mages, I decided.

Spinning about, I raced towards the spellcasters, forgoing stealth altogether as I hurtled through their magelights.

Two hostile entities have detected you!

"There he is!"

"Freeze him!"

Expecting an attack, I bobbed and weaved. To further confound the mages' aim, I drew on my psi again to cast one-step.

You have failed to one-step.

Predictably, I failed to cast the spell the first time, but I persisted in my efforts and eventually managed the casting. The spell didn't slow me down and added to the randomness of my trajectory, which was enough to make the effort worthwhile. Halfway into my charge, another message arrived.

You have lost control over Darnell.

I didn't let the latest Game report dissuade me. I was committed to my course now, and besides, the elven fighter was injured. And when it came down to it, even three-to-one odds were better than what I would face in the cavern.

A bolt of ice rushed towards me. Not slowing down, I sidestepped the projectile. Another spell—a fire dart—flew at me. Rolling forward, I ducked beneath it. From up ahead, I heard the lizardman chanting, starting a more complex, and likely more dangerous, spell.

I sprang out of my roll and risked a glance backward. Distracted by their own attacks, the spellcasters had not redirected their magelights. The two orbs hung stationary a few yards behind me, leaving a pool of shadow between them and the guard station.

I smiled. *Careless.* I changed direction abruptly, breaking my forward momentum to dash to the right. After two steps, I stilled suddenly and drew the shadows around me.

You are hidden once more.

"Where'd he go?" I heard Darnell mutter. The elven fighter sounded as if he was in pain.

The lizardman broke off his chanting. "Locate him!" he hissed. "I can't cast my spell without a target!"

The elven fighter stumbled forward, his steps dragging. The magelights began moving my way as well, but I was already deep in a casting and ignored them. My spell completed, and I reached out with my will.

Cathar has passed a mental resistance check! You have failed to charm your target. Your mental intrusion has been detected!

I growled in frustration at the failure and, swapping targets, started again.

"He's in my mind!" the elven mage screamed, sounding panicked. "Find him quickly!"

"I'm trying," Darnell wheezed, "but the coward is hiding."

A heartbeat passed, then another, then the magelights reached me. Hovering over my still form, they revealed my location.

Three hostile entities have detected you!

"There he is," Susa hissed. "Get him!"

"I'm going," Darnell snarled and limped forward. A dagger was stuck in his thigh, and he was moving poorly. The fighter wouldn't reach me in time to stop my casting, I judged.

But the two mages weren't waiting for their companion. Lowering their wands, they sent their own attacks racing toward me.

In the midst of my casting, I watched wide-eyed as the ice bolt and fire dart hurtled toward me. I couldn't dodge away from the projectiles. If I did, I would interrupt my own spell. With only a split second to decide, I braced myself for the impact and hurried through my spell as fast as I dared.

An ice bolt has injured you! A fire dart has injured you! You have passed a physical resistance check! Spellcasting uninterrupted.

Fire splashed over the bare flesh of my thigh, and ice crackled over my torso, seeping into my bones. The pain was excruciating. But despite the twin blows, I didn't drop the weaves of the spell I was constructing in my mind.

"He's still casting!"

"Hit him again!"

My spell completed, and I flung it at the lizardman.

Susa has failed a mental resistance check! You have charmed your target for 10 seconds.

I smiled thinly. I'd done it. *Now to finish this.*

"Attack, Darnell," I ordered my minion, then set off running. My body protested. The burnt skin on my legs tore open further, and my torso felt unaccountably heavy. I gritted my teeth against the pain and kept going. Angling around the approaching fighter, I ran toward the mages.

Darnell was still a few feet away and moved to intercept me. But with his leg injured, he was not fast enough to stop me.

Another set of magical projectiles erupted out of the mages' wands, one rushing toward me, the other toward the fighter. I twisted out of the way of the fire dart and resumed my charge.

Darnell was not so quick. The elf was unprepared for the attack and was hit squarely in the chest by the ice projectile. With a groan, he collapsed to his knees. He was far from dead, but the attack had slowed him further.

The elven mage's eyes widened, only then realizing his fellow spellcaster had been charmed. He spun about and lowered his wand at the bewitched lizardman. The threat went unheeded by my minion. Raising his wand again, Susa sent another ice bolt hurtling towards Darnell, even as his companion's fire dart sizzled into him from point-blank range.

I ignored the trio's three-way battle and made straight for the dead human fighter. His shortsword had fallen by his side. Dashing forward, I picked it up. My target was preoccupied and had his back turned to me.

Lunging forward, I plunged the blade into Cathar's back. The elven mage shrieked and tried to turn around, but using my momentum and body weight, I bore him to the ground. Slapping my left hand across the elf's shoulder, I stunned him before cutting into him again with the sword in my right hand.

I had to repeat the combo twice more before the elven mage finally died. Rolling off the corpse, I took stock of the battle. Darnell, still some way off, was barely moving, and Susa's entire left side had been burned to a crisp. But despite that, the lizardman hadn't let up with his attacks, and as I watched, another ice bolt raced toward the downed fighter.

I rose to my feet and positioned myself behind the mage. Seconds later, my spell lapsed. The lizardman crashed to his knees with a whimper of pain as the weaves of psi around his mind dissipated. He was too far gone to even stand, I realized. My spell had been all that was holding him up.

Pitilessly, I drew back the unresisting mage's head and slit his throat. Then I strode to Darnell's side and did the same.

It was over. I had triumphed.

CHAPTER 76: TWELVE HOURS TO LIVE

Multiple Game messages awaited my attention, and I perused them quickly.

Your insight has increased to level 26. Your telekinesis has increased to level 7. Your telepathy has increased to level 13. Your chi has increased to level 9. Your sneaking has increased to level 39. Your dodging has increased to level 26.

Warning! Your psi is at 10%. Warning! Your health is at 80% and will not recover without healing.

I had to meditate and restore my psi at some point, but first, I had to loot the bodies and put some distance between me and the guard post. My health, I couldn't do anything about, not until I found a healing potion.

I looted the two fighters first, and between their gear, managed to put together a full and undamaged leather armor set.

You have equipped a set of basic leather armor. This item set reduces the physical damage you sustain by 15% and, based on your current light armor skill, penalizes your Magic and Dexterity by 45%. Current modifiers: Dexterity skills and abilities limited to rank 4.

The mages carried nothing of value to me, not even a coin pouch. Still, their robes and wands would possibly be of use to Morin and Tantor, and I stripped the bodies of both.

Martin's dagger and sheath I took as well, even though the weapon was of limited use to me.

You have acquired 1 basic steel dagger. You lack the proper skill to wield this item. Weapon bonuses will not be received, and weapon-based abilities will be disabled. Abilities can only be used with a weapon with which you are proficient.

I added Darnell's longsword to the items I took from the mages and bundled the pile together. Carrying the bundle on my back, I headed back up the passage and concealed myself. Then sitting down, I began to meditate.

~ ~ ~

Meditation completed. Your psi is now at 100%. Your meditation has increased to level 24.

A short while later, I opened my eyes. I had finished meditating without being disturbed, and my psi was fully restored. About to rise to my feet, a patch of white attracted my notice.

It was Gnat. The familiar was back.

I turned his way, feeling sudden trepidation as I wondered about the message he carried. "The Master wishes to speak to you directly," Gnat said without preamble. "I will act as his conduit."

Before I could respond, a cloud of dense black formed beneath the skeletal bat's hovering form.

"Michael," a softly spoken voice called through the swirling darkness. It was the Master. "Gnat tells me you wish to bargain?"

"I do," I replied, straining to keep my voice firm.

"And what makes you think I would be interested in a deal with you?" the Power asked, coldly amused.

You're here, aren't you? I thought but didn't voice the words out aloud. "I will bind myself to the Dark," I said instead, ignoring his question altogether, "in exchange for your non-interference while I pursue my vengeance."

"Revenge," the Master mused. "It is a worthy goal for a Darksworn."

"Then we have a deal?"

The Power did not reply immediately. The dark cloud from which his voice emanated pulsed ominously while I waited in anxious silence. "No," the Master said at last.

"No?" I repeated, my heartbeat quickening. *Why not?* I wanted to rant but managed to restrain myself. What would I do if he refused to deal?

"It is not enough," the Master said.

"Then what is?" I asked tersely.

"Your allegiance—sworn directly to me."

Dread curdled in me. The Master was asking for more than I'd bargained. I'd known venturing down this path would be risky, but there was no backing out now. I had no illusions. If I didn't manage to strike a deal with the Power, I fully expected to be dead within the hour.

"If I do as you ask, will you give me the freedom to do what I must?" I asked. *This is madness,* an inner voice protested. I ignored it.

"I will not stay my hand indefinitely," the Master replied. "I will give you twelve hours only. "Will that suffice?"

A vein throbbed at my temple. Twelve hours? Would it be enough? *It will have to be.* I nodded slowly.

"Excellent," the Master said, his voice still emotionless. "Step forward and place your hand in the cloud then, and I will form the Pact between us."

I hesitated. How much did the Power want this deal? Up to this point, his manner had given nothing away. But that he was here indicated more than a modicum of interest. *How much room do I have to maneuver?* I exhaled softly. "Not yet," I said.

The black cloud stilled. "Do not toy with me, boy," the Master replied, the first edge of anger entering his voice. "I am here at your behest. If you refuse my bargain, you will not enjoy the consequence."

"I have a counter-proposal," I said hurriedly.

For a drawn-out moment, there was no response. "Go on," the Master said finally.

"I will accept your time limit," I said, speaking rapidly. "But I have a condition of my own. Our Pact will only be valid while I remain in the sector."

The Master laughed. "You think to escape the dungeon?"

There was no point denying the truth. "If I can."

"How?" the Master asked, sounding genuinely curious. "I can see that you carry no Dark Mark. The portal will not open for you. And lest you think to purchase a Dark Class from my merchants, they've been instructed not to sell to you."

So even the deal that Stayne offered me was rigged, I thought. I shrugged. "Still, I will try. Are we in agreement?"

"What of your vaunted vengeance?" the Master asked.

"I will pursue it, too," I said, allowing my determination to show.

The Master chuckled. His attention seemed to shift upwards. "Do you believe him?"

"I do, Master," Gnat replied.

"Do we have a deal?" I repeated.

The Power was silent for a moment. "We do. Step forward, and I will seal the Pact between us."

My nerves tingling, I placed my hand in the dark cloud. A game message opened in my mind.

Initiating a Pact between the Power known as the Master and the player, Michael...

~ ~ ~

Agreeing upon the exact wording of the Pact took longer than expected.

The initial phrasing was at the Master's direction. I found it too vague and outright rejected the proposal. To my surprise, the Power did not protest my refusal, and before I could blurt out a hurried explanation, a new Pact appeared in my mind, one whose revised wording I found *far* more palatable.

I accepted immediately.

Only for the Master to refuse the proposal.

It turned out that the process of forming a Pact was mediated by the Adjudicator. It made me wonder if I could have altered the original terms of the Pact formed between Gnat and me, but I suspected the Master would not have allowed me any leeway then.

It took several iterations, but finally, the Master and I reached a consensus on a Pact whose terms we both found agreeable.

You have sealed a Pact with the Power known as the Master. The terms are as follows: For the next twelve hours, all players and creatures sworn in service to the Master are forbidden from attacking you. This only holds true while you take no hostile action against said creatures and players. At the end of the allotted time, if you remain in sector 14,913, you will swear allegiance to the Master, and the Pact will be fulfilled. Alternatively, if you leave the sector any time before the allotted time, the Pact will also be considered fulfilled.

This Pact may not be terminated by either party. Once the Pact has been fulfilled, a 7-day non-aggression Pact will be enforced between the parties.

The non-aggression Pact had been the biggest sticking point—I had wanted a year, the Master, none—but finally, seeming to be annoyed by the entire process, the Master had agreed to a week. Once the Pact was sealed, he vanished immediately, leaving me alone with Gnat again.

"Phew," I muttered and wiped the sweat from my brow, feeling drained.

"You play a dangerous game," Gnat murmured. "If you somehow escape pledging yourself to the Master, he will not let you go. He will hunt you down, and his punishment will be merciless." Gnat's luminous white eyes pulsed. "Believe me, Michael, you don't want to experience the Master's wrath."

I nodded in wholehearted agreement. I had gotten what I was after, though, even if the consequence of failure was a bit more than I had bargained for.

Twelve hours to kill Saben and Sigmar and find a way out of the sector. It was not a lot of time, but it would have to be enough.

I rose to my feet. It was time to get to work.

~ ~ ~

I returned unseen to the safe zone cavern first and dropped the bundle of looted items down the crater at the same spot from which I emerged. That way, if the worst befell me, then at least Tantor and Morin would have something to work with.

Having done what I could for the pair, I raced through the north passage, only slowing down when I reached the gang's camp.

Concealed in the darkness and ready to flee at a moment's notice, I crept into the cavern. Saben's original gang had numbered about seventy, and given the two dozen in the safe zone cavern and the four guards I had just killed, that still left as many as forty unaccounted for—which was a lot for little old me to take on my own.

Of course, some of those forty had probably not been resurrected after suffering final death in the earlier battle. The problem was I had no way of knowing how many that could be and had to be prepared for the worst.

But after long moments of scrutinizing the gang's camp, I realized it was empty. I frowned. Where was everyone? I expected to find at least a token guard in the cavern, but it was, to all appearance, completely deserted. With nothing to hold me back, I slipped into the camp, passing silent rows of tents and dead campfires. At the camp's center, I paused.

Equipment of all types and sorts had been piled high in a large heap. Where the gear had come from was no mystery. It had to have been looted from the dead. I was surprised, though, that no one was guarding it. I studied the surroundings with a wary gaze but spotted nothing that smelled of a trap. I inched closer to the discarded equipment.

Still, nothing jumped out at me.

I shrugged and, accepting my good fortune for what it was, began rifling through the pile. It became apparent pretty soon that all the gear in the heap were basic starter items, which partially explained why it had been left unguarded. Still, I managed to get another serviceable sword and a belt with potion slots on it.

You have acquired a basic steel shortsword. This item increases the damage you deal by 10%.
You have acquired a slotted-potion belt. This item can hold up to 10 potion flasks.

Of course, there were no potion flasks on the belt itself, but I hadn't lost hope yet of recovering my lost gear. Discarding the dagger I had been carrying, I sheathed my new shortsword and felt new confidence fill me now that I was properly armed again.

Straightening, I considered my next move. The tunnel to the east was where I had to go to find Bornholm's people. Given my time limit, I needed to hurry, and my first instinct was to head that way directly.

But almost of my own volition, my eyes were drawn west, in the direction of Saben's chambers. If my backpack was to be found anywhere, it was likely there. While time was of the essence, I knew I could not afford to die again. The eight hours spent resurrecting alone would wipe out two-thirds of my deadline. And more than anything else, I needed my healing potions.

Searching Saben's chambers shouldn't take long. An hour, no more. Then I'll go looking for Bornholm.

Decided, I slipped into the western tunnel.

~ ~ ~

The passage to Saben's chambers was just as deserted as the camp. Even so, when I reached the first strands of spiderwebs, I redoubled my efforts at caution. I was *not* about to be caught out by the same trick again.

Halting every few steps, I prodded the silk strands with my swords and confirmed nothing lurked beneath. My caution proved unnecessary, though. The webs were empty. But three feet from Saben's chamber, a booming laugh broke the silence, giving me fresh cause for concern.

I froze.

The laughter was shockingly loud and appeared to be coming from within the chamber. "You idiot! Stop fooling around!" a voice growled.

"You should have seen your face," another said.

I frowned. The voice sounded familiar, but I couldn't place it.

"That was childish," the first protested.

"It's your own fault," the second pointed out. "You shouldn't have dozed off."

My eyes widened, finally recognizing the speaker. It was Markus. My lips tightened in an unpleasant smile. It was time for payback.

"I was not sleeping!" the first protested.

Bracing my back against the chamber's entrance, I peered carefully around the edge of the wall.

"You were!"

Markus and another gang member I didn't know were alone inside. They were guarding a small pile of looted equipment and appeared oblivious of my presence.

I took my time and rechecked the cavern. I still didn't detect anyone else. I tightened my grip on my swords, wondering if this was some sort of trap. But a trap here didn't make sense. For all Saben and Sigmar knew, I was still stuck in the safe zone.

I slipped inside the room, exploiting the thugs' distraction. Given that there were only two enemies, I didn't bother with charm. Drawing on my psi, I cast one-step as I closed the distance.

I was still a few yards away from the pair when Markus spotted me out of the corner of his eye. His head whipped around, and his eyes widened.

"You should see your face," I murmured in mockery of his earlier words. I didn't give him time to react, though, and dashed forward.

The gang member fumbled for his still-sheathed blade, but before he could draw it, I lunged and buried my sword in his throat. I withdrew the blade, and Markus fell lifelessly to the floor.

I sensed a weapon rushing down on me from my right. I sidestepped, evading the blow. The thug attacked again, swinging his broadsword in a mighty arc. I dodged the second attack just as easily, but instead of darting in to seize the glaring opening my opponent had left, I stepped back. "Can we talk?"

The thug snarled and lunged at me in response.

I slipped past the blow with laughable ease. "Look, if you tell me what I want, I'll let you go."

Once more, I was ignored. Hefting his broadsword above his head, my foe brought it crashing down—on empty ground. I was long gone.

I sighed from behind the fighter. He really wasn't any good, and even though he was in full chainmail, I foresaw no problems with disarming him. But given the thug's reticence, I suspected I would have to question him quite harshly to get the information I needed.

Thinking about what I might need to do made me a little queasy, but I didn't let it deter me. If I was going to take down Saben's gang, I needed to know more about their numbers and whereabouts. I had other reasons too. Reasons less certain but no less important.

Enough of this, I thought. Dashing forward, I touched one of my blades to the fighter, crippling his arm and causing him to lose hold of his sword. Dropping my second blade, I stun-slapped the thug, then rammed my shoulder into him.

The fighter stumbled but didn't fall. I repeated the maneuver, and this time, he fell face forward. Before he could recover, I straddled my foe's body and proceeded to beat at his skull with the pommel of my sword, only stopping when he fell unconscious.

~ ~ ~

The fighter—his name was Jorin—came too to find he had been stripped of his armor and that his hands had been tied together.

"Ready to talk now?" I asked from my position across from him.

A hard stare was my only response.

"Where is the rest of your gang?"

He glared back silently.

"How many men does Saben have?"

No response.

I sighed. "It's better if you cooperate. Don't doubt that I won't resort to harsher measures if necessary."

"Do your worst," Jorin spat. "Hurt me as much as you wish. I won't talk!"

"Oh, I'm not going to hurt you," I replied evenly. "You're going to do that all by yourself."

A frown flitted across his face, before he replaced it with a sneer. "You're some sort of fool, or what?" he mocked.

"Maybe I am," I murmured. Forgoing further banter, I drew on my psi and cast simple charm.

Jorin has failed a mental resistance check! You have charmed your target for 10 seconds.

Yanking on the mental leash I held around his mind, I directed Jorin's attention to one of the chamber's walls. *"Run,"* I ordered.

The fighter staggered to his feet, and obedient to my will, ran full tilt towards the solid, rock wall. He hit hard, and I winced at the impact. As Jorin collapsed to the floor, the expected Game message dropped into my mind.

You have taken hostile action against your minion! Control of target lost.

Rising to my feet, I approached the dazed fighter and knelt by his side. He gazed up at me, his eyes still unfocused.

"Now," I said gently, "if I can make you do that, imagine what else I can force you to do."

It was all a lie of course. The simple charm spell didn't allow me to direct my minions to self-harm. The imperative for self-preservation was too strong to be overcome by such a basic spell. The best I could manage was to make Jorin indirectly injure himself. But I was betting Jorin knew none of this.

Jorin blanched, finally comprehending my threat. "W-w-what did you do to me?"

"Mind control," I said succinctly. "Shall we find out what else I can do?" I asked, letting a cruel smile dance on my face.

The fighter just stared back at me, his face white.

"Still won't talk? Oh well." I rose to my feet. "Let's try this again."

Jorin's eyes bulged. "No! Wait, please! I'll tell you whatever you want. Just don't do that again!"

I smiled coldly. "Good, then let's begin."

CHAPTER 77: BACKUP GEAR

Jorin had a lot to say.

Most of it was irrelevant, and much I simply didn't believe. According to the fighter, Saben and Sigmar had already lost half of their gang to final death.

If Jorin was to be believed, other than the two dozen fighters in the safe zone cavern, only ten more gang members remained. He even claimed that Bornholm and *all* his people were alive and unharmed—which was preposterous. The dwarf, I was sure, would never side with the gang.

I compelled Jorin to run into the wall twice more after that, but sadly his tale didn't change, and eventually, I was forced to concede it wouldn't—not unless I took more drastic measures. Which I wasn't prepared to do. Despite my determination to eke out what information I could from the thug, I had already gone as far as I was willing to.

I had to be satisfied with what I had.

I rose to my feet and looked down at my captive. "Thank you, Jorin," I said gravely. "You've been a great help."

He jerked his head upwards towards me. "Are you going to let me go now?"

I shook my head. "No," I said softly and sliced open his throat.

~ ~ ~

I stayed with the fighter until he gasped his last breath. I wasn't pleased with what I had done, but I thought my actions were warranted.

A necessary evil.

I swallowed back bile at the thought. Such justifications were a slippery slope, I knew, and I had to be careful with how far down this path I went, or I could lose my way entirely. Putting the fighter out of my mind, I turned my attention to other matters.

A few more Game messages had opened in my mind. Some of my skills had advanced, and I had gained another level. I didn't have to think too hard about deciding how to spend my new attribute point.

Your Dexterity has increased to rank 11. Current modifiers: -5 ranks in Dexterity. Dexterity skills and abilities limited to rank 6.

After seeing to the changes, I pulled up my player profile.

Player Profile (Basic): Michael

Level: 21. Rank: 2. Current Health: 80%.
Stamina: 70%. Mana: 100%. Psi: 90%.
Species: Human. Lives Remaining: 2.
Marks: Wolf-friend, Lesser Shadow, Lesser Light.
Classes: Nightstalker Rank 1, Psionic Rank 1.
Class point: 1 available.

Attributes (0 points available)

Strength: 2. Constitution: 5. Dexterity: 11. Perception: 8. Mind: 5. Magic: 0. and Faith: 0.

Traits

Undead familiar, Wolven, Beast tongue, Metamind, Marked, Nocturnal.

Skills (1 slot available)
Dexterity: Dodging: 27. Sneaking: 39. Shortswords: 35. Two weapon fighting: 31. Thieving: 1.
Constitution: Light armor: 20.
Mind: Chi: 9. Meditation: 24. Telekinesis: 10. Telepathy: 15.
Perception: Insight: 26.

Abilities
Crippling blow, minor backstab, simple charm, stunning slap, basic analyze, one-step.

Known Key Points
Sector 14,913 exit portal and safe zone.

Equipped
2 basic steel shortswords (+10% damage each).
slotted-potion belt (empty).
basic leather armor set (+15% damage reduction, -50% Dexterity and Magic).

With my progression seen to, I rose to my feet and searched Markus and Jorin's corpses. Other than their weapons and armor, both thugs carried little upon them, and I moved on to the heap of equipment they had been guarding.

The pile turned out to be the very gear our party had lost in this chamber. The items looked like they had been dumped here for sorting later. Morin and Tantor's equipment had been basic, consisting of items looted from the goblin complex, and I didn't bother recovering any of it. Decalthiya's armor was too heavy to lug away and I left it behind too.

Which left only my own gear.

I spotted my backpack buried underneath Decalthiya's armor. Pulling it free, I peered inside anxiously.

A relieved smile lit my face when I saw everything was exactly as I had left it. After popping a ration cube in my mouth and quenching my thirst with water, I filled my belt slots with my healing potions. Then, I searched for my remaining gear.

It didn't take me long to find my fighter's sash and thief's cloak, and I equipped both. My money pouch, though, was nowhere to be found.

I grimaced at the thought of my lost coins. I hadn't been carrying much, but still—

I paused. Something else occurred to me. Neither Markus nor any of the other gang members I'd just killed had had any money on them either. I frowned. *So where is all the money that the gang looted?* I had questioned Jorin repeatedly about the gang's treasure trove, but he'd insisted that the gang had none. I still wasn't sure if I believed him, though.

Straightening, I scanned the chamber. The only furnishings in the cavern were the bed and table on the left side. It didn't take me long to examine both, but I came up empty.

I pursed my lips. The only other spots to hide something were behind the spiderwebs, but considering the volume of silk in the chamber, searching them would be a mammoth task and not something I had time for.

Returning to the center of the chamber, I turned a slow circuit and scrutinized the walls. Nothing stood out to me, though. *Oh well,* I thought, *it would've been nice to find the gang's stash.* I was sure they had one, but it didn't look like I was going to find it now.

Still, for the sake of thoroughness, I tried one more time. Walking along the perimeter of the room, I paused after every step to run my gaze along the webs enveloping the walls. Halfway through, I began to regret my decision. *This is useless. I have what I came for, and it's time I got—*

You have found an anomaly! Your insight has increased to level 27.

I froze as the Game message popped into my mind. At the edge of my vision, I'd noticed an oddity. The thing that had attracted my attention was not something within the webs as I'd expected but was instead a curiously-straight groove cut in the floor less than a yard from me.

Bending down on my haunches, I inspected the spot in question more closely. The groove was definitely not natural. With a gentle hand, I brushed away the concealing dirt and uncovered three more straight-cut edges.

A hidden compartment had been set into the rock beneath. Sitting back, I scrutinized my find again, but nothing else triggered my insight.

Is it trapped?

I couldn't tell, and I didn't have the time necessary for a more careful and thorough examination. I bit my lip, wondering if I should open the compartment.

I have to.

I drew my shortsword and readied a full healing potion in my left hand. If I *did* trigger a trap, I would down the potion immediately. I knew opening the compartment was risky, but I needed to see what the gang kept in it. It could make all the difference between the success and failure of my mission.

Without further delay, I wedged my blade between one of the grooves and levered up the covering rock plate. It came free easily. Gripping the healing flask tightly in my left hand, I waited for a reaction.

The seconds ticked by slowly. Nothing.

I exhaled and felt my pulse return to normal. The compartment wasn't trapped, only hidden. Reaching inside, I retrieved a handful of items.

You have acquired 3 full healing potions, 3 moderate healing potions, and 3 minor healing potions.

You have acquired a coin pouch containing 91 golds, 4 silvers, and 9 coppers.

You have acquired a rank 1 shortsword, +1. This item increases the damage you deal by 15% and has been enchanted to increase the wielder's shortsword skill by +1 rank (10 skill points). This item requires a minimum Dexterity of 4 to wield.

You have acquired a rank 1 priest's robe. This item decreases the faith-based damage you sustain by 10%. This item requires a minimum Faith of 4 to equip.

You have acquired a master Class stone. This stone contains the path of: a blood siphon. It confers a player with four skills: dark magic, light resistance, scimitars, and leech. This Class also permanently boosts your Faith attribute by +2, your Strength by +2, and your Magic attribute by +2. This is a Dark Class.

I couldn't believe it. I had found the very item I needed to escape the dungeon, but I left its examination for last. I turned my attention to the rest of my new possessions.

There were no skillbooks or ability tomes, which was no surprise really. Those, I assumed the gang had found ready use for. In fact, given the items in evidence, it appeared the compartment was Saben's stash of backup gear.

I was rich too, and assuming I could make it back to the safe zone without dying, I would not want for more skills or abilities. The enchanted blade was of the most immediate use, and without hesitation, I replaced one of my basic swords with it. Then, I downed two of the minor healing potions and restored myself to full health. Finally, I inspected the Class stone.

It was the only item that didn't belong. Saben already had a master Class of his own, so he didn't have any need for it. What I couldn't figure out though, was why he hadn't given it to one of his elites.

"Wow, what stone is that?" Gnat asked.

I glanced at the familiar. He likely knew what it was already. "You know what it is, don't you?"

Gnat ducked his head sheepishly. "It holds the blood siphon Class."

"Tell me about it."

"It is a lucky find indeed," Gnat said, "and comes equipped with the leech and light resistance skills."

I had been wondering about the skills myself. I hadn't come across them before. "What do you know of them?"

The bat snickered. "Only that they are amongst the rarest skills in the Game. Both are master tier skills."

My brows drew down. "What do they do?"

"Light resistance increases your resistance to light spells, and leech allows you to siphon any form of energy—including health—from your foe with each hit."

My eyes widened. "Really?"

"Really," Gnat said with a chuckle. "Most players would kill to get their hands on the Class."

My gaze slid back to the marble in my hand. The desire to absorb the Class was nearly unbearable. The leech skill alone would make the Class worthwhile.

It was the perfect Class. Almost.

I couldn't ignore the fact that it was force-aligned. I had bought myself some time through my Pact with the Master, but I wasn't ready to commit myself yet. I would not be the Master's puppet, nor the Dark's if I could help it. I still held out hope of finding another way of escaping the dungeon. Reluctantly, I dropped the item into my backpack.

Gnat was watching me closely. "You aren't going to assume the Class?" he asked, surprise lacing his voice.

"Maybe later." I glanced at him. "You will report this to the Master?"

The skeletal bat nodded. "I must. Although, it will make no difference. The Master is constrained by the Pact from acting against you. Besides, he would likely award you with a similar Class once you swear allegiance to him." He hesitated. "You *should* claim the Class, Michael, but you *shouldn't* try using it to escape the dungeon."

I shrugged noncommittally. "I'll deal with the stone later. For now, I have work to do. How much time do I have remaining on the Master's deadline?" I asked, changing the subject.

"Eleven hours, fifteen minutes."

"Then, there is no more time to lose. Let's go find Bornholm."

CHAPTER 78: SPINNING FOR CONTROL

I made my way back to the gang's camp without incident. My pockets were full, and my gear was better than it had been at any stage since I'd entered this world.

I felt ready for anything.

Reaching the camp, I found it still deserted, and I crossed the barren space quickly before ducking into the eastern tunnel. There I paused and took stock.

The tunnel was wide, and torches had been set at regular intervals along the wall. All were lit and burning. No one was in sight, so I crept up to the nearest torch and inspected it more closely.

Its reservoir of oil was nearly full, which meant someone had been this way in the last few hours. With renewed caution, I advanced down the corridor. A hundred yards later, I stopped again. The tunnel had begun to snake sharply, but that was not what had caused me to stop.

There were people up ahead.

I could hear their voices, muffled by the distance but distinct nonetheless. I drew both my blades. Slowing my steps further, I kept going. The voices grew louder, and I strained my ears for the least hint of danger.

A voice rang out. Louder than the others, the speaker's words reverberated through the stone tunnel. "... let us out of here, you wretched fools!"

I paused. I knew that voice. It was Bornholm. Hope rekindled in my chest. If the dwarf was alive, then likely more of his people were as well. I hurried forward again, and presently another's words became clear too.

"Stop your damn hollering, you blasted dwarf. I'm trying to sleep over here."

"Just wait till I get my hands on you, witch!" Bornholm bellowed.

"That's not happening," the first speaker said, her voice oozing boredom. "You and the fools with you are never getting out of there. Now be quiet!"

Bornholm, of course, did not stay silent. Swearing fit to wake the dead, he spewed out a long litany of curses. But I stopped listening as my surroundings changed abruptly.

I was no longer in a tunnel.

The passage's floor and sidewalls had fallen away, and I found myself standing at the top of a slope, looking down onto an immense cavern. A deep chasm ran from left to right along the cavern's far end, and on the other side of it lay another tunnel. Bornholm was standing in the tunnel mouth, and facing him across the chasm was his heckler.

Not wanting to be seen, I dropped into a crouch while I studied the scene below. Ten gang members were one hundred yards ahead of me, on the near side of the chasm. They were sitting at ease, laughing, and talking quietly amongst themselves—except for the one throwing rejoinders back at Bornholm. She was screaming nearly as loudly as the dwarven fighter.

Bornholm himself was thirty yards away from the thugs, separated from his foes by both the chasm and a lowered portcullis guarding the tunnel entrance. Through the latticed grille metal, I spied others by the dwarf's side, although they remained silent, letting him do all the talking.

Our lost army. So Jorin wasn't lying, I thought.

A drawbridge spanned the darkness separating both groups, which explained how the dwarf and his people had gotten across the chasm in the first place, but it was presently raised. The controls for both the drawbridge and the portcullis were on the near side of the chasm.

Bornholm and his people were trapped, and the ten thugs I saw were guarding the controls. I let my gaze rove over the area, searching for a way to free the trapped candidates.

A pathway lined with torches led down from the top of the slope to the bridge area, which itself was overflowing with torches. In my present position, I was in no danger of being seen, but creeping up unseen on the gang squad was out of the question. I would have to depend on charm instead. But even assuming I charmed one of my foes, two against nine were not great odds.

I could not defeat the guards alone. I needed help. I rested my gaze on the two control wheels for the drawbridge and portcullis.

I have to free Bornholm's people first, then we can take care of the guards together.

Lowering the drawbridge would be a simple enough matter. I only needed to sever the ropes holding it up. Raising the portcullis, on the other hand, would take time. I would have to rotate the control wheel manually and, bit by bit, haul back the ropes holding it down. At the same time, I would have to prevent the guards from interfering.

Aargh, this is not going to be easy.

~ ~ ~

I spent a minute analyzing the ten thugs. All were between level ten and twelve, which left me with a distinct advantage in combat, at least one-on-one.

Next, I worked to contact Bornholm. The only way I could think of getting the dwarf's attention without alerting the thugs was by using charm.

On Bornholm himself.

I grimaced. I was sure this was not going to be pleasant for the dwarf, and I doubted he would appreciate the need, but it had to be done.

Drawing on the shadows to hide me, I crept around the top of the slope until I was far from the torchlit path. Then I padded softly through the darkness until I reached the chasm's edge. Bornholm was still hollering nonsense at the gang and was squarely in my sights.

I drew in a breath. *Here goes.* I reached out with my will and attempted to charm the dwarf.

Bornholm has passed a mental resistance check! You have failed to charm your target. Your mental intrusion has gone undetected!

My lips turned down, and I tried again.

Bornholm has failed a mental resistance check! You have charmed your target for 10 seconds.

Midstream, the dwarf's flow of curses cut off. I issued no commands. Sitting back on my haunches, I waited.

"What's wrong?" his heckler called back. "Cat got your tongue?"

Bornholm didn't respond. The seconds ticked by until, eventually, the psi leash around the dwarf's mind dissipated.

You have lost control over Bornholm.

Now to see what he does.

The moment he was free, Bornholm pressed his face against the gate and clenched its bars in his mailed fists. Turning his head left and right, he scanned the cavern.

As his head turned in my direction, I rose to my feet and let my stealth lapse. It was a risk but a small one. I was standing in pitch darkness, and that alone was enough to conceal me from all but those with night vision. Even they would have to be looking directly at me to spot me.

Bornholm's eyes widened as he caught sight of me. I jerked my chin towards the control wheels. The dwarf's gaze darted that way, and he nodded slowly, seeming to understand what I meant. I gave him a thumbs-up, then faded back into hiding and slipped toward the bridge area.

It was time for the next step.

~ ~ ~

My plan was simple. Tried and trusted too. I intended on charming the biggest and most well-armed of the thugs and setting him on the others to act as a distraction while I released the drawbridge and unhinged the lever keeping the portcullis lowered.

With Bornholm and his people pushing up the gate on their end and with me turning the control wheel, together we could hopefully release enough of the trapped candidates before the guards realized what was happening. But halfway to the bridge area, I was forced to revise my plans.

Bornholm was shouting again.

"Hey, you!" the dwarf bellowed. "Yes, I'm talking to you, lass! I've just about had it with your insults. I'm coming over there to wring your neck!"

Maria, the lass in question, laughed uproariously. "Of course you are."

What is he up to? I wondered.

"Just you wait," Bornholm promised. Turning around, he motioned the mages and archers behind him forward. The spellcasters stuck their wands out of the grille, and the archers shoved the points of their arrows through.

Seeing this, some of the guards got up. "What are they doing?" I heard one hiss.

"Whatever it is, it is bound to be something stupid," Marcia muttered.

"FIRE!" Bornholm ordered in an earth-splitting roar that caused some of the gang members to twitch involuntarily. About a dozen mage and archers released their attacks. Given the awkward angles involved, the projectiles were poorly directed, and most ended up falling into the chasm, but a few of the missiles splattered on the end of the bridge near the guards.

More guards got up.

"Should we retaliate?" a thug asked.

Maria rounded on the speaker. "Of course not, you fool! From that distance and angle, they stand little chance of hitting us. Sit back down."

But the guard didn't sit back down. Neither did any of the others. Forming a line across the bridge, the thugs warily watched the trapped candidates.

I smiled, finally realizing what Bornholm was up to. The dwarf had come up with a much better distraction than I could have managed on my own. *This will make my task much easier,* I thought and crept towards the control wheel for the portcullis.

~ ~ ~

Bornholm's efforts had served to get all the guards watching the trapped candidates across the chasm and not the control wheel behind them.

Ten hostile entities have failed to detect you!

Courtesy of the guard's distraction, I slipped right up to my goal without being spotted—despite the brightness of the surroundings. The rope to raise and lower the portcullis was wound around a toothed wooden wheel that had been locked in place by a metal lever.

Kneeling beside the device, I gently eased the lever out of position and released the portcullis. Bornholm's people could now push up the gate on their end unimpeded. Given the dwarf's swift response to my appearance, I was betting he had his people ready to do just that once I gave the word. Next, I snuck up to the drawbridge control wheel.

Ten hostile entities have failed to detect you!

There I paused. Before I released the bridge, I intended to add my own efforts to Bornholm's distraction. Picking out a half-giant armored in plate mail from amongst the thugs, I cast simple charm.

Wuxi has failed a mental resistance check! You have charmed your target for 10 seconds.

I rose to my feet and drew my swords. *"Attack,"* I ordered. The half-giant pulled out his axe and, with a roar of rage, smashed the heavy weapon into the mage standing by his side.

Your minion has killed Gavin.

Chaos erupted amongst the guards. Not waiting to see how they reacted, I released the drawbridge lever and chopped down on the rope holding it up to speed its descent. It took two blows before the rope severed. With a resounding crash, the drawbridge crashed into place to span the chasm.

A hostile entity has detected you!

My head whipped upwards. Maria was staring at me wide-eyed. A second later, her eyes narrowed, and she lowered her wand in my direction. Dashing forward, I stepped upwards and over the acid spit she hurled toward me.

You have successfully one-stepped. You have evaded Maria's attack.

On my next step, I touched down on the ground. Seeing me escape her attack unscathed and still rushing towards her, Maria turned to flee. She was too slow, though. Before she had taken more than a step away, I plunged both my blades through her back.

You have killed Maria.

An axe swept towards me from the right. I dived left and rolled away. Bouncing back to my feet, I risked a glance across the bridge.

Bornholm was watching me. Our gazes met, and he raised his hammer in fierce salute. I nodded back, noting in passing that the dwarf's people had already lifted the portcullis a foot above the ground, and the leanest amongst them—gnomes and elves—were already slipping beneath its sharpened ends.

Good, I thought. *This battle is won. All I need to do now is survive.* Returning my attention to the growing skirmish, I searched for another target.

CHAPTER 79: THE CLOCK IS TICKING

The battle did not last long after that.

With their leader Maria dead and Bornholm's people streaming across the bridge, the remaining guards were helpless to stop us. I killed a few more of them before disengaging altogether and leaving my allies to mop up.

When the last guard was seen to—his helm caved in by Bornholm no less—the dwarven fighter rushed up to me. I smiled in welcome as I saw his enthusiastic approach.

Too late, I realized that the dwarf wasn't slowing down. *Uh-oh. What does he mean to—*

Before I could dodge away, the metal-clad fighter wrapped his thick arms around my waist, trapping me in a dwarfish bear hug. Lifting me off my feet, Bornholm swung me around. "Lad! I can't tell you how glad I am to see you!" he crowed.

"Me too, Bornholm," I managed to squeak. "Uhm, can you put me down?" I wheezed.

"What? Oh, sure," he said, setting me down. He looked beyond me. "Where are the others?" Not waiting for my answer, he scowled. "What is Morin thinking, letting you do all this alone? Where is she?"

My smile faded. "No one else is coming, Bornholm," I said sadly. "Your people are it."

The dwarf looked at me as if he thought I was joking. "You're kidding, right. They can't all be—"

I laid an arm on his shoulder, interrupting him. "I have a lot to tell you." I swallowed, wondering how I was going to tell him about Sigmar's betrayal and Decalthiya's death. "Come, you will want to sit down for this."

~ ~ ~

Bornholm took the news badly.

He bawled. He yelled. He pounded the ground with his fists.

I sat on the slopes with the rest of the candidates and let him mourn. He was not alone in his grief. Many of the other candidates were in the throes of similar emotions. I was acutely aware of our time constraints, but I knew the candidates needed to come to terms with what had happened to their fellows before we could regroup and take the fight to the gang.

While I waited, I quietly questioned a few of the candidates about the prisoners they had gone in search of. It turned out they were all dead. The prisoners' wrists had been slit, and they had been left to bleed out slowly. When Bornholm and the others had found them at the end of the eastern tunnel network after hours of searching, the prisoners' bodies were still warm. It explained why none had been resurrected in the safe zone yet.

After that, I perused the changes to myself from the last skirmish. Once more, I had advanced, although, for some of my skills, the growth was minuscule. Most of my dexterity-based skills had reached rank three, and their development had slowed significantly. Nonetheless, I was pleased with how my training was progressing.

My psi skills, in particular, were advancing apace. Even the lowest had reached rank one. As a result, my spell failures had greatly reduced, and I could now use them with greater confidence in battle.

I'm about as ready as I can be, I thought.

I turned to my familiar. "Time?" I asked softly.

"Ten hours, thirty minutes left," Gnat replied.

I nodded and turned back to the dwarf. It was time for me to intervene. But Bornholm was done with his grieving and already stomping back towards me. "Where is he?" he demanded, yanking furiously at his beard.

I didn't have to ask who he meant. "In the safe zone cavern with Saben."

Bornholm's eyes narrowed. "You have a plan?"

I nodded.

"Tell me," he demanded.

I did. The dwarven fighter scowled when I was done. "That's more complicated than this needs to be, lad. We have numbers on our side. We should just rush in and overwhelm them—quick and dirty."

I shook my head. "Too risky. If Sigmar and Saben decide to retreat to the safe zone, our plan will be in shambles. They can stay holed up in there indefinitely. We do it my way."

What Bornholm suggested *was* actually the safer option, but I was not about to tell him that, nor was I willing to debate the issue. I was on a time limit, and since I would be bearing the brunt of the risk with my plan, I had no compunction about forcing the others to go along with it.

Bornholm eyed me for a moment before nodding curtly. "Alright, we'll follow your lead." He paused. "But Sigmar is mine."

"No," I said firmly. "Like it or not, Bornholm, I'm better suited to face Saben and Sigmar. Leave them to me."

The dwarf glared at me through reddened eyes before finally relenting. "Have it your way then, lad." He heaved me to my feet. "And this is no time to be sitting on your arse. Let's be about it."

~ ~ ~

It took longer than I would have liked to get everyone organized and briefed, but an hour later, I was crouched in the north tunnel entrance of the safe zone.

A squad of scouts was hidden behind me, their arms and backs laden with equipment. When things kicked off, their task would be to throw the gear into the safe zone to equip the thirty candidates there.

Bornholm and the sixty-odd remaining troops lay in wait about fifty yards back in the tunnel. They would only charge into the cavern once the scouts gave them the go-ahead.

I peeked into the cavern, studying it intently. Nothing seemed to have changed in the nearly three hours since I had left, and both gang squads were exactly where I had last seen them. Obviously, none of the guards had been missed yet. *Good.* I looked over my shoulder at Cyrus, the scout who was serving as my second-in-command for this mission. "Ready?" I whispered.

He nodded.

I clasped his hand briefly. "Remember the plan. I'm heading in." I glance down at myself again, making sure for the umpteenth time that I hadn't forgotten anything.

I was in newbie gear once more.

I had already stashed my backpack and gear somewhere safe, keeping only my coin pouch on my person. Assuming everything went according to plan, I would retrieve my other stuff once things got going, but for now, I couldn't afford to rouse the gang's suspicions by being spotted in armor.

Right, no use delaying then. I cloaked myself in shadows and slipped into the cavern.

Let's go play bait.

You have entered a safe zone.

I reached the crater's edge without incident and climbed down unseen. Letting my stealth fade, I slipped through the camp, searching for Morin and Tantor.

"Michael!" Tantor called, spotting me first.

I hurried to his side. Morin was with him. "You got the gear I dropped earlier?" I began without preamble.

The pair nodded.

"You've found Bornholm," the painted woman stated, somehow divining my news.

"I have," I said and proceeded to fill them in on the plan as rapidly as I could.

"It will be dangerous," Morin said, her face serious. "For you. Are you sure you want to take such a risk?"

"I am," I replied, not explaining why I deemed it necessary or my deadline. "Besides, if the worst happens, the rest of you can still finish this."

"Very well," she said, not questioning me further.

"Good," I said. "Now, there's one more thing I need to do before we get started. Ready the others. I have to go repay a debt."

~ ~ ~

"You're back!"

I smiled. "You sound surprised, Hamish. Don't tell me you thought me a bad investment?"

Consternation flitted momentarily across the merchant's face, then he laughed ruefully. "I didn't think I would be seeing you again," he conceded. He shook his head sadly. "Sometimes, I think I'm too soft-hearted for a merchant."

"Perish the thought," I replied with a grin. I glanced around carefully to make sure no one was watching, then stepped up close to the merchant and placed some coins in his hands.

"What's this?" Hamish asked, looking down in surprise.

I chuckled. "The money I owe you. And this—" I placed more coins in his hands— "is for the items I wish to purchase."

~ ~ ~

You have bought 1 master tier skillbook and 4 basic ability tomes. You have lost: 40 golds. Total money carried: 46 golds, 4 silvers, and 9 coppers.

"Oh, my," Hamish said when we concluded our transaction. "You've done better for yourself than I expected."

The merchant reached into his wagon and pulled out the books I had bought. Thankfully, he had had the foresight to obtain most of them from his partner in the Nexus after our first discussion, and I didn't have to wait for their arrival.

"Thanks," I said, taking the items. "Now, I have another request to make."

The dark elf's eyebrows rose. "Another favor? I'm almost afraid to ask."

I grinned. "It's nothing onerous," I assured him and placed my coin pouch into his open palms. "Can you hold this for me?"

Hamish's eyes darted downwards. "What is it?"

"Money," I said, then hesitated before adding, "And a master Class stone."

The merchant's eyes widened, but he didn't refuse the pouch. "Why give me this?"

"I'm heading back into danger," I said. "And if I die again, I don't want to be trapped here without resources." I gestured to the coin pouch in his hands. "Call that insurance."

"And the other item?" he asked.

"It's part of it, too," I said, not explaining further.

I was hedging my bets. I was playing for high stakes and knew I needed an alternative plan in case things went horribly wrong. The gold coins and the Class stone were part of that plan. In my own mind, I had four hours—and not twelve—in order to kill Saben and Sigmar.

The other eight hours were my reserve. In the event of my death, it would allow me to resurrect, assume the siphon Class, and flee the dungeon before my time ran out. I was hoping it wouldn't come to that, though.

If I succeeded in the first part of my plan, then I would have enough time to enact the second part of my strategy. All this meant I had little more than an hour left to kill Sigmar and Saben, and I was painfully aware I was cutting things close.

I met Hamish's gaze again. "Will you do this for me?"

The merchant's fist closed around the pouch. "I will," he affirmed.

You have lost: 46 golds, 4 silvers, and 9 coppers. You have lost a master Class stone.

"Thank you!" I said, pumping his hand vigorously. Bidding him goodbye, I swung around and began hurrying away.

From behind me, I heard Hamish mutter to himself, "I don't know why you would entrust me with this, though."

"Because you're soft-hearted," I murmured. "And a friend."

CHAPTER 80: BAIT AND SWITCH

Finding a quiet spot, I sat down cross-legged and read three of the ability tomes.

You have acquired the basic ability: lesser trap detect. This ability consumes stamina and can be upgraded. Its activation time is average. You have 6 of 8 Perception ability slots remaining.

You have acquired the basic ability: basic trap disarm. This ability consumes stamina and can be upgraded. Its activation time is very slow. You have 8 of 11 Dexterity ability slots remaining.

You have acquired the basic ability: simple lockpicking. This ability consumes stamina and can be upgraded. Its activation time is slow. You have 7 of 11 Dexterity ability slots remaining.

I gave my mind a moment to adapt to the new knowledge I had just absorbed before turning to the next book I intended on reading: the master tier skillbook, deception.

I exhaled a soft breath before opening the tome. This was a momentous occasion in my player growth. I was about to complete the configuration of my second Class and find out if my first two Classes would meld together.

I disliked that I had to rush into this, but time was passing, and the Game wasn't going to wait for me. *Onwards, Michael,* I thought and opened the skillbook.

You have acquired the master skill: deception. Deception is the art of deceit, disguise, distraction, and trickery. With it, a player can use his intuition offensively to fool others. In addition, this skill allows you to conceal your own actions and abilities and to resist or detect the scrying and analyze attempts of other players. You have 0 of 6 psionic Class skill slots remaining.

You have fully configured your second Class. Congratulations, Michael! Synergies exist between your chosen paths of a nightstalker and psionic. You now have the option to combine the two into a blended Class.

Do you wish to meld your original Classes into the bi-blend Class: mindstalker? Note, none of your existing skills or characteristics will be lost through your Class melding.

This was no time to hesitate, and with little deliberation, I willed my choice to the Game.

Your Classes have melded! You are now a mindstalker!

The mindstalker is a path for those who lurk in the dark and can kill not only with their blades but with their minds too. The mindstalker is said to live as much in the consciousness of others as in the world itself. Infiltrator. Assassin. Hunter. Deceiver. The mindstalker is all that and more. Only a handful have ventured on this path before, and in time, it will deepen your Wolf Mark.

Your Class base traits have melded together to form the new trait: psi wolf heritage. In ages gone past, wolves were renowned not only for their physical prowess but for their psicasting too. You share the legacy of those venerated ancients and, in time, may acquire more of their gifts. Your Dexterity is increased by +2 ranks, your Strength by +2 ranks, and your Mind by +4 ranks.

You have gained the ability: simple mindsight. Mindsight is the foundation upon which all other mindstalker abilities are built.

Simple mindsight is an activated ability that allows you to sense the unshielded consciousness of other entities within a 10-yard radius of yourself. Minds detected in this manner can be targeted by your mental abilities without direct line of sight. This ability consumes psi and can be upgraded with Class points. Its activation time is fast. This is a Class ability and does not occupy any attribute slots.

"Well," I murmured, studying my new Class. Other than my new ability, I hadn't gained any new bonuses from the melding, but that was all right. I suspected that when I eventually spent my Class point, I would be quite pleased by the options the Game offered me.

I turned to the last book in my hands. Opening it, I began to read.

You have acquired the basic ability: conceal small weapon. This ability allows you to disguise the presence of a weapon on your person. This ability consumes stamina and can be upgraded. Its activation time is average. You have 5 of 8 Perception ability slots remaining.

My latest ability was not one I had originally shortlisted for purchase, mostly because I had been strapped for cash then, but now that my pockets were full—figuratively speaking—I decided to splurge a little and get the ability.

I didn't have any direct need for the conceal weapon ability, but it would speed up the training of my deception skill, and that in itself made conceal weapon worth the five golds I had spent on it. I rose to my feet. With my Class configured and my new abilities acquired, I was ready to proceed.

It was finally time to kill Saben and Sigmar.

~ ~ ~

I returned to the same spot where I had scaled the crater hours ago, but this time I made no attempt to hide as I hurled myself at the wall. My telekinesis skill had improved sufficiently that I managed the feat on the first try, and shortly I was dragging myself out of the crater.

You have left a safe zone.

The first cry of alarm was sounded as I stood erect on the cavern floor. With a small smile, I glanced in the direction of the shout. The thugs at the western ramp were gazing my way and gesturing frantically to one another. Sigmar and Saben were amongst those staring.

I waved.

Then I took off running southwards towards the door of the goblin complex. Pursuit was instantaneous from both the western and eastern ramps. *Excellent*, I thought. I only hoped Sigmar and Saben were amongst those chasing me.

I ran a twisted path, turning left, then right, and one-stepping up, then down, to further muddle my pursuers' aim.

You have evaded an unknown assailant's silken shot.

I smiled grimly as strands of white sailed past me to bury into the ground a few feet to my right. I didn't turn around to see who had fired the projectile, but given the spell's description, I suspected it was Saben. He was also the only enemy spellcaster who I was certain could see well enough in the dark to target me from that far out.

Two more projectiles splashed nearby, and the darkness behind me began to brighten as half a dozen arctic-white magelights rose in the air, making me easier to target. But I was already at the metal door, and I ducked inside the tunnel before the magical attacks could escalate further.

I didn't slow down. Racing flat-out, I made for the second door. Only when I was safely beyond it did I slip into the shadows.

You and your familiar are hidden.

Hands on knees, I took a moment to regain my breath. Stage one was complete. The gang had taken the bait and pursued me into the goblin complex. Some, I was sure, had remained behind to watch the ramps, but I wasn't concerned about them as long as my primary targets had followed on my heels.

Time for stage two, I thought. *Staying alive.* At a quick walk, I turned left and padded through the darkness, making for the small cavern where I had hidden my gear.

~ ~ ~

I reached the empty chamber with my equipment before the gang found me. The tunnel to my rear remained dark and unlit, from which I concluded my pursuers had slowed down.

Saben and Sigmar were being cautious.

Given the size of the tunnel complex, even with magelights to assist them, I was confident the gang would not easily find me. They would have to disperse into smaller groups and hunt me down. But well before that, I expected Bornholm's people to arrive and blockade the north metal door.

Once that happened, we would have the gang imprisoned. When I had hidden my gear, I'd also made certain to remove the rope ladder leading down from the maze and to lock the gate to the sector's exit portal. The only way out now for Saben and his people was through the north metal door.

We had them trapped. *Like rats in a barrel.*

I grinned to myself. Reversing the situation on the gang had a certain irony to it, and I relished the idea. I finished dressing and took a moment to check that my gear was in order. Both my swords rested in their sheaths, and my potions were close to hand on my belt. I was ready to begin my own hunt. "Time?" I asked softly.

"Eight hours, forty minutes remaining," Gnat replied.

I nodded in response and slipped back into the tunnel. The passageway was still dark. Tilting my head to the side, I listened.

From the south, I detected no whisper of sound. From the north, I heard the tramp of many feet and shouted orders. That had to be my allies arriving. Straining my ears, I thought I heard the clash of weapons too.

Saben and Sigmar were trying to break out.

Turning north, I hurried to join the fight.

CHAPTER 81: RATS IN A BARREL

A battle was raging in the tunnel between the two doors.

I wasn't sure what had happened, but something must have caused the gang to suspect a trap, and they had turned around sooner than I expected.

Concealed in the darkness shrouding the first door, I peeked cautiously around the threshold. The tunnel beyond was brightly lit by magelights. A hundred yards into the passage, I made out a dozen gang members, with Saben, Sigmar, and a handful of summoned undead at their fore, facing off against the packed ranks of Bornholm's people. In their midst, I spotted Tantor and Morin too.

But despite the disparity in numbers, the gang was winning.

Step by step, they were pushing back the candidates who were attempting to hold them at bay. In the tight confines of the tunnel, Saben's spells were especially devastating. As I watched his bouncing black orb—the same one that had felled Decalthiya—cut another swath through the defenders, leaving dead bodies in its wake.

My allies were trying their best to reach the gang leader, but with Sigmar and the undead shielding him, they were making little headway.

My face hardened. Saben had to die fast or singlehandedly, he might just turn the tide. I crept forward, drawing psi as I went. I needed to be closer before I acted. Ten yards into my approach, my spell was ready, and I reached out to my chosen target.

A glint of steel distracted me.

My head whipped around to the right. A dagger was hurtling through the air toward me. Reacting instantly, I threw myself out of the way.

You have evaded an unknown assailant's attack. Spellcasting interrupted!

I bounced off the hard stone wall and regained my balance. Where had the dagger come from? Ignoring my bruises, I scanned the tunnel.

You have detected a hidden entity. Goral is no longer hidden!

Twenty yards ahead of me, Goral emerged into sight. His face was twisted in rage, and his eyes seethed with hate as he glared at me. "The bastard is here!" the thug yelled. "He's found me!"

"Damnit," I growled. Saben had anticipated me and prepared accordingly. Drawing my blades, I charged toward Goral. Out of the corner of my eye, I saw Sigmar leave Saben's side and head my way. I had to kill Goral fast. I would have company soon. But Goral didn't wait for Sigmar. Drawing his daggers, the thug rushed to meet me.

It was a mistake.

I waited for him to strike first. Goral slashed at me simultaneously from the left and right. Sidestepping the first attack, I parried away the second before ducking inside his guard and plunging my sword under his chin and upwards.

You have killed Goral.

The blow was instantly fatal. Withdrawing my blade, I let the corpse fall to my feet. I lifted my head and saw that Sigmar was closing fast but still thirty yards away. I risked a glance beyond him. Saben had stopped hurling magical projectiles and was chanting again, seemingly in the midst of a more intricate spell.

I swore unhappily. I had to try stopping whatever the gang leader was up to, which didn't leave me much time to deal with Sigmar. My gaze darted back to the inquisitor, only to see his form suddenly blur.

What the—?

Like an angry streak of red, Sigmar blitzed through the air. One second, he was over twenty yards away; the next, he was crashing into me. I barely had time to bring my swords up in time.

Not that it made any difference.

The inquisitor struck me with the force of a bull's charge, and I flew backward.

You have failed a physical resistance check! Sigmar has knocked you down. You have been stunned for 2 seconds.

I landed on my back, staring at the ceiling. My eyes were frozen open in shock. I couldn't move my hands or feet or so much as twitch a finger. I had been snared by a spell.

I was helpless.

Feet hurried towards me. Sigmar. "I wish I had more time to enjoy this," the inquisitor hissed. Pointing his longsword downwards, he wrapped both his hands around the hilt. "But you are too dangerous to let live any longer," he finished and brought the blade crashing downwards.

A heartbeat before the sword bit into me, Sigmar's spell lapsed, and I shifted desperately.

It was not enough. Not nearly enough.

I managed to foil the inquisitor's aim slightly but still bore the brunt of the blow. The sword point tore through my leather armor and sank deep into my chest, piercing my heart.

Sigmar has critically injured you. Warning! Your health is dangerously low at 5% and falling. Death is imminent.

Pain engulfed me, and my world turned white with agony. Blood gurgled from my mouth and pumped out of my chest in copious amounts as Sigmar withdrew his blade.

"Die, you filth," I heard the inquisitor snarl as he walked away.

Death beckoned, and I felt myself fading. "No," I croaked. *Not like this.* Straining to remain focused, I blindly felt for one of the potions on my belt and unstoppered it. With a trembling hand, I brought the flask to my mouth. Just as it touched my lips, a wave of dizziness passed over me, and I dropped the potion. Still, some of the contents made it into me.

You have consumed 10% of a moderate healing potion and restored 3% of your lost health. Your health is now at 6%.

A sliver of new energy coursed through me, far short of what I needed but enough to reinvigorate me for a second attempt. With more care, I popped open a second flask and downed its contents.

You have restored yourself with a full healing potion. Your health is now at 100%.

I gasped, and my back arched, the sudden shift from agony to pain-free leaving me momentarily disorientated. But I had no time to revel in my restoration.

Move Michael.

Rolling onto my knees, I pulled the shadows around me.

You and your familiar are hidden.

Sigmar was still hurrying away from me, oblivious to my revived state. I dashed forward with only one blade in hand. My footfalls were muffled, and my presence was unnoticed as I drew up behind the inquisitor. Reaching upwards, I yanked Sigmar's head around, activating stunning slap as I did.

You have stunned your target for 1 second.

Before the larger man could recover, I buried my sword in his throat.

You have killed Sigmar. You have slain a priest of Ishita, increasing her ire towards you!
You have dealt final death to Sigmar and fulfilled 1 of 2 objectives of the task: <u>Vengeance for the Fallen!</u>

So, the inquisitor was another of Ishita's creatures, I thought absently. Flinging away the corpse, I surveyed the battle.

With Sigmar's absence and with Saben no longer actively throwing spells, our forces were doing much better, and now it was the gang members who were dying. A second later, Saben spun around to stare my way. Our gazes met. Somehow the gang leader had sensed his fellow priest's death.

He has stopped chanting too, I noted. *Why has he stopped chanting?*

A moment later, I had my answer. The gang leader's limbs began to bulge, and new appendages grew out from his torso. Four more to be precise. I swallowed. *He is transforming.*

In a handful of heartbeats, Saben morphed from a slim human male to an enormous black hairy spider that towered over even the half-giants amongst the candidates. The spider's gaze fixed on me. Dancing forward on his eight legs, Saben scurried towards me.

Uh-oh.

I threw myself sideways, barely dodging the spiked legs that reached out to skewer me. Bouncing back to my feet, I watched the creature skid to a halt. Saben's own momentum had carried him a few yards beyond me, but now he was pivoting around.

How the hell am I going to defeat that? I wondered, drawing my second blade. I had known Saben was overpowered for his level, but this was ridiculous. Saben-spider flew back towards me. Tightening my grip on my swords, I waited. *Perhaps if I cripple him as he rushes by...*

But this time around, the spider slowed his approach when he got within striking range. Standing up tall, Saben raised his forelegs until they touched the ceiling. Then he stabbed down. Once. Twice.

I dodged, left then right, nimbly avoiding the descending appendages before lunging forward in counterattack. The only parts of Saben-spider within range of my blades were his legs, and I slashed hard against the closest. To my surprise, my swords clanged off.

What the hell? The spider's legs were armored.

What now? I wondered, momentarily nonplussed. At movement from above, my gaze whipped upwards. The spider's mandibles were turning in my direction. Sensing danger and not waiting to see what attack was forthcoming, I leaped backward.

A torrent of violet energy spewed out of Saben's mouth to splash the ground, but my own maneuver had carried me to safety, and I avoided the spell.

I grinned at my oversized foe. "Missed me this time, you ugly bastard," I mocked.

A silk strand shot out from one of the spider's spinnerets. I rolled left. Another followed as I got to my feet. I slashed downwards with my sword and severed the sticky web before it could reach me. Saben fired again.

Staggering back, I twisted out of the way. "God damn," I muttered. *How many different bloody attacks does he have?* Changing tactics, the spider charged forward. Thinking Saben meant to run me over, I threw myself at the nearest wall and out of the way.

It was a mistake.

The charge had been a ruse. Two steps into his maneuver, Saben spun to a halt and fired another volley of webbed shots. The first missed. The second too. The third wrapped its clinging tentacles around me just as I collided with the wall.

You have been immobilized.

The webs clung to me, trapping my arms and pinning me to the wall. The scariest aspect, though was the attack was not magical in nature. It had no spell duration. I was trapped indefinitely unless I could free myself. Saben-spider tiptoed slowly towards me, his multi-faceted eyes glinting evilly.

I imagined he must be chuckling right now.

I had managed to retain hold of my swords, but they, too, were ensnared inside my silk prison. Straining desperately against my bindings, I turned the blades until their sharpened edges rubbed up against the strands. Working frantically, I sawed at the webs.

Ever so slowly, they began to loosen. But far too gradually for me to get free before Saben reached striking range. Refusing to look at the spider, I kept at my task.

I am not going to die here, I told myself adamantly. *I'm not.*

But no matter how I wracked my mind, I could see no way out of my predicament.

CHAPTER 82: SPIDER STOMPING

Saben was only a few yards away from me when the complexion of our encounter changed again.

The ground shuddered.

Saben paused, forelimbs raised questioningly.

Before he could react, thorn vines burst out of the ground. The spider attempted to dance away from the sudden surge of magical growth, but they encircled him completely.

A vine lashed out. The gang leader skittered back, reflexively warding off the attack with a forelimb, but his movement only triggered more attacks from the vines behind him.

My foe was trapped.

"Thank you, Morin," I whispered.

The vines were well-matched against the spider. Neither Saben's size nor his many limbs seemed to be helping him escape the magical growth. More of the vegetation wrapped itself around the spider's limbs. But while Saben appeared unable to escape the vines, the thorns were no more able to penetrate his armored skin than my blades had been.

Saben might be trapped, I thought, *but he isn't taking damage.*

I glanced up the tunnel. The last gang member was dead, and the rest of my allies were rushing toward our skirmish. Saben saw the same thing, and his efforts to extricate himself grew more frantic.

I picked out Tantor from the approaching candidates. Meeting the battlemage's gaze, I jerked my chin downwards to the webs binding me. "Burn it," I shouted.

"But-but—" He stopped. "I won't be able to protect you from the spell's damage," Tantor warned.

"Doesn't matter," I yelled, quelling my spurt of fear. "I have to get back in the fight. We have to kill the bastard quickly."

Tantor's eyes darted toward the trapped spider. Our mages had begun throwing magical projectiles, and our fighters were moving cautiously to form a second perimeter around the circle of vines, but despite the storm of spells being hurled at him, Saben did not appear unduly bothered.

In fact, the spider was ignoring the assault altogether. Facing southwards and with his back to me and the mages, Saben was launching webbed shot after webbed shot at the ceiling. Realizing he could not go through the thorn vines, Saben was trying to go over them. *He is spinning a web to escape.*

Morin and Tantor came to the same conclusion. "Destroy those webs!" Morin shouted, redirecting her people's attacks from Saben to his silk strands.

Tantor reached my side. "You sure about this?"

I nodded. "Do it."

The high elf nodded. Muttering the words of his spell under his breath, the battlemage pointed his hands toward me.

I closed my eyes, waiting.

Droplets of fire splashed against my lower body. I held in my scream. But the web strands holding me captive were tougher than I expected and resisted the burning heat. Still, they began to weaken, and I sawed harder against them. I heard the whisper of steel as Tantor drew his own blade and added its edge to my efforts.

"Again," I muttered.

Tantor's sawing paused. He didn't question my request, though and sent more globs of flames dashing against me.

The pain was gut-wrenching. I ignored it. My skin blackened under the heat, but so too, did the web. My hands came free, then my arms, and finally my legs.

Opening my eyes, I staggered out of the webs and sheathed my blades. Without pause, I pulled out a potion and downed its contents. My gaze flew to Saben. Despite the efforts of Morin and the others, the gang leader looked little worse for wear. There were splotches of damage on his abdomen and thorax, but other than that, he was remarkably undamaged.

Saben's tether to the ceiling appeared complete too. *He will free himself soon.* All that was holding the spider back were the vines wrapped around two of his forelegs. Vines that he was biting through with his mandibles.

I swung back to Tantor. "Tell Morin to be ready to release the vines. She will know when. And prepare the fighters. They must attack on my order."

The elf nodded. "What are you going to—"

"You'll see," I replied and took off running towards the still-trapped spider.

There was no use in me attacking Saben's legs again. They were too well-armored for my attacks to harm them in any meaningful way. His torso, though... with it already weakened in places by our mages, perhaps I could punch through the armored shell there and do real damage. But the challenge was getting to it. Taller than even a half-giant, the spider's height alone put its central body out of my reach, and with the way the creature was moving, scaling him would be near impossible.

But I had a plan.

I ducked through the vines. With most of their attention focused on Saben, only one of the vines lashed out at me, and I evaded its thrashing grasp easily. The spider hadn't seen me yet. Distracted by his own attempts to escape, Saben did not have attention to spare for the lone figure at his rear.

I slapped a hand onto one of the spider's hind legs and channeled stamina. Energy gushed out of me and through the appendage in my grasp.

You have crippled your target's leg for 3 seconds.

The limb went slack, temporarily crippled. The spider's other legs shuddered slightly before firming as they took up the added burden of the creature's weight.

I wasn't done yet, though. I disabled another leg. Then another, channeling stamina in quick succession from one to the other.

You have crippled your target's leg for 3 seconds. You have crippled your target's leg for 3 seconds.

With three of his legs crippled, and another two trapped aloft by the vines, the weight of his own torso suddenly became too much for Saben's remaining three legs to bear.

Saben has been knocked down.

My own vision had gone blurry from draining a hefty portion of my stamina, but I had been expecting it. Fighting off my dizziness, I leaped upwards and onto the downed spider. Saben would not stay down for long.

I flew across the creature's torso, making for the weakened spot near its head. One step. Two. I felt the spider shudder beneath me. His crippling had worn off. I was only midway across Saben's abdomen and was not yet where I wanted to be. But I had no choice. *It has to be now.*

I crashed a closed fist down onto Saben's armored shell, channeling psi simultaneously.

You have stunned your target for 1 second.

I flung up my head. The vines were retracting back into the earth. Good. Morin had caught onto my plan. "Now, Bornholm!" I ordered. Not waiting for his response, I slapped my other hand down onto Saben.

You have stunned your target for 1 second.

I heard the roar of the fighters as they charged forward, but I didn't let them distract me. I had only one task now: timing my blows and keeping Saben stun-locked. I waited for a heartbeat, then lashed downwards again.

You have stunned your target for 1 second.

Another heartbeat later, I repeated the attack with my other hand. Around me, I sensed the fighters close in and get to work, hacking at every limb they could get to.

It was only a matter of time now.

Soon Saben would be dead. I smiled to myself, imagining what this must feel like to the gang leader. He had to be in agony—and fuming at his helplessness.

I chuckled. *It couldn't be happening to a nicer person.*

CHAPTER 83: PICKING UP THE PIECES

A little while later, the gang leader met his end.

I hadn't been able to keep the spider stun-locked the entire time, of course, but I managed to do so long enough for the fighters to bring their own disables into play.

When the spider finally met his demise, the oversized body disappeared, leaving behind only a slim human corpse that looked as if it had been pummeled to death.

Saben has died. You have slain a priest of Ishita!

The cheering was deafening. The candidates were elated. Their nemesis had been slain—again. I, though, had another concern. "Time?" I croaked to Gnat.

The familiar looked at me curiously. "Why are you so concerned about the time? You have plenty remaining, and you've already accomplished what you set out to do."

"Time," I repeated insistently.

Gnat sighed. "Eight hours, twenty minutes."

I nodded. *Good enough.* I sheathed my blades and wiped the sweat off my brow. Toward the end, I had joined the fighters in hacking at the spider and was both sore and tired from my exertions.

Popping a ration cube into my mouth, I looked inwards and perused the most important of the waiting Game messages.

You have reached level 22!
Your sneaking has reached rank 4.
Your chi has reached rank 2.

Most of my skills had advanced again, and two of them had even ranked up. I was especially pleased about the increase to my chi. From what I recalled reading in Hamish's catalog, I knew that there were a few other chi basic abilities I could now learn.

"Michael!" Morin called. "Come here, please."

I turned around to see that the painted woman and her companions were gathered around Saben's corpse while the other candidates were busy stripping the gang members' bodies.

I walked up to join them. Bornholm grasped my hand and pumped it vigorously. "Nice job there, lad. I don't know if we would have managed to bring down the big bastard without you."

I smiled tiredly. "All in a day's work."

Morin was holding something out to me. I looked at her questioningly.

"It's your share of the loot. Take it."

You have acquired the rank 1 shortsword: spider's bite.
You have acquired a rank 1 set of enchanted leather armor. This item decreases the damage you sustain by 20% and has been enchanted to reduce the armor's base Magic and Dexterity penalties to 35%. This item requires a minimum Constitution of 4 to equip.

I took the items. It was Sigmar's armor and Saben's sword. "Thank you," I murmured. Both items complemented my own skills nicely. I hesitated before adding, "You should know I've already looted Saben's stash. What I retrieved from there was more than ample compensation."

Morin shrugged. "Whatever you've found, you've earned." She gestured to the items in my hands. "This too, you've earned."

I inclined my head in thanks and stored the items in my pack without further protest. Morin was being generous in the spoils she'd awarded me. I doubted any of the other gang members carried anything as valuable as the equipment I now bore.

"There is something else we wanted to show you," Tantor added.

I looked at him curiously.

"These," he said, holding out his hand. There were two rings and a medallion resting on his palm.

This is a rank 1 spider acolyte's ring. This item has been enchanted to allow its user to communicate through the aether with other ring bearers in the same sector. Its enchantment can be replenished with mana. This item may only be worn by a priest of Ishita and requires a minimum Faith of 4 to use.

This is a rank 2 spider disciple medallion. This item has been enchanted to allow its user to transform into a steel-skinned giant spider, a replica of one of Ishita's own clutch. Its enchantment can be replenished with mana. This item may only be worn by a priest of Ishita and requires a minimum Faith of 8 to use.

"Well, well," I murmured. "That explains a few things."

Morin nodded. "It does. That spider-form was much stronger than it had any right to be. Now we know why."

"What will you do with the items?" I asked.

"Sell them and split the proceeds amongst the rest of the candidates," the painted woman said. "Hamish should be able to get a tidy sum for the lot at the Nexus, the medallion especially."

"Well, then it looks like we are done here," I said.

"We are." Morin ran a tired hand through her hair. "What will you do now?"

I shrugged. "For starters, explore the tunnel with the trolls." I glanced at the other candidates. "And your people?"

"A few want to wait and see if any of the gang resurrects." Morin grimaced. "And kill them again. "Many, though, have had enough of this dungeon and only wish to leave. With the proceeds from the gang's loot—both here and in their camp—there should be more than enough for all the survivors to buy a Dark Class and leave." She sighed. "It is not what most want, but it's better than being stuck here."

I nodded, understanding what she meant. "And what about you three? What are your own plans?"

Morin exchanged glances with Tantor and Bornholm. Both nodded in response to her unspoken question, and she turned back to me. "We will join you in exploring the troll tunnel—if you will have us. Some of the others too."

"Of course," I said with a smile. "I must visit Hamish first. Then we can get going. I'll meet you in the safe zone."

~ ~ ~

I cleaned up, equipped my new gear, and also took the time to invest my new attribute point.

Your Dexterity has increased to rank 12.

Then I headed back to the safe zone, pondering my next move as I did. I hadn't been completely honest with Morin and the others about my own plans. I had eight hours to wait before I could further my own agenda. During that time, I certainly wanted to explore the troll tunnel, but once we were done, I intended on returning to the safe zone.

To kill Saben again and send him to his final death.

I hadn't mentioned this to Morin because I was wary of discussing the matter outside the safe zone. The walls of the dungeon had ears, and despite our Pact, I would not put it past the Master to try to foil my plans if he knew what I intended. As it was, the Power knew about the siphon Class stone, so I suspected I was being watched closely. I wasn't sure if he would attempt to stop me if I assumed the Class and left, but I was certain the Master would not simply let me go if I tried escaping *without* a Dark Class.

There were other things I had to discuss with Morin, too, not least being the issue of the familiars. But they would all have to wait until we could talk safely.

You have entered a safe zone.

The crater was mostly deserted, with most of the candidates out looting the camp or the gang members, and I made my way directly to Hamish.

"Michael, you're back!" he greeted me.

I nodded in response.

"How did everything go?" he asked.

I smiled. "We won."

"Excellent," the merchant said, beaming. "Now, what can I do for you?"

"I've come to retrieve my pouch."

"Ah," Hamish said, pressing his hands together. "About that..."

Dread curled in me. *What now? I hope Hamish hasn't stolen my goods. Was I a fool to trust him?*

"No, no, it's nothing like that! Your money and item are still safe," Hamish assured me, seeing my expression and correctly interpreting my fear. The merchant uncurled his hands. "It's just... I took the liberty of storing your gold in the Albion Bank. It seemed like a good idea then. Now I'm wondering if perhaps I had been overly hasty. It was not my decision to make after all."

I stared at Hamish; my mind momentarily stuck on the first part of what he'd said. Then the sense of the rest of his words penetrated, and relief warred with confusion on my face. I glanced around. "There is a bank in the safe zone?"

Hamish laughed. "No. This little corner of the world is too remote to attract the interest of any of those illustrious organizations."

My brows furrowed. "Then how did —"

"My partner opened the account on your behalf," Hamish said in a rush. "At the bank's head office." He paused. "You're not angry?"

"No, I'm not," I said. But I was still perplexed. "How do I get the money out?"

Hamish held out a hand. A rectangular stone lay in his palm. Elaborate sigils that pulsed a dull blue had been carved onto its surface. "This is a keystone. Every reputable merchant will carry one. It has the ability to record transactions and read the identity of players. This particular stone is linked through the aether to every major bank of Shadow and the only major non-aligned bank in the Forever Kingdom: Albion."

"Non-aligned?" I asked.

Hamish shrugged, looking apologetic. "I'm sorry, Michael, but I didn't know which of the Forces you intended on joining and thought it safest to deposit your money in a bank that serves players of all Forces. You can move the money to another bank as soon you have a chance."

I waved aside his apology. "No, you did the right thing. In fact, I already feel more relieved knowing I don't have to lug around all that gold. What can you tell me about the Albion Bank?"

"The institute is one of the oldest of its kind in the Game. They have no affiliation to any particular Force or faction, and their branches can be found in every major settlement." The merchant made a face. "Their fees are a touch expensive, though."

I smiled. "I knew there had to be a catch," I murmured. "How much?"

"Five hundred gold. Payable annually, with the first installment due at the end of this year. The account comes with free storage for three items as well."

My eyes widened. At that sort of fee, the storage space certainly didn't sound 'free' at all. "Five hundred?"

Hamish nodded. "It's a lot, I know, especially for a new player like you, but I assure you, your money and items couldn't be safer, and I've managed to get them to waive the registration fee." He paused. "You can cancel at no cost to yourself anytime during the first month, but thereafter you will be indebted to the bank for the full year."

I sighed. I didn't even want to ask what the registration fee was, but I hadn't misspoken earlier. I was relieved at not having to carry around all my wealth. "So, how does it work?"

"Place your hand on the keystone. It will record your identity, ascertain your location, and link the account to you."

I did as he bade.

Identity confirmed. Albion Bank account 42,247,212 has been registered in your name.

"That's it," Hamish said, beaming.

"That's it?"

The dark elf nodded. "Your profile has been registered with the bank. The next time you visit a merchant with a keystone linked to the Albion Bank, you can transfer money directly from your account to his and even withdraw your items through the merchant. Although, it's best to deal directly with the bank when you have the opportunity. Most merchants will charge you a fee for acting as an intermediary."

"I see," I said. Assuming I got out alive from the dungeon, the bank would make things much easier for me in the future. "Thank you, Hamish. I appreciate this."

CHAPTER 84: WANTED

I didn't buy any equipment from Hamish. Given my new gear, I didn't feel the need. But I did retrieve the blood siphon Class stone. If things didn't go as planned, I would have need of it soon. Hamish refused to charge me a handling fee for removing the item, and I gladly made two additional deposits to my bank account.

You have stored a stack of full healing potions (2) and 2 x basic steel shortswords. You have acquired a blood siphon Class stone.

With my wealth secured, I had no reason to rush my future purchases. I could afford to be more conservative in my spending. For that reason, I bought only one additional ability.

Minor reaction buff spellbook. Governing attribute: Mind. Tier: basic. Cost: 5 gold. Requirement: rank 2 chi.
You have acquired the basic spell: minor reaction buff. This is a self-use ability that increases your Dexterity by +2 ranks for 10 minutes. This ability consumes psi and can be upgraded. Its activation time is slow. You have 1 of 5 Mind ability slots remaining.

Bidding the dark elf farewell, I went in search of the others. The safe zone was filling up again as candidates returned loaded with loot. Walking away from Hamish's wagon, I felt a prickling on the back of my neck as if I was being watched. I glanced over my shoulder.

Four candidates were staring at me, their faces impassive. I recognized two of them. They were Morin's followers. I nodded politely. They didn't nod back.

I frowned. *Now, what's got into them?*

"There he is!"

I turned around at the shout. It was Bornholm. He and Tantor were hurrying my way. I began to greet the pair, but Tantor shushed me.

"Not here," the elf hissed. I closed my mouth with a snap, realizing from his tone that something was wrong.

We hurried to Morin's tent. "Inside," Tantor said as soon we got there. "She's waiting for you." I ducked within. The dwarf and elf didn't follow and instead turned around to stand watch.

Morin rose to her feet at my entrance. "Good, they found you."

"What's going on?"

"It's Ishita," she said.

"Ishita?" I frowned. "The Power?"

Morin nodded. "She's posted a bounty." She paused. "On you."

I blinked, startled. "What?" I didn't ask why she would do that, though. That part was obvious. I had killed two of her priests, after all, one of them twice. What I wasn't sure about was whether that was her only reason for the bounty. *Has the Master prompted this move?* But would he risk her interference? Ishita was another Power and not bound by our Pact. "How much?"

"One thousand gold."

My eyes widened. "You're joking."

Morin shook her head. "I wish I were."

I rubbed at my chin, understanding now the looks the candidates had been casting me and the reason for Tantor and Bornholm's behavior. *One thousand is a lot of gold.* And more than enough to tempt even the most loyal.

I was not afraid of the other candidates, but I was not so foolish as to believe I could take them all on, especially not when many of my own capabilities were now common knowledge. "You're not considering claiming it?" I asked half-jokingly.

"Of course not!" she snapped with the first real display of anger I had seen from her.

I waved apologetically, then bowed my head thinking through the implications. "I'm not sure I understand," I said finally. "If I've angered the Power this much, why isn't she acting against me directly."

Morin snorted. "I doubt you've gone so far as to anger her. Mildly annoyed, perhaps. As to your question... under normal circumstances, a Power can't act directly against a player. Only a Pact grants them the leeway to do so. Hence, they usually work through intermediaries."

"I see," I said, understanding now why the Master himself had not acted against me. *So I am safe from Ishita herself, but likely not from her minions.* "It's time I left then. If I am not here, perhaps the others will feel less tempted by the bounty." I grimaced. "After so recently fighting by their side, I have no desire to slay any of them." I met Morin's gaze squarely. "I guess this is where we part ways. I'll slip away—"

"No," Morin cut in.

I paused. "No?"

"Tantor, Bornholm, and I will still join you," she said. "But none of the others. I won't trust any of them that far, not with the bounty in play. Will you have us?"

I nodded slowly. The trio had proven themselves trustworthy, and I could use the help clearing the tunnel network beyond the trolls. Eight hours seemed like a lot of time, but I had no idea how extensive the remainder of the dungeon was, and it would be foolish to die in an encounter with some random creature now.

Morin smiled. "Thank you. When do we leave then?"

"In a moment," I said. "There is something I must tell you first." Morin needed to understand what she and the others were risking before they joined me.

~ ~ ~

Morin, Tantor, and Bornholm left the safe zone the normal way, and I slipped out using my 'backdoor.' The three exited the cavern, walking openly through the passages while I traveled in the shadows.

We took the shorter router to the trolls, heading straight through the gang's camp, then back to the final chamber of the third leg, and finally down the left fork. The journey passed without incident and with little talking. Like me, I assumed the others were preoccupied with thoughts of the future.

When we neared the troll cavern, I slowed and allowed the others to catch up.

"We're here?" Morin asked.

I nodded. "Their cave is just up ahead."

Morin's brows crinkled. "How do you want to do this?"

I rubbed at my chin. "I'll sneak ahead and analyze the creatures. Once we know what we're up against, we can decide how to tackle them. Sounds good?"

"Just be careful," she warned.

I nodded in return and crept forward into the darkness. I navigated the winding tunnels much quicker than I remembered doing the first time around. *I have grown,* I thought. No tremor marred my steps, and no fear gnawed at my mind. I felt confident, eager almost for the challenge ahead.

I paused when the field of glowing mushrooms came into sight. Candidate corpses still decorated the cavern. I couldn't see the trolls, though, but that didn't mean anything. They could be hiding or even sleeping.

I took a second longer look at the cavern, scanning every inch of its interior. Nothing stood out. But I was still not satisfied. Funneling stamina to my senses, I sharpened my focus and rechecked the area.

You have failed to detect any traps.

Hmm, I mused. To all intents, the cavern was safe. So where had the trolls gone? Rising from my half-crouch, I tiptoed into the cave. Avoiding the field of mushrooms, I kept to the shadows and skirted the cavern's edges.

A quarter of my way across the room, I froze. I had found the trolls.

They were dead.

~ ~ ~

"What's happened to them?" Bornholm asked.

The four of us were gathered around the bodies of the two trolls. The corpses lay concealed by the surrounding mushrooms, which explained why I hadn't spotted them at first. The pair was quite obviously dead, yet the how of it remained a mystery.

"I don't know," Tantor murmured. "There are no wounds on their bodies—magical or otherwise."

I nodded in agreement. I had inspected the bodies earlier and hadn't perceived anything either.

"The mystery will have to wait," Morin said. "Bornholm, did you find anything on the dead candidates?"

The dwarf grunted. "Junk mostly, nothing of use to us."

Morin turned my way. "Let's move on then. Some of the other candidates knew we planned on heading this way, and if they are serious about claiming your bounty, they will follow after us sooner or later."

I nodded. The troll cavern had only one other exit. I had peeked inside earlier and seen nothing but empty tunnel. With the others following behind me, I slipped into the passage.

A few hundred yards later, the tunnel came to an abrupt end, terminating in a door. I drew to a halt in front of it. It was a most unusual door.

The door was wooden and painted in muted shades of grey. There was no lock, only a polished golden handle. The strangest thing about the door, though was the image sketched on its center.

It looked for all the world like a jester—one who appeared to be laughing at me.

I studied the figure intently. The jester was dressed in a tight-fitting white costume patterned with black diamonds. A grey cape, many times too long, was draped across his shoulders, and on his head was a black and white striped cap with grey bells dangling at the ends. He wore pointed black shoes, and his face was a mask of white paint. His lips and eyes, though, were painted black in sharp contrast to the whites of his eyes and grinning teeth.

In the tunnel, the door and its logo looked altogether incongruous. I sighed. *Another mystery?* I couldn't even begin to imagine what this one heralded. Settling down, I began the laborious task of inspecting the area for traps.

~ ~ ~

"I have no idea what to make of it," I admitted a short while later. I turned to the others crowding behind me. "Anyone else?"

They all shook their heads, looking just as puzzled.

"Do we open it?" Bornholm asked, tugging at his beard.

Morin shook her head. "I don't know." Her eyes darted to me.

I shrugged. "What else can we do?" There was nowhere else for us to go except back to the safe zone. We had explored the rest of the dungeon already.

The painted woman glanced at Tantor. "Michael's right," he said. "We don't have any choice but to go on."

Morin nodded to me. "Alright, open it."

I turned back to the door and reached out to the handle with a tentative hand. Every test I had run on the door had come back negative, suggesting that it was nothing more than an ordinary door, yet not for a second did I believe that.

My hand closed on the handle. I paused, waiting for a reaction. Nothing.

Slowly I turned the golden knob. Still nothing.

Finally, I swung back the door, my every sense alert and my other hand gripping the hilt of my sword.

The door creaked open.

No ambush or trap lay waiting for us. In fact, there was nothing beyond the door's threshold.

Nothing but solid rock.

"What in the world?" I whispered.

"Is this the Master's idea of a blasted joke?" Bornholm growled. "It's a bloody dead-end!"

Even Gnat snickered. "Well, I guess you have no choice now, Michael, but to—"

The world flashed white.

Gnat has been frozen.
Txal has been frozen.
Mazi has been frozen.
Hurn has been frozen.

CHAPTER 85: OLD FRIENDS, NEW FACES

My head whipped sideways to see the skeletal bat topple off my shoulder and clatter against the ground. Out of the corner of my eye, I saw the familiars of the other four do the same.

What the hell is going on?

Whatever trap I had triggered, it had not affected me or the other candidates. Only the familiars. This couldn't be the Master's doing. But if not him, who? *Ishita? And what—*

A merry chuckle floated out of the darkness.

I spun about, drawing my blades. The others followed a hairsbreadth after. Standing ten yards behind us was the jester's spitting image. *This just keeps getting stranger and stranger.*

"Who in blasted hells are you?" Bornholm bellowed.

The figure blinked out. Then reappeared *much* closer. One moment, he was yards away; the next, he was bent over Bornholm, his painted face inches from the dwarf's own. "I, you rude fellow, am the Harlequin." He paused theatrically.

No one responded.

"Ah, you don't recognize me. How disappointing." The stranger pouted. "Very well, I see introductions are in order."

The jester blinked out and back in, appearing at Morin's side. "By the by, I like your colors, my dear. Very lovely," he murmured. Before she could respond, he vanished again, only to reappear ten yards away again. "I am Loken, Power of Shadow, member of the Shadow Coalition, connoisseur of the jest, master of disguises, ruler of the emerald sea, and so on, and so on..."

My eyes widened. *Another Power?* I recognized this one's name, though. The Power before me was the same one whose notice I had attracted after freeing the wolves.

Loken's gaze met mine across the distance. "Finally, it seems I am known!" he exclaimed. His eyes twinkled. There was something about them... something familiar...

Wait a goddamn minute!

My mouth dropped open. "Hamish?!" I blurted. "It couldn't be, yet it was. The mannerisms, the build, it all fit. The grey merchant was Loken!

The Power bowed with a flourish. "You've seen through my disguise. I had a bet with myself about that, you know. And I've won!" He clapped his hands together in delight.

The others were shocked. I was too. I stared dumbfounded at the Power. "What? Why?" I finally managed to get out. I wasn't sure what exactly I wanted to be explained, but I knew I needed *some* sort of answer.

"All in good time," Loken said. He waved his hand delicately. "But come away from those ugly things. We can talk by the mushrooms. I *so* love their color."

I frowned, thinking at first the Power meant my companions but then realizing he was actually pointing to the familiars. "What's happened to them?" I asked, prodding Gnat's body with my toe.

"I've frozen the foul creatures. They can neither see nor hear. And they will stay that way until we are done," Loken said. "Still, I dislike the sight of the things. Now enough questions. Follow me!" Pivoting on his heel, the Power skipped down the tunnel, back to the trolls' cavern.

I glanced at the others. Bornholm's jaw worked soundlessly, Tantor was rubbing his lips nervously, and even Morin, tugging at her hair, appeared distressed. "Do we follow him?" Bornholm finally asked in a loud whisper.

"I can hear you, you know!" Loken called out, his voice floating through the darkness.

Morin and Tantor looked at me, waiting for me to take the lead.

I had no idea what the right course was. My mind was still struggling to come to terms with the Power's revelation. Unbelievably, Loken was Hamish—the person whom I had grown to trust most in this world.

But if Loken is Hamish, Hamish isn't real—and never was. He was just a role played by the Power. Which meant... I shook my head. I had no idea what it meant. I glanced at the frozen familiars, wondering at the repercussions when they woke up.

I sighed. Matters were growing complicated. "Let's go hear what he has to say." At this stage, I didn't see how any of us had anything to lose.

~ ~ ~

Loken was tapping his foot impatiently by the time the four of us stole into the troll cavern. "Quickly now," he said. "I don't have much time."

"What's the hurry?" I asked cautiously.

"I've blown my disguise," he harrumphed. "Every minute longer that I spend here increases the chance of Erebus detecting my presence."

Morin's brows drew down. "Erebus?"

Loken slapped his palm to his forehead. "I forgot. You people know him as the Master."

Ah. I had a name now for my nemesis.

"How are you even here?" Tantor asked quietly. "This sector belongs to the Mas— err... I mean Erebus. I thought the Powers couldn't enter each other's realms uninvited?"

"Oh, I *was* invited, alright." The jester grinned. "Or at least, Hamish was. Even other Powers struggle to see through my guises when I don't want them to."

"Was anything about Hamish even real?" I asked. I was slowly coming to terms with the Power's deception, but still, I couldn't help but be hurt by the betrayal.

"Hamish was real, my friend!" Loken said. "As real as you and me." He paused. "Or you, anyway. When I play a role, I assume the part *fully.*" He bowed his head. "Alas, the poor merchant must be retired now. His cover is blown, and the others will be hunting him." He met my gaze. "Hamish wishes you to know he enjoyed your company and regrets that you had to part ways. You have my word that he never lied to you."

I didn't know which disturbed me more, the fact that Loken was speaking of himself in the third person or that I believed him.

"Now, I'm sure you are all wondering—" the Power began.

"Did you do that?" I asked abruptly, pointing to the trolls.

Loken frowned at me. "It's rude to interrupt, you know," he said primly. "I've killed players for less."

I just stared at him, not sure if he was joking.

He sighed. "Yes, if you must know, it was me. I did it, so we might have this little chat. Now, can I continue?"

I nodded.

"Excellent," he said. He held up a gold marble. "Now I'm here because of this."

My face drained of color as I began to suspect what he held. Frantically, I felt my pockets, searching for the stone I had retrieved from Hamish so recently.

"What Class stone is that?" Bornholm asked, unaware of my sudden panic.

"A blood siphon," Loken said at the same time as I withdrew the gold marble from my pocket. In front of my eyes, the stone in my hands turned to dust.

I lifted my eyes slowly to the Power's.

He shrugged contritely. "The one I gave you was a fake. I apologize for the deception, but I needed to buy some time to speak to you first. I couldn't let you assume a Dark Class until we had a chance to talk."

The others turned around to stare at me. "The stone is yours?" Morin asked.

I nodded curtly. "I looted it from Saben." My gaze darted to Loken. "Before he stole it."

"I did not!" the jester declared. "I'm no thief. I will give it back to you."

"When?" I demanded.

"After we're done speaking."

I studied him suspiciously for a moment before letting go of my anger. It was useless against a Power anyway. *But is he one?* We only had his word for it, after all. Reaching out with my will, I cast analyze on the jester.

You cannot analyze your target! This entity is a Power and immune to this ability!

Huh. Well, that answers that.

"That was rude," Loken said. "But given that you are upset, I will forgive you." His mask of affability slipped, and his expression turned cold. "This time. Do we understand each other?"

I lowered my gaze. *Calmly, Michael,* I told myself and bobbed my head meekly.

"Good!" the jester said, his tone light again. "Now I see that perhaps I erred in my choice of mask. Perhaps a serious face will be more conducive for this conversation."

Loken blinked out.

CHAPTER 86: THE TWO STONES

"Huh, where'd he go?" Bornholm asked, scratching his head.

"I don't know," Tantor said, shaking his head. He stepped forward to tentatively run his hand across the space the Power had so recently occupied.

Morin stepped up to my side. "What's going on, Michael?" she whispered. "Why is a Shadow Power interested in you as well?"

I bit my lip, not sure how much to tell her. I hadn't told Morin about my Class evolution or about the wolves, but she knew that both Ishita and Erebus were after me. "I think—"

"Greetings, children."

The four of us spun about. Standing behind us was a figure dressed in a cowled robe of charcoal grey and leaning on an oversized white ash staff.

This time, I resisted the urge to cast analyze on our visitor. "Loken?" I asked uncertainly.

The stranger drew back her hood, revealing a human face seamed with age, silver hair, and pale, colorless eyes. The old woman smiled. "In this aspect, I prefer the name Gestala."

Alright, so he is a woman too.

"Come sit," Gestala said, seating herself unceremoniously and patting the ground beside her. "Let us begin. I have much to tell you."

The four of us did as she bade, forming a half-circle around the old woman.

"I shall start at the beginning," Gestala said gravely. "Erebus lied to you." Her old eyes twinkled. "I realize you must have figured out this much already, but perhaps what you've not realized is the extent of his deception." She raised an aged hand and began ticking off points. "You are, all of you, players already. You were so the moment you set foot in the Forever Kingdom. You were never candidates.

"Two, neither Erebus nor any other Power knows who you were in your past life. Some of you certainly have no predisposition to violence. Others, perhaps. But your destiny is your own to forge.

"Three, you have all been trapped in a game of Erebus's own making. Every so often, the cosmos introduces new blood into the Grand Game. From where players come, no one knows." She smiled ruefully. "Not even the Powers. Players usually begin their journey in one of the central counties of the Kingdom—neutral territory unclaimed by any faction or Force. This time, however, Erebus managed to divert a group of you to his own domain."

Gestala looked over the four of us carefully. "Are you all following?"

We nodded.

"Good," she said approvingly. "Now, here is the most important part. The essence of the Game is choice. The Game, while oftentimes brutal and unpredictable, is fair. Erebus has come perilously close to revoking your choice, but he has not done so completely. What he did in this sector is frowned upon by all the Powers, *but* it is not against the rules." Gestala leaned forward. "Do you know what he has done?"

We shook our heads mutely.

"Erebus has manipulated events to force the outcome he desires, robbing you of many of your choices and leaving you with only two options: death or becoming Darksworn." She leaned back. "There is only a single exit from this area, the sector portal, and none of you may use it without taking upon a Dark Class and forsaking the other Forces."

The old woman's gaze flitted to me briefly, but she didn't add anything further. She knew, of course, that unlike the others, I was Marked, but did she know that the Adjudicator had awarded me two more tasks? I hadn't told anyone about them.

How far does a Power's knowledge extend? I wondered.

"And is that why you are here?" Morin asked in the pause that followed. "To offer us a different path?"

Gestala eyed Morin shrewdly. "Smart girl. You are quite correct. It is because the Game prizes choice that my intervention here is allowed. The Adjudicator is not best pleased with the Crow at the moment, and because of that, it has acceded to my petition to intervene more directly. I am here to offer you four another choice."

The old woman closed her eyes briefly. When she opened them again, a gold marble rested on the floor before each of the others. In front of me, there were two. I picked up both and examined them carefully.

You have acquired a master Class stone. This stone contains the path of: a blood siphon. It confers a player with four skills: dark magic, light resistance, scimitars, and leech. This Class also permanently boosts your Faith attribute by +2, your Strength by +2, and your Magic attribute by +2. This is a Dark Class.

You have acquired a master Class stone. This stone contains the path of: a shadow operative. It confers a player with four skills: shadow magic, light resistance, regeneration, and dark resistance. This Class also permanently boosts your Faith attribute by +3 and your Constitution attribute by +3. This a Shadow Class.

My eyes widened at the description of the shadow operative Class. It was as tempting as the blood siphon one, which Loken had returned as promised. I looked up to find the disguised Power smiling at me.

"I told you I would return your stone," she said.

"I don't understand," Tantor said slowly.

I glanced at him. He and the others were staring in fascination at their own Class stones. I assumed the stones Loken had given them were different from my own, but if the trio's expressions were anything to go by, what the Power had offered them was just as good.

"How do these Class stones help us escape the sector?" the elf asked. "It is a magnanimous gift, no doubt, but I don't see how it will let us pass through the sector portal. With this, we will become Shadowsworn, not Darksworn."

Gestala cackled. "Oh, it's not a gift. It's a requirement."

Silence.

"A requirement?" Morin asked finally.

The old woman nodded. "For me to open a portal to the outside world for each of you." On the tail end of Gestala's words, a message unfurled in my mind.

Your task: <u>Find your own way out</u>! has been updated. You have discovered another way out of the sector. Revised objective: Adopt a Shadow Class and use the portal provided by Loken. This task and the task: <u>Escape the Dungeon</u>, are mutually exclusive.

The others gasped, which I took to mean they had been given tasks of their own.

"Now," the disguised Power said with a smile. "You have another path before you. How will you choose?"

~ ~ ~

I placed the golden marbles gently back on the ground and stared at them for a drawn-out moment while I pondered my choices.

Two Class stones. Two tasks. Two means of exiting the sector.

Yet I was not sure I favored either.

"I must have your answers now," Gestala said, intruding on my musings. "I don't know for how much longer I can shield my presence in the sector from Erebus."

I glanced up to find the old woman looking at me. "I'm not sure yet," I admitted.

Wordlessly, the disguised Power turned her stare from me to Morin. The painted woman bit her lip and glanced at me. I kept my face expressionless. This was her decision to make.

"I need your answer, girl," Gestala prompted.

Morin's eyes flitted between me and the old woman, the struggle on her face clear. I could see that she was drawn to the gift Loken offered, and I couldn't blame her. Her own choices were more limited than mine.

The druid sighed. "I accept." The marble in her hand dissolved, fading into her skin as she absorbed the master Class it contained.

"Excellent," Gestala said, a pleased smile on her face. She turned to Bornholm and Tantor.

Tantor's eyes lighted briefly on me before he followed Morin's lead. "I accept."

Bornholm bobbed his. "Aye. I do, too."

"Wonderful," Gestala said. "Welcome to the Shadow Coalition, recruits." She waved her arm negligently over her head. In response to her gesture, the air was rent apart, and a glowing door of light appeared. "Step through the portal and enter the domain of Shadow."

Morin, Bornholm, and Tantor rose to their feet. I did too. The painted woman approached me and mutely clasped my hands.

"I guess this is goodbye," I said.

"It doesn't have to be," Morin replied, her eyes resting on the Shadow Class stone at my feet.

I shook my head. "I have something that still needs doing. I'm not ready to leave."

She smiled sadly. "I thought that might be the case." She exhaled a breath. "Michael, I hope you understand why we had to make this choice. We don't—"

"I understand," I said, cutting her off. I raised my gaze to take in Tantor and Bornholm. "And besides, this may not be goodbye forever. I may see you three again." I didn't believe that, though. And from their unhappy gazes, neither did they.

Tantor clamped a hand on my shoulder, and Bornholm swallowed me in a bear hug. Then as one, the three entered the portal and disappeared from the dungeon. The glowing doorway closed, and I swung back to the old woman.

She was gone, and in her place sat Hamish.

He was staring at me. "Sit down, Michael. Let's talk. It's past time we had a franker discussion."

CHAPTER 87: A WISE OLD MERCHANT'S TEACHINGS

I stared at the dark elf. I could not deny that I was put at ease by Loken's latest persona, even though I realized the Power had only assumed Hamish's guise to manipulate me.

"Why have you rejected my proposal?" he began. "It is a good one. Better than most would offer."

"I haven't," I replied, sitting down cross-legged from across him. "Not yet, anyway."

The dark elf studied me carefully. "You want more information before deciding, is that it?"

I shifted. "Partly," I admitted.

"Ask your questions then."

"Why did you come here?"

"For you, obviously," Hamish replied. "The others were a bonus."

I shook my head. "No, I don't mean this cavern. I mean, why did you come to this sector?"

"Ah," the dark elf said. "That's simple enough to answer: I was spying. I came to see what Erebus was up to and to frustrate his plans if I could." He smiled. "And in you, I found the perfect opportunity."

I frowned. "I don't understand that part. What is your interest in me? Or Erebus' and Ishita's, for that matter."

"Your evolution," Hamish answered promptly.

I had suspected as much, but I still didn't know why. Seeing my confusion, Hamish added, "It's my role to maintain the balance."

My brows drew down. "That's awfully cryptic, Hamish," I replied irritably.

He chuckled. "I know. Nevertheless, it's all I am prepared to say on the matter. Now is there anything else you wish to ask?"

I chewed over the question for a moment. This was an opportune moment, I realized, to finally get an answer about something I had been wondering for a while. "What are the Forces?" There was more to my question than I was letting on. Understanding their nature was integral to my escape plan.

Hamish smiled. "A complex question, and one with no easy answer. If I recall, you've asked about them before."

"And you refused to answer."

The disguised Power laughed. "Well, I shall answer you this time. Let's see where to begin," he mused and fell silent. "The Forces are the building blocks of the cosmos," he said a moment later. "Energy in its rawest form and oftentimes in conflict with one another.

"Light seeks to perpetuate itself and shine on all. Dark is less intent on spreading and more focused on deepening its own nature. Shadow lies in the middle and attempts to bridge the gap between the other two."

I bit my lip, chewing over Loken's words. What he described was not at all how I had been thinking of the Forces—and did not bode well for my plans. Something else struck me about what he had said. "You talk of them as if they are alive. Are they?"

Hamish smiled. "That is something philosophers are fond of pondering, my young friend. But no, the Forces are not alive in the manner you mean. They cannot be slain, defeated, or even contained, nor do they possess sentience."

"Then the Dark is not evil?" I asked, voicing the question that concerned me the most. *If my assumptions are wrong...*

"Bah!" Hamish said dismissively. "That's superstitious drivel. The Forces have no morality. Many—including some Powers, sadly—assign motives to them, labeling Light good and Dark evil, but those are misconceptions. The Forces simply are."

My face troubled, I stared at Hamish. *Is he being honest with me?* "But—" I began.

The dark elf held up a hand, stilling my protest. "I know where you are going with this, Michael. But remember, you are new to this world, and your experiences thus far have been skewed. As much as Erebus may want you to believe otherwise, the Dark of itself is *not* evil." Hamish's grey eyes burned into mine, driving in his next words. "The Awakened Dead Faction *is*, but there are factions amongst the Light that are arguably just as evil."

"And amongst the Shadow too?"

Hamish's look turned wry. "And amongst the Shadow, too," he agreed.

I bowed my head, pondering the elf's words while I tried to come to terms with the concepts he explained and their implications for me. "If all you've said is true," I said, articulating my thoughts slowly, "if the Forces have no morality, what does it matter which Force I follow?"

Hamish made a face. "That's another difficult question to answer. In their purest forms, the Forces are simply different types of energy, and in a world devoid of life, that is all they would be.

The elf sighed. "But the Forces don't exist in isolation. They coexist in a cosmos filled with people. People with their own ideologies and beliefs. Over time the natures of the Forces have become... tainted with their followers' beliefs.

"Light's propensity for spreading has become synonymous with life and favoring the welfare of the many over the one. Today, Light embodies unity and order, and its adherents primarily wield mass buffs and area-wide effects. Light factions, rarely if ever, compete amongst themselves. It is not in their nature. To be Lightsworn means championing the cause of the many, even unto the detriment of the individual.

"Dark's inwards focus has become tantamount to individuality and conquering death in all its forms. Darksworn value the self over the collective. An individual Darksworn is usually stronger than a single Lightsworn, but in a group, the Light often triumphs over the Dark. The Dark and its factions favor chaos, and indeed they actively pursue it, both amongst their own numbers and in their conflicts with other Forces."

Hamish held my gaze, his face unwontedly serious. "To Erebus, you are a commodity, one whose worth is measured by how much stronger you can make him. If he feels threatened by you, he will have no compunction about destroying you, regardless of whether you become Darksworn or not. Do you understand?"

I nodded slowly, accepting the warning for what it was.

"Lastly, we come to Shadow," the dark elf continued. "Shadow tries to balance Light and Dark and can draw from either, yet at the same time, it is weaker than both in direct confrontation. Where Shadows excels is in misdirection and containment. We of the Shadow pursue balance, seeking to hold the Dark at bay while also preventing the Light from spreading unchecked."

I narrowed my eyes. "By your description, Shadow sounds to be the best of the three."

Hamish shook his head ruefully. "I only wish that were the case, but there are many amongst Shadow who believe that both Light and Dark should be subordinate to Shadow, that Shadow's true place is to rule over both, not so much maintaining the balance as enforcing it."

"I see," I said. "And I take it your faction's approach is different."

Hamish chuckled. "You could say we prefer to work unseen." He smiled. "We try to guide events to their proper course while always seeking to keep our hand hidden." He met my gaze. "You will be well suited to our work, Michael."

"So is that what this is? A recruitment pitch?"

The dark elf shrugged. "If you wish to perceive it as such."

I thought for a second before asking another question. "Who is Artem?"

"You've attracted her notice too?" the disguised Power asked. "How did you manage that?"

So the Powers don't know everything. Well, that or Loken's surprise was faked, which could very well be the case. I ignored the question, not willing to reveal more of myself than necessary.

"Ah, still secretive, I see," Hamish replied. "But despite your mistrust, I will deign to answer. *She* is the goddess of nature. Far be it for me to speak ill of a fellow Power of Shadow, but I must warn you, she can be a trifle... stiff at times. Best you stick with me," he finished with a grin.

I pursed my lips. "She is a goddess? And you're what? A god?" I asked disbelievingly. "Is that what you Powers are? Deities?"

"That's exactly what most of my kin have deluded themselves into believing." Hamish sighed. "My colleagues would not appreciate me revealing this, but we are not, in fact, gods. Consider us... highly evolved players, if you will."

I frowned. Had Hamish used the words he just did by happenstance? Or was further meaning hidden beneath? The implications were both scary... and intriguing.

"But enough small talk," Hamish said. "Time is passing. I cannot stay here longer, and once I leave, my offer expires. Do you accept my bargain?"

I rubbed my chin, thinking hard.

On the face of it, Loken's deal sounded a good one. I glanced down at the two Class stones on the ground.

Do I want to bind myself to Shadow?

Not particularly, I answered myself truthfully, *at least no more than I want to become Darksworn.* I liked Hamish—I suppose that meant I liked Loken too—and though the bait he offered me was sweeter than Erebus', it boiled down to the same thing: forswear the other Forces and follow the path I set for you.

So if it came down to choosing between two unpalatable options, why pick Shadow over the Dark?

If Hamish's explanation of the Forces could be trusted, the Dark was no worse than the Shadow. And I had made a promise to our dead. One that I still intended on keeping. If I took up the Shadow Class and left now, I could not honor my vow. Loken, I was certain, would not wait eight hours for me to wrap up matters here.

There was something else that made me hesitant to accept his offer as well: achieving a tri-blend. I didn't know if the Shadow Class Loken offered would synergize with my existing paths. Until I had a chance to learn more about my lupine heritage, I did not want to blindly pick my Master Class—be it Dark or Shadow. I had to speak to the dire wolves first. And that meant rejecting Loken's offer and possibly the siphon Class too.

I picked up the Shadow Class stone and rolled it back to Hamish.

"No," I said at last. "I do not."

~ ~ ~

Hamish's perpetual half-smile faded. "Why?"

I sighed. "I have unfinished business here," I said, deciding to be truthful. "I intend on returning to the safe zone and killing Saben again once he is reborn."

The dark elf's eyes flitted over my face. "I believe you would do that," he said softly. "Do you understand the consequence, though?" he asked, his gaze dropping to the Dark Class stone.

"I do," I replied. "Will you stop me?"

Hamish shook his head ruefully. "Even if I wished that, the Game would not allow me to interfere so blatantly." He rose to his feet. "Besides, I am not in the business of forcing myself on anyone." Turning around, he called over his shoulder. "It's been a pleasure. Goodbye, Michael."

"Wait!" I shouted.

The dark elf paused and swung around, one eyebrow raised questioningly.

"About the familiars," I asked, then hesitated. "Are they still frozen?"

"Why I believe they are," Hamish said. He tilted his head to the side and studied me curiously as he seemed to divine my intent. "You have five minutes. Good luck, my friend."

Not waiting for a response, the Power vanished.

CHAPTER 88: WHAT COMES NEXT

I rose to my feet and raced back up to the tunnel with the painted door, counting down the seconds as I went.

Reaching the downed skeletal bats, I ground to a halt. The four undead remained frozen and motionless. Hands on knees, I took a moment to regain my breath. *There is still time,* I told myself. *Better to do this carefully.* I drew my blades and knelt over the nearest familiar.

Then I slashed downwards.

You have injured Txal! Warning, you have taken hostile action against a friendly entity. Txal is no longer bound by your Pact with Erebus and is now your foe!

Ignoring the Game message, I kept hacking. With every hit, my blades dug deeper into the frozen body, sending bits of ice flying. Eventually, the notice I had been waiting for appeared.

You have killed Txal.

Without pause, I moved on to the next familiar. Loken's intervention had given me a priceless opportunity, one I could not ignore. With the familiars senseless, I could attack them with impunity and without fear of the creatures alerting Erebus through the aether. I could finally rid myself of the Power's observers.

You have killed Mazi.
You have killed Hurn.

Only one skeletal bat remained. I had deliberately left him for last. "I'm sorry, Gnat," I breathed. "But I have to do this." Plunging my swords downwards, I struck at the undead.

You have injured Gnat! Warning, you have taken hostile action against your familiar, voiding your Pact. You have lost the trait: undead familiar. Gnat is now your foe!
...

...
You have killed Gnat. You have reached level 23!

I rolled away from the corpses and lay on my back, chest heaving. It was done. I was free of Erebus' spy. Now there was no turning back. One way or the other, my path was set.

And I had to finish what I set out to do.

~ ~ ~

Nearly eight hours later, I was back in the safe zone cavern.

I'd spent four of those hours sleeping in a small, out-of-the-way cave. The other four, I'd spent sneaking around the crater and observing those within.

Players moved freely in and out of the safe zone. Most, I recognized. Some were former followers of Morin. Others were gang members. And without fail, they all sported Marks of the Dark.

I didn't act against any of them or do anything to reveal my presence, even when some passed only a few feet away from me on their way into or out of their safe zone.

Instead, I stayed hidden and trained those skills that I could: sneaking, meditation, insight, and deception.

I was biding my time.

When Saben was finally resurrected, I wanted him stupid and unconcerned. I had less than twenty minutes to kill the gang leader after his rebirth, and I couldn't risk him delaying his departure from the safe zone. After that, anything could happen. I shivered—including Stayne showing up. If I could help it, I wanted to be long gone from the dungeon before that occurred.

Without Gnat, I had no exact measure of the passing hours, but from sitting on the crater's edge and observing the players that emerged from the resurrection tent, I knew when the time drew close for Saben's rebirth.

Three elites emerged from the tent together. All had been with Saben in the goblin tunnel complex, and if I recalled correctly, they had died not long before him. I loosened my swords in their sheaths and cast minor reaction buff.

Your Dexterity has increased to 15.

I had invested the attribute point I had earned from my last level in Dexterity once more. For this encounter, speed would be my ally.

I checked the latest Game messages waiting for me.

Your sneaking has increased to level 42. Your meditation has increased to level 31. Your insight has increased to level 32. Your deception has increased to level 9.

Good, I thought. *Now only to wait.*

~ ~ ~

Saben emerged from the resurrection tent a few minutes later.

I saw players turn and whisper at his appearance, but surprisingly no one approached the gang leader. *Former gang leader,* I thought as I observed one of the elites turn his back on Ishita's priest.

I smiled. *That has to hurt. Poor Saben. I guess defeat isn't looked on too kindly by the Dark.*

Even from where I sat on the crater's edge, I could see Saben's face turn purple with rage as he realized he was being ignored. The priest took a step toward the player in question before seeming to rein in his anger. Muttering something under his breath, Saben made for one of the crater's exits.

I noted the direction and tiptoed that way. When Saben reached the west ramp, I was concealed ten yards away and out of his direct line of sight. The priest didn't even glance at me.

A hostile entity has failed to detect you!

I let Saben get a few yards ahead before I crept after him, stalking him patiently. Only when he reached the north tunnel mouth did I draw closer. *He is probably planning on returning to his chambers for his stash,* I thought.

I closed rapidly. Ten steps separated us. Still, Saben didn't sense me. Then six.

Two steps. One.

I struck.

You have backstabbed your target for 50% more damage! You have critically injured Saben. A hostile entity has detected you! You are no longer hidden.

My blade slipped easily through the former gang leader's back. Saben gasped and his back stiffened. Withdrawing the blade, I slapped my left hand on his shoulder before plunging the blade into my target again.

You have stunned your target for 1 second.
You have killed Saben. You have slain a priest of Ishita, increasing her ire!

Saben's lifeless eyes stared uncomprehendingly at me as his corpse fell to my feet. "Now we are even," I whispered softly.

More Game messages scrolled through my mind. I closed my eyes and swallowed nervously. The moment of truth had come. Now I would find out if my plans had come to fruition. After what Hamish had told me, I worried that I had gone about things all wrong and that everything I had done since resurrecting was for naught.

Turning my focus inwards, I scanned through the messages.

You have dealt final death to Saben and fulfilled 2 of 2 objectives of the task: <u>Vengeance for the Fallen</u>.

You have completed a task! Your deeds have attracted the enmity of Ishita and furthered the interest of Loken. The Marks on your spirit signature have grown.

Your actions have redressed the imbalance in the sector and have met with the approval of Shadow, deepening your Mark therein.

You have punished the killers of those who you claimed as your pack. This is the true path of the wolf. The pack is all. It is your duty to protect the ones you've claimed for your own and avenge them when necessary. Your Wolf Mark has deepened.

Your true motives for fulfilling this task have not gone unnoticed. You sacrificed your familiar and abandoned your companions for personal benefit. The Dark approves. You have acquired the Mark: <u>Lesser Dark</u> and have begun to tread the ways of Dark.

Despite forsaking your companions, you acted for the betterment of all allied players in the sector at great personal risk. Light is satisfied. Your Light Mark remains unchanged.

Your task: <u>Escape the Dungeon,</u> has been updated. You have been Marked by the Dark and have been granted access to the sector's exit portal. Revised objective: Use the sector 14,913 exit portal within 10 minutes.

If you fail to complete this task before then, your Pact with the Master's minions will be enforced.

I read through the Game messages with a sense of stunned shock. My plan to gain a Dark Mark had worked, yet not in the manner I had anticipated.

I thought of Jorin. What I had done to him had been as much to earn the Mark as it was to extract information. Yet the Adjudicator's messages made clear that my preconceived notions of the Dark were wrong. The Dark was not evil.

Loken had been truthful, it seemed. The knowledge the Power had provided was invaluable and, in the future, would let me navigate the ways of the Forces more clearly. I had rejected his offer, but the Power was still my most reliable source of information in the Game.

Perhaps I should seek him out. Assuming he didn't find me first, of course. But these were all matters for future consideration. I still had to get out of the sector. And I had only ten minutes to do it. I sheathed my blade.

Time to leave.

A white shape descended steeply out of the cavern's darkness and hovered before me. "Where is your familiar?" he demanded.

I turned around. It was a skeletal bat. "Who are you?"

The undead creatures scowled. "Answer the question."

I folded my arms, affecting a nonchalance I didn't feel. Where had the bloody creature come from? It could ruin everything. *Play it cool, Michael.* "You first," I insisted.

The bat descended onto the corpse at my feet. "I'm Saben's familiar."

Aargh. Of course. "Well, your master is dead," I said, mustering all the scorn I could. "Best you get out of here."

"Where is Gnat?" the familiar demanded.

"Busy," I said curtly. "Now go."

"You're lying," the bat screeched.

I turned my back on the creature. This was no use. And I was wasting time. I took off running. Behind me, I heard the familiar squawk in protest and take off after me. Putting my head down, I ran flat out, trying to open the distance between us. The familiar pursued.

I reached the metal door ahead of the undead and tried dropping into stealth.

You have failed to conceal yourself from the nearby entities.

I bit off a curse and resumed my running. The familiar kept up easily. "Where are you going?" he called.

I didn't answer. Feet pounding against the ground, I hurtled down the passages of the goblin complex.

"You're heading to the exit portal, aren't you?" the bat asked, gliding effortlessly by my side. "Why?"

I didn't look at the creature.

"You don't have a Dark Mark, so why go there?" the bat asked suspiciously. It paused. "Or do you?"

The bat winged in silence by my side for a drawn-out moment. "The Master must be told," he declared before flying away.

Bloody hells! I swore. Exhorting myself to greater effort, I ran even harder. There was nothing I could do now but escape before the Master, or his minions figured out a way to stop me.

~ ~ ~

Less than a minute later, I was hurtling down the passage with the sector portal, and presently, the exit's shimmering curtain of bright white came into sight.

But so, too, did the figure standing before it.

Stayne.

I skidded to a halt. "What are you doing here?" I gasped. My lungs were on fire, and my chest heaved uncontrollably.

The undead player's eyes sparked ominously. "You are reneging on your deal with the Master."

"What? Of course not."

"Don't lie to me, boy."

"I'm not," I insisted and began walking forward again. I was ten yards away from the portal.

"Stop," Stayne barked.

"No," I replied.

The undead appeared momentarily flummoxed by my response, and I closed another two yards to my destination. "Are you crazy? If you refuse, I will cut you down where you stand!"

I laughed shakily, my breath still not fully under control. "Do that, and you will be the one breaking the Pact Erebus forged with me. And the Adjudicator, I suspect, will not look kindly upon that." I was six yards away now.

Stayne's eyes narrowed. "You will address him as the Master."

I snorted but didn't say anything. Four yards.

The undead drew his blade.

I stiffened but made no move to draw my own weapons. Fighting Stayne would be beyond stupid. There was no way I could win. I kept walking.

Now, let's see how much the Game's vaunted rules actually mean.

I was two yards away. Stayne raised his blade to strike. Unflinchingly, I kept walking.

One yard to the portal. I was beneath his weapon. Stayne's arm flashed downwards.

My heart skipped a beat, but I didn't let my fear show. I lowered my gaze. The undead's open hand had stopped inches from my chest. His weapon had disappeared, but he was still barring my way. I lifted my gaze to his own. "Well, Stayne?" I asked mildly. "Are you going to risk the Game's wrath?"

"You will regret this, Michael," he growled.

"Perhaps." I smiled and stepped forward. "Or perhaps not."

Before I could bump into his hand, the undead player whipped his arm out of the way.

I exhaled a careful breath.

I am free.

"Goodbye, Stayne," I called over my shoulder and entered the portal.

Transfer through portal commencing...

...

...

Passage granted!

Leaving sector 14,913. Entering the Forever Kingdom.

Your Pact with Erebus has been fulfilled.

You have completed the task: <u>Escape the Dungeon</u>.

You have failed the task: <u>Find your own way out</u>.

~ ~ ~

THE END.

Here ends Book 1 of the Grand Game.

Michael's adventures continue in **<u>Way of the Wolf</u>**!

I hope you enjoyed the story! If you did, please leave a review and let other readers know what you think.

<u>Click here to leave a review.</u>

Happy reading!

Tom Elliot.

MICHAEL AT THE END OF BOOK 1

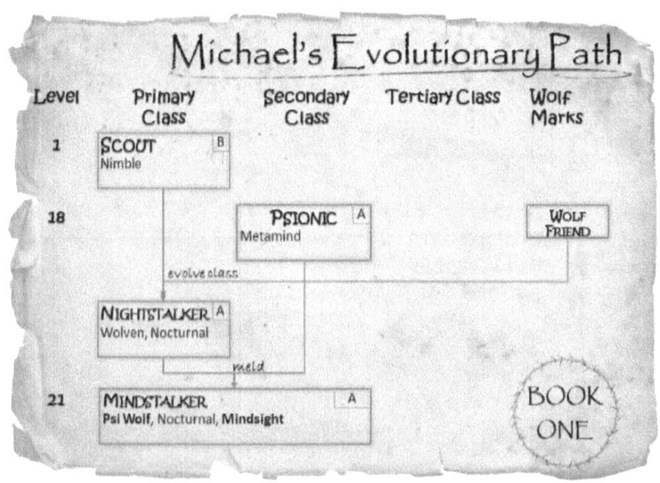

Player Profile: Michael

Level: 23. Rank: 2. Current Health: 100%.
Stamina: 100%. Mana: 100%. Psi: 100%.
Species: Human. Lives Remaining: 2.
Marks: Wolf-friend, Lesser Shadow, Lesser Light, Lesser Dark.

Attributes

Available: 0 points.
Strength: 2. Constitution: 5. Dexterity: 13. Perception: 8. Mind: 5. Magic: 0. and Faith:
0.

Classes

Available: 1 point.
Primary-Secondary Bi-blend: Mindstalker.
Tertiary Class: None.

Traits

Psi wolf heritage: +2 Dexterity, +2 Strength, +4 Mind.
Beast tongue: can speak to beastkin.
Marked: can see spirit signatures.
Nocturnal: perfect night vision.

Skills

Available skill slots: 0.
Dodging (current: 31. max: 130. Dexterity, basic).
Sneaking (current: 42. max: 130. Dexterity, basic).
Shortswords (current: 38. max: 130. Dexterity, basic).
Two weapon fighting (current: 33. max: 130. Dexterity, advanced).
Light armor (current: 22. max: 50. Constitution, basic).
Thieving (current: 1. max: 130. Dexterity, basic).
Chi (current: 20. max: 50. Mind, advanced).
Meditation (current: 31. max: 50. Mind, basic).
Telekinesis (current: 13. max: 50. Mind, advanced).
Telepathy (current: 16. max: 50. Mind, advanced).

Insight (current: 32. max: 80. Perception, basic).
Deception (current: 9. max: 80. Perception, master).

Abilities

Crippling blow (Dexterity, basic).
Simple charm (Mind, basic).
Stunning slap (Mind, basic).
Basic analyze (Perception, basic).
Minor backstab (Dexterity, basic).
One-step (Mind, basic).
Lesser trap detect (Perception, basic).
Basic trap disarm (Dexterity, basic).
Simple lockpicking (Dexterity, basic).
Conceal small weapon (Perception, basic).
Minor reaction buff (Mind, basic).
Simple mindsight (Class, basic).

Known Key Points

Sector 14,913 exit portal and safe zone.

Equipped

common thief's cloak (+3 sneaking).
spider's bite shortsword (+15% damage, webbed).
shortsword,+1 (+15% damage, +10 shortswords).
common fighter's sash (+3 shortswords).
enchanted leather armor set (+20% damage reduction, -35% Dexterity and Magic).

Backpack Contents

26 x field rations.
2 x flask of water.
3 x minor healing potions.
2 x iron daggers.
1 x bedroll.
7 x moderate healing potions.
1 x coin pouch.
1 x keyring.
3 x full healing potions.
1 x basic fire-starting kit.
1 x Catalog of Skills and Abilities.
1 x rank 1 priest's robe.
1 x blood siphon master Class stone.

Bank Contents

Money: 46 gold, 4 silvers, and 9 coppers.
2 x full healing potions.
2 x basic steel shortswords.

Books by the Author

By Tom Elliot

The Grand Game
Book 1: The Grand Game: ebook | audiobook
Book 2: Way of the Wolf: ebook | audiobook
Book 3: World Nexus: ebook | audiobook (coming soon!)
Book 4: Wolf in the Void: ebook (**releasing 1 March 2023!**)
Empyrean's Rise (a novella).

By Rohan M. Vider

The Dragon Mage Saga
Book 1: Overworld: ebook | audiobook
Book 2: Dungeons: ebook | audiobook

The Gods' Game
Crota, the Gods' Game Volume I
The Labyrinth, the Gods' Game Volume II
Sovereign Rising, the Gods' Game Volume III
Sovereign, the Gods' Game, Volume IV
Sovereign's Choice, the Gods' Game Volume V

Tales from the Gods' Game
Dungeon Dive (Tales from the Gods' Game, Book 1)

AFTERWORD

Thank you for reading the Grand Game!

If you enjoyed the book, please consider leaving a review on amazon [click here]. I'm already working on Michael's next adventure. If you have any questions or comments, please feel free to contact me through my Patreon.

Regards,
Tom
Support me on PATREON[2]
Amazon Author page[3] | Goodreads | Facebook[4] | Reddit |

---

[2] https://www.patreon.com/grandgame
[3] https://amazon.com/author/tom_elliot
[4] https://web.facebook.com/TomLitRPG